THE EX I'D LOVE TO HATE

NADIA LEE

The Ex I'd Love to Hate

To you, for opening this book.

ACKNOWLEDGMENTS

When I needed help with the first part of the book, I asked for brave volunteers from my Facebook reader group Nadia Lee's VIP Hangout. So many raised their hands and generously offered their time. Thank you from the bottom of my heart for your support, ladies! You're the best!

Also, I'd like to thank the following beta-readers for their amazing feedback:

Mary Lou Alvarez-Garcia
Theressa Baumann
Madelaine De Geest
Mercedes "Sadie" Fonorow
JoHanna Hale
Melena Torretta

You're awesome.

PART I

THE BEGINNING

1

ASPEN

I have worked *too hard* to get to where I am, and nothing's going to derail my plans, especially not some trust-fund boy born with a silver spoon stuck up his butt!

I march to Professor Taylor's office after Culture and Music in History to discuss the fact that my project partner, Grant Lasker, hasn't been to class in weeks. Actually, I don't think he's come since the first day. I've never met him or spoken to him, but he had to have been there. Students who miss the first day are dropped, and Professor Taylor took attendance by passing out a sheet of paper, asking everyone to write down their name. On the other hand, somebody could've done it for him. The class has fifty-eight students—who'd know?

We have four days left until the paper is due. I've emailed, texted and even tried to call Grant after getting his number from a guy in the class who took pity on me. Grant wasn't my first choice, but when Professor Taylor asked us to pair up, I was the only one without a partner. And Grant was the only one available, since he was absent. *Again.* Professor Taylor told me we were to do our paper on the tango and its impact on modern culture, while scrunching his face in distaste like he couldn't believe he was throwing pearls in front of swine.

With my other professors, I'd assume I was the pearl and Grant the swine. But it's hard to tell with Taylor. He shows overt annoyance every time I ask a question in class. He seems to believe that I'm challenging his authority with my questions, when all I want is clarification and deeper explanation. This is a 300-level college course, not high-school-level music appreciation, but he treats it like a kindergarten music class.

I check my phone again. Nothing from Grant. *Damn him.* That lazy jerk has ignored all my attempts to get in touch. He isn't avoiding me because he thinks I'm one of those girls who drools over him like a starved dog over a bone. I made it crystal clear in my subject lines that I only want to see him about the project we're doing for class.

He probably doesn't care if he flunks the course. But I do. I have to maintain a 3.5 GPA or better to continue to receive my scholarships. Unlike him, I wasn't born with a moneyed mommy and daddy. Actually, I don't have any parents, rich or otherwise. And I couldn't bear the thought of asking my grandparents to dip into their retirement savings because I couldn't keep my grades up. They've already done so much.

There's nobody outside Professor Taylor's office, which doesn't surprise me. It's an easy course to meet the minimum degree requirements, after all. I knock on the plain wooden door and wait.

"Come in."

I push the door open, resulting in a hair-raising creak. Professor Taylor peers at me over his round, gold-rimmed glasses with disapproval—like it's my fault the hinges need oil. I clear my throat and shut the door, wincing as it creaks again. But I don't want anyone overhearing our conversation and creating unnecessary drama.

Professor Taylor sighs, but doesn't say anything. He's in his mid-thirties, his hair slicked back with wax. He's clean-shaven except for a mustache a shade darker than his chestnut hair. I've never seen him in anything but a suit and a tie, but they aren't your standard academia outfit—staid and serious. Today, his jacket and pants are azure, his shirt lemon cream.

He doesn't bother to offer me a seat, although there are three empty chairs. He merely steeples his long fingers, which remind me of spider legs. As he studies me, his eyes narrow, as though he's just thought of something unpleasant.

"Alisha, what can I do for you?" he says finally.

"Um...actually, I'm Aspen Hughes."

Three lines create deep gorges between his eyebrows. "I see. Thank you for that *important* correction." His tone says it was anything but. "What is it you need?" His voice is colder now.

Despite the annoyance bristling in every syllable, I remind myself I did nothing wrong by telling him my name. "I need to talk to you about my group assignment."

"It's still due in four days," he says thinly.

"Yes, I know. I need to talk to you about my partner."

He waves a hand, gesturing for me to go ahead.

"I'm paired with Grant Lasker, but I haven't seen him in class, and he isn't responding to my emails or texts. I tried calling, but he's ignoring me."

His well-trimmed eyebrows jump an inch up his wide forehead. "And what do you suppose I should do about that?"

I pause for a second, stunned by his reaction. I thought he would at least show some concern over the fact that my partner is ghosting me. Not to mention, is he not bothered that Grant's been missing his class?

I struggle to figure out what to say for a moment, then finally manage, "I was wondering if you could let me do it by myself."

Haughty annoyance twists Professor Taylor's face. "Aspen, it is *your* job to do this assignment *with* your partner. You're in college. You should know better than to run to your professors every time you can't get what you want. Maybe you should try to track down Grant yourself, and talk to him about the assignment. Being able to work together effectively is a large part of the grade."

I can't believe this. "So you want me to chase after Grant all over campus?"

He looks at me. "That would seem to be the inference. Unless you don't mind getting an F on the assignment."

Okay, I'm not going to get any help. "I see."

I turn around to leave. *What a jerk.* I wish I could drop the course, but it fulfills two of the academic requirements I need to graduate—three credits each from social sciences and historical studies. There aren't many classes that do both.

This time, I open the door with more force than needed. The hinges shriek in protest. Not caring, I shut the door just as carelessly, and its screech makes the hair on the back of my neck bristle.

It's my little revenge against Professor Taylor. Asshole. He didn't have to be so unsympathetic and rude.

As I walk down the hallway, I text Grant again.

–Me: This is Aspen from the Culture and Music in History class. We really do need to talk about our assignment. Are you available anytime soon? It's due in four days!

I wait a few heartbeats. Nothing. I check my inbox. Nada there. I'm pretty sure at least one of my emails has reached his inbox. Just in case, I sent him emails using multiple accounts.

Bastard!

–Me: If I get an F because of you, I'm going to kick your ass!

Texting that little threat feels good, but it's not going to be effective. There can't be any ass kicking if I can't find him!

As much as I hate Professor Taylor's attitude, I have no choice but to track Grant down. He can't ignore me if I show up in person and demand that he pull his weight on the project.

Assuming I can find out where he is.

I'm not part of his social circle, which is mainly kids with wealthy parents. The rumor is that even though he parties all night and sleeps all day, professors give him A's anyway because his parents are important. But I don't know how much of that is true, since not all the staff are like Professor Taylor. From what I overheard, Grant's mom is a famous photographer and his dad is some hotshot movie producer in Hollywood. Every girl on campus thinks he's God's personal gift to them, and every guy wants to be him.

I snort. They only care about him because of his incredibly cool parents. And if there's any justice in the world, he'll be short, ugly and smelly.

I open one of the social media apps, and go into the group for my graduating class. I type:

Has anybody seen Grant Lasker recently?

As soon as I hit post, a photo from another girl pops up on my feed. It's of some guys on horses. Her post reads:

#Polo #Hot

She's tagged all the players. I see Grant Lasker in bold.

Yes! I delete my post and look up where the polo team practices. The field is forty minutes from the campus. If I leave now, I might be able to catch him.

I start huffing as I dash across campus to the student parking garage. God, I'm out of shape, but I pump my legs faster. There's no way I'm missing my delinquent partner.

I locate my ten-year-old blue Mazda3, hop in, dump my backpack on the passenger seat and peel out.

The two-lane road to the polo field cuts through several large vineyards. So much green, stretching away like God shook out a blanket of landscape and left it rumpled before the wine growers came in and arranged everything into orderly rows. And so much blue above—the sky is cloudless, the weather absolutely perfect, giving me a little pang of missing sunny SoCal. But unlike in L.A., the roads here aren't congested. I see all of three other cars along the way.

About thirty minutes later, I pull into a large lot with several gleaming sports cars and sedans from luxury European manufacturers. My unwashed and unwaxed car stands out like a homeless child at a fancy ball.

The huge rectangular blue and green sign in front reads:

Napa Polo and Equestrian Club

To all visitors,

Welcome to our lovely club!

I climb out of the car, trying to shake off a vague sense of unease and shame over how I don't fit in, despite the sign. I'm not going to be poor forever. Napa Aquinas College isn't just a place for me to chill out and discover myself before I get out into the world and have to start adulting. It's a stepping stone to the bigger and better things I've planned for my future. A fabulous job, and a comfortable and stable life. So long as I work hard, everything is within reach.

Beyond the parking lot is a white two-story building by a huge field. Shaded stands spread out on each side of the building, and pristine ivory tables with matching parasols dot the white metal fence that encircles a massive outdoors area.

The polo team is easy to spot. They're on the gigantic ground—almost ten times the size of a football field—and making enough noise to rouse the deceased. Eight players on sleek horses gallop back and forth in groups.

I straighten my back and start toward the white metal fence. Several girls from the school are seated at the tables, their designer sunglasses covering their expertly made-up faces. Pitchers with iced drinks sweat on the tabletops.

One of them says something, and there's laughter. I wince inwardly at an exceptionally high-pitched giggle. *Sadie Woodward.* The bane of my existence.

The college paired us as roommates our freshman year, when we all had to live in on-campus housing. She wanted to trade me for Bronte, one of her best friends, but without my agreement, she couldn't. And I wasn't going to agree, especially since Sadie wanted me to take Bronte's room. Bronte's dorm was old, away from the main campus and had subpar plumbing that everyone knew about. The joke is that the boys can't poop there because it'll clog the pipes.

My refusal set Sadie off. She told me she needs a roommate with "class and gloss," and some poor kid from L.A. wasn't going to cut it. It pissed her off even more when her boyfriend stared at my ass too long. As if I wanted that gross Neanderthal near me!

Later, I overheard her tell her friends she'd rather live with a cockroach. The feeling was *almost* mutual. I'd have gladly traded her for a small spider.

Sadie tosses her golden hair and pauses, wrinkling her nose. She lowers her sunglasses to peer at me, like she can't believe what she's seeing. "What are *you* doing here? Get a job shoveling horse shit from the stable?"

Other girls look at me and start giggling.

"No." I tilt my head, gazing at her thoughtfully. She'll know which one of the boys is my delinquent partner. And given her temper, she might blurt out something that can help me locate him. "I'm actually here to talk to Grant Lasker."

The superior hilarity vanishes from Sadie's face, and she glances at the field.

So. He's one of the riders.

"For what?" The tight set of her mouth and shoulders says that if I don't answer to her satisfaction, I won't be seeing him.

She's insane if she thinks she can stop me with her sticklike arms and legs. "None of your business."

"He's too busy to talk to somebody like you," she says.

"Sure, your nosiness. But I don't think he needs you to speak for him. He's a big boy." I hope he can act like an adult and agree to work on the paper.

I turn away and go to the fence to look at the players. They're swinging mallets around, trying to hit a ball. One of the riders in particular is extra aggressive, moving in between two players without slowing down. Some of his maneuvers look dangerous to me, but nobody's stopping him, so I guess they're legal...? Or maybe they're too intimidated to complain, since he's almost half a head taller than them—and wider, too, with lots of solid muscle.

Stop ogling him, my internal voice warns.

Right. Focus on the mission. Which one is Grant?

Sadie marches over. "Get out! It isn't like you're a member of the club."

I point at the sign to the left of the parking lot. "That actually says 'all welcome.'"

"There's all, and then there's *all.*"

"You planning to drag me out?" I look at her fingers. "You might break one of those pretty nails." I'll make sure of it if she tries.

Her jaw drops. She likely believes "small people" shouldn't talk back.

Suddenly, her expression flips from sneering to pleasantness. I blink at the abrupt change, then look around to see what could've caused it. A tall guy on a horse has stopped right in front of us.

Based on his uniform and the white, star-shaped spot on his horse's forehead, I realize this is the super-aggressive one I was admiring earlier.

I put a hand over my eyes and squint. The sun's directly behind him, and it's hard to see his face, although I can tell his features are extra fine. It's the strong jaw and eyes, I decide. I can never resist them, and he has the best I've ever seen, although I can't quite tell his eye color from here. And the body can't be faulted, either. He looks like a medieval warrior on that huge horse, his shoulders broad and thighs powerful.

I wonder if there's a name embroidered on his shirt. Actually, it'd be easier if I just ask him about my never-to-be-found project partner.

Sadie steps forward, pushing me to the side with a hard swing of her hip.

"Ow! Hey!"

But she isn't paying attention. Her focus is on the guy on the horse. She smiles, her overbleached teeth blinding in the sun. "Hey, Grant."

I swivel back to the guy. "You! You're Grant Lasker?"

God is unfair. This guy has a trust fund *and* looks? And I've been mentally drooling over him. *Ugh. No, no!*

Grant cocks his head, his eyes on me. I can feel him studying me from head to toe, but I can't tell what he's thinking. "Who are you?"

"She's nobody," Sadie says loudly. "We need to talk, Grant baby. It's important."

"I'm Aspen Hughes." Whatever flirting she wants to do can wait. The paper is more important! "We're in the same class— Culture and Music in History—and we're doing the group project together. Did you get my texts and emails?"

"I was thinking we should attend the gala in San Francisco together!" Sadie's trying to talk over me...and doing a pretty good job. She sounds like a banshee on crack.

Grant's eyebrows pull together, and he winces like he's getting a headache. Wonder why he's acting like he's pained. I'm the one in pain from him and her!

"I don't check texts and emails from people I don't know," he says finally.

"The gala—"

"Well, now you know me. And the project's due in four days. So we need to get together as soon as possible."

"Meh." He shrugs. "I have other things to do."

"What the hell could be more important than a major school project?" I say.

Sadie tries to stand in front of me. "I really think that the gala—"

If she says "gala" one more time, I'm going to drag her to the stable and throw her into a pile of horse manure! "You'll have to cancel them," I tell him, placing a hand on my hip.

"Why?"

His seemingly genuine confusion makes my blood boil. Didn't he hear anything I said? Maybe God made him stupid. Or maybe he got hit by polo balls once too often. Regardless, I'm not letting his lack of IQ get in the way of maintaining my GPA.

"Because it's *your* fault that we only have four days left. If you'd checked your emails or even come to class sometime in the last two weeks, we could've already been done with all this."

He shrugs. "If it's that important, *you* do it. And feel free to keep my name out of it. I don't care."

I ignore Sadie's smug laugh. "This is a *team* project, Grant. Professor Taylor expects us to do it *together*. You know, teamwork?"

"That's what they always say." He lifts a shoulder and drops it. "There's no I in teamwork." He starts to trot away on his horse.

Damn it! "Yeah? Well, there are *four* in irresponsible idiot!" I yell at his back. He keeps going. "And two S's in *asshole!*"

2

GRANT

The market is moving as expected. *Excellent.* I smile with satisfaction as I thumb through the charts on my phone.

Everything in life is about timing, what you know and what you can predict. And I'm about to clear a little over twenty grand in two days.

It isn't luck that's going to net me that sum. It's perseverance, determination and an appetite for smart risk. I have all three.

I block out the sound from the crime show that Will put on the TV. Silence apparently gives him anxiety. But given how high-strung he is, white walls could probably make him nervous. The apartment is painted mustard yellow—probably Will's doing. I bet the campus housing division doesn't know about it and won't be too happy when they find out.

Shots are fired on the TV, and people make dramatic noises as they keel over. How can Will watch crap like this all day and not have his brain rot?

I wish I were back in the quiet two-bedroom apartment that I leased for myself in the fall. However, a bolt on one of the toilets broke three weeks ago, resulting in a leak. The sound of the fire alarm from the unit below woke me up, the wiring in the alarm having been short-circuited from all the water. When I got off the bed, I stepped into two inches of cool puddle.

Half my stuff got soaked, but that's what insurance is for. The real problem was I had no place to live, since my apartment required significant work to make it habitable again. The general contractor claimed it would take six weeks, which is probably going to mean more like six months. I got in touch with a realtor, but unfortunately, all the decent off-campus places are taken. What's left are dumpster rejects. Even when they look sort of okay and my realtor smiles reassuringly, I'm suspicious. There's a reason they're still available in early February.

The only acceptable option that remained was sharing this on-campus three-bedroom suite with William Thornton IV and Heath Harringer. Their other roommate got suspended at the end of last semester for some hushed-up scandal. My money's on drugs or girls —possibly both.

I pray that the realtor comes through with something decent fast, although so far he's been failing. Nothing he showed me in the last few days has been acceptable. Money isn't a factor. My time and sanity are—I don't know how much longer I can tolerate the endless TV noise.

Thinking of time and sanity reminds me of the redhead from two days ago. Aspen Hughes was in a ratty T-shirt and faded denim shorts. No makeup or fancy hairdo. But I couldn't take my eyes off her as she placed her hands on her hips and demanded I do the group paper, her moss-green eyes flashing. Sadie seemed like a lifeless prop by comparison.

That doesn't really explain it, though. My usual taste is girls with toned bodies who are relaxed and carefree. A girl wound tightly enough to chase me to the polo field and call me an asshole over some dumb project neither of us is going to remember in a month is definitely not my type. Even if she does have curves more fitting for a Vegas stripper than a college kid. That body could revive a corpse, and my dick obviously isn't immune because it's getting hard at the thought of her.

It's not the body, my gut whispers. I've been around women who were even hotter. It's just...Aspen looked at me like I was an annoying pest, which people simply *do not do*. They're too impressed by my parents—and their fame—to notice or care that I don't like or respect them. I shouldn't put too much significance into her actions, though. She probably doesn't know who my parents are. Once she finds out, she'll smile and gaze up at me like I'm some kind of minor deity, like everyone else.

For some reason, the possibility annoys me.

It's perverse that I want her to continue to hate me over the stupid class assignment, even though her reaction was over the top. The entire point of taking Culture and Music in History is to slack off. Everyone on campus knows this. Taylor is a pussy who wants to feel important. He's a total tyrant to students he deems of no consequence and nauseatingly sycophantic to those he thinks are special.

I happen to fall into the latter category, because of my parents. It's amazing how useful they are—for once. I don't even need to show up for class to get an A.

After the first class, Taylor came up to me and said, "I'm so glad you're in this course, Grant. I have such admiration for your father's work. And your mother! What a treasure to humanity." He laid his hand on my shoulder and gave me a we-are-different-from-*them* smile. But the hungry edge to his expression betrayed his desperation to *be* special. "Just the fact that you're here elevates everything."

"If you want, I'll see if I can show you Mom's 'Twenty-Seven.'" There are fifty photos in the series, and Mom gave me "Twenty-Seven" on my eighteenth birthday. It's never been shown publicly, and the mystery surrounding it makes it one of her most talked-about works.

He gasped. "Would that really be possible?"

"I can ask," I said, not making any promises. "Twenty-Seven" is in a climate-controlled vault in Geneva. And I'm not taking it out, certainly not for Taylor.

"It'd mean the world to me."

And it means a lot to me that I don't have to lift a finger and will still get a good grade in the class. It's a pointless course a lot of students are forced to take. There are better professors for it, who could make the material more interesting, but Taylor is the dean's nephew.

However, you can get a good grade in his class even if you don't have fancy parents. Suck up to him a little, and he hands out A's like an overly generous granny on Halloween. So I don't understand why Aspen was acting like she's on the verge of getting some shitty grade.

"What are you doing? Planning a hot date?" Will positions his head so close to me that I can feel the hot air coming out of his flaring nostrils. Gross. Even if I played for the other team, he wouldn't make the grade. He's okay looking, with straw-colored hair, average blue eyes and an average nose and mouth. But his social skills are awful.

I shift away, not bothering to point out his obnoxious intrusion. If he hasn't learned the importance of respecting other people's personal space by now, he's not going to. "No. I'm trying to cover my position."

"For what?"

"For a trade. I have to do that before the market closes in half an hour."

He scoffs. "Nothing has to be done today. Do it tomorrow."

"The trade won't be good by then. The window will be closed."

He makes a *whatever, dude* noise in his throat. "How much are you trying to make?"

"Twenty grand. At least."

"Pssh. Pocket change. Tell your dad's assistant you need some money."

"I'd rather get tied to Starfire and get dragged for a mile." Starfire is one of my horses. She's gorgeous and loves to gallop down the polo field like a goddess of victory.

"Hey, is it true Sadie dumped you?" Will asks, apparently having decided he doesn't want to talk about my trade or how much I despise asking for money from my dad. He has more interesting things to gossip about. Like my ex-girlfriend, who's the queen of the campus. But this makes sense because he has only one priority: getting laid. If the college offered a degree in it, he would be a dedicated doctoral candidate. "She says she did because she got tired of you taking her for granted, but nobody believes her."

I make a vague noise in response. Campus gossip is boring.

"Gretchen said she saw Sadie texting you, like, a hundred times during Victorian Lit yesterday."

She might've. I blocked her number following her tenth text, after *she* walked away because I wouldn't agree to go to that dumb gala with her. Apparently, my refusal to cater to her every whim makes me a shitty boyfriend. All the other boys she's dated must have kissed the ground she walked upon.

I only do as much as I want for the girls I date. If they don't like it, they're welcome to go find somebody else. I've never stopped a girl who wanted to move on. Life's too short, and there are plenty of fish in the ocean.

"She isn't acting like she dumped you." Lurid excitement puts an odd hitch in Will's tone.

"She wanted me to be a better boyfriend, but I didn't know how. So she walked. End of story," I say.

"You didn't try to stop her? She's hot!"

"Not that hot." There are thousands of attractive women around, especially when your mother is a photographer and your father is a movie producer. But the more important thing is, Sadie isn't worth the effort. I've never met a girl who was.

"Man, I'd do anything to have those lips wrapped around my dick."

"Still not worth it," I mutter.

"Wait. She gives bad head?" He sounds stunned.

"No comment." I don't rate girls. It's crude, and they're all the same. Mildly interesting at first, but they become progressively boring. The story never changes. When they look at me, they see my parents and what they represent. I could be a hunchbacked troll, and the girls would still act like I was somebody.

Actually, it isn't just girls—it's everyone. Sometimes I wonder what would happen if I announced that my parents disowned me.

"Come on! Just a little hint?"

I ignore him and execute the trade. The position is as good as it's going to get. "If you want to get your dick sucked by a hot chick, hire an escort."

"Dude—"

The door slams closed, and I glance up. Heath marches in like a pissed-off rhino, drops his ass in an oversized armchair and heaves out a loud sigh. The left half of his face has a huge bandage over a large scrape that looks to be a few days old.

"You need a bigger bandage," Will says.

"What happened?" I say, more out of reflex than curiosity. It's a habit I acquired dealing with Mom. Athena Grant doesn't handle being ignored well. "A fight?"

Even as I ask, I know the probability is low. Heath is a trust-fund baby, just like Will. His way of dealing with conflict is to throw money at it. Or a lawyer, whichever is easier.

"He tried to grab some girl a few nights ago. When she pushed him away, he fell." Will snickers.

"I did not! The bitch pushed me for no reason," Heath says.

"Then sue her," Will says.

Here we go again. More girl convo, now devolving into toxic stupidity.

"She'll probably countersue and win," I tell them, then turn my focus to my phone. Twenty-five thousand and some change pops into my account. I smile with satisfaction. If things go as planned, I'm going to be at least five hundred K richer by the end of the semester, and clear a million after taxes before the year's over.

A text flashes on my screen.

–Mom: You must transfer to Harvard.

I look at the text for a few moments, mildly curious and annoyed. She doesn't *really* want me to transfer to Harvard. There's something else here.

–Me: Why? Nobody goes to Harvard after experiencing the beauty of Napa Valley.

–Mom: What beauty?

–Me: The weather, for one.

–Mom: Nobody picks weather over Harvard.

–Me: Like Odysseus with the Cyclops, just call me...

–Mom: Don't try to change the subject!

–Me: Okay, what happened?

That will get her to her point much quicker than my telling her Harvard isn't that desirable. Massachusetts is cold and disgusting.

How am I going to ride my horses when the ground is muddy with slush?

–Mom: Jerry is an insufferable bitch!

Okay. So she spoke with Huxley's mom, Huxley being my brother. Dad had a vasectomy fail, and fathered sons with seven different women before he discovered it. We were all born within four months of each other, named after our mothers—because Dad couldn't bother to come up with seven original names—and spent our formative years together, exiled to fancy European boarding schools that Dad paid for to make himself look good.

Most of the mothers get along, but mine has a personality conflict, especially with Huxley's mom. Not sure why. Jeremiah is a sensible woman.

However, Mom must be furious with her to call her Jerry. She loathes the nickname, claiming she isn't some cartoon mouse.

–Mom: She's acting like she's hot shit because her son's going to Harvard.

Jeremiah's "hot shit," all right, not because of her son's accomplishments, but because *she* attended Harvard, then went on to graduate summa cum laude from Harvard Law. But I refrain from pointing that out. Gasoline and fire and all that.

Plus, Mom can claim the same hot-shit status, since she also got accepted to Harvard. She just chose not to go because she thought it'd be boring. A smart decision. Mom has a two-hundred-plus IQ. Everything bores her, and Harvard wouldn't be an exception.

–Mom: I want you to go there.

–Me: Absolutely not.

Should I remind her that I—thankfully—got my brain from her and I'd be bored in that cold, dank institution?

–Mom: If you don't want to be around Huxley, then pick another Ivy League school.

I actually like Hux. When Mom's mad at one of the mothers, she takes it out on their son. Huxley can handle himself, but I don't need the embarrassment.

–Me: Mom, all of New England comes with atrocious weather.

–Mom: I want to show Jerry that Harvard isn't that special!

–Me: It isn't. It's not even that hard to get in.

—Mom: So do it! Don't make me fly over and talk to you about this in person.

Ah, God no. Mom's appearance on campus would be awkward. She's an *artiste* of the worst variety—temperamental, with a fragile ego. My brother Griffin often says *his* mother is dramatic. He hasn't seen anything until he's seen mine go into a temper tantrum.

Will says something to me, and I just nod. He's probably asking about something inconsequential, like the homework from Fixed Income Securities, which we're taking this semester. He doesn't understand a thing about the math required for mortgage-backed securities pricing. I, on the other hand, mastered it before my sixteenth birthday.

Right now, the more pressing matter is Mom's need to show Jeremiah up.

—Me: Fine. I'll apply to them all.

And once they say yes, I'll turn them down. That should satisfy her, if what she's looking for is simply a way to outbrag Jeremiah.

—Mom: Excellent. Oh, and apply to Stanford, too!

—Me: Why? Are you having issues with Emmett's mom, too?

—Mom: What are you talking about? Emma's fabulous. It's Jerry! Her new boyfriend's son applied last year and got waitlisted! Ultimately he didn't get in, and had to settle for UCLA.

I roll my eyes at her pettiness. But I know better than to try to improve her character. People don't change.

—Mom: Let me know if you need anything.

I start to tell her nothing, then change my mind.

—Me: There is one thing. I need a quiet place to live.

—Mom: What happened to your apartment?

—Me: A minor incident. But can't live there now.

Another parent might ask something like "What happened?" or "Are you okay?" Not mine.

—Mom: I'll see what I can do. I have some friends in Napa.

I hope she isn't making empty promises. She does that often, then claims she "forgot." I don't care if she can't give me sympathy, but I need results.

Just as I put the phone down, Heath and Will erupt.

"All right! So we're all in!" Will says with glee, looking at me and Heath.

"In what?" I ask.

"The bet to see who can sleep with Aspen before the semester's over."

"Aspen who?" My mind immediately goes to my Culture and Music in History partner. But she's probably too smart to bother with these two.

"Aspen Hughes," Will says, pointing at the bandage on Heath's face. "The girl Heath wanted to bang but crashed and burned with."

Well, well. My esteem for her goes up several notches. Heath has the manners of an orangutan when he's around a girl he wants to screw. For some inexplicable reason, he believes that'll get them to give it up.

"She should've been grateful I bothered. She's just a cheap bitch! Ask anybody," Heath grouses.

Well. If he asks me, I'm going to say she's worth more than both his balls and his prized Porsche put together. But he doesn't ask.

He continues, "Like I said, I got a new angle going, and it's solid."

I'm glad I wasn't paying attention. His "angle" has to be moronic. Besides, if you need an angle to get chicks, you're already doomed.

"I doubt either of you will be able to fuck her before the semester's over. She's a real ice queen." His tone says there's no way we're better than him.

I shrug. It's not worth the effort to tell them I'm not interested in the bet, especially with Will and Heath looking at me like pulling out isn't an option. None of us are going to sleep with her before the semester's over—and a week from now, none of us will even remember this conversation.

3

ASPEN

After my lunch shift ends at the café on Sunday, I head to my dorm. I got lucky this year and managed to grab a single room at Howell Hall—no sharing with anybody! Having another roommate like Sadie would make me want to mix myself an industrial-strength bleach cocktail.

Of course, hearing that I live there makes most of the kids wince in sympathy...or snigger. Howell Hall is at the edge of the campus and was built when the college was founded. And it shows in the old, crumbling exterior. Moss actually grows on the shaded side. Everyone calls it *Hovel* Hall, and some frat boys filled in the second V in the W in the engraved hall name over the main door, so it reads HOV ELL. They were probably too drunk to remember how to spell "hovel" and so left the second L. The administration never fixed the name, but they updated the security on the door, so people who don't live there can't just go in and out.

I take the stairs to the second floor, where the girls' rooms are. There's a common lounge with a kitchenette for everyone on the floor. Three worn couches in sage and purple—the school colors—sit flush against the gray tiled walls. A big window wraps around the corner, providing natural light, and a table that can accommodate five or six students is in the section opposite the window.

I wave at Suyen, who occupies the room directly across from mine. Currently she's reclining on one of the couches and reading a huge paperback. She prefers to spend as much time as possible in the lounge because of her claustrophobia. Our rooms are just big enough for a twin bed, a small wardrobe with a single drawer underneath and a desk. Having two guests over would violate the fire code for overcrowding.

Suyen was the first real friend I made on campus. Her family moved to San Jose from Datong, China when she was seven. She got into Yale, but turned it down to come here. The move apparently didn't go over well with her parents, who expected her to become a doctor or a lawyer. If all else fails, she might opt for engineering. But that would be a last resort—her dream in life is to run a vineyard.

Her phone pings. She doesn't bother to check it.

"Hey, girl. You done at the café?" she says, putting the book down on her flat belly, the pages still open. *The Enchanting History of Champagne.*

"Yup."

Her phone pings three more times. "You working again later?"

"No." Her phone pings a fifth time. "Shouldn't you answer that?"

"Nope. It's just my parents, wanting to see if I've course-corrected. I don't have to read their texts to know what they're saying." She puts her hands on her hips and frowns exaggeratedly, her shoulders raised in mock indignation. "'Suyen-ya, we aren't spending hundreds of thousands of dollars so you can be a grape farmer!'" She shakes her head. "It's so clichéd, it's embarrassing."

"They probably just want the best for you." I met her parents a few times last semester. They seem strict but caring. And incredibly worried that she's starving because her mom brought four giant Tupperware containers full of food, while Suyen protested she'd gained five pounds since she started college.

Her mom, wisely, didn't believe her. I wouldn't have, either. Suyen could make a chopstick look fat.

"Trust me, you're lucky you don't have grandparents who want what's 'best' for you the way my parents do," she says.

"Our families have different ways of expressing their love."

"I guess. Anyway, if you aren't working the evening shift, wanna go catch a movie? I just saw a trailer for something awesomely, mindlessly violent. It's gonna be fun."

"I'd love to, but I have a paper due tomorrow." I would've finished it earlier, but I had to cover a couple of shifts at the library for a freshman who came down with a stomach bug.

"Aw, man..."

"Maybe next time?"

"All right. But it'll be *two* movies."

I laugh. She can be a bit childish in her demands, in that confident way only a person who's been loved all her life can be. "Fine. If I finish early, I'll let you know."

Anticipation sparks in her eyes. "Deal! Now go write. Chop-chop!"

Smiling and shaking my head, I go to my room. It's as sad as the building itself. When I first came in, I was shocked at how depressing it looked. The blank white cinder-block walls made the tiny space look like a prison. The mattress is thin, with no box spring. The bed comes with drawers on the bottom for extra storage. There's one large circular fluorescent bulb on the ceiling, and it casts a harsh light over the room.

Still, it isn't too terrible now that I've beautified it. I grabbed some free concert posters from the music department to put up on the walls to cover up the cinder blocks. On my desk is a tiny, clear vase with a fake yellow daisy in it. I bought both from a yard sale, and they add a bit of a happy vibe.

I boot my five-year-old laptop. It struggles to come to life, but after a few minutes, it's ready.

I pull out a blank sheet of paper and jot down the points I want to make. Then I review the assignment sheet *again* to make sure I'm hitting everything to get the highest grade possible on the paper.

The grading criteria section reads:

Teamwork and cooperation will be worth fifteen percent.

Damn Grant. Since there's none of that, the best I can aim for is eighty-five. "Asshole" is too good a word for him. He's such a butt-fucking-hole.

I exhale. *Calm. Let it go.* It's probably best he isn't here to whine about the fact that he's working on a paper he doesn't care about. I'll get it done faster without his dead weight around my neck.

I start typing the paper, referencing the books I borrowed from the library a couple of days ago to prep for the project. Thankfully, the topic is the tango, something I'm very familiar with. My grandparents used to dance professionally, even winning a few tango competitions. Now they put all their focus on teaching, not just the tango but other dances, too, although their tango classes are very popular. People who want to study with the best come to them.

They taught me when I became old enough to walk. But then, it would've been impossible to grow up with them and not learn it. They're always dancing—when they're happy, when they're sad. It's how they express themselves, and the tango is their favorite. It's mine, too.

On the blank Word doc, I type, backspace, then type some more until I have a good ten pages plus the bibliography. My phone plays a soothing sound to alert me that it's time to call my grandparents. I make an effort to call them every Sunday at five—unless I'm working, in which case I text them ahead of time.

They're worried about me being in Napa alone, and they're doubly worried because they haven't visited the campus since freshman orientation. I tell them I'm a big girl, but Grandma says that no matter how old I am, I'm always going to be their little baby. They fret that they can't do more to watch over me, but I don't want them to make the long trip from L.A. They're busy with the dance studio, something I feel guilty about. They would've retired years ago, but are continuing to work until I'm done with college because they want to help out with the tuition.

I open Skype and call. Grandpa answers, his warm, friendly face filling the screen. His hair is totally gray now, but still full and bushy. A few lines cut across his high forehead, and his bright blue eyes crinkle as he smiles.

"Hi, Grandpa!"

"Aspen!" He laughs, then looks to his left. "It's Aspen." He turns back to me. "Your grandmother is in the kitchen getting some iced tea. Wait, here she is."

Grandma appears on the screen, leaning in until she's almost cheek to cheek with Grandpa. She doesn't wear makeup except for some mascara, but she glows brighter than many women a third her age. Her long silver hair is up in its usual daytime bun—she'll let it down once the sun sets. A joyful smile splits her face. "Aspen! How have you been?"

"Oh, you know. Studying, working and keeping myself busy. I just finished a paper on the tango."

"Great!" Grandpa smiles. "Speaking of the tango, all our classes are full. We're thinking about adding another."

"Really?"

"Yeah. Some people just seem really into it. I was a little worried after I kicked that guy out last winter. Harry? Barry?"

Grandma rolls her eyes. "Barry. Horrible fellow."

I remember that incident because I happened to be at the studio, waiting for them to wrap up the class before we went out for dinner. Barry was a big guy, maybe six-two, with beefy arms and hands. He was rough with his partner, dragging her around, rather than letting her follow his lead. He also didn't understand why she wasn't picking up which direction he wanted her to go to.

Grandpa stepped in before Barry grew too frustrated and got nasty with his partner. "You have to signal by shifting your torso, and make sure your partner gets it. You can't just drag her. Some of these moves, you could end up hurting her."

"It isn't like she fell," Barry argued. "I'm just trying to lead. You know, take charge."

"Your job as a male partner isn't to take charge." Grandpa held Grandma to demonstrate. "Lead her gently, pay attention to her response, support her, make her shine and ensure she feels pampered in your arms. Tango is a sensual dance. Think about how you'd treat a beautiful woman on a date."

Barry didn't like that. He wasn't shy about expressing his feelings, either.

Grandpa had to ask him to leave and refund his money,

although Barry shouted profanities and made a scene. He even promised to bad-mouth the studio on social media.

Thankfully, one of the female students in the class recorded the entire exchange and posted it. But my grandparents were worried anyway. It takes a decade of hard work to build up a business, but some jerk can tear it down overnight.

"So are you doing anything fun?" Grandma asks.

"Maybe I'll go watch a movie with a friend later," I say.

"Good for you. You're only young for so long, so you should make it count." And to her, that means playing too. She and Grandpa worry that I work too much.

"I know. Suyen invited me. It should be fun." She's great at picking out entertainingly mindless movies.

We chat a little longer, about their little getaway plan—they want to go to San Diego for their anniversary.

"We have to go now, but you have fun with that tango paper and movie," Grandpa says.

"Love you." Grandma blows me a kiss.

I smile and make a kissing motion at the screen. "Love you both back!"

After the call ends, I go back to my paper and read it over. There are a few typos, some awkward phrasing and a couple of paragraphs that could be more clearly set out. I correct everything and save the paper so that it's ready to be turned in.

You were right about Grant. You got it done faster because you didn't have that asshole weighing you down.

Yeah, that's probably true. Grant would make a terrible tango partner—selfish, careless and self-absorbed. Probably worse than Barry.

I create a cover page for the paper. After placing the title and the course name, I put my name on the lower right-hand corner. Then I hesitate, thinking about the fifteen percent of the grade and the fact that Grant didn't do crap. And he told me to keep his name out of it, like I wouldn't dare. *What a jerk.*

I can hit save now and upload it to the class server. Or...

Fifteen percent of the grade. Or spiting Grant.

Nothing demonstrates the "no free lunch" concept from my Econ 301 class better than this. I purse my lips, then hit a few keys.

That done, I go out and look for Suyen, determined to have fun at the theater and not think about the paper or Grant.

4

GRANT

A few days after the confrontation at the polo field, I get a notification that my grade has been updated. Curious, I click on the alert to see what's going on.

HIS 343 Culture and Music in History – Group project A+

A+? Didn't Aspen turn the paper in with only her name on it?

We should have a chat about the paper, Grant. My office, when you get a chance?

No mention of Aspen anywhere. *Hmm...* Maybe the alert is wrong, and he gave me a big fat zero. He might be pissed off that I didn't show him and his class enough respect. He seems like the type to care about that sort of stuff.

Since he really wants to talk and I've got a minute to spare, I'll drop by his office and dangle "Twenty-Seven" in front of him again. Or mention that my mom is very interested in his class—she isn't. She only knows I'm taking it because the subject came up once last fall. But I don't feel bad about using what I have to get what I want. It's Taylor's own fault for not treating his students equally. The kind of bullshit I pull with him wouldn't work with someone like Professor Pettit, who teaches Corporate Finance.

I walk over to Taylor's office. The famous chorus from Beethoven's Ninth Symphony is blaring through the open door.

Eyes closed, Taylor is leaning back in his chair, feet propped up on the desk. He strokes his mustache, and the blissful expression on his face is more fitting to a man masturbating than listening to Beethoven. He's waving his index finger like a conductor's baton. Sadly, he's off-beat.

There's another reason I quit going to his class, other than the guaranteed A. I don't want to see his slimy face with a bad nose job. I mean, no nose could look that ugly naturally. He must've found a plastic surgeon offering a fifty-percent-off coupon.

"You wanted to talk?" I say, walking into his office and closing the door behind me.

His eyes fly open, and he puts his feet down flat on the floor and immediately straightens his posture. "Grant! Of course, of course. Good of you to come by." He gestures at one of the chairs with a grin so big, it makes him look like the Joker. "Please. Have a seat."

"Thanks. Hopefully, this'll be short. I have to get to polo practice." A lie. I just don't want to talk to him more than is absolutely necessary.

"Of course not. I know your time's valuable." He leans forward, his eyes overeager. "Before we start, I want you to know that I was quite impressed with the paper you did. Exceptional work. Your insight on the tango's impact on Latin America is quite insightful. Truly excellent."

He thinks I wrote the paper?

He continues, "I wanted to tell you in person. When I was assigning topics to students, my gut told me you were the person for the tango."

I smile to hide my distaste at his toadying. I'm saving it for the class evaluation at the end of the semester. "My name wasn't on the paper, was it?"

"Of course it was."

"Really? Are you sure?"

Taylor laughs. "Of course! I saw it myself."

"Did you compliment Aspen on the paper, too?"

"Oh, please." He laughs. "Generosity and team spirit are sterling qualities in a young man such as yourself, but there's no need to praise her for typing up what you dictated, unless you want to give her credit for no typos. She's lucky she got an A+ just for working with you. It's not as though someone from her background knows anything about culture or music."

This guy's crossing the line. And his general snobbishness is irritating. So what if Aspen isn't rich? That doesn't mean she's stupid. "Actually, I didn't do anything for that paper. She did all of it."

"Grant, you're simply too kind. I'm sure all she did was ask endless questions. She's good at that, you know," he says. "Clearly considers herself a brilliant thinker, challenging authority and all that, when what she *really* is is an annoying know-it-all."

My esteem for him drops even lower, if that's possible. "She never got to ask me anything, since I didn't show."

"Smart of you!" He beams. "It would've been a waste of your time otherwise."

The idiot isn't listening. He's almost as bad as my dad's assistant, Joey. "I deserve a zero on the paper."

Taylor laughs it off. "Nonsense. It's group work, so everyone gets the same grade."

"Not when one person did nothing."

"Your name *is* on the paper. She put it after hers, as if that would make me think she did more of the work." He laughs.

Sudden disappointment settles over me. Aspen probably found out about who my parents are and freaked out, thinking she made a mistake in calling me irresponsible, an idiot and an asshole. This is probably her way to making up for that transgression.

She's just like everyone else. That shouldn't bother me, but for some reason it does. "Well," I say with a sigh. "Her name is on the paper too, so she should get the same praise."

"I don't know why you're bothered by this. Wait... Did she complain?" His tone says, *How dare she!*

"No. I just want to set the record straight. I thought you would understand and appreciate that. Don't you care about fairness?" Why do I care so much about him treating Aspen better? I've never given a damn about fairness before. Life's supposed to be unfair— you can never have everything you want.

"Of course." He inhales, with all the patience in the world. He looks at me fondly, like an adult might at a child too innocent to know any better. "Grant, I appreciate your honesty. As a matter of fact, I'm giving you extra credit for this."

"Are you not listening? The extra credit you're about to give me should really go to Aspen."

He quickly pastes on a smile to mask the confusion and irritation fleeting through his eyes. "I'll give it to both of you. Does that address your concern?"

Not even a little, but I give up and leave the office so he can get back to fondling his mustache. If Aspen gets extra credit too, it isn't a hill worth dying on.

Snob.

Taylor's condescension annoys me. He has a rep for treating students from less privileged backgrounds with subtle contempt. But seeing it in action is much worse. So what if she doesn't come from money? I'd trade her upbringing for mine. At least people who want to be her friends aren't doing it to be friends with her parents.

I go to a nearby café. It's run by the college, and if it weren't for the fact that I need to wash down the gross aftertaste of talking with Taylor, I wouldn't bother. It's generally too crowded, and the drinks are mediocre and overpriced. The place does a good business only because of its on-campus location.

I walk inside and see Sadie in one of the booths over on the left. She's with her friends Tanya and Bronte. They chat and thumb through their phones at the same time. Will hovers over them, probably trying to get Sadie to blow him.

Hopefully they're too self-absorbed to notice me. I head straight to the counter, where a barista in a sage and purple uniform is working alone. A cap with the café logo is pressed low on her head, but I know that lush, tempting body.

Aspen Hughes.

She hands a coffee order to a girl, who dashes out, then comes over. "Hi, what can I get for you?" she says without glancing up.

I expect her to notice me and start fawning. Maybe even apologize for the way she yelled at me on the field because that's what anybody else would do.

And then she does look up. Her smile fades and the corners of her lips turn down. Weird. Didn't she find out about me and my parents? Why else would she have put my name on the paper?

She's pretty even when she's frowning. And intriguing. It's the eyes. That cool green gaze that says I'm full of shit and she's not buying.

I can't remember a time when a girl wouldn't go along with more or less whatever I wanted. Maybe she's a little pissed off because I didn't tell her about my background, but all it'll take to get her out of her snit is flashing a smile. Maybe dinner, if I want to be extra nice.

For some weird reason, I want to see her smile. Maybe it's because I'm curious about what it will do to her eyes. I bet they'll lighten and sparkle like finely cut emeralds.

Or maybe it's because she was sensible enough to rebuff Heath. He's a complete dick. He's taken nude photos of his girlfriends without their permission. He hasn't plastered them all over the Internet—his conscience isn't totally dead—but that doesn't excuse his behavior.

He reminds me of my dad.

"Didn't they train you to smile at the customers?" I give her an easy grin.

"Customers." Her mouth remains flat. "Not pests."

I laugh. She wants to play a game. Cute, very cute. It's been a while since a girl tried that. "One grande iced Americano, to go. Now, how about that smile?"

Her mouth curves upward like it's being pulled by puppet strings while her eyes flash a sincere *fuck you*. "Anything else?"

Still laughing, I shake my head and put my credit card into the reader. She goes off to deal with the espresso machine. I watch her move, those long limbs like a symphony. She dominates the small space behind the counter, all confident and in charge.

She comes back and places the iced Americano in front of me with more force than necessary, but without spilling a drop. "There. Your coffee."

She's about to say, "Take it and fuck off." Or at least she's thinking it really hard. But I want my curiosity satisfied first. "Why did you put my name on the paper?"

She blinks slowly, then looks at me like I'm weird. "Because Professor Taylor expected it."

"So? I told you to leave me out of it."

"Hate to shake you up here, but sometimes a girl might not do what you tell her. In this case, cooperation and teamwork are part of the grade. If I'd only put *my* name on it, I wouldn't have gotten an A+." Her fake smile grows even faker. "Trust me, I didn't do it out of love for you."

I take a sip of my Americano. It's quite good. Must be the girl, because the one I had last year tasted watered down. But the entire time she's looking at me like I'm unworthy. Apparently she really has no clue about my background. "You can't be afraid to bloody your knuckles if you want to knock the other guy out."

She rolls her eyes. "Listen, I don't care if you got an A+ you didn't earn, as long as it doesn't take anything from me. I know this is going to be news, but you're really not that important. So. You're welcome." She flutters her eyelashes at me, while her gaze is saying, *Now get the fuck outta here, asshole.*

I stare at her for a moment, trying to fathom how her mind works. In my experience, cutting off your nose to spite your face is, in fact, vastly desirable. It's a matter of principle. Showing the other guy that you aren't anybody to mess with. I've internalized this since I was old enough to understand what was going on around me. Mom would cut off her own arm if she could shove it up the other person's ass.

But Aspen isn't like that. I want to get to know her and figure out what makes her tick. Or if she's hiding some nefarious plot to screw me over later.

"Have dinner with me."

She blinks. "What?"

"I said, have dinner with me."

She gives me the wary look she might give a feral—and possibly rabid—dog. "Are you high?"

"No."

"No."

When she doesn't elaborate, I say, "No what?"

"No, I'm not having dinner with you."

Did she just turn me down? Girls never turn me down, no matter how angry they are. "I'm paying."

"Yeah, well, I'm not eating."

"It's a free dinner." The magic words that would make most college kids ecstatic.

"And?" She scoffs. "What am I? A charity case?"

"I just want to thank you for the A+."

She shrugs. "It didn't cost me anything. And I already said you're welcome." But the tightness in her voice betrays her annoyance. I bet she ground her teeth as she added my name to the paper. "If you really want to thank me, show up for class. That way, the next time I'm forced to do a project with you, I won't have to track you down to some polo field."

5

ASPEN

I huff as I hurry to Culture and Music in History. I don't believe for a second that Grant really wanted to thank me for putting his name on the assignment. It isn't like he cares about what grade he gets. If he did, he wouldn't have ridden off after hearing that we had to work on the paper together. For all I know, some of his polo buddies gave him shit about the scene I made and he wants revenge.

He could take me to an expensive restaurant and conveniently forget his wallet. It happened on a date with a guy last year. He acted embarrassed and contrite, promised to pay me back and then ghosted me. I was out nearly three hundred bucks I couldn't afford, not just for the meal but the valet parking for his car, too. In retrospect, it's obvious he pulled the move because he realized halfway through the dinner that I wasn't going to sleep with him. He wasn't special enough to punch my V-Card. The right guy is going to be someone who makes me feel like the center of the universe.

Anyway, what that jerkwad didn't count on was how much I wanted that money back. I hounded him, then embarrassed him in front of his frat brothers to the point that he had to cough up the parking and his portion of the meal and drinks. His buddies call me That Cheap Bitch, but the money mattered more than their opinion, especially since I'm not going to see them again after I graduate.

With Grant, if he pulls something similar, it'll be impossible to get a hold of him. I was only able to track him to the polo field because somebody posted where he was. I'm not going to count on being lucky again.

Besides, even if I did manage to corner him again, there's no guarantee he'd pay. If our personalities were tattooed on our foreheads, his would read SHAMELESS. He's the type who never understands why what he did is bad because how could he be in the wrong? He's led a charmed life where everything's been handed to him, including girls. A guy who looks like that doesn't go without.

I read the comments Professor Taylor left directly on the paper. He kissed Grant's ass so hard, it wouldn't shock me if his mouth smells like ass for the next decade.

Let it go, I tell myself. I have the grade, and I only need to suck it up for two more years and one semester before I get my econ degree. Then I'm going to get a job as a stockbroker. It seems like a doable career, and it pays well. My grandparents have sacrificed so much, and I need to pull my weight. Move out and let them finally have their retirement.

I walk into the lecture hall with its huge stage, from which Professor Taylor lectures. I take my usual seat in the front, second from the aisle. Nobody else sits on the row, which is perfect. No distractions.

I pull out my textbook, tablet and papers and position them just so on the fold-out desk, then lay down my plain black ballpoint pen, ready for class.

"Hello, Aspen."

I jerk my head up. The greeting is smooth, said in a low voice that makes my skin prickle—probably with unresolved rage.

"What are you doing here?"

Grant smiles. "You told me to show up if I wanted to thank you."

I stare, trying to process. *He's actually following through?* This guy doesn't strike me as the type to be nice to anybody. Plus, why does he look so damn good? All those bold lines, the high cheekbones and surprisingly full lips. The bridge of his nose is straight. I guess he never got smacked in the face with a polo mallet. His shoulders look even wider this close, and he smells nice—some expensive, spicy cologne.

Which I must be allergic to. That's the only explanation for the weird tingly feeling I'm getting in my chest. It's too warm and uncomfortable.

He smirks. "Didn't think I'd do it, did you?"

"No." Abruptly, I turn my attention back on the textbook, which is closed. I open it and pretend to read.

"Is this taken?" He points at an empty seat next to me.

Oh no. "There are plenty of seats over there. Next to the sorority girls, who will probably be more to your liking." Sadie's there too, and maybe they can discuss going to that gala thing she wanted him to take her to. I'm sure she'd be thrilled if he offered to buy her dinner.

He glances over, then makes a face. "No thanks."

As he lowers himself into the seat next to me, I can't help staring. Is he just obtuse?

Sadie jumps up and struts toward us, her golden ponytail swishing left and right. "Hey, Grant! *We're* all sitting over there." Her tone says he could do better than sitting next to me. And for once, I agree with her.

"I'm good," he says.

Sadie turns her attention to me. "Why are you sitting here?"

"I *always* sit here."

She pulls back, obviously stunned. To hide her initial reaction, she rolls her eyes with an exaggerated sigh. "*You* need to move."

I bare my teeth. "Make me."

Her lips tighten, and calculations are taking place in her head. She's probably trying to figure out if she can successfully force me.

"You should go back to your seat," Grant says.

Yes. And you go with her.

"But I need to talk to you!" Sadie whines.

"Whatever—just take your conversation away from me," I say. Her perfume is starting to give me a headache.

"If you continue to bother me," Grant says to Sadie, "I'm going to get a restraining order."

She pulls back like he just slapped her. "*What?*"

"Stalking, excessive texting, excessive calling, trying to talk to me when I don't want to..." He shrugs. "The family lawyer will have a lot to work with."

"But we're dating!"

They are? He isn't acting like a boyfriend.

"No, you 'dumped' me. Remember?" he says.

"That was a misunderstanding!"

Grant gives her a look. "I didn't misunderstand anything."

Huh. So maybe *he* dumped *her*? I wonder if it happened before or after I saw him at the polo practice... And what would make a girl like Sadie throw away her pride and cling to him like this? Doesn't she know some other guy who can take her to the gala?

Grant sighs. "Sadie, *everyone* is watching."

She flinches, then glances at her crowd. All they need is a tub of popcorn. Her cheeks flaming, she walks away stiffly.

"I don't mind if you want to sit with her." I feign disinterest, although all my senses are hyperalert to every move he makes.

"Nah. If there's another assignment, you can just talk to me right here instead of chasing me down," he says magnanimously.

He looks innocent, but I don't buy it. Not after blowing me off on the polo field. Why would he change all of a sudden?

Professor Taylor walks in. He's in a white dress shirt and black slacks that fit too tightly around his hips. They aren't flattering—his ass is as flat as a year-old balloon.

His pale blue eyes skim the audience, then flare with shock at the sight of Grant. He falters for a second, then frowns when he notices me, like somehow I'm the cause of whatever's bugging him.

"Today we are going to review some of the more interesting papers I received," he starts. "Sadie and Bronte, why don't you start?"

They clear their throats and tinker away on their laptops. Sadie starts on the impact of flamenco on other cultures and dances. She reads about half the paper out loud, then Bronte handles the rest. They don't do much to hide the fact that they're bored reading it.

But Professor Taylor beams proudly like they just recited the *Odyssey* in the original Greek. He gives us a long and unnecessary rewording of their paper, and makes us watch a few clips of flamenco dancers. Then he looks around the class with a huge grin. "The tango would be an excellent follow-up, since it's been influenced by flamenco. And the paper done by Grant and Aspen is particularly insightful."

Huh. So now he remembers my name.

I pull up the paper I wrote on my tablet so I can read it out loud.

"For this particular subject, it'd be more interesting to have the dance demonstrated by someone who seems knowledgeable." Instead of moving toward the control for the huge screen behind him, he takes a step forward and extends a hand toward me. "Come on up."

"Me?" I squeak. I steal a quick look at Grant, but he seems uninterested. He's probably daydreaming about horses. And hitting a ball.

"Yes. You did the paper, so I assume you know how to tango." Professor Taylor cocks a supercilious eyebrow.

I start to stand. So does Grant.

Professor Taylor waves him down. "No need, Grant. Aspen and I will do it together."

Ugh. So annoying that he's speaking like he's doing Grant some huge favor. I'm certain the professor expects me to make a fool out of myself. *Asshole.*

Grant frowns a little, but sits down.

Everyone's eyes are on me now. I walk stiffly to the stage, then stand next to Professor Taylor. He gestures animatedly, his fingers and arms flying everywhere. "The one we're about to demonstrate is an Argentinian tango." He drones on for a bit, reading directly from the paper that *I* wrote.

Why can't he just stick to the paper, rather than have a demonstration? I'm not dressed properly. I'm in sneakers, and they're the worst because of excessive traction. If I'd known, I would've put on a loose knee-length skirt and strappy heels suitable for smooth gliding and turning.

"Now, Aspen. Get ready."

Professor Taylor fiddles with his phone, pairing it with the Bluetooth speakers in the class.

He extends a hand, and I place mine on it. His palm is slightly sweaty and unpleasant to the touch, but I keep my expression neutral. He might be just nervous. He puts the other hand at the small of my back. My whole body tenses. Something about his touch makes my skin crawl. His gaze doesn't help because he's staring down at me like I'm a bug he's dying to crush.

I exhale. Most tango music doesn't last longer than three minutes or so. I can put up with him and his stare for that long.

The familiar strains of "La cumparsita" start. I keep my eyes on him, waiting for some signal that he's about to start.

Suddenly, he yanks me hard to the side as he takes his steps. I catch myself and follow along. Abruptly, he changes direction, without any sign that he's going to do so. He doesn't seem to understand that leading doesn't mean yanking me around. My guess is that he took maybe one or two tango classes a long time ago. If he didn't quit because he decided he was too awesome, he probably got kicked out for being a dick partner, just like Barry in my grandparents' class.

When I nearly stumble for the third time, Professor Taylor stops and lets me go, pushing me away like I'm a piece of trash. Irritation burns through me. What an ass. Who the hell dances like this?

Professor Taylor looks out toward the other students, "Aspen writes well enough but obviously hasn't learned how to follow a tango lead properly. Unfortunate, because it is a beautiful and elegant dance when done correctly."

Giggles and snickers come from the students. Sadie in particular seems to be enjoying herself.

Humiliation burns my cheeks. I open my mouth to tell him that I was taught by my grandparents, who've won several tango competitions. But Grant stands up first.

"She probably needs a better partner," he says to Professor Taylor. "Why don't you let me try?"

"That won't be necessary, although I admire your desire to defend your project partner," Professor Taylor says. "We wouldn't want to impose on you that way." He winks at Grant like they're in this together.

What's going on here? Is Professor Taylor doing this to embarrass me because that's what Grant wants? But in that case, Grant wouldn't have interrupted.

"No, no. I would hate it if they"—Grant glances toward the other students—"got the wrong impression."

He climbs up on the stage, then comes to me. I watch him warily. I don't know what he's planning.

"You okay?" he asks, his voice low.

I shrug, feeling way too vulnerable. I don't want to tell him I'm not, but for some reason, I don't want to lie, either.

"This is going to be quick. Don't worry—I'm a *much* better dancer than that scarecrow with a bad mustache."

I snort-giggle, then cover up my reaction by fake-coughing. I look at Grant. His eyes are a gorgeous aquamarine, and I feel like I could get lost in them.

Pull yourself together.

Everyone's watching us now, and I have no choice but to tango again. I pray Grant doesn't pull a dick move as he extends a hand. I place my hand there, feeling his other hand on my waist. Why is he siding with me against Professor Taylor when he has nothing to gain by it?

Grant's palm is dry and warm, and touching his bare skin sends a frisson of warmth through my core. *Nerves,* I tell myself, even though it doesn't feel like nerves. *It's the anxiety,* I insist, even as my belly flutters and my mouth goes dry.

Grant gives Professor Taylor a meaningful look. "We're ready."

The professor clears his throat with a dark scowl at me, then starts the music.

Grant lets the music go on for a few beats, then exerts a gentle backward pressure on my hand and shifts his torso subtly before starting to move. I relax and match his steps. When the music changes, he turns his hips and torso just enough to let me know where he's going to take me. I follow easily.

My heart is pounding with anxiety as I wait to see if he's going to do anything showy. He seems like the type who'd love to exhibit his awesomeness. But he's making sure I'm okay and doesn't try to do any fancy turns or abrupt changes in direction. I'm grateful because it's difficult to turn smoothly in sneakers. The soles grip the floor too hard, and a quick turn could make me stumble.

Once I realize he's actually going to lead me to the best of his ability, I start to relax. He's a fabulous partner. His body heat warms me all over as we move closer, our eyes on each other, like we've choreographed and practiced the basic tango moves since forever. Goosebumps break out, and the air tastes thick and sweet as I inhale through my parted lips.

The music ends, and we stop. I try to breathe evenly, calm my racing heart. Grant's eyes are on mine, and I can't look away.

"Well. That was indeed quite well done. Great job, Grant," Professor Taylor says, clapping and jerking me out of the paralysis.

Ass, I think, looking at the professor, but say nothing. As long as he ignores me and doesn't bug me, I'm not going to complain.

Grant shoots him a cool look. "Aspen did amazing. What a difference a better partner can make, eh?"

Professor Taylor flashes an awkward smile. "I'm sure you showed her the steps when you did the paper together."

"Like I told you, all the great insights in the paper came from her," Grant says, although his eyes are hard now. "I did nothing except lend my name."

The professor looks lost. "Uh... I see. Well. Lending one's name is important, too."

The man is an idiot. But I want Grant to stop, since I don't need the professor to realize I did all the work and lower our grade to spite me. Grant may not need scholarship money—if he's even getting any —but I do.

Thankfully, before I can intervene, one of the guys raises his hand. "Professor Taylor, we gotta go. Class time's up!"

Professor Taylor says, "Yes, yes, go on. Do the reading for next class!" and waves everyone away. The students start to stuff their belongings into their bags and leave. Sadie looks at us like she wants to say something, but Bronte pulls at her, and they go out together.

I tap Grant on the shoulder. "We should get going. I'm sure Professor Taylor has more important things to do now."

Grant looks at the man like he isn't finished, but finally he nods.

I let out a small sigh of relief, then make sure he leaves without saying another word to our red-faced instructor.

6

GRANT

I leave the lecture hall together with Aspen, just in case Taylor tries something. His behavior in class reminds me so much of Dad's assistant, who's only nice to people who he thinks are important and treats everyone else like shit. I don't know who Taylor thought he was fooling by jerking Aspen around like a rag doll. It made him look like an idiot, not her.

It was offensive. And I hated the way he put his hands on her and yanked her close twice in what he must've believed was a dramatic gesture. I loathe the fact that he heard her gasp as he did so, felt her breath on his skin, even if the situation wasn't sexual.

The more I think about it, the more irritated I become. The bastard obviously didn't warn her about having to demonstrate a dance for the class. It's clear he wanted to humiliate her.

Asshole.

Once we're outside the building, she stops and turns. "Thank you."

I shrug. "You were my partner for the project, so..." I can't tell her that the way Taylor treated her pissed me off because I don't know precisely why it bugged me so much. Normally, I try to keep drama at a distance. The only stuff I get involved in is with my brothers and my mother, but that's expected. They're family.

Aspen isn't. And she isn't even a friend. As a matter of fact, she made it clear I'm not worthy of buying her a thank-you dinner.

"Yeah, but still. You didn't have to do that." She looks torn as she says it, but I don't know what could be so conflicting about thanking me.

"True." I was going to say goodbye and go, but now I don't want to. "Feel free to pay me back if you like."

She regards me warily. "What do you want?"

"How about dinner?"

"*Me*"—she points at herself—"taking *you* out?"

"Uh-huh." She couldn't be more surprised if I told her I was a Martian with X-ray vision.

She cocks her head. "I'm not taking you to French Laundry."

"I guess I'll settle for Morimoto, then," I say with a heavy sigh, full of feigned dejection.

"*What?*"

I laugh. "I'm just kidding. Anywhere's fine. You choose."

"You don't know what people say about me, do you?" She puts her hands on her hips.

"Probably not." Not going to count what Heath and Will said. Or Sadie.

"I'm cheap." *There*, Aspen's voice says in a dare to not find fault in that.

"Cool. I like cheap women."

"Hah. No, it's going to be a cheap *dinner*."

"A free dinner, for me."

"You sure you can do without a fancy tablecloth?"

"Free dinner," I singsong.

"They only have canned pasta."

"Still free."

"And I'm not paying for your drinks." *You still want me to take you out?* her eyes challenge.

"I don't drink." Well, I don't drink cheap or bad alcohol, but I'm not giving her an excuse to back out. She's probably one of those scholarship kids the college takes in to be "diverse" enough. It looks bad if the entire student body consists of trust-fund babies. So the college accepts several students from average backgrounds and gives

45

them scholarships and financial aid that are directly tied to their grades. Which would explain her desperate attempt to get me to do the paper with her.

She huffs. "Fine. I don't know why you're so intent on dinner, but..."

"Awesome."

"I'll text you."

———

I realize she's ghosting me after four days of silence. I didn't get to see her in Culture and Music in History, since Taylor canceled the class after the tango debacle. Probably too ashamed to show his face. Or maybe he overslept. Who the hell knows?

I text her, but it goes ignored. If she was like anybody else I've dated, I'd assume she was playing a game to try to demonstrate who was in charge of the relationship. But she doesn't seem like the type to waste energy over such triviality. If she wants to have a little revenge over how I ignored her texts and emails, she's doing a pretty good job... Although it annoys me that she's not following through on her promise, as I did when she asked me to go to that pointless class.

Since I know exactly how to find her, I go to the café where she works. But there's a different barista at the counter today. Some guy who looks vaguely familiar.

"Hey," he says with a friendly smile. "What can I get you?"

"Actually, I'm here to talk to Aspen. Is she here?"

"Oh. No, she's off today."

"Do you know when her next shift is?"

"Tomorrow, maybe? She called in sick for two days in a row, so I don't know." He shrugs apologetically.

Okay, so maybe she isn't ghosting me just for the hell of it. I don't like hearing that she's sick. It must be serious for her to miss work. Bet she also missed classes. "I have a project I need to pick up from her. Do you know where she lives?"

He squints and looks off into the distance. "Howell Hall?"

I make a face. That place is a dump. Nobody understands why

the college hasn't demolished it yet. They had a room there on the boys' floor I could've taken, instead of the three-bedroom suite with Heath and Will. I picked the Frat-Stereotypes-R-Us duo rather than a dorm cell. "You sure?"

"No, man. I don't have Aspen watch." He shrugs.

So Hovel Hall is my best lead. Maybe somebody in the housing division hates her, just like Taylor. Snotty assholes are everywhere.

I text her before heading out, in case she's recuperating at a friend's.

—Me: Heard you're sick. You okay?

It stays unread, like my other messages.

This doesn't seem like her. She's the type to come after someone rather than ignore them like this. If she's too sick to check her phone, maybe she's really got something bad. So I shouldn't go empty-handed. Mom taught me better.

But I've never been really sick. A minor cold once in a while doesn't count.

—Me: What's something to take to make somebody feel better?

There. My brothers should have some suggestions.

—Noah: An Aston Martin. It never fails to cheer me up.

Most girls would offer to suck me off for an Aston Martin. Aspen? She'd run me over with it once she recovered from whatever's ailing her.

—Me: No. For someone who's sick.

—Emmett: Mom's chicken noodle soup.

Should've known. Unlike me and some of our other brothers, Emmett has a normal mother who does motherly things for him.

—Me: Where am I going to get your mom's chicken noodle soup right now?

—Sebastian: Chef-made isn't bad, either.

—Me: No chef on campus.

—Nicholas: Campbell's. For God's sake, don't try cooking for whoever it is.

Dick. I'm not *that* bad.

—Me: Fine. Campbell's it is.

—Emmett: Call and see if he needs any meds?

Well, well. Emmett must not know me as well as I thought if he thinks I'm doing this for a guy. On the other hand, he probably can't believe I'm doing this for a girl, either.

–Me: Not answering, so I dunno.

–Noah: Texts are better.

–Griffin: You could've been blocked.

–Me: Shut up.

I shove my phone into my pocket and stop by a store on campus. They're out of Campbell's, so I have to pick a different brand I've never heard of—not that I'm an expert on canned goods—but it's probably okay. The label claims it's made with quality white meat and organic noodles.

With two cans and some crackers, I head to Howell Hall. The school says it's named after one of the founding families, but if that's the case, they should've done a better job of maintaining the structure. A thick layer of moss looks like wet, green slime on the dingy white walls—which could've used a fresh coat of paint twenty years ago. One corner is covered with soot. Maybe somebody tried to perform a public service and burn it down so the college would be forced to rebuild it.

I hang out at the main entrance, waiting for somebody to let me in. Once I'm inside, it shouldn't be hard to find Aspen's room. The dorm is only four stories, two for girls and two for guys.

A skinny Asian girl in a thin hoodie and jeans swipes her ID to get in. I try to sneak in with her, but she stops and turns around.

"Scan your own ID," she says, looking up at me like I'm a serial killer.

I give her a charming smile that never fails to win people over.

She merely narrows her eyes.

"I'm a student here," I begin, "but my friend isn't answering my texts. I want to see if she's okay."

She looks me up and down, head to toe, studies my face and takes in my clothes. "You have a friend who lives here?"

"Yeah."

"I don't believe you." Her dark gaze rests on my Harry Winston watch.

"Don't be a reverse snob."

She puts a hand on her hip. "Who's your friend?"

"Aspen Hughes."

Her demeanor changes instantly, from skepticism to shock. "Wait. You're Aspen's friend? Like a friend-friend, or a friend?"

I laugh a little. "Just a friend."

Vague disappointment settles over her. "I see. Well, that's too bad. On the other hand, if you were a friend-friend, you would've known."

"Known what?"

"That she's sick. Come on."

I step inside, letting the door close behind me. "What's up with her? A cold?"

"I don't know. Kind of looks like the flu, but she says it isn't." She shrugs. "Probably just exhaustion from having to do a group project all by herself."

I doubt that's the case, but I keep my mouth shut.

"She told me about it Sunday evening on our way to a movie, and I was like, 'Girl, you should've punched that shithead.'"

"She didn't." I don't tell her that the shithead is me, in case she decides to punch me for Aspen.

"She's just too nice. That's her problem." She walks up to the second floor, then stops at a room at the end of the hall. "That's her." She points at a door. "If she doesn't answer after a few knocks, just chill out in the lounge, or you can go. She's probably napping, which she needs more than you, as pretty as you are."

I quirk an eyebrow at how disapproving she sounds while calling me pretty. "I'll keep all that in mind."

The girl goes into her room. I knock softly on Aspen's door, not wanting to wake her up if she really is sleeping.

Nothing.

After waiting a few moments, I start back toward the lounge to scroll through news about the Asian markets on my phone for an hour or so before I check again.

The door opens to reveal Aspen. "Suyen...?" She blinks. "Grant?"

"Yeah." I take a good look at her. Dark circles under her eyes like bruises. Chalky complexion, no color to her chapped lips. Hair like a rat's nest. Her black shirt and yellow shorts are wrinkled to the max.

"What are you doing here?" she croaks.

I wince and clear my throat, feeling a little awkward all of a sudden. We were partners on a project, which I didn't work on. And we aren't friends or anything. There's no real reason for me to be here. "Heard you were ill, so I decided to stop by. Thought you might like some soup." I lift the bag I'm carrying.

She looks at it, her expression unreadable.

"It's canned. But better that than half-killing you with my cooking." I hope she's not offended. Mom would rather die than touch anything canned or instant. She prefers everything to be cooked from scratch.

Aspen tries to swallow, then gives up. "Thanks. Um. Wanna come in?"

"Sure." Every time she speaks, her eyebrows pull together tightly. Her throat must be killing her.

Her room is dimly lit and awfully small. The blinds are the color of horse shit—literally—and I shake my head inwardly at just how awful the housing division people are at the college. Cinder-block walls don't particularly alleviate the effect.

But there are bright posters covering those walls, and a yellow daisy on her desk that makes the place feel less like a jail for students whose only crime is not being able to afford expensive off-campus housing. Her room's tidy as well, nothing out of place. Bet she's the type to make her bed the second she gets up in the morning, which, for some reason, feels oddly endearing. Other than a bottle of Advil with a label so worn that it's almost white, there doesn't seem to be any medicine around.

She sits on the bed, then gestures at the hard wooden chair that came with the desk.

I promptly park my ass on it. "You got anything for your throat? And other stuff for whatever you have? The flu, right?"

She shakes her head. "It's nothing contagious. I get it sometimes. I should be fine by Friday night. I have to be."

"By Friday? Got a big exam to study for over the weekend?"

"No, a call with my grandparents. I don't want them to start worrying."

"I see. So...no fever or anything?"

"Just a headache. And my throat hurts. No appetite."

"You should probably eat something, though." Emmett always makes a point of eating even when he's sick and doesn't feel like it. Says you can't recover otherwise, and he does seem to get better rather quickly.

"Yeah... Maybe later." She doesn't meet my eyes.

"Did you take anything?"

"An Advil this morning."

"Then take some more and you'll probably feel okay enough to eat." I pick up the Advil bottle and shake it. The pills rattle, but I notice something. "Hey, these are expired."

"Only by six weeks," she says defensively.

I don't understand how anybody can shrug off taking something that's gone past its due date. "They've probably turned into poison by now."

She gives me a look. "I Googled. It's fine."

"No, it isn't. No wonder you're still sick. I'll be back."

She opens her mouth to argue, but I stuff the bottle into my pocket—just in case she's stubborn enough to take one to spite me—and head back to the store to grab some over-the-counter stuff for her.

Once I step inside the store, I realize I have no idea what I'm doing. The only thing I buy is aspirin for the rare occasion when I get a mild headache.

—Me: What's the best OTC medicine for when you feel bad? Like a headache and your throat hurts.

—Emmett: Are you sick?

He adds a shocked emoji.

—Noah: Brain tumor? That might explain your unnatural IQ.

I roll my eyes. Leave it to Noah to jump to not only the wrong conclusion, but the *most* wrong conclusion.

—Griffin: Cough drops. Advil or Tylenol?

—Sebastian: My grandmother swears by cholera septic.

I pull back. *What the fuck?* I'm not buying Aspen anything named "cholera septic," no matter how good it is. Her opinion of me has improved somewhat since the tango fiasco, and I don't want it dropping back down to *asshole*.

—Sebastian: Dammit, Chloraseptic! Stupid autocorrect. It's a throat spray.

—Me: I was wondering about your grandmother.

Now armed with knowledge, I stare down at the OTC med aisle. Jesus. It's full of stuff. Cough drops, Advil and Tylenol in all sorts of variations. Gels. Tablets. AM. PM. *Dual Action*...which sounds kind of dirty.

Since I'm not sure, I just grab one of each variety of Advil and Tylenol, including Dual Action just in case regular old single action doesn't do it for her. Plus that Chloraseptic spray, and three bags each of the different varieties of cough drops.

Armed with supplies, I head back to Aspen's place. The door to Howell Hall is once again locked. I debate texting her, but don't want her leaving her bed and having to come all the way down the stairs to let me in. Thankfully, a student is on his way out, and I go in, trying to look like I belong in the dorm. Unlike that chick earlier, this guy doesn't seem to notice or care about me.

When I go to Aspen's room and triumphantly lift the bulging bags to show her what I brought, she blinks dully.

"What am I supposed to do with all that?" she croaks.

"Take some, and then take more." I feel like an unlicensed doctor. "Get better."

She takes the bags in slow motion and dumps them on her bed. Spread out, the haul takes up at least a third of the mattress. "Eight bottles of Advil? And Tylenol? And how many bags of cough drops did you...? Oh my God, there's, like, *twenty*." She collapses back onto her pillow.

Maybe I did go a little overboard. But how was I supposed to know what she needs? "Just think of them as gifts," I say, feeling a bit ridiculous. I've never given girls OTC drugs. When the occasion demands, I go with roses because they're easy. But then everything with Aspen's been irregular.

"Thanks."

A small smile comes over her wan face, and it breaks something inside me. Even though she's been sick and hasn't showered in days, she's so pretty when she smiles, her green eyes crinkling with warmth. My heart and belly feel funny, like with heartburn, except it doesn't hurt.

"Why don't you start with that throat spray, and I'll heat the soup up for you?" I need some time to figure out why I'm reacting like this. It's like the air in Howell Hall is tainted with hallucinogenic drugs or something.

She nods.

The second I leave her room with a can, I realize I have no clue how to operate the stove. Actually, I've never been to any kitchen except to grab something from the fridge or use the microwave. I know you can't microwave metal.

Since my brothers are as worthless in the kitchen as I am, I knock on the door of the Asian girl who let me in earlier. She doesn't answer.

Shit.

All right. Maybe I'll just Google. I stare down at the can in my hand. How hard can it be?

I walk along the hall until I hit a lounge with a kitchenette. The Asian girl I was looking for is lying on a couch, reading. She lowers her book.

"You still here?" she asks.

"Left and came back, actually. Aspen needs some food."

She looks at the can. "Soup?"

"Yeah."

"Don't you know canned soup is bad for you? Too much sodium and preservatives."

"Positivity. Good! Just what Aspen needs to get better."

"Just sayin'." She gets to her feet. "So. Do you know how to turn on the stove?"

"Do I look that helpless?"

She smiles. "Yes."

"I can probably turn it on, but beyond that..."

She snorts. "Figures. Lemme show you. But not because I want to help you, because I love Aspen."

It's a good thing, too. I have no idea what I'm doing. The can isn't that big. Also it isn't condensed, which, according to Suyen, means no adding water.

"It's barely a bowl." I'd be starving if this was all I got.

"That's all she needs," Suyen says. "She probably doesn't have much appetite right now." She gestures at the dish drainer by the sink. "You can use the stuff there, but you gotta clean everything up before you leave."

The drainer has a few plates and a couple of cups that are big enough to hold the soup. I pour it into the cup and put some water in the pot.

After grabbing a spoon, I take the food to Aspen's room. When she opens the door, I search her face, wondering if anything I brought is helping. She looks to be about the same, though. They need to invent meds that deliver instant results.

"How are you feeling?" I ask. "Did the spray help?"

She nods. "A little, yeah. Thanks."

She put the bags of stuff away already. There's only a bottle of Advil, throat spray and some cough drops by her bed.

"Why don't you sit on the bed?" I say, since the room is tiny and doesn't have a good place to eat. She settles down, the sheets over her legs. I hand her the soup. "Careful. It's hot."

She holds it gingerly. "Thanks." She takes a small spoonful to her mouth. Her eyebrows rise. "It's pretty good."

I smile with satisfaction. It's such a small thing, but I like feeding her.

Then she looks at my empty hands. "You want some?"

"Nope. It's all yours." I sit on the hard chair in front of her desk again. "I'm going to wait until you're done so I can clean up."

"You don't have to. I can do it later," she says.

"Nah. That's the nurse's job."

She gives me a small smile. "Are you a nurse?"

"For you, yes. And an awesome one."

Shaking her head a little, she finishes the soup. I take the empty cup and spoon and place them on the desk next to the daisy.

"Don't you have anything better to do than buy me soup and stuff?" she says, looking at me like I'm a curious animal. Her voice is still a little rough, but she doesn't seem to be in as much pain.

"Nothing I can't do over the phone." I wave mine.

"Trying to get girls to buy you dinner?"

I laugh. "No. Just checking the market and making sure I'm making money."

"How come? Doesn't your Hollywood daddy give you as much money as you want?"

I tilt my head. "You know who my parents are?"

She nods.

Well. There goes my theory that she doesn't know my background. "Since when?"

"I don't know. A while." Her tone says she doesn't know why it would be important.

"Before you yelled at me on the polo field?"

She nods again.

"But...you weren't very nice," I say slowly, trying to process.

She shrugs. "You weren't either."

"Yeah, but...most people don't care." When they look at me, they see my parents—and all that they represent.

"I'm not most people." Suddenly, her eyes grow wide. "Wait, did you think I should've been nice to you because of your rich parents?" She shakes her head and laughs. "That's... Wow. Listen, I don't care who your parents are. They aren't here—you are. I'm talking to you, not them. So if you act like a jerk, I'm going to treat you like a jerk."

I stare at her. She's serious. She doesn't give a shit about anything but me—*my* behavior, *my* attitude. When she lays her eyes on me, she sees *me*, Grant Ares Lasker, not Ted Lasker or Athena Grant lurking in the background.

The world seems to tilt. *I* matter to this woman. But the feeling is quickly followed by embarrassment. I've been a dick to her because I let my assumptions color our interactions.

Well, maybe not a *complete* dick. I did show up for class like she asked. Showed Taylor what a shitty dancer he was and made her look good. But is that enough to pull me out of the Jerk Zone?

She shifts a little, like she's given up on getting a response. From her rather calm expression, she doesn't seem to understand the bomb she's just dropped on me.

Her eyelids droop a little. Her cheeks are flushed from having eaten something warm. I like the sight of her looking rosy and sleepy after consuming what I've provided.

I make her lie down and tuck her in so she can get some rest. Then—because I can't stop myself—I press my fingers to her forehead. "Just checking your temperature."

But what I really want to press there are my lips.

7

ASPEN

By Friday afternoon, I feel like myself again. After coming over to buy me enough painkillers to supply the entirety of Howell Hall for a year—and heating the soup for me and making sure I ate the whole thing—Grant drops by once more in the morning before classes to check up on me and see if I need anything. Then he texts me in the afternoon.

It's the oddest thing to have somebody doing this for me. Other than my grandparents, nobody's ever been this attentive. And Grant can't be doing it to get laid—he has hundreds of girls who want him. I don't think it's for a free dinner, either.

Maybe he's just being nice, although the possibility seems a bit remote, given how he was when we first met. But then again, he defended me against Professor Taylor, so Grant might actually not be *too* terrible.

I know I'm softening because I keep waiting for his texts. It's lovely to be taken care of. It makes me feel like I'm not alone on campus, especially when I know he has to be busier than he lets on. He plays polo, and from what I've seen on some of the pictures posted, he also plays tennis. Suyen's a great friend, but she's too busy to check in on me more than every once in a while, especially with the new job she started a couple of weeks ago at a local vineyard.

–Grant: How are you feeling?

–Me: Much better. Thanks.

–Grant: Good enough to call your grandparents this weekend?

Huh. He remembered.

–Me: Yes.

–Grant: Told you that expired Advil wouldn't work.

I can just hear his smug tone. For some reason, it makes me smile a little.

I start to type something snarky, then stop. He deserves better for his acts of kindness. He said he wanted me to buy him dinner after our last class. Maybe I should do that. Combine thanking him for that and the "nursing."

–Me: Fine, you were right.

–Grant: Thank you.

–Me: Are you free tomorrow evening?

–Grant: Maaaaaaybe. Are you asking me out?

Wait—did I sound like I was asking him out?

–Me: I wanted to know if you could bring me more canned soup.

After hitting send, I stare at the screen, something hot and exciting blooming in my chest as I wait.

–Grant: We can do better than canned soup. For variety.

He sends me a picture of canned spinach. The caption reads: *If it's good enough for Popeye, it's good enough for you.* I laugh.

–Me: How does cheap pasta sound?

–Grant: You paying?

–Me: Told you I would.

–Grant: I dunno...

He probably wants something fancy. Like his watch. Suyen told me that thing's worth over fifteen grand, and I almost fell off the lounge couch. Who just casually wears that kind of stuff on their wrist? I would have a dozen anti-theft devices on the strap!

Oh well. If he doesn't want to...

–Grant: Screw it. :shrug emoji: I should probably play hard to get, but who am I kidding? What time?

I laugh.

–Me: 7?

–Grant: Works for me. Pick you up in front of Howell?

I hesitate. That feels too much like a date, rather than just an innocent thank-you dinner.

–Me: Let's meet at the diner. I'll text you the directions.

–Grant: I shall wait with bated breath.

I Google the small Italian bistro where I waited tables last year, and send him the link. That done, I look around my room. I have today off from my job at the library.

The air feels stuffy and stale. *Okay. Time for action.* I open the window, throw out the piles of cough drop wrappings and start cleaning my room.

I email some classmates to see if I can borrow their notes. Most of them email me their notes, no problem. Clara, who likes to hand-write, sends me pictures, with a warning: *No guarantees you can read this!* It turns out to be pointless, because her cursive is superb.

On Saturday, I call my grandparents. They moved the day because tomorrow is their fiftieth anniversary. They were thinking about going to San Diego, but changed their mind at the last minute. They're going to celebrate in town at a nearby restaurant instead.

"Happy early anniversary!" I say.

"Thank you," Grandpa says. He holds Grandma's hand and grins.

"Doing anything special?" I ask innocently. The daisies I ordered should arrive tomorrow morning. But I'm not saying anything because it's a surprise. Grandma adores yellow daisies—they're the flowers Grandpa gave her on their first date. Her eyes light up every time she tells me the story. My grandparents are so cute.

"Dinner. Dancing. Celebration." Grandma says with a contented smile.

"That's awesome," I say, even though a small pang pinches my heart. If it weren't for me and my college tuition, they'd be able to afford a nice getaway for the occasion. But as soon as I graduate and get a job, I'm going to send them on a nice trip with the money I make.

"So, how's your week been?" Grandma says. "You seem a little pale."

Damn it. I thought I was doing a great job of faking a haven't-been-sick mien. "It's the light. The maintenance guy swapped out the bulb, and I think it's harsher than the one I had before. By the way, guess what outrageous thing happened to me!" I say quickly, trying to get her mind off my paleness. There's no need to worry them. I come down with a sore throat and general achiness occasionally when I'm stressed or working too much or something. But it only happens once every two to three years, and I recover, no problem.

"What?" Grandpa asks, leaning closer to the camera.

"I did this paper on the tango, and the professor had me dance with him!"

"Oh my." The skin around Grandma's eyes crinkles. "You must've done an amazing job! But did you have the right shoes?" She turns to look at Grandpa. "Did she take her dance shoes with her...?"

"No, I was in my sneakers. But it didn't matter. He was awful. Worse than Barry."

Grandpa frowns. "Did you twist anything? Get hurt?"

"No, because my partner for the paper stepped in and tangoed with me." My voice goes slightly breathless.

His frown deepens. "I can't decide if that's good or bad. College kids can get a bit reckless and showy."

"Oh, it was good. Most definitely good. He was amazing at it, actually. Didn't try anything fancy and was careful to make sure I was okay the entire time."

While Grandpa nods with relief, Grandma props her chin in her hand and squints at me. "You like this boy?"

"What? That's such a...random question." *Me? Like Grant?* Come on. I let out a laugh. "No."

"Then why did you get that look in your eyes?"

"What look?"

Grandpa points at me. "That dreamy look."

I laugh. "The camera must be glitching."

"I know the difference, child. And yes, I recognize it because I see that look in the mirror every time I think about your grandpa," she says with a slightly teasing smile.

"I mean, okay, sure, he's a nice guy. But *like*?" I shake my head, trying to hide something light and bubbly inside me.

"It's difficult to like a not-nice guy," Grandpa says. "And I hope, for your own safety and happiness, you get yourself a nice young man."

"No, no, no." I wave them away.

"You're nineteen. Plenty old enough for boys and love," Grandma says softly.

"Ha. I don't have the time or energy."

Boys are... Well, they're *boys*. And most are only interested in sex or...more sex. I'm not saying this out of some preconceived notion. That's just how it's been in high school and college so far. I don't know why I should sleep with a guy just because *he* wants it, especially when there are so many risks involved. STDs. Unwanted pregnancy. Okay, so you get an orgasm if the guy is decent in bed, but that seems like a consolation prize. And orgasms aren't worth the hassle of sleeping with a boy, especially if you aren't really sure.

If I sleep with a guy, it's going to be with somebody I can't imagine *not* being with. Someone who I feel happy and content with just by being together. I want what my grandparents have.

"Such an unromantic child." Grandma sighs, half serious, half teasing. "We tried to fix that by teaching you how to dance."

"Which I appreciate, since I'll be dancing like a dream when I meet the love of my life." I smile. "I'm sure it'll happen when I'm ready."

My grandparents start laughing for some reason. Grandpa actually wipes a tear from one eye. "Aspen, little darling, love comes when you least expect it, not when you're *ready*."

"Exactly." Grandma nods. "If it comes only when it's convenient, then it isn't love."

8

GRANT

After getting Aspen's text about the restaurant, I set my expectations low. It's the best way to avoid disappointment. So long as there aren't rats scuttling around my feet, I'll be fine.

I step out of the cherry-red Maserati Dad gave me when I got into college. Actually, he gave a Maserati—our choice of color—to every one of my brothers. That's how he parents, and I'm perfectly happy with it. Things might have gotten awkward if he tried to act like he cared all of a sudden.

The restaurant isn't fancy, but it isn't dilapidated or anything. It's a quaint little place with a sloped red roof and faux-stone walls that fit right in with the whole Napa Valley Tuscan vibe.

I walk inside, and immediately get hit with the mouth-watering aroma of sizzling garlic and butter. Unlike the hoity-toity places that Mom likes to drag me to, which would have a string quartet playing Verdi or something, this joint has Ed Sheeran coming from the sound system.

For that alone, I like it.

A smiling hostess appears in a black-and-white uniform. "Hi! Can I help you?"

"There should be a reservation for two under Aspen Hughes," I say.

"Oh yes, she's here. This way."

"Actually, hold on a minute." I give her some instructions, making sure she understands she isn't to let Aspen know what I'm doing.

"My lips are *totally* sealed," she says, making a zipping motion across her mouth.

"Thanks."

She leads me to a small round table for two by a window that overlooks an illuminated garden full of flowering rosemary bushes. Aspen's already seated, in a white Aquinas College T-shirt, faded denim skirt and strappy sandals. Although she isn't wearing much makeup, she looks so pretty that I can't even blink. Her coppery red hair is down and flowing softly around her shoulders, and the mellow light from the candles on the table gives her moss-green eyes a tender glow.

I don't know why I thought she had the body of a Vegas stripper. She's more like an erotic pagan goddess men must've worshipped in an earlier era.

Without thinking, I pick up the plumeria from the small center-piece on the table and tuck it behind her ear. "Perfect," I murmur.

Her cheeks turn pink, but she doesn't remove the flower. "Is this how you hit on girls who give you a free dinner?"

I smile as I take the chair opposite her. "Only when they're pretty."

She stares at me, her plump lips slightly parted, as though she can't decide what to make of the comment. Or me, for that matter. I hold her gaze and give her time to process.

Our server interrupts the moment. "Welcome to Benedicto's! And Aspen, nice to see you again."

She turns to him with a relieved smile. "Hey, Zack."

The guy can't be older than twenty-one. Maybe a college kid working part-time. Not somebody she's ever dated, not from the soulful look he's giving her. But he'd love to.

What a dick.

"How've you been?" he asks.

"Pretty good," she says.

"Awesome." The asshole's eye-fucking her. I don't know how she can miss the way his eyes follow her curves, lingering on her breasts and hips.

Would it be weird if I gave him a short, sharp punch in the nose? Eye-fucking without consent should be illegal. This isn't the Dark Ages.

"So, *Zack,* you have any recommendations?" I shoot him the bland smile of reprimand Mom taught me when I was three. It never fails to put the other person in their place.

He turns to me like he's just realized Aspen isn't sitting at the table alone. "Oh. Uh, yeah, actually." He drones on and on. He's trying to pronounce the dishes the way an Italian would, but he has a high voice and unfortunately sounds like he's been sniffing helium.

Wonder what he'd say if I told him, "Your face looks like your ass," in Italian. Would he understand or just stare blankly?

"Can you give us a moment to look at the menu?" I say when he's finally finished.

"Yeah, sure. Want anything to drink?" He looks at Aspen as he asks.

"Lemonade," she says.

I want to say scotch, but I'm not in Geneva. "A Coke for me."

He lingers for a second, obviously hoping for some sort of further interaction with Aspen, but she's looking at the thin menu like the sensible person she is.

Once he's gone, I open my menu as well. "Wow. Look at that. Chicken parmesan. Fancy."

She smiles. "Did you honestly think they'd have nothing but pasta?"

"Nothing but *cheap* pasta. I expected only three items—cheap, cheaper and cheapest."

She laughs, the sound sweet. "I wouldn't treat you *that* badly."

"You certainly set my expectations very low."

"Didn't want to disappoint you."

"You couldn't have disappointed me."

She cocks a skeptical eyebrow, although her mouth remains curved into a smile. "I don't know if you would've said the same thing at the polo field."

"Ah, about that." I clear my throat. "The fact is, you surprised me. I didn't think you'd go the distance to track me down. Most give up."

"Do you ghost your project partners a lot?"

"Case by case, but I basically don't like group projects and avoid classes with them. I didn't realize Taylor was going to assign a group paper. If I had, I would've thought twice about taking his class."

Zack returns with drinks and a bread basket. Then he claims he wants to know if we have any questions about the menu, while gazing at Aspen like a dog begging to be acknowledged.

Thankfully, Aspen orders clam pasta without indulging him. I get the chicken parm, while wondering if I should suggest he go work in the diet industry. He'd be able to guarantee effortless results. His face alone would kill the appetite of his clients.

He takes our menus, then sighs a little before heading toward the kitchen.

"So you're ordering fancy," Aspen says.

"Hey, you said you were paying. If that isn't an invitation to splurge, I don't know what is."

She laughs.

"So how did your call with your grandparents go?"

"Great! They're doing so well. And I suspect they're probably having the most romantic time right now."

"How come?"

"It's their anniversary. I usually call them on Sundays, but this week I did it a day early."

"Really? If I had to call my folks every week, I'd go bald from stress. What do you talk about?"

"Anything and everything. Sometimes it's enough just to say hello. But this time, we talked a little bit about you," she says.

"That I saved you from getting poisoned from expired Advil?" What would she have told her family about me? Someone like Sadie would say, "He's *really* important. His dad is *the* Ted Lasker and his mom is *the* Athena Grant." It wouldn't be that critical to her what kind of person *I* was. Part of me wants to know what Aspen thinks of me, but there's also a part that doesn't. As long as I don't know, I can pretend she thinks I'm as amazing as the creators of the tango.

"No, never! That'd make them worry too much. I told them you saved me from Professor Taylor. They were...impressed. They danced professionally and won some tango competitions when they were younger. They teach now." Her gaze grows tender with affection, and a weird aching sensation spreads through me.

"That's awesome. So you must've been horrified by how Taylor 'led' you around." I make a mental note to file an anonymous complaint with the college about his behavior the second I'm done with the transfer applications, which are due soon.

"Yes." Aspen rolls her eyes. "I have no clue what he was thinking. By the way, this is one of the reasons why I haven't danced since I came here, even though I love it. It's hard to find a partner who's good and has the right schedule."

Bad as it sounds, I'm happy she hasn't been able to find a decent partner. I don't like the idea of some other guy holding her.

Our server returns with our food. He asks Aspen if she wants freshly grated parmesan, and she turns it down. He then asks her if she'd like freshly ground black pepper, which she also declines.

I ask for both. His face collapses a little, but he takes care of me well enough.

Once he's gone, I dig into the huge portion. The sauce has the intense flavor of tomatoes and herbs you can get only if you make it from scratch. The chicken is tender and perfectly cooked. It's one of the best chicken parmesans I've ever had.

"How do you like it?" she asks after my first bite.

"Fantastic. The sauce reminds me of a home-cooked meal I had at a friend's place in Tuscany, although chicken parmesan isn't really Italian, the way General Tso's chicken isn't really Chinese."

"You know what? Suyen complains about Chinese restaurants in America all the time, for the same reason!"

"Because she knows." Then I gesture at her pasta. "How's yours?"

"Good. I waitressed here last year, and this is my favorite."

"So how come you don't work here now?" *Say it's because Zack is a creeper.*

"Because they needed somebody to work during the summer and winter vacations, but I couldn't. But it doesn't matter. I got a different job to make up for it." She takes a sip of her lemonade, then clears her throat. "I feel like I'm talking too much. So...I guess you don't talk with your parents too often?"

"No." *God no.*

"A nanny, then?"

I almost choke on my chicken. "I'm a little old for a nanny."

"I thought you might've had one when you were younger and kept in touch or something." She shrugs a little.

"My parents didn't do nannies. I was shoved into a boarding school when I was old enough to talk."

She stares at me for a long moment. "That didn't bother you?"

"Nah. It was for the best. Helped me become independent. Figure out what I want to do."

"Which is...?"

"Enjoy the moment. Not worry about stuff that doesn't matter. And most things don't matter." *I have a feeling you're becoming one of the very few things that do matter.* And I like that. It's new and exciting. "Do you talk to your parents often too, like you do with your grandparents?" I ask, wanting to turn the conversation away from my folks and also to get to know her better.

"They passed away when I was little," she says.

Oh, shit. "I'm sorry."

She gives me a small smile. "It's okay. It was a long time ago. I don't even really remember them, you know?"

"So, is that how you ended up with your grandparents?"

She nods. "There was nobody on my dad's side of the family. He went through the foster system, so... If it weren't for them, I wouldn't have had anybody."

That explains her affection for them so much, and I admire them for their dedication to her. If I'd been left alone as a little orphan... I just can't picture any of my grandparents stepping up. They're too busy with their lives, and they wouldn't have wanted to be bothered with a child.

We split a tiramisu for dessert. I'm a little full, but she says it's the best tiramisu in the state, so I have to take a bite.

"Wow. Fabulous," I say with a nod of approval.

"Told you." She closes her eyes for a moment, lost in the sweetness, then lets out a soft sigh. "It's the best thing I've ever had.

Thank God I don't come here all the time. Otherwise, I would've gained a Freshman Fifty or something."

I laugh. "You'd still look pretty."

She flushes. "Yeah, but my grandparents would've worried. They might've assumed I was stress-eating."

"Do you do that?"

"Depends. But generally, no. I prefer to mull things over or just go out for a walk to clear my head."

I can see her doing that, actually. She seems too practical to gorge on sugar to soothe herself.

Dinner ends, and she asks for the check.

"It's been taken care of." The server beams proudly, like he had something to do with it.

She frowns up at him. "How?"

"I don't know." He gives her a small black folio with my credit card sticking out.

The hostess should've told him to hand it to me, but I guess she forgot. The food gets an A+, but the service? A big fat F.

She opens it, reads the name on the black AmEx and looks at me. "You paid already?"

"Uh-huh." I smile.

"But I thought I was buying you dinner for the medicine and all that when I was sick."

"I still owe you one for putting my name on the paper."

She laughs. "If I'd known, I would've taken you somewhere classier."

"That's why I didn't tell you." Since Aspen's watching, I quickly do the math and tip Zack twenty percent. If I were alone, I'd give him nothing for being a fool who tried to hit on Aspen every time he came by.

I scrawl my signature on the slip and put it into the folio. "Ready?"

"Yup."

We head out together. I walk her to her car. Although the lot is well lit, it's the principle of the matter. Plus I feel the need to come up with a reason to see her again. It's a surprisingly unfamiliar feeling—but I've never had to bother before. Girls almost always try to score more time with *me*.

"Hey, you free next Saturday? There's a polo match. Thought you might be interested." I play it cool and all, even though inside I'm dying for her to come. I want to celebrate with her after we spank the other team.

She considers for a second. "I have a shift at the café until two."

"That's fine. The matches generally go on for hours. Besides, we need you there to win."

She shoots me a mildly skeptical look. "How come?"

"We'll need a little sass to beat the other team."

"And I'm supposed to supply this sass?"

"Seems like it'd be right up your alley."

She laughs. "Fine. I'll see what I can do. But no promises."

9

ASPEN

Per the polo club's website, the match starts at one. It'll take at least forty minutes to get out there, so it'll be almost three by the time I arrive. But I should be able to catch the last couple of periods or so. No, wait—the last couple of *chukkas*. That's the term.

So after my shift is over, I reapply my mascara and lipstick, then drive to the field where I met Grant. The section for spectators is nearly full. The best tables, closest to the field, are taken, so I decide to stand near the huge fence around the green. It's probably better this way anyway. I prefer to be away from Sadie and her friends, if they're here—and I have a feeling she's stalking Grant, just like she did in Culture and Music in History. I'm counting on them missing me in the crowd. If nothing else, they might not want to make the trip out to an unshaded section. They're most likely lounging at a cool, shaded table with ice-cold drinks.

I start toward the white fence, my eyes roaming, looking for Grant. There are eight riders, and I realize our team is wearing green, and the other team burgundy.

Then I find him—on a horse with a white star on the forehead. He's so tall and powerful on the mount, absolutely in control of the two-ton animal. I stay rooted to the spot and stare as he plays with skill and confidence.

Ten minutes in, he moves aggressively through the narrow gap between two riders and swings his mallet, connecting with the ball. It shoots forward, but another player gets in the way. Grant charges faster; others gallop after him. One of the horses to his left bumps into him, jostling him hard enough on his saddle to push him off to the side, and another one to his left smacks his horse's rump.

His horse stumbles and goes down. Grant is thrown, landing on his side, then rolling once. Fear crushes me, a shocked breath hissing between my lips. The other players veer off so they don't trample him. But before he can get up, his horse rolls over him. My hands fly to my face. The animal gets up almost instantly once it's finished rolling, but Grant stays on the ground.

Terror closes my throat, and my heart hammers. A flood of adrenaline and desperation suddenly crests, making it impossible to feel anything except panic.

Grant is lying there, his eyes closed. What if... *Oh my God, what if he's seriously injured? Or even dead?*

I immediately try to climb over the fence, but a uniformed official stops me.

"Hey, you can't go in there. It's dangerous!" a huge guy says, blocking my way.

"But he fell!" I gesture behind him—or try. He isn't just blocking my way; he's blocking my view.

"We'll take care of him," he says, unmoving. "The medical team's coming."

People are shouting behind me, and the commentator is indeed calling for a medical team. But it seems to take them forever. Why aren't they on the field instantly? What if Grant never gets up because they were too late?

I clench my hands, barely hanging on to control. I hate it that there's nothing I can do.

"Oh my God! I have to go!" Sadie screams dramatically from behind me.

I turn and spot her standing. Her friends jump to their feet and start saying things I can't quite catch to console her. Pretty tears stream down her face as she dabs at her eyes.

She starts moving toward a white building labeled "Medical." I follow her through the crowd, which is on its feet to get a better view of the field. I maintain several yards between us. She's too self-absorbed in shock to notice me. If you didn't know better, you'd think her best friend had just had a stroke.

The remnants of terror cling to me like a sticky film. The possibility of Grant being injured enough that he might not be able to play —or even walk—again is just horrifying. When I was growing up, a neighbor who used to ride every weekend fell from a horse and became wheelchair-bound. And that was *without* the horse rolling over him.

I run a hand over my face. Maybe Grant will get lucky. Not everyone who falls off a horse gets crippled.

The clinic is smaller than it looks from outside. It's just an open space with five beds, some unrecognizable medical equipment and a few chairs. The air smells faintly of antiseptic. The place is probably designed to give basic care before sending the injured athletes off to a real hospital for further treatment.

The medical team carries Grant inside on a stretcher. He isn't moving and his eyes are still shut. He looks impossibly pale this close.

I look for blood, but don't see any. There are huge grass stains on his pants. A small scrape on his cheek.

Sadie rushes toward him. "Grant!" She tries to grab his arm, but the medical staff heave a sigh and block her. A nurse rolls her eyes. Maybe this is a familiar scene to them.

Grant stays still. I go to him, wanting to see how he's doing for myself.

"What are *you* doing here?" Sadie says.

"I just want to check if he's okay," I respond, ignoring her hostility. Grant is so much more important than her issues with me.

"Nobody invited you."

"Actually, Grant did."

A guy in a white uniform says, "Sadie, you mind helping us by grabbing the bandages for Grant from over there?"

I don't think the man needs any help. He probably just wants to separate us, and she's closer to him than I am. On top of that, he doesn't know me.

She looks at me like she's torn, not wanting me near Grant, but also not wanting to look like an unhelpful bitch. Finally, she stomps away.

I place a gentle hand over Grant's cheek. "Come on, Grant." I bite my lip. "You're scaring me."

His eyelashes move a little, then he opens his eyes. They wander for a moment, then meet mine.

Relief pours through me. Something wet trickles down my face, and I realize I'm crying. "Are you okay?" I ask, wiping away my tears impatiently.

He looks up at me mutely. He seems vaguely confused and stunned.

It's probably a concussion. Anybody would have one when they've fallen off a horse and then gotten rolled under it.

He opens his mouth. After blinking once, he licks his lips. "Aspen," he whispers softly, like he's in awe.

"Out of the way!" Sadie says, shoving me away with her hands and hips.

I stumble and almost fall. Damn it.

"*You* need to get out of the way," a guy with a nametag that reads *Dr. Wilson* says to Sadie.

"But—"

"Unless you have a medical degree, I suggest you let me do my job."

I'm too restless to take a seat, so I just stand there. We wait for what feels like forever. Sadie shoots me a dirty look from time to time from her plastic chair, but she stops with the verbal abuse. When she tried, she got shushed by Dr. Wilson, who said he can't work with shrill noises.

Finally, he announces, "Nothing seems to be broken." He starts packing up his medical equipment.

"He could be concussed," I say. What kind of doctor thinks no broken bones is enough?

"I'm not," Grant says from the bed.

"You don't know that," I say.

"I didn't hit my head."

"Grant, baby, who cares what she says?" Sadie sticks close to him, now that Dr. Wilson is done.

I stay in the corner I was occupying, since it feels ridiculous to follow her lead. I'm not going to create a scene from some third-rate love-triangle drama and beg for Grant's attention when he seems perfectly okay with her wrapped around him.

But even as I tell myself that, I feel like crap. Not sure why. Maybe it's the shock of seeing him get rolled like dough.

Be honest. You hate the way her long, manicured nails are digging into him.

Fine. I don't like it. But I'm not acknowledging it out loud.

Sadie makes a weird noise that she must think is super cute. "Lemme take care of you. I can drive you home and nurse you back to health!"

"That's a good idea," Dr. Wilson says.

"I don't need a nurse." Grant scoffs. "And I can drive myself."

"You should *not* be driving," the doc says. "Even though you aren't exhibiting signs of a concussion at the moment, they don't always manifest immediately after a trauma. Sometimes it can take hours."

"Oh, come on," Grant says.

"So someone should watch you for the next day or so," the doctor continues. "Also, the pills I had you take were muscle relaxants. You aren't supposed to drive."

"Why the hell did you do that?" Grant complains. "Tylenol's plenty good enough."

Dr. Wilson shakes his head. "Because you're going to be very, very sore. You're extremely lucky that nothing was broken."

"Starfire is a good horse."

The doctor squints. "I don't think—"

"You heard the man!" Sadie loops her arm around Grant's. "I'm totally ready and willing to drive you anywhere."

"I don't think that's necessary." He pulls his arm out of her grip. "And your Aston Martin's too cramped."

Her eyes light up. "No, Daddy just got me a Maserati for my birthday! It's just like yours, except newer!"

Must be nice. I watch those two—so well suited to each other.

Both rich. Both privileged. Both pretty. I don't even recognize the brand logos on their clothes, while I'm in a cheap outfit and have a car that's ten years old.

Grant looks pained. "New-car smell? Ugh."

"We can open the windows!" she says.

"Sadie, your voice is going to give me a concussion for real."

I stifle a laugh.

Sadie looks at him like he just called her ugly. "How could you say that?"

"There. That shrill tone." He puts a finger at his temple and groans. "How can anybody *not* get a concussion?" He turns to me. "Aspen, would you mind?"

I blink at the abrupt shift in his focus. "Mind what?"

"Driving me home."

"No!" Sadie screams.

I wince at the screech, but I'm not going to say no just to soothe her. Besides, Grant's seen my car already. Guess not even a just-like-Grant's-but-newer Maserati is good enough to beat my not-at-all-new Mazda3. "Of course. Nothing would give me more pleasure."

———

"We don't have to go right now," Grant says as I fold him into the passenger seat of my Mazda3. But he doesn't resist much as he goes in.

"Yes, we do." I don't need Sadie bringing backup. Bronte and Tanya only exacerbate Sadie's impossible personality.

He puts a hand on the door to stop me from closing it. "But the match isn't over yet."

"It's about to be. Move your hand."

"I want to know the score," he says as the crowd erupts.

"Ask a teammate to text it."

"But I want to be here."

I put my hands on my hips. "Okay, *look*. I'm not letting you stay here and do whatever that you do after a match. You need to get horizontal on your bed and *rest*! Didn't you hear what your doctor said?"

He smiles. "I did. Nothing's broken."

"Yeah, except for your common sense."

He laughs. "Come on."

"No." I swat his hand until he lets go of the door. I close it, go around and take a seat behind the wheel. "I'm taking you home."

"What about my car?"

"Later." I peel out of the parking lot before he decides to hop out.

"Doc's just covering his ass so he doesn't get sued. I'm telling you, I feel great."

"It's the muscle relaxants talking."

"Nobody gets loopy on two pills."

"And nobody feels great when they've had a horse roll over them."

"You worry too much."

"You worry too little."

He sighs, then falls silent. He's probably feeling the pain—or the pills Dr. Wilson gave him—but trying to be manly. It's the stupidest thing in the world. Even Grandpa does that, and it's asinine. Drives Grandma insane.

I don't turn on any music, so Grant can reflect on the unreasonably casual way he's treating himself. And this is the guy who freaked out over some barely expired Advil!

When we're close to the campus, I say, "Where do you live?"

"Burton Quad," he says.

It's one of the newest and nicest on-campus housing options, each unit designed to accommodate three students, but I'm surprised he opted for on-campus housing. He seems like the type to have his own place, based on what he said during dinner about being independent. Maybe he craves companionship more than he lets on.

I park my car in one of the three visitor slots. As he undoes his seatbelt, I say, "Stay there."

"Okay..."

I get out and go around the car. I open the door for him, then hold out a hand. "Come on. Let me help you out."

"I'm not an invalid."

76

"Uh-huh. I'll believe that when the memory of you under that horse stops making me panic."

He looks at my hand for a second, then wraps his bigger, warmer hand around it. "Thanks."

"You're welcome. Are your roommates around?" *Please let the question hide the hot tremor him holding my hand has caused.*

"No. They're out of town for the weekend. Hanging out with some girls at a couple of vineyards, drinking wine."

"Aren't they underage?" No matter how cool Grant is, I can't imagine seniors rooming with a sophomore.

He shrugs. "Fake IDs."

Of course. Probably half the students have them.

I take Grant to the first floor. The interior of Burton Quad is all warm wood—both the walls and floor. A wood floor is wasted on college kids, though; this one is scuffed and marred to the point that there's more scar than wood. But the overall feel is upscale and welcoming, rather than dank, jail-like claustrophobia.

It's sort of interesting in a sad way that, even in college, money matters, and the students are separated into the haves and have-nots.

Grant gestures at a door to our right, and we enter a three-bedroom suite together. The place could fit eight of my room. No wonder everyone calls Howell Hall "the Hovel."

The suite is comfortably furnished, but very college-boy-like—lots of game consoles piled in front of a huge TV, a couple of Bluetooth speakers, a mountain bike leaning against the wall behind the TV and a huge bowl about a quarter-full with stale popcorn. Even the air in here smells like testosterone.

"Sorry it's a bit messy." The tips of his ears actually go red. "We weren't expecting a visitor."

"Don't worry about it. Which one's your room?"

"There." He points to a room on the other side of the TV.

I gird my loins. Grant doesn't come across as the type to clean up after himself, and given the condition of the common area, his room probably isn't that much better. I'll be happy if it doesn't have a jumbo-sized bottle of Vaseline lotion and a box of extra-soft Kleenex by his bed. One of the boys who wanted to get into my pants in high school came up to me during lunch and told me how he kept those for the times he couldn't stop thinking about me. He ended up wearing my pasta.

But Grant's room is astonishingly neat. No trash. No dust. No lotion. His Kleenex is the standard kind. There are three large cardboard boxes neatly stacked by his desk, which has nothing but his laptop and tablet. The walls are barren—no posters of hot girls or fancy cars. Or maybe he doesn't need them because he already has a Maserati.

He pulls off his polo boots and grabs a towel and a couple of things off his desk chair. "I need to shower."

"Yeah. You probably should." He smells like horses and sweat. Not that that's necessarily terrible, but he probably feels gross. Then I realize I made it sounds like he's stinky. "I mean, just to make yourself more comfortable."

"Right." He nods slowly. "Are you still nervous about me being loopy or something?" A corner of his mouth tilts up.

"No, I'm not going to hover over you in the shower. I'll be right here. If you need anything, holler."

"I don't know. What if I feel faint and collapse before I get a chance to holler? Or I could slip."

"I'll call 911 if I hear you fall and crack your skull open for real."

Laughing, he vanishes into the bathroom. Meanwhile, I pull out my phone and Google what happens when you experience what Grant has.

The articles are dire. The only thing they don't bring up is epilepsy, which isn't really comforting.

I have a shift at the library later today. Should I call and ask for time off? On the other hand, wouldn't it be presumptuous to assume that *I'm* the one who should be keeping an eye on him? Sadie could come barging in later. Or any of the other girls who'd love an opportunity to get close to Grant. But I don't like the idea.

What's wrong with me? It's weird to act like I have any kind of hold over him. He's just... Okay, so he's a surprisingly nice guy, and he bought me a thank-you dinner. But that doesn't mean we're in a position to feel jealous about the opposite sex's interest.

Is this how stalkers are born?

Grant comes out of the bathroom in a gray shirt and black

shorts. His hair is slightly damp—probably towel-dried, since I didn't hear a dryer—and he looks incredible. The little scrape on his left cheek looks redder, but not infected.

He smells like his shampoo and body wash—some subtle musk and wood. It isn't anything I've ever sniffed in a supermarket. He probably uses some ultra-exclusive brand. It's the kind of scent that makes me want to bury my nose in the crook of his neck and inhale.

"So, no need for 911?" I try to joke, so I can quit thinking about how delicious he smells. I'm not here to sniff him like a pervert. He's injured, for God's sake!

"Nah. Told you I'm not that hurt."

I shoot him an I-don't-think-so look. "Into bed, please."

"Join me?" He smiles charmingly.

"Uh, no."

"Can't blame a guy for trying." Grant crawls into the bed. I wait until he's settled, then pull the sheets all the way up to his chin. "Happy?" he asks.

"Almost." I peer into his eyes. They seem focused. And clear. That's a good sign, I'm sure. "Are you feeling okay? No dizziness or anything?"

10

GRANT

I stare up at Aspen. She looks like an angel, the light creating a bright, coppery halo around her head. I thought I must've gone to heaven when she hovered over me in the examination room, too. Because having Aspen fussing over me is my idea of heaven. Well, sex is up there too, but I doubt the angels strip and fornicate with the mortals who've recently arrived.

I should definitely get some reward for my restraint, though. I considered faking an accident just to get her to come into the shower. But that might have made her freak out, so I thought about coming out in nothing but a towel instead. That's what I normally do, anyway. However, that would probably make her extra skittish. I didn't miss the way she stayed in the corner while Sadie did her best to stake a nonexistent claim to me. I know Aspen feels something for me, but she isn't acting on it. Not sure why.

I haven't done anything to repel her, have I? Or am I simply not as appealing without my parents' radiance behind me? Ugh, I'm not giving that thought any credence. It's too depressing. Besides, I've done a lot to make up for my initial standoffishness.

Aspen's eyebrows pull together, creating three lines between them. She slips her hand under my head, runs her fingers through my hair and traces the curve of my skull. I don't know what she's doing, but it feels *great*. Maybe this is why cats and dogs like to have their heads scratched.

Thank God Will and Heath are out of town. They'd ruin the moment. Especially Heath, who would have a temper tantrum because he's still bitter that she wouldn't sleep with him. I wouldn't sleep with him either if I were a girl. Guys like him are the reason women have vibrators.

Aspen frowns. "I'm not feeling any bumps."

"I *was* wearing a helmet."

She withdraws her hand, leaving me feeling bereft.

"So? That doesn't mean it can completely block the impact from a fall. Not to mention a horse rolling over you."

"Well. Starfire is a big girl, so it probably looked worse than it really was," I say, with all the affection I feel for the mare.

"You know horses weigh, like, two tons, right?"

"Starfire actually weighs a little more."

Her lips tighten. "I don't think that's something to smile about."

"Sure it is. She's a healthy girl."

Aspen rolls her eyes. "Do you fall off horses a lot?"

"No. Those two guys who were flanking me are known for playing dirty. They're mad because we beat them last time." And they don't care if the horses get hurt during a match. I do.

"Is there anything I can do? Maybe get you something?"

"Nothing yet. Just sit with me." When she looks around, I pat the bed next to me. "Just stay here for a little bit."

"Okay." Her gaze drifts toward the desk. "Are those moving boxes?"

It's my chance to let her know I'm not Will and Heath's buddy. At least not close enough to want to room with them if I had a choice. Although she didn't seem to recognize Heath's mountain bike in the living room, she might hear that we're rooming together later.

"Yeah. And they're not getting unpacked," I say casually. "Not while I'm here."

"How come?"

"Because this place is temporary. I actually have an apartment off-campus, but it got flooded a few weeks ago."

"How?"

"One of the toilets broke. Anyway, I needed a place to crash, and this was the best I could find. Their third roommate is gone for the semester. So as soon as my place is fixed or my realtor finds me something, I'm moving out." I should text Mom and see if she's found anything.

Aspen nods. "That explains a lot."

I quirk an eyebrow.

"I didn't think you were the type to share a space. Not that I think you're picky, but you seem like someone who wants privacy to do whatever you want, anytime you want, without worrying about anyone else."

"Well... Yeah." She's pegged me pretty well.

My phone pings. I check it and see a text from George from the polo team. We won. *I knew it!*

–George: Can you join us for a celebration? We'll be hitting Bad Bastards.

That's a pub we generally head to. Normally, I'd say yes, but right now, I have Aspen in my room.

–Me: No.

–George: You okay? I thought it wasn't serious?

–Me: It isn't, but I'm already back in my dorm, and don't feel like heading out.

–George: Who is this texting me in place of Grant?

–Me: LOL. It's me, asshole. I just need some sleep. See you next practice.

I put down my phone. Aspen tilts her chin. "What was that?"

"One of the guys from the team. He wanted to know if I was up for a victory celebration."

"Most definitely not," she says sternly. "Didn't he see what happened?"

"Exactly." I don't tell her that's why he asked. He knows I'm not really hurt if I'm well enough to walk to the parking lot. But I'm not going to waste this opportunity. "Just because I'm not hooked up to a machine and stuff doesn't mean I'm okay."

"Precisely."

I give her a sweet smile, the one Emmett says could fool

anybody into thinking I'm an innocent angel. "You could probably kiss it better."

Her eyes narrow. "Kiss *what* better? I thought nothing was broken."

"That doesn't mean I haven't strained anything." I give her my most innocent and serious expression, although my thoughts are anything but. I suffered a fall from a horse, not castration.

"If you tell me it's your groin, I'm going to smack you."

"I thought you were worried about my injuries."

"Obviously you aren't *that* injured."

"I think my lips have a concussion."

She gives me a prim look, but her eyes twinkle. Her good humor pierces my heart, already vulnerable after her concern for me.

I push myself up, bracing my weight on one hand. I reach out slowly and cradle the back of her skull with the other, threading my fingers through her silky hair. Her eyes widen with surprise, but her lips are soft as I bring her in and fit them over mine.

I keep the kiss sweet and tender as I taste the lovely honey of her lips. Her breath mingles with mine, and then her tongue darts out, shyly stroking.

My hormones surge, and my heart booms in my ears. It's an effort to control myself. Aspen Hughes might have a body that could tempt a saint, but she has a gentle soul that deserves to be cherished and loved. I lick her back, and lead her tenderly, letting her tell me what she wants, how far she wants to go with her lips and tongue. Her breathing grows shallow, and mine matches hers. She lifts her hands, placing them on my shoulders. The heat from her palms through my shirt sends a hot rush of lust through me, and I groan against her mouth.

She slides her hands down my biceps, then up to my neck before linking them behind it. She opens her mouth more, inviting me inside. She tastes like fire and need. Sugar and spice. All the things lovely and beautiful. Things so precious they have no price.

It's crazy I'm falling for her this fast, this helplessly. But logic has no meaning when it comes to my heart.

I want to give her everything. I want to take her all.

I want to make her mine, and mine alone.

She tilts her head and fuses her mouth to mine. Something pings in the background. I ignore it and focus on making her feel good.

It pings again. *Fuck.* The team doesn't need me at Bad Bastards that bad.

It pings again. *Argh.*

Aspen pulls back, blinking. She licks her wet lips.

"It's my alarm." My body heats even more at how husky her voice has become. "The shift I have at Clemson Library."

I want to beg her to call in sick. Fuck, I can give her more money than the dumb job at the library. But I know that would ruin everything between us. She has her pride. My trying to buy her time would be a slap in her face, especially after what we just shared.

She clears her throat. "I'll, um, be done at eight."

"I'll call you if I feel sick." I give her a reassuring smile.

"No. You're going to call 911 if you start to feel bad. Promise."

She's really cute when she's worried and gets all firm and bossy. "Okay."

"I'll stop by after work to make sure you're okay."

"Awesome. I'll wait up." I smile like I'm not desperate for her.

———

As soon as I'm certain Aspen's gone, I grab another shower, this time *cold.* I gotta do something about this damn hard-on. She probably didn't notice because of the strategic way I placed the sheets, but I can't leave my dick like this. It's cruel and unusual.

The chilly temperature isn't doing anything, though. *What the hell?* This is anti-scientific. Not to mention, cold showers never failed before.

My hard penis bobs. *Hey, bud, you gotta do better.*

The water spraying over me, I grip my dick hard and jerk my hand up and down. The kiss was rather chaste, considering what I really wanted to do, but my hormones are more excited than a kid at a rave doing ecstasy. I imagine her mouth over my lips, my neck, my chest. I fantasize her mouth trailing down until it reaches my dick.

"Fuck," I mutter as my cock aches so hard, my vision dims for a second.

And I come. Jesus. That was embarrassing. I don't think it took more than a couple of decent pumps. It was just the thought of her lips on my penis that did it.

I breathe out, my whole body descending from the sexual peak. I don't think I've ever lost it like this. But Aspen does something to me that nobody else can.

I get out of the shower and wrap a towel around my hips. I check my phone and see a bunch of texts. I ignore them all, until I get to the ones from my brothers.

–Noah: You aren't dead, are you?

Huh?

–Sebastian: Hello? Do you think Grant's in the hospital right now?

Oh. They must've seen a video of me falling off the horse. I should've known somebody would record it and plaster it all over the Internet.

I look for it, and sure enough. I hit play.

Damn. I whistle. It's interesting to see it from a different angle. The tumble I took looks spectacular, especially with Starfire rolling over me. She gets up, then shakes her mane like a diva. George told me I need to stop feeding her so much because she's getting fat, but she's still a sleek goddess from every angle.

–Nicholas: Shouldn't they be calling us about that, then?

–Huxley: Why would they call us? We aren't his mother.

–Emmett: I can ask my mom to call his mom.

–Griffin: She won't answer. Athena never does.

Griffin knows my mom well. She doesn't bother unless she wants something in return. Forwarding this video to her won't cut it.

–Sebastian: I hate it that nobody has any answers!

Ask and you shall receive!

–Me: I'm fine.

–Nicholas: Seriously? That fall looked pretty bad.

–Noah: You don't have to lie.

–Emmett: How hurt are you? Are you in the hospital?

–Me: I'm fine. Nothing's broken. No concussion, just sore. The doc forced me to take muscle relaxants, but I think he went overboard. I feel great.

—Huxley: He probably fed you morphine.

—Emmett: You didn't drive yourself, did you?

Emmett knows me pretty well.

—Me: I'm a responsible human being. I had somebody drive me back to my dorm.

—Emmett: Good.

Of course, if Aspen *hadn't* driven me, I would absolutely have gotten behind the wheel of my Maserati. But I don't need a lecture from anyone.

—Me: Anyway, I'm fine. Quit worrying.

I toss the phone on the bed and get dressed, then open my laptop. It's barely five, which means I have about three hours to kill before Aspen comes over. I should use the time productively and wrap up the transfer applications. All I need are some finishing touches, so there's absolutely no reason for them to reject me.

As I review the one for Harvard, my mind wanders briefly to what Will said when he saw me fill out the app last week.

"You really think you can get into Harvard?" He looked like he couldn't believe my audacity.

"Not just Harvard, but Stanford, Brown and Yale, too." I didn't list all the Ivy League schools. No need to have him faint. Given his lack of respect for personal space, he'd fall on me.

"Damn. If I got into any of them, my dad would give me anything I wanted."

"Get your grades up and try. You might surprise yourself. And your father." I gave him a pat smile, knowing he wouldn't. He's obsessed with Sadie—or the blowjob he can get from her—and won't bother with anything else.

I submit all the transfer applications, along with the fees, then text Mom.

—Me: Any progress on a place for me?

She probably won't respond anytime soon, so I drop the phone on the couch next to my laptop, go to the kitchen and grab the huge tub of pistachio ice cream. It's Heath's favorite, so of course I take it instead of the chocolate ice cream Will bought for himself. The asshole thought nothing of grabbing Aspen, so this small payback is the least I can do. It's too bad he doesn't play polo—I'd trample him with Starfire.

I return to the couch with the ice cream and start digging in. There's nothing exciting on Netflix or TV. It's like the world wants to punish me for having finished all my work early.

Normally I don't mind being alone, but right at the moment, the quiet is annoying. I wish Aspen were here. I want to hear her bossy voice. Then I want to feel her against me. Taste her. Smell her.

She's a billion times better than this lousy ice cream. Tastes better, too.

My phone pings. I look down, wondering if it's one of my brothers again, but it's Mom.

–Mom: Patience. Acceptable places don't just magically fall from the sky.

Ugh. So, no progress.

–Me: Come on, hurry up. I'm working on the transfer apps to make you happy.

I don't tell her I've already submitted them. I need something to hold over her or she'll never bother.

–Mom: They're for your own good.

–Me: Nice try. Basically, they're busywork.

–Mom: I haven't been able to find anything decent that's close enough to your campus. There are a couple near the polo club, but...

–Me: That's too far out.

–Mom: Exactly.

–Me: Do you know how much time it's taking me to do these transfer apps?

There's no immediate answer, but I can just imagine her huffing.

–Me: Quid pro quo. Give and take. You told me how important it is to give something back.

–Mom: How about I let you use my Malibu mansion for your spring break? But only if you promise to leave it in the exact condition you found it in when you walked in. I'll require pictures.

Wow. Either she feels terrible about not having a place for me in Napa or she really wants me to wrap up my applications. Possibly both. She never, ever lets me bring friends over to the Malibu place.

—Mom: No more than 3 guests. Actually, 2. And you'll pay for the extra housekeeping.

I almost laugh. Should've known.

But the place is gorgeous, and now that things are progressing with Aspen... I haven't asked her what she's up to for the break, but I doubt she has plans other than working. She seems to work way too much. *Two* jobs, good God. And those are the ones I know of. There could be a third.

I should see if she can take a day or two off. It isn't like the college café will need a lot of workers with most of the students gone. And they probably won't give her that many hours during the break anyway.

—Mom: Also, you can have a bag I left there. A burgundy Hermes from this event I went to in Paris, but you know I don't do croc leather.

True. Crocodile skin creeps her out because she had an unpleasant encounter with a crocodile during a fashion photoshoot in Paris once.

—Mom: It's supposed to be some special edition, but that still doesn't mean I'm carrying anything crocodile. So unbecoming. Anyway, give it to some girl you're banging. I'm sure she'll be extra bangy for you.

I choke on my ice cream, then start coughing. The pistachio ice cream shoots into my nostrils, which makes me sneeze.

Ugh. Great. Now I have disgusting green goo on my shirt.

—Me: OMG. Please, Mom.

—Mom: What? Aren't the girls today grateful when they get a $70k bag?

I'm too busy wheezing, and I guess my response didn't come quickly enough to suit her.

—Mom: So entitled!

—Me: It's not about that.

I can't think of how to put it.

—Me: Never mind.

She's not going to get it, and I'm not going to try to explain.

—Mom: Are you being a prude? I know you have sex. I'd be worried if you were still a virgin because that would mean you're suffering from erectile dysfunction or some psychological disorder.

I'd rather have Starfire sit on me for an hour than get a text on sexual dysfunction from my mother.

–Me: It's one thing for you to KNOW, and another for you to SAY IT!

–Mom: How many times have I told you? Reality doesn't care about your hang-ups.

Time to end this before I get some kind of PTSD.

–Me: I gotta go. Thanks for the offer of the mansion. And the bag. I'll take both.

–Mom: Okay. I'll have the property manager get in touch.

–Me: I have her number. I'll text her.

Mom doesn't respond. She's probably just happy she doesn't have to bother with her property manager. And I'm relieved Mom's done traumatizing me. At least she's letting me use the beachfront home and gave me the bag. The ones those fancy event organizers hand out aren't something you can buy on the street. Aspen will look rad carrying it. Griffin's mom says a woman should always have a great purse, even if she's dressed in rags. She's a fashion model, so she should know.

I throw the empty ice cream carton into the trash and stretch. My muscles are a bit achy, but they're always a little sore after a match. I change out of my soiled T-shirt and shove my feet into a pair of sneakers. After grabbing my phone and wallet, I head to the library. It would suck to be in my dorm like a loser on a Saturday night when I could be hanging at the library, where Aspen is.

Professor Pettit told us to read up on—and analyze—the events leading up to Black Monday. I already know a lot about the stock market crash, but I can always get more material...with Aspen's help. A quick refresher would be great.

Clemson Library is only about fifteen minutes on foot. It's a four-story structure with red brick walls and windows set into white wooden frames. It's one of the original buildings at the college, but the interior is brand new, with over thirty computers right as you walk in. There are also comfy couches and armchairs for reading. The second floor has a huge area for group studying, and the third and fourth floors have individually partitioned desks. Although the first floor smells like fresh air and plastic, the rest of the building is musty from all the old books.

Aspen is at the information counter opposite the entrance. She's so pretty, her hair glinting like spun fire as she studies something on her desk. She purses her full lips. The sight makes me think of the kiss, and how soft and sweet she felt against me.

I let out a rough breath. Shit, it's hot. The A/C here must be broken.

A trio of girls approach her—Sadie, Bronte and Tanya. *Oh fuck.* Now what?

Sadie says something to Aspen I can't quite catch. Aspen shakes her head, which is not a response Sadie likes. She doesn't handle rejection well.

"I don't know why you won't let me check out *The History of Medieval Mathematica*," she says loudly, her voice high-pitched with annoyance.

Does she know the phrase "silence is golden" was invented for her?

"It's for my Medieval Europe class!" she adds.

"I understand," Aspen says, "but we only have one copy, and Professor Levine specifically instructed the library not to let anybody check it out. You can snap photos with your phone."

"I'm not studying on this tiny screen!" Sadie says.

"Then there's the old-fashioned way." Aspen points at a copy machine.

Go, Aspen! I love it when a girl can handle herself so well.

Sadie stamps her foot. "She told me I could check it out!"

"Last time you said that, it turned out you lied and we had an unpleasant situation. Plus, you had the gall to tell the professor *we* were the ones who made the mistake, not you," Aspen says. "So, no."

Does it make me a perv that watching her take charge is turning me on?

"Are you calling me a *liar*?" Sadie hisses. Tanya and Bronte put their hands on their hips and move forward. I have no idea what they're trying to do. There's a counter that comes to my chest between Aspen and them. They aren't athletic enough to jump over, although I'd love to see them try and break something.

"If the shoe fits," Aspen says blandly.

Sadie huffs. Nobody treats her like this, and she probably doesn't know how to handle it.

Aspen pulls out her phone. "If you really want to check it out, just say into my phone here that you received permission from Professor Levine to check out *The History of Medieval Mathematica* for the Medieval Europe class."

Sadie starts tittering. "Oh my *God*. Do people still use phones that old? I mean, did you steal that from a museum?"

I roll my eyes. As exciting as it was to watch Aspen put Sadie in her place, it's time for Sadie and her friends to fuck off. "I used the same model until last year," I say, approaching the counter. I smile at Aspen. "Hey."

"Shouldn't you be in bed?" she says, her eyes sweeping me up and down.

"Maybe, but I don't have a nurse to keep me there."

Aspen sighs like she's exasperated, but her cheeks turn pink.

Sadie tries to latch on to me, stretching her hands out. I let her take my arm earlier because I was stuck on that tiny-ass infirmary bed, but I'm not letting her touch me now, especially not in front of Aspen. I recoil like she's been rolling around in a pigsty since the polo match.

She looks at me. "What's wrong?"

"Your voice. It's giving me a concussion. I warned you about it."

"My—"

"Why don't you just either make the recording or take pictures of the pages you need? Oh, and you were being way too loud. This *is* a library."

Just then, the librarian comes strolling over. "Hello, Sadie. Is there a problem here?"

Took the old man long enough. I turn to Aspen. "Now you're free."

She clears her throat. "Shouldn't you be resting?"

"No. I'm great. Wanna grab some dinner?"

She looks skeptical, but glances at the clock behind her. "I have another hour."

"No problem." That pistachio ice cream turned out to be good for something because without it, I'd be dying from low blood sugar. "I'll just go read some Shakespeare," I say, deciding that that sounds more impressive than Black Monday.

She frowns. "It's going to be late. Almost nine by the time we get to eat."

"I love late dinners."

"Grant Lasker. The man with an answer for everything."

"What can I say? I'm a smart guy." I give her my most charming smile.

"Fine. But you don't have to force yourself to read Shakespeare. Wouldn't want you to break anything."

I put a hand over my chest. "Thou woundeth me, fair lady."

Aspen snorts. "There are some comic books in the contemporary culture section over there. I'll see you in an hour."

11

ASPEN

I keep an eye on Grant while I organize the returned books and help a freshman find a volume on modern Russian history. Clemson Library can be overwhelming, and its stack system isn't the most intuitive.

So far, Grant seems to be okay, sitting in an armchair in my line of sight. He didn't look like he was in pain when he more or less told Sadie and her friends to go away. On the other hand, testosterone makes men do stupid things—like pretend they aren't hurt when they really are.

Why is he here instead of waiting at his place? He isn't reading comic books like I suggested. He's scrolling on his phone. His mouth is curved into a small smile that makes my heart want to do a cartwheel, and he's running a finger along his lower lip. It reminds me of how his mouth felt.

Thinking about the kiss makes my lips tingle. It's the craziest thing because that's never happened before. Just because I'm a virgin doesn't mean I haven't kissed guys. But the act had been sort of weird and awkward. A wet, slippery lump of flesh—a tongue— gliding over my mouth, and the experience left me unmoved. I couldn't understand why girls in high school swooned over some guy's kiss. I didn't get it last year either, when Sadie said her boyfriend—the one who stared at my ass one too many times—kissed like a dream.

Until Grant.

There was heat with him. Something that made my breath roughen, my senses go unsteady, my world tilt. The hair on the back of my neck prickled, and every cell inside me quivered at the unfamiliar and wondrous feelings he aroused.

I don't know what that makes us. To be honest, I don't know why he kissed me. I think he likes me, but I don't know if it's a serious-like or casual-like.

But most importantly, I don't know how far I want to take this thing between us. I can laugh when I'm with him and forget all my worries—my grades, my scholarships, the love-guilt I feel for my grandparents. It's a new experience, just being a college girl having fun with one of the most popular guys on campus. And when I'm with him, I don't feel like I'm alone—like I often do with others because I'm not really being seen or heard. It's a casual type of disrespect—because I'm poor or lost my parents early.

Being with Grant comes with some nuisances—like Sadie, who obviously has a thing for him. But I've never let a roadblock get in the way, and I'm not letting her stop me from exploring possibilities. I'm not trying to marry this guy, just figure out how I really feel about him. I can let things progress naturally and see where we end up, even though part of me wonders if I'm moving too fast.

At eight, I clock out. Grant immediately jumps up from his armchair and comes over.

"Where are we going?" he asks.

"I don't know. All the dining halls are closed." That's not quite true. There's a shitty one by Howell Hall that's open until nine thirty, but he hasn't waited this long to go *there*.

"How about Serrano's?" he says.

It's a popular Mexican restaurant. Their food is great and reasonably priced. The fact that they're only a ten-minute drive away from the campus is a bonus. And the company? Even better. "Sounds good."

We take my car, since Grant's is probably still in the polo club parking lot. But even if he got his Maserati back, he shouldn't be driving. I haven't forgotten the doc's warning.

The traffic is minimal—it's Saturday, and the kids have already had dinner and arrived at whatever party is on their social calendar. Grant looks at my playlist in the car. Paloma Faith's "Do You Want the Truth or Something Beautiful?" fills the interior, and I tap my fingers to it. Grant doesn't comment, but listens to it in silence with me.

"Are you lip-syncing?" Grant asks suddenly.

"What?"

"Your mouth is moving."

It is? He must've been watching me closely, and the thought makes my lips tingle. "I sometimes sing along when I drive."

"Hey, don't hold back on my behalf."

"Ha. I'm not embarrassing myself. I sound better in my head than in reality. You sing."

"I would if I didn't have to hit those high notes."

A corner of my mouth quirks. I wonder if he sounds like one of the early contestants for *American Idol*. Most of them sound awful. The worst thing is that all their humiliating displays are preserved forever on YouTube.

On the other hand, it's hard to imagine him being bad at anything. If I pick the right song, he might be able to sing pretty well, especially with that gorgeous baritone voice of his.

By the time Paloma Faith's second song ends, we're at Serrano's. A cheery Mexican folk song rings from the speakers, and the scent of chili, lime and sizzling meat and veggies wafts along the cool air. The restaurant's more than half-empty. The host shows us to a table, and a waiter shows up immediately after.

He introduces himself, offers us some chips and salsa, then wants to give us time to decide on the entrées. But I'm starving. I look at Grant. "You know what you want?"

"Yup."

I order the dinner special—chicken and shrimp fajitas with an extra order of guacamole—plus pink lemonade. Grant gets the steak burritos and a Coke.

After the waiter's gone, I lean across the table. "By the way, thanks for earlier."

"For what?" he asks, genuinely confused.

"Getting Sadie and her friends to back off. They can be very persistent."

He shrugs. "You were doing fine by yourself."

I dig into the chips and salsa. *God, I'm so hungry!* I haven't eaten anything since lunch. "Yeah, but when Sadie gets upset, Bronte and Tanya tend to join the fray. Not my idea of fun." Administration tries to look the other way when Sadie's being bitchy because her father graduated from the college and donates regularly. They don't want to upset one of their more generous ATMs.

"It's not anybody's idea of fun. Those three could make a pack of rabid dogs look well balanced."

I bite my lip so I don't start giggling. Still, the sound escapes anyway.

"You can laugh."

"Didn't you and Sadie used to date?"

He makes a vaguely pained noise in his throat. "Yeah. So?"

"You must've seen something in her."

"For a while. But then she got...boring."

It's an unexpected response. "Because she asked you to take her to that gala thing?" Sadie is one of the most popular girls on campus. A lot of guys would give up a kidney to date her, including a couple of the baristas at the café.

Weirdly enough, the fact that Grant found her boring enough to dump makes me feel oddly satisfied. It's a bit of a shock—I've never experienced such petty vindictiveness over somebody else's relationship gone wrong.

"No. She was boring before that. But the gala is a good excuse. I really don't feel like going."

"Something doesn't add up, though. She's a proud girl. She wouldn't be clinging if you were the one who dumped her, saying you don't want to be her date to the event."

"I didn't. *She* dumped *me*," he says.

"She did?" Wow. That's...surprising. And the weird satisfaction I felt starts dissipating.

Our waiter returns with the food. The service is extra fast today, probably because we're eating so late. I wrap my chicken and shrimp in the warm flour tortilla and take a bite.

"I let her," Grant says with a nonchalant shrug. "Generally, it's easier. When the girl gets to be the dumper, they're less stalkerish because they know I spared them their reputation."

"You don't care about what people think of you?"

"Why would I? It's just some college drama nobody's going to remember or care about. So what if I dated Sadie at some point? There were other girls before her, and there will be others after." He pauses to take a sip of Coke, then looks at me. "One of them might end up meaning something."

The air in my lungs seems to go still. I don't know why it suddenly feels like he's talking about *me*, specifically, not some woman he might meet some day. It's probably the intensity of his gaze. But, of course, anyone would get serious about the love of their lives. My grandfather is super serious when he talks about how lucky he was to have met Grandma.

I'm pretty sure I'll meet someone that special at some point, but I'm not sure when or how. It probably won't be in college, though. I'm just too busy to meet the love of my life right now.

"That's great." I take a quick bite to avoid having to say more.

Grant looks vaguely let down—or maybe annoyed about something—but then he smiles again, so maybe I imagined his disappointment. His phone pings, and he looks down at it briefly and purses his mouth.

"What is it?" I say, glad to have another topic to hop to.

"It's the Investment Society alert. Someone's freaking out about the team ranking after this week's tally."

"You're a member?" I say, surprised. He seems too active to sit down and do market analysis.

He nods, tapping a few times on his phone.

I try not to sigh with envy. The Investment Society is a club for students interested in stock and bond trading. I've been trying to join for two years, but failed.

"Somebody made a trade I asked them not to, and now we're

falling behind," he explains, putting his phone down. "*This* is why I don't like group work."

"Is there a team competition?" It's impossible to totally hide my envy. I'd die to be in the group, even if I had to deal with people doing things I asked them not to.

"Yeah. Every semester, we're put into a team of two or three to make trades. Well, paper trades—we don't use real money. We just place the number of shares and price into the app, and it automatically tallies our profit or loss. Normally I wouldn't bother with a club like this, but George—a polo teammate—begged me to."

Could this man and I be more different? Grant has people begging him to join clubs he isn't interested in, and I have nobody asking me. When I tell people what I'd like to do, they laugh and brush me off, like the future I'm dreaming of just isn't within my reach. Or maybe they think I can't be smart enough or serious enough to have it.

"So you're mad at George?" I ask.

"No. He isn't even my team." Grant sighs. "He would've shorted, like I said. I'm leaving after this semester."

"Oh." I pick at my food. "I wish I were in it," I blurt, my tone crabby despite myself.

He raises his eyebrows. "Why aren't you?"

"I tried, but they said I needed an invitation." My mouth tightens. The two guys I spoke with laughed a who-do-you-think-you-are laugh.

"Dicks," Grant mutters. "You don't have to have an invitation. You can just tell them you're an econ major."

"I did. I told them I wanted to work in finance. Stockbroker."

He scowls. "And they still said no?"

My face burns. "They just laughed. I guess they couldn't believe I knew anything about the market."

"I'm sorry," he says. "I swear, some of the guys in that society act like they're still in high school." He leans forward. "You still interested in joining?"

"*Yes*. I know some of the people in there are going to be nasty, but my advisor said it'd look good on my résumé." I'm already sucking up. I can endure a bit more.

"We take in new members every semester. I'll invite you."

I blink in shock. "Really? But didn't you say you're going to quit?"

"I don't mind," he says. "It doesn't cost anything to be in it."

He shrugs like it's nothing, but it has to be something for him, who is headstrong and used to doing what he wants. "They said whoever invites me has to vouch for me too."

"Yeah, it's a rule. But why wouldn't I vouch for you?"

"You aren't afraid I might not know anything and embarrass you?" Those are what the two guys said when I tried to apply. *Sorry, we don't accept people who don't know anything.* And in a way, they're correct—I'm familiar with some of the terminology, but some of the words they were throwing around were totally new to me.

Grant scoffs. "Like most of *them* know anything? They're dabbling. It's just a game to them."

"Isn't it to you, too?" I keep my tone neutral.

"No. I actually risk my own money. I make the same trades in the market that I do in the society. And I'm way, way ahead of the team, since some of them execute trades I wouldn't." He smiles. "Why don't you join next semester, and we can be on the same team —just you and me? That way, if you aren't sure about anything, I can help."

"For real?" I ask, my heart fluttering with hopeful joy. "What if I make a bad trade?"

"Everyone makes some bad trades," he says with a shrug. "The key is, are you making money overall? If you know what you're doing, the market can nosedive, and you can still make money hand over fist. I'm going to make sure we're going to be the best team next semester, and those assholes who laughed at you are going to kiss your butt." His eyes sparkle.

I laugh. But there's more than just humor running through me. I'm also touched and reassured that he's unconditionally in my corner. He doesn't talk about the difficulties or how much work it's going to be. As far as he's concerned, I'll be in the Investment Society, and he and I will team up, and we'll kill it. No other option exists.

I suddenly realize that, other than my grandparents, Grant is the only one I feel comfortable talking about what I want to do when I'm out of college. On top of that, his belief in me boosts my confidence.

He doesn't see somebody poor when he sees me. He sees somebody with limitless potential. My heart swells, seems lighter than a balloon. I feel like I can reach up and pluck stars from the sky.

I'm falling for him. But then, how can I not fall for a guy who makes me feel like I can do anything?

"Thank you," I say. "I'd love to join the society and show them."

"Awesome." He beams. "That's a promise."

I nod, laughing, as excitement bubbles in my heart.

Our server comes over and refills our drinks. Once he's gone, Grant asks, "By the way, what are you doing for spring break?"

"Probably staying here," I say with a shrug. "You?" He's undoubtedly jetting off to Mexico for a week or something. He probably won't hit Cancun, since it'll be full of other college kids. He'll pick someplace more exclusive and upscale that peasants like me have never heard of.

"No particular plans," he says, surprising me. "But you aren't working during the break, are you?"

"I have three days off, but I have to work the other days."

"Three back to back?"

"Yup. Our supervisors decided we need a break." Which is ridiculous, since we're staying on campus for hours, not for "a break." "Why?"

"Your bosses aren't going to call and ask you to come in, right?" He waves the question away. "Actually, tell them you won't be available."

I look at him warily. "How come?"

"So we can do something fun together."

"For three days?"

"Why not?"

"What're you going to be doing for the rest of the week?"

"Don't worry. I'll find something to fill the time." He grins. "I'll plan everything, to make up for scaring you so much today."

I'm not sure what we could do for three days that would also fit his lifestyle. And there's the other issue. "I'm broke," I tell him so he doesn't plan anything too extravagant. He has a Maserati and talks oh-so casually about his horses. It's clear that he exists on a completely different financial plane.

He waves it away. "It won't cost you a penny."

I don't buy it. Anything "fun" costs money around here, especially if it's something that can keep us occupied for three days. "You aren't going to make me ride, right?"

His eyes twinkle. "You afraid of horses?"

"Not the animals themselves. They're gorgeous. But riding them? A little, after what I saw."

He laughs. "Fine. No riding horses. I promise."

"Can you tell me what we'll be doing?"

"No, it's a secret. Mainly because I don't know yet. But prepare to be wowed."

———

The next two weeks pass in a blur. All my midterms are taking place right before the spring break. That's a good thing, since I won't have to worry about studying for the tests while I'm with Grant. But it keeps me crazy busy. I only get to spend time with Grant in the evenings on days I'm not working, and that's only because he comes over to my dorm carrying food.

On his mind are things other than feeding me. Like sitting near me, wrapping his free arm around my waist, finding the gap between my shirt and jeans with his thumb, running the warm pad along the bare skin. Goosebumps spread along my spine, followed by a hot, tingling sensation.

I always think he's going to go straight for my mouth, but he never does what I expect. Sometimes he spends what feels like forever laying kisses all along the back of my neck, the side of my neck, behind my ears—I never knew how sensitive my neck and that spot behind my ears could be.

"Grant," I sigh softly, urging him to give me what I want.

He ignores me and continues to rain hot kisses along my shoulder.

Now I'm the one squirming and sliding my fingers through his hair and taking his lips. Our tongues tangle as we taste each other. Every time he plunders my mouth, my senses start to spin out of control. All I can feel is the heat of his skin, the hot need building inside me, the vibration in his chest when he groans. The soft moan that tears from my lips.

But when he slips a hand underneath my shirt, I stiffen, like someone getting pulled out of a dream. He withdraws, his breathing rough and his eyes dark. His tongue glides over his lips like he's savoring the lingering taste of me, but he doesn't push or demand I give more than I'm comfortable with.

Which may be why I keep seeing him, keep letting him into my dorm and keep letting him touch me...and keep letting myself touch him back. It's like he's taming me—getting me used to his caresses so I crave them.

I feel like I can trust him to stick to my boundaries.

When I ask him if he doesn't need to study—he's spending a lot of time with me—he tells me he has some free time. He still won't tell me what he's planning for the break, but I don't press. He says he wants to surprise me, and I'm certain it's going to be good.

Thankfully, my work shifts are light. Since my bosses are used to dealing with college kids and their schedules, they're flexible when they know we're under pressure. I head to Clemson to study. It's open twenty-four seven for two weeks when there are midterms and again for two weeks during the finals. I have to make sure I do a good job on every exam.

–Grant: Still studying?

I see the text he sent about an hour ago. I missed it while going over my notes on intermediate microeconomics. The professor wants us to do multivariable calculus, and I need to do some extra review to make sure I'm comfortable with it. He has a rep for allotting no more than two minutes per question on average, and his tests are *long*. It's like you need both speed *and* endurance to survive the ninety-minute exam.

–Me: Yeah.

I hit send, then realize it's after midnight. Hopefully I'm not waking him up.

–Grant: Need a study buddy?

Although I'm tired and need more caffeine and food, I smile.

—Me: I'm done studying for Culture and Music in History.

—Grant: I'm good for other subjects, too.

—Me: Don't you have to study for whatever midterms you have before the break?

—Grant: You gonna say no to coffee?

I shoot him a raised-eyebrow emoji. I was about to text him that I need to go grab some snacks.

—Me: You didn't mention that.

"I am now."

I look up. Grant gives me his signature killer smile—it never fails to make my belly flutter, and now *he's holding two cups of iced coffee*. It's like he knew what I needed even before I told him.

"How did you know where I was?" I whisper, then move my backpack from the seat next to mine.

Grant takes the hard plastic chair. "I got mad skills." He winks, handing me one of the cups.

"Thank you." I take a sip. The caffeine floods my system like some divine elixir, and I have to stifle a moan. "I needed a little boost."

"And that's not all..." He lifts a brown paper bag.

"What's in there?"

"Chocolate-cream-filled croissants from Sunny's."

My mouth waters. They're my favorite. Actually, they're everyone's favorite. They aren't always easy to get because they sell out almost as quickly as they're taken from the oven. You have to wait in Sunny's parking lot for the "Fresh Croissants" light to go on if you want to grab them. The bakery stays open until one during the midterms and finals because it does so much business with college study-zombies desperate to jack up their blood sugar.

"Oh my God, you are the *best*."

"I know." He hands me the whole bag.

I grab a croissant as he watches me with an amused smile. Suddenly, I feel self-conscious about digging into the food like a starving pig. "You want one?"

"If you think you can spare it."

"There are four. I'm not eating all of them." I grin. "Just three."

Laughing softly, he takes one and bites into it.

"So. You're on a break from studying?" I ask as I enjoy my croissant. The chocolate cream is rich, the pastry light. It's the best thing to pair with the slightly bitter coffee.

"I'm done." Grant shrugs.

"Wait, you're done with all your midterms?" I ask, stunned and envious.

"I'm done studying. Two more tests tomorrow, but I'm not worried about them."

"How come?" I give him a flinty stare. "They aren't group projects you ditched, are they?"

He rolls his eyes but has the decency to look slightly abashed. "No. But they're easy. I don't really have to study."

"At *all*?" Color me skeptical. He has one undemanding course— Culture and Music in History. But he couldn't be taking *all* easy classes. It wouldn't meet the minimum requirement to graduate. On top of that, although someone like Taylor might dole out good grades to him, most professors aren't like that. There are those who are proud of their reps as super assholes who rarely grade on a curve.

"I already know everything."

"Either you're super arrogant or super smart. Which is it?" I ask jokingly, expecting him to say super smart.

"Do I have to pick one?" He laughs and shrugs. "I'm serious—I already know most of what they're teaching here."

Even though he said "most of," I have a feeling what he really means is *all of.* "Then why are you here? This place costs a fortune." Maybe he honestly doesn't care about money because his family's rich. "Are you here to just screw around for four years before you have to get a job or something? Take over your dad's business?"

"I'd rather die than work in Hollywood with Dad. Ugh." He shudders, his face scrunching. "I think I'm going to be sick."

I raise my eyebrows. "*Sick?*"

"Sick. Puking. Body parts dying, falling off. Nah, I just need a piece of paper that says I graduated from some college. So I'm here to have fun."

It's amazing how different we are. For him, college is a lark, something to kill four years. But for me, it's a once-in-a-lifetime opportunity that I can't afford to waste. There's a weird mixture of feelings welling in my chest. Not anger or resentment. Just... sadness? And some slight envy, maybe? Part of me wonders if things could've been different for me, too, if my parents hadn't died when I was just three years old. I doubt my parents would've been able to treat my college education as "killing time and having fun," but maybe I'd feel less pressured to be perfect because I'd have a little margin for error.

I shake off the tightness in my heart. Life isn't fair, and my wondering *what if* doesn't change anything.

"We can have fun together as soon as these exams are over," Grant adds.

"Right. The break," I say with a smile, happy he ended one of my rare moments of self-pity. "What do I need, since you said there's no horseback riding?"

"Some toiletries if you want. Some clothes. Oh, and a bikini if you have one."

"We're going to the beach?" I didn't think we'd be hanging out in Napa for three days, but I didn't realize we'd be heading to someplace that warm.

"Yup. It's probably too cold to swim, but there's a hot tub."

"That sounds like fun." I finish the last bite of the croissant and wash it down with the coffee. "Now I need to go back to this." I gesture at the textbooks on the table. I have an econometrics class to study for. Not something I'm looking forward to, since it's my weakest subject.

"Study away. I'll just sit here with my mouth zipped."

12

GRANT

I shouldn't have told Aspen I was screwing around here at school, even if it was true. Her eyes dimmed a little, damn it.

I'm just not used to opening up about the reason for my being at Napa Aquinas College. It isn't a bad place—it's one of the nicer liberal arts colleges. But it can't teach me anything I don't know already. Mom pressured me to start skipping grades at age seven—and my teachers were certainly amenable, since I was years ahead of my peers—but I resisted. I didn't want to be ahead of my brothers. I liked hanging out with them at boarding school. Even though we're at different colleges now, I enjoy the fact that we're all going through the experience at the same time.

But after being a dick about the group paper, telling Aspen that my college education is more or less a joke doesn't put me in the best light. Most of the guys I hang out with generally admire that I don't have to do much and still set the curve, because that's what *they'd* like to be able to do. But Aspen is different.

I bite into the croissant and watch her pore over the econometrics textbook. She frowns, then checks her notes, then frowns again.

It's on the tip of my tongue to say that econometrics is ridiculously easy, and she shouldn't act like the book is written in Latin. But her opinion of me matters, so I keep my mouth shut. Only econ majors take econometrics—it's boring as hell, although my brother Griffin loves it because he's weird like that—so I should let her frown all she wants.

She lets out a frustrated breath and taps the page with her pen.

"Problem?" I ask tentatively.

"A little. I just don't understand this. Actually...I don't understand this either." She flips several pages back to the offending section and huffs with frustration. She *thunks* her forehead against the book. "I'm so screwed."

"Lemme see," I say, keeping my voice neutral as I slide closer. Our arms touch. Her bare skin's soft against mine, and a prickling sensation spreads over me. My heart thuds. I want to tell her to forget about econometrics and kiss me until we're both out of breath. But that's only going to make her think more poorly of me, so I bottle it up. Solid.

"Have you taken this already?" Her tone is skeptical.

I hesitate for a second. "No."

She sighs, her shoulders slumping. Her arm slides along mine, and the blood goes south, leaving the barest minimum for my brain.

"Have at it," she says. "But it isn't going to make any sense."

I take a look at the pages she mentioned. "Which problem doesn't make sense to you?"

"This one." She points, leaning closer to me over the textbook between us. Our shoulder brush. But I know econometrics, so I can still parse the text despite the distraction. "And *that* one." She sticks her finger on a page with another question and long, boring explanation with resentful force.

"Okay. Well, let's see if I can make them a little simpler." I then explain the concepts to her without using the terms from the book. No need to make them drier than they already are.

Her stare says, *I don't think you really know this, but I'm going to humor you,* but then her eyes change and she slowly starts nodding. Eventually her jaw drops. "Oh my *God!* That makes perfect sense!"

I smile, happy she gets it. I don't generally bother explaining things because it's usually too much work for hardly any return.

That's why I just let Will copy my homework. But seeing Aspen's eyes light up is its own reward.

"You're amazing!" She hugs me, then places a quick kiss on my mouth.

Before she can pull away, I put my hand at the back of her head and fuse our lips for a proper kiss, sweeping my tongue in for a taste of her—coffee, chocolate and all her, laced with a hint of shy heat. She feels so warm and sweet, and I could stay like this until dawn, but she has to study—killing the midterm is important to her—so I pull back before I lose control. I want to respect her needs and boundaries, but it's really starting to become difficult. I've never had to be this patient with a girl before.

But Aspen's worth it. She's worth everything.

"Wow," she says, looking at my lips, then at me.

"You're welcome." I wink.

She flushes, laughing softly. "Thank you for the explanation." Then, reluctantly, she turns her attention back to the textbook. "Okay... Okay..." She goes through another couple of problems. "Okay! Now that I understand that, the rest of it makes sense!"

"Good."

She exhales softly, moving slightly away to reach for the croissant bag. I narrow my eyes. *Should've kept the bag closer.*

She takes a big bite, then shakes her head and turns to me. "You seriously haven't taken it? For real? You aren't just messing with me?"

I shake my head. I know what she's thinking. Will reacted the same way when he realized I already knew how to price fixed-income securities.

She takes another bite of the croissant like her soul needs soothing from the chocolate cream. "It's so unfair. But no wonder you said you're just here for a piece of paper. You could be teaching this class."

I shrug, since I have nothing to say. Teaching a bunch of unmotivated college kids is my idea of hell. I could be doing something more productive. Like flossing my toes.

"You saved me a lot of time. And some sanity." She hesitates for a second. "Is it okay if I ping you if I get stuck again? You can get back to me whenever."

I grin. "Of course." That's precisely what I'd love.

So I read something on my phone while she studies, our arms close enough to brush each other. At around three a.m., she can't keep her eyes open anymore and falls asleep over a notebook. I smile as her adorably soft mouth moves likes she's whispering to herself in her sleep, and send a few texts to the concierge service I'm using to make some minor adjustments to our spring break.

————

D-day.

My Maserati convertible is spotless and gleams like a pigeon-blood ruby. Freshly washed and waxed. The drive to the airport is short, but I'm not picking Aspen up in an unwashed car.

I park it by Howell Hall and text her to let her know I'm here. Then I get out and wait for her by the door, trying to look cool even as excitement crackles through me.

–Aspen: Coming now!

Within a few minutes the door to the hall opens and she rushes out, carrying a small black bag stuffed so tight that it looks like a ball. Her eyes are bright, her step springy. She's in a casual blue T-shirt and denim shorts that show off her long, shapely legs. Her feet are narrow and pretty in flip-flops, and pink nail polish is on her toes.

"Hey," I say with a smile.

"Hi!" She beams at me. "You could've stayed in your car. I know where the visitor lot is."

"Well, yeah, but what would that make me?" I pull her close to steal a quick kiss.

She flushes. I love how bright her eyes are, how pretty she is when she's flustered about something as innocent as a peck in public.

"Let me take that for you." I reach for the bag.

"Thanks. It isn't that heavy, though," she says, handing it over.

"Still." I carry it, putting a hand at the small of her back as we walk to the car.

She tenses for a fraction of a second. The reaction makes me question if I should've put my hand on her elbow, but that's so... distant. Like she's somebody's grandma. But then she relaxes into my palm, and I feel like I have everything I could ever want.

I open the door to the Maserati, then wait for her to climb in and shut it. I place her bag in the trunk, settle behind the wheel and get on the road. Aspen is gorgeous and cute, studying the leather interior and surreptitiously running her hands over the seat. I like how she's confident and carefree but still a little shy.

"Aren't we going to the beach?" she says after a while.

"Yup."

"I'm pretty sure this isn't the way."

"It is. Trust me."

"Uh-huh. Are you going to be unhappy if I need to use GPS to give you directions?"

I grin. "All that 'fragile male ego' stuff? Doesn't apply to me. And in any case, no GPS is needed. I know exactly where we're going."

She looks skeptical. She wants to say something, but pulls her lips in instead. I try not to laugh. I don't want to ruin the surprise.

I pull into the hangar at Napa Airport, where the sleek jet I chartered is waiting for us, and stop the car.

She stares out the windshield for a moment, then points at the aircraft. "Uh... That's not... We aren't flying in that, are we?"

"Of course we are."

"But...isn't that a private jet?" Her voice is thin with shock.

"Mm-hmm."

"Holy shit. I said I'm broke."

"So?"

"Broke people don't fly private." Her tone says she can't believe she has to spell it out for me.

"But I do." And I have every intention of pampering her. She deserves it. "Consider it hitchhiking...? No, wait—plane-pooling!"

She blinks slowly, then bursts out laughing.

"And sharing is good for the environment," I add with a little shrug. I love the sparkle in her eyes. "Look, whether you were going to come or not, I would've chartered a plane." That much is true. I hate flying commercial. The security alone is enough to drive you insane. "And the fee is the same no matter what. It's really not a big deal. Didn't your microecon professor teach you about marginal costs?"

"I think I remember something about it."

"Yeah, well, here the marginal cost is zero." I make an O with my thumb and forefinger to emphasize the point.

She runs a hand through her hair, which makes it spill over her shoulders like a silken cape. I resist the urge to grab some, pull her close and take her mouth. I don't think I can stop if I start. There's too much pent-up need ready to erupt.

She looks slightly lost. "I don't even know what to say."

I feel like the fairy godmother spoiling Cinderella. But I'm a guy, so maybe I'm the god*father*. "You don't have to say anything. Just enjoy it."

13

ASPEN

After we get out of the car, I look for our bags. Grant says, "What do you need?"

"Our bags."

"They're already loaded on the plane."

I stare in shock. "How?"

"I popped the trunk when we pulled up."

He escorts me straight to the jet. I guess when you're flying private, you don't do TSA.

A blonde cabin attendant in a navy uniform gives us a sunny smile. "Welcome aboard."

I murmur my thanks and look around at the eight seats on the plane. "Which one am I supposed to take?" I ask Grant.

"Whichever you like."

I sit in the front row, next to the window. The seat is huge and made of pale leather. It cushions my body like a cloud. I stroke the leather, marveling at how soft it is. "Wow. This feels great."

"It's too bad the flight's so short. It has a bedroom in the back," he points out matter-of-factly.

"What? For real?" I turn my head to see if I missed something when I walked in. I see the door at the end. "That's a bedroom?"

"Yup."

"I thought it was the, uh, lavatory."

He nods. "There's a bathroom with a shower in there, too."

"Wow," I say again. I think I'm going to say a lot of wows on this trip. Then I lower my voice and blurt out, "Isn't the door sort of thin?"

Grant blinks at me, like he's trying to compute. "Are you thinking what I'm thinking?"

"I've heard about what people do on planes when they get frisky," I say, my cheeks warm. "I used to think doing it in the bathroom was pretty gross. And cramped."

His shoulders shake. "Oh my God. I don't think people charter a jet just to join the Mile-High Club."

"I was just thinking about the logistics of your average person's excitement on a plane."

"Why? Wanna test it?" His eyes appear darker, with heat underneath, but there are sparks of humor there, too.

"No," I say primly, then tilt my chin in the direction of the cabin attendant, who's bringing us welcome-aboard virgin margaritas and some snacks.

"No champagne," Grant says with a wistful sigh. "Stupid age limit."

"Do they normally give you champagne?"

"Yes, if you're twenty-one." He sips the margarita. "But this isn't bad."

I taste it too. Although it doesn't have any alcohol, the flavor is intense. I like the saltiness that lingers on my tongue.

The jet takes off smoothly. As soon as the pilot says we can move around the cabin, the cabin attendant appears with a platter of fancy finger food, including smoked salmon and caviar. I've never had caviar before, but I think I like it. It isn't fishy like I thought. More like briny, with a hint of nuttiness.

"Now can you tell me where we're headed to? If it's an overseas destination, you may need to turn back the plane. I don't have a passport."

"Nothing as exciting as Formentera. We're going to Malibu. Mom's letting me use her beach house."

"Are we going to be running into her?" I mentally go through what I packed for the trip, wondering if any of it is good enough for meeting his mom. I have a feeling she's sophisticated and glamorous.

"No," he says. "She's not in the country, as far as I know. And she's hardly ever in California. She only has the Malibu home for the few times a year she's in SoCal."

"Like Christmas?"

"She spends her Christmases in Malta. Or some other warm place."

"Must be nice to spend your holidays overseas." I sigh with longing. I've never been outside of the country. Maybe when I get a real job and have some savings, I might hit Buenos Aires. Maybe bring my grandparents, too. They'd love that.

"Eh. Europe is a lot like the U.S. now," he says. "And if you go into the southern hemisphere, it's basically like summer. So, it's just Mom."

Wow. I can't imagine spending Christmas alone. My grandparents always decorate for the holidays, and I love the quality time we spend together. "You don't go with her, ever?"

"Not anymore. We like different things during the holidays."

"Like what? Hanging out with your dad in Hollywood?"

Grant's gorgeous face twists like he's just bitten into sand. "*No.* He goes out of the country, generally to the Bahamas or something. And I don't join him. We have what you might call irreconcilable differences in taste."

Guess he doesn't get along with his parents. Maybe they like really weird stuff. Since the topic seems to make him uncomfortable, I decide to shut up and have more caviar.

Soon enough, it's time to land. Apparently, we had a strong tailwind, but it's a shame the flight's ending so quickly. It's probably the first and only time I'm going to feel this way about getting off a plane early. I could fly for days in this type of luxury, especially when the cabin attendant keeps refilling our drinks and food without anyone having to ask.

A ground crew member is there with our bags as we deplane. No baggage claim carousels to mess with. A silver Mercedes convertible is waiting for us on the tarmac. Holy cow. I didn't know you could rent a Mercedes. A crisply dressed man hands Grant a tablet. He scrawls his name on the screen with a finger and gets the key to the Mercedes.

"Thanks," Grant says.

The man smiles. "Enjoy your car."

Another person places our bags in the trunk, and we get inside the car. As soon as the engine roars to life, a soprano starts belting out some tragic song, hitting several high notes loudly enough to shatter a wine glass.

"Wow. Is this your jam?" I say.

Grant sighs, although his eyes are bright with good humor. "Of course not. She sounds like a banshee."

"Can I pick something else?" I gesture at the controls.

"Please. Anything is better than this."

I laugh and pair my phone with the car's system. The soprano's singing cuts off abruptly, replaced by the Arctic Monkeys.

"Much better," Grant says with an appreciative sigh.

I grin. "I have excellent taste."

"That you do." He smiles back, and I feel like a balloon flying in the warm sky.

We head to Malibu. Grant doesn't rely on the GPS for directions. He already seems familiar with where we're going. I grew up in Los Angeles, but don't know this area at all. There was never any reason to visit such a wealthy neighborhood.

The drive along the Pacific coast is gorgeous. The ocean stretches endlessly, a bed of fractured sapphires under the sun. The sky is cloudless and blue, with a few seabirds dotting the horizon. I wrap my hair around my fingers so it doesn't fly everywhere. The unexpectedly warm, briny wind ruffles Grant's dark hair.

For once, I feel like my age. Not worried about money or grades or any of those things. It's just me and a gorgeous guy I think I'm falling for, the infinite ocean and bright, happy sun.

"Did you spend any time in the house we're about to visit after you left Europe?" I ask.

"Not really. I got my own place. My mother and I don't like to be in each other's hair. Like I said, I've always been independent. Besides, even if I weren't, she would've hated having me around. She doesn't like having people over."

"Okay, but you aren't just 'people.' You're her son."

"But not part of her inner circle."

What? "Who's in the inner circle if not her family?"

He shrugs. "Her cameras and lenses? Her agent, maybe?"

I don't understand how he can brush it off. If my mom were around, and if she acted like I was a bother, I'd be hurt. Even though I have no memory of her, thinking about her not wanting me is just painful.

He glances at me, then laughs a little, probably more as an attempt to lighten the mood than out of amusement. "Come on, don't give me that pitying look. It's not a big deal. I accepted my situation years and years ago. It doesn't bug me." He points to his left. "Look at that coastline instead. We'll be on it soon."

After a few more minutes, he pulls into a private driveway dotted with palm trees and hits a few keys on a security keypad. The gates open, letting us onto a slightly curved road. He stops in front of a large two-story structure that stretches away to either side. Grant pops the trunk, and I climb out. The salty breeze carries the sound of crashing waves.

"Wow." I take a few steps back to see the place better. The walls are white, but the windows are small and not so numerous. Blinds are lowered, covering every window.

"It looks sort of boring from out here," he says. "It's better inside."

We walk up to the main entrance, which is framed by two white columns. A huge potted palm stands next to the door, in front of which is a giant blue doormat with dolphins and waves that reads, *You've Been Warned: Trespassers Will Be Shot,* lying on the tiled entry.

Grant reaches under the upper-left corner of the mat and pulls out a key.

"That's so...ordinary," I say, "like it's something my grandparents might do."

"What were you expecting?" he says with a laugh.

"I don't know. Something that very rich people would have. Like 'Beam me in, Scotty.'"

He laughs harder. "Beam me *in?*"

"Well, they can't beam us *up*."

He unlocks the door. "You're killing me. Just so you know, we don't actually light our cigars with hundred-dollar bills." He hits a few numbers on the security keypad in the foyer and then waits until the light turns green.

"Right. You just eat caviar."

"You ate it too," he counters good-humoredly. "We aren't that different."

"That's true. We aren't." And the fact that he thinks this way is probably why I've been able to relax around him. It's hard to be standoffish around a guy who doesn't treat you different because of money or anything else—refreshing after having dealt with people like Sadie and her friends and some of the frat boys who thought I should be overcome with gratitude if they rubbed shoulders with me.

Grant holds the door and gestures grandly. "After you."

"Thank you." I step inside.

The interior is cool and surprisingly dry. It's mostly decorated in chrome with black accents. Everything is sleek and expensive-looking, and there isn't a speck of dust anywhere.

Directly ahead is a floor-to-ceiling window that shows a spectacular view of the ocean. The dark blue waves rush the shore and break over the soft-looking sand. The house must be soundproofed, because I can't hear anything.

"Wow," I whisper, my face only a couple of inches from the spotless window.

"It's prettier when the sun sets," Grant says, coming up behind me. "If you want to hear the waves, you just hit this button here." He gestures at a white switch to our left. He flips that, and the sound of the waves rolls in.

"So that disables the soundproofing?"

"Sort of. It opens some small windows to the side." He points out a couple of small sections of the window-wall near the ceiling.

"It's amazing," I whisper. "I've never been in a place this gorgeous before."

He smiles, like he's happy I'm in love with this beach house. "Want to see the rest of the house, or do you want to relax for a bit?"

"Let's see where everything is," I say. I want to know which room I'll be taking. Part of me says Grant would be a fabulous choice if I want to lose my virginity. He makes me laugh, he makes me feel carefree and he makes every cell in my body flutter with sweet anticipation. But the cautious part of me wants to be double damn sure, because it's a huge step.

You're just being a coward, part of me whispers. *Just admit you want him already.*

I surreptitiously run my palms over my pants. Okay, fine. *I want him.* But is it weird to feel just a tiny bit of trepidation?

The place is sparsely furnished, almost shockingly so. Although the dining room has a table big enough to seat twelve, the living room has only a couple of armchairs.

The lack of furniture and the open-floor design make the entire first floor look even more gigantic, and the two-story-high ceiling gives everything an airy feel. An indoor balcony with smooth chrome and glass railings wraps the area from two sides, connecting several rooms on the second floor. Nothing except elegant matte wallpaper is on the walls, which makes the place feel even more cavernously huge.

Grant gestures at the space to my left. "As you can see, that's the main kitchen, and there's a back kitchen through there." He points to an arched hallway.

"A back kitchen?"

"It's sort of a pantry as well. That's where Mom likes the actual prep and cooking to happen so that the main kitchen looks pristine when everything's served." He takes me to a place in the back that is better equipped than the one in my grandparents' home.

"Then why have a kitchen in front? Why not just have a serving area?" It's gotta be a complete waste to have an entire extra kitchen.

"Looks prettier in pictures," Grant says, like it's the most logical and normal thing to have two kitchens in a house. "Mom likes her subjects to be neat without looking staged."

I can't help shaking my head. But it's her money, so...

He leads me out and points to a room to the right. "That's her darkroom. Of course, these days almost everything is digital. But when she does more traditional photography, that's where she handles the film. She occasionally paints in there, too, although that's not something most people know about, so I'd appreciate it if you keep that to yourself."

I nod, feeling like I'm part of a special group. Surely he doesn't share his mother's semi-secrets with everyone.

"Anyway, she doesn't let anybody go in there, not even housekeeping."

"I'll make sure to stay out."

"Yeah, it's better that way. You'd think she was hiding bodies in there. She went ballistic one time when my dad's assistant went in by mistake. The only reason he didn't die is because Dad bought her a telescope she always wanted."

"Seriously?"

Grant nods. "My mother can be soothed with the right gifts and gestures. They just cost you a kidney and some pride."

"I'll keep that in mind," I say. Even though the woman isn't here, it's her home. I'm not doing anything that could come back and bite me in the butt.

He takes me into a sizable room with double-glass doors. "And this is the mini-gallery where she displays some of her work. This area is even more carefully climate-controlled to preserve the photos."

Ooh. Is that why there aren't any pictures of him or his mom out in the living room and so on? Eager to look at the pictures from his childhood, I rush over to the rows of frames on the walls. I bet he was super cute.

But none of the pictures feature him—or anyone that could possibly be him from years and years ago. They're mostly scenes from the ocean, some of them underwater. Every single one is stunningly beautiful, but... My shoulders sink as confusion ripples through me. Doesn't she love her son? Is she somehow ashamed of him?

"What's wrong?" he asks.

I gesture at the walls. "There aren't any pictures of you."

"Oh. Well, no. They wouldn't fit the theme."

"But you're her son. I mean, what's the point of having a special room for photos if she isn't going to display *you*?" A sudden thought strikes me. It's preposterous, but I don't know if it's *that* outrageous for his mom. "Don't tell me she's never taken a picture of you."

"She has. They're probably in storage somewhere."

"What's the point, then?"

He shrugs. "The point is, she took the pictures, and me from a newborn to now is preserved somewhere. I'm pretty sure they're artistically done."

What the—? It doesn't even sound like he's *seen* them. "How do you know if she stuck them into storage?"

"Because she gave me one on my birthday."

Now we're getting somewhere. "Can I see it?" I ask.

"I'd love to show it to you, but it's in a vault in Geneva."

"Geneva."

"Uh-huh."

"I don't suppose that's a little-known neighborhood in the Greater Los Angeles area?"

"No. Switzerland."

I shake my head. "You're as bad as her."

He shrugs again. "Displaying photos of each other isn't something we do."

"So you don't have any pictures of your mom on your phone?"

"Nope."

I can't imagine. I have lots of photos of my grandparents on mine. "You know how to use the camera on your phone, right?"

"Of course." He pulls it out and snaps a picture of me. "There. Took one just now."

Laughing, I run to him. "Show me!"

"Nope. It's mine."

I reach out to take the phone from his hand, but he raises it out of reach.

"Show me! I want to know if I look weird."

"You look great. I'm a fantastic photographer."

I shake my head. "You're just..."

"Wonderful. Amazing. Thoughtful. Sweet."

I laugh again. "Full of it."

"Exactly. 'It' being manly awesomeness, of course."

He snakes his arm around me and pulls me close. A gasp tears from my lips, and he takes my mouth. I kiss him back, wrapping my arms around his neck. My heart accelerates, and my God, he feels so, so good. What's crazy is how it feels as natural as breathing to have his lips on mine. I would've never thought I'd feel that way when we first met. I can feel him growing hard against me, and it makes me ache. It's like my body knows he's the one.

When he lowers his other arm, I press closer against him...until a wayward thought hits me. Suddenly, I make a grab for the phone.

But he's too quick, jerking it out of reach again. "Nice try." He smiles, shaking a finger at me. "Sneaky girl."

"I just want to see my picture." I flutter my eyelashes. "Pretty please?"

"No. It's my prize." He kisses my forehead. "Now behave and let me show you the rest of the house."

He leads me up the floating stairs with the elegant handrails. I run my hand along the thin, smooth surface.

"The original stairs didn't have a rail," he explains.

I shudder, imagining walking up and down without any safety measure. "Nobody fell off?"

"Not that I know of. But Mom had one installed because her lawyer said she was inviting a lawsuit."

I can see that, especially when somebody sees Grant's mom as a means to score some easy money.

I look down from the indoor balcony. If you hate heights, you'd hate this place. The floor is clear glass reinforced with cables. The doors to the bedrooms are ornate, with different pink seashells at eye level.

"So this is one of the guest bedrooms." He opens the door, and we stick our heads inside...

...to see an empty bedframe.

I blink. Grant makes a vaguely confused noise. "Weird. The house should be fully furnished. Maybe Mom's getting a new mattress for this room."

We go to the next room, and then the next. No beds. Except for the master bedroom suite—I presume this, since it's locked—which we obviously can't take, since it's his mother's. Even if Grant had a key to the room, I would totally decline after having heard about her temper. I'm pretty sure sleeping in her bed would be an infraction.

But now what?

Finally, on the opposite side of the house from the master suite, we find a gorgeously appointed ocean-view bedroom. Thankfully, it does have a bed—and sheets! At the foot of the bed is a pearl-gray velvet bench with a burgundy crocodile leather bag sitting on it. The bag looks brand new.

"Is that your mom's bag? Is this room also reserved for her?" She has two kitchens. It's possible she has two bedrooms and just forgot to lock this one.

"Not really," Grant says, looking at the bag thoughtfully.

Okay, maybe it belongs to his aunt or something, but this room most definitely isn't for guests in that case...

Or is it? I pull my lips in as another thought crosses my mind. Does this mean there's only one bed for us in the entire house? The living room doesn't have a couch. Just two armchairs.

Grant frowns. "You know what? Let me see what's going on real quick."

14

GRANT

I pull out my phone and text the property manager as I walk out of the bedroom. I have a feeling whatever I hear is going to be annoying or embarrassing. Probably both. Mom didn't get rid of all those beds for me.

–Me: What's up with the house? Mom doing a renovation or something?

——Carmen: Not that I know of. Why?

–Me: Every guest bedroom except for one is missing a bed.

–Carmen: Oh. She asked to have the mattresses removed while you were there.

What the hell? I start to type, *Why would she do that?* then delete the question. How the hell would Carmen know? She's just following instructions, and Mom doesn't explain herself to the people who work for her.

–Carmen: If you want to discuss the timing of the mattress delivery, she's probably still up, because I spoke with her just moments ago.

Carmen's too innocent if she thinks this is just a coincidence, or Mom did it so Aspen and I could have new beds. But she's right about contacting Mom to get some answers. I text her thanks and type up my question for Mom.

—Me: What's up with the beds?

Three dots appear, then vanish. I count to five, but nothing. *Oh no, you don't.*

—Me: If you don't answer, I'm going to withdraw my transfer applications. And then I'll tell Jeremiah I couldn't get in.

Within a second, Mom calls.

"What do you mean, withdraw your applications?" she demands. "I only let you use the place because you promised to transfer!"

I move farther from Aspen and lower my voice. I don't want her to know how galactically weird my parents are. "Why did you remove all the mattresses?"

"I got that tip from Nikki." Nicholas's mom. "She told me it's the best way to ensure you don't host a three-day-long orgy."

"I don't do orgies. I'm not Dad."

"Then why are you upset? Did you bring a herd of college kids?" Her voice starts to rise. "I told you no big parties! No—"

"*One,*" I say. "I brought *one* person with me!"

"Then what's the problem? The guest bedroom has a California king."

"I don't want her to feel like she has to sleep with me." I want Aspen to do it because she wants me, not because she wants to thank me. There's a big difference. I don't want our first time to be transactional. Aspen deserves the best.

"Why did you bring her if she doesn't sleep with you?" Mom sounds lost. "Don't tell me you've made a platonic friend. Such things don't exist between men and women. Either you want to do her but got friend-zoned or you're just waiting for an opportunity."

"I'm *not* having this discussion with you."

"Well, you should. You might learn something." She huffs. "I know better than you. Much more experience."

Ugh! I don't want to think about how much she knows or how much experience she has. "Because it's *weird,* okay? Anyway, we haven't... We aren't..." I fumble for words, then bite back a frustrated curse. Why the hell am I trying to explain my sex life to my mother?

"Dear God, Grant. I haven't raised you to be a fool. And I didn't let you use my home so you could reinforce a friend-zoning. I totally wasted that purse, then. I had Carmen put it on the bedroom bench in the guest room, so the sight of it would make the girl ovulate on the spot. Of course, I expect you to be smart and use a non-defective condom."

"*Mother.*" There's plenty of warning in the word.

"Just say, 'Thank you for thinking of everything even though I can't rise to the occasion.' If she's being difficult, get her a room at a hotel. You don't want some ungrateful bitch whining the entire time. And if you need help, just tell me. I know plenty of girls who'd be happy to fuck you for a bag far cheaper than what I left, and in a home far inferior to mine. Now, I have to go. Unlike you, I'm about to get laid."

Before I can make a gagging noise, she hangs up. Mom is certifiable. Why couldn't her high IQ come with a normal personality? Thank God Aspen's sitting in the reading nook by the window in the guest bedroom, looking at the ocean. I'd have to jump off the second-floor railing if she heard anything coming out of Mom's mouth.

Even my phone feels filthy now. I wipe it on my pants and shove it back into my pocket before going to Aspen and giving her a heavily edited version of the conversation I just had. "I'm really sorry, but my mother was worried I might host a huge party here, so she, uh, kind of removed all the beds. Except for one."

She nods slowly as she processes the news. "And left only two armchairs."

Fuck. I realize I made myself sound like an irresponsible asshole. "Basically. She's a little paranoid about some things. Like couch surfing." Either Mom thought of everything, or Nikki told her. *And I used to like Nikki.*

"I see," Aspen says slowly.

"You can take the bed." Never let it be said I'm not a gentleman.

"And where are you going to sleep? Your mom's bed? The door's locked."

"I can probably pull the armchairs together and sort of make a bed. I used to do it as a kid."

"I don't know how old you were, but they won't be big enough for you now." She shifts a little. "I don't want you to feel uncomfortable in your own mother's home."

"No, no, no. You're the guest, and I don't want *you* to feel awkward."

She clears her throat. "I guess the bed is, you know...pretty big."

My mouth dries. The realization that we're actually going to be in the same bed rolls through my mind like Viagra laced with steroids. I alter my posture to hide the effect on my dick. "Yeah, um. A California king."

"We can probably share it without touching each other. You on one side and me on the other."

This probably isn't the time to tell her I sleep naked. "Right," I say, wondering if I packed something that can be used as pajamas. I should just call Mom's personal shopper in the city and have her bring something over.

"Okay. So. Cool." Aspen clears her throat again.

"Okay." I pause. "So, uh, you want lunch?"

"Uh, yeah. Sure."

My phone vibrates in my pocket. I pull it out. A normal person might assume it's his mom texting to say she's sorry, but I know better. Athena Grant is *never* wrong.

It's actually a message from the AmEx concierge service that comes with my black card. A couple of weeks ago, I asked them to get us a reservation at La Mer, an upscale seafood restaurant in L.A. that opened last week. There's a long waiting list, and I wasn't sure if they could do it, but apparently they came through. Tonight at seven.

The note specifically states that there's a dress code, which I didn't think about. I didn't tell Aspen to pack something fancy, and I didn't pack anything, either.

But such a minor inconvenience isn't going to get in the way of splurging on Aspen.

"Is everything okay?" she asks.

"Yeah. It's actually the concierge letting me know about our dinner reservation. I totally forgot about it because there's a waiting list, but apparently, we're in."

"Awesome!" She smiles.

"The thing is, there's dress code. And it's sort of formal. You didn't pack anything that could pass for a cocktail dress...?"

"Oh." She bites her lip. "I didn't. Um. I thought it was going to be a casual vacation. Maybe we could drop by my grandparents' place and grab something? I left some stuff there."

It's a sensible solution, but I don't like it. Knowing how frugal and careful Aspen is with money, it's probably some basic item she bought on sale years ago and has worn a lot already. Nothing wrong with that, but I want to spoil her and get her something new and pretty to add to her wardrobe. I'm still annoyed over how rude Sadie was to Aspen about her old phone, and if I had a good excuse to get her the latest model, I would. "No need. I'll just ask Marketta to bring us something."

"Who's Marketta?"

"My mother's personal shopper. Convenient when you don't have much time, and her taste is great, too. Plus, *I* need something to wear. I didn't pack anything suitable either."

"Um... How much is it going to be?" she asks, her cheeks going slightly pink. "I mean, you know. Approximately."

"Don't worry about it." I say it casually, like I don't notice her reaction. "Mom's paying."

Her eyes go round. "She is?"

"She told me she'd foot the bill for everything. That's probably why she didn't want me bringing a lot of people over." The lie rolls from my tongue easily. I'll be providing for my girl, not Mom. But Aspen will never accept it if she knows it's coming from me because she'll feel like she owes me.

"But why? We've never even met."

"You helped me get an A+ on the group assignment, remember? Mom takes my grades seriously. Way more seriously than I do." Only because she wants me to successfully transfer to a fancy school so she can rub it in Jeremiah's face, but Aspen doesn't need to know that sort of boring and unimportant detail. "And you made sure I was okay after my fall on the polo field. Mom feels terrible about not being there for me. You know how mothers are when their kids are injured."

I'm laying it on thick—the reality is, I have no idea how Mom gets when I'm injured. I've been healthy as a horse all my life, and even if I were to be deathly ill, she'd probably just put me in a hospital with some super-famous specialist and get back to her life.

But Aspen's nodding slowly, seemingly convinced. "Well...okay, I guess."

"In fact, you see that bag?" I point at the burgundy bag sitting on the bench. "It's yours."

Aspen's jaw slackens. *"What?"*

I nod. "Most definitely. She reminded me again on the phone just now. She loves to give presents to people who've been kind to me. Brings her joy." Against all odds, my pants do not burst into flame.

"I don't know what to say. It's so extravagant."

"You don't have to say anything because you deserve it. Think of it as something you earned because of your good work. Go on. Take it. Enjoy it."

Aspen picks it up and runs her hand along the leather, her eyes bright. I'm no bag expert, but even I can tell it's really nice. I can only imagine how it must look to a woman.

She opens the bag and checks inside, probably to make sure it's empty. She doesn't think I'm lying, but she probably can't believe she's getting a brand-new purse just for putting my name on the paper and driving me home after the fall. "Wow. I need to write your mom a thank-you note."

"If you give it to me, I'll forward it to her," I lie. Then I text Marketta.

—Me: I need something to wear to La Mer tonight. Plus some pajamas.

—Marketta: PJs for you?

She adds a shocked emoji.

—Me: Yes. Also my date needs a dress, shoes and everything else a woman needs for a night out.

—Marketta: If you have a date, why would you need pajamas?

—Me: Har har. Just do it, okay?

I'm not explaining my personal life to Marketta even if she is like the grandma I never had.

—Marketta: All right. Her coloring, height and size?

—Me: Red hair. Green eyes. Really pretty. 5'6". I dunno her dress size.

—Marketta: But you know her bra size.

I can just picture her stifling a laugh.

—Marketta: I can't dress her if I don't know her size, but I can see why you don't want to ask. Just send me pics of her, then. Full body. Front, side and back. Make sure she's standing straight. I need her shoe size, too.

—Me: I can do that.

—Marketta: Where are you staying?

—Me: At Mom's. In Malibu.

—Marketta: She must love you.

Marketta is delusional.

—Marketta: Don't go anywhere. I'll be there in 2-3 hours.

———

While Marketta does her shopping magic, Aspen and I have a leisurely lunch at a small beachside restaurant that has the best cheeseburgers and fries in the area. But better than the food is her smile, the relaxed twinkle in her eyes as she looks at me. Getting away from the campus was a genius move. No pressure, no friends around, and we aren't concerned about anything but us. And I want there to be an *us*, because she's making me feel things I've never felt before, things that make me high.

When we're back in the house, I get a text from Marketta.

—Marketta: Arriving in ten.

Perfect timing.

Marketta shows up with her assistants, who get busy rolling in racks and racks of clothes and boxes of items—probably shoes and accessories. Marketta's a petite blonde in her sixties, but you'd never know from looking at her. Her thick platinum hair is pulled into a tight chignon, and she's fashionably thin and wrapped in a purple Versace, her favorite brand. Her motto is she has to look as good as her clients—if not better.

"Grant. You always look amazing." She comes over and gives me air kisses on both cheeks.

"Good to see you." I return the air kiss on her cheeks, careful not to touch the pristine layers of makeup.

Her eyes land on Aspen. "And your date for the evening...?"

"Hi. I'm Aspen." Aspen extends a hand.

Marketta gives her a hug instead. "Hello, sweetheart. Oh my, you're so *pretty*." She means it. She never issues empty compliments, and she's never afraid to tell a client the truth.

Aspen looks slightly taken aback. "Thank you."

"I have a few things you can try, although I think they're all going to be fantastic. But first, Grant, Penny's going to take care of you. I also brought a few Harry Winstons because I figured it's time you got a new one." Her gaze falls to my wrist. "Not that there's anything wrong with that, but sometimes you just need a new watch to go with a new outfit."

Aspen looks at Marketta the way she'd look at a used-car saleswoman. Marketta is many things, but she never, ever recommends something she doesn't believe in. That's why she has tons of clients who adore her. The fact that my mom likes her says everything.

"I'll take a look," I say, squeezing Aspen's shoulder reassuringly. "Aspen, don't worry. This lady is going to take good care of you."

15

ASPEN

Marketta's assistants set up partitions and mirrors, creating a couple of impromptu dressing rooms. They also have enough racks to open a small clothing store.

Two of her assistants fuss over Grant, but I don't get to watch for long.

"Let's see. Your proportions are better in person than in photos. You have a black cocktail dress?" Marketta asks.

"Not with me, but yeah."

"Good. Every girl needs one." She crosses her arms as she squints. "Your hair... The color's all natural, yes?"

I nod.

"Excellent. I love it."

"Thanks." I flash a smile at her, then glance at the racks, wondering if I need to go through them and pick one out. There are an awful lot of dresses.

"Let's try a purple Dior," Marketta begins. "And that Chanel and a turquoise Givenchy—not the one with sheer sleeves but the adorable one with a great bustline."

One of her assistants picks out three outfits like she knows exactly what Marketta wants from the countless dresses she's brought. The colors are vivid, but I don't know... They sort of hang limply, and I struggle to visualize how they're going to look on me. I don't have the kind of lean body that models who wear these kinds of clothes on the runway do.

"Let's put these on," Marketta announces like a queen.

I merely smile, knowing I don't have any say in the matter. She's wearing the confident expression of a woman who's convinced she's never wrong, and I know too little about high fashion to offer an opinion.

I take the Dior into the "dressing room" and try it on. The fabric feels amazing against my skin, like it's made of spun cloud. It hugs my torso like a glove, then flares out with an asymmetrical skirt. Wow. Marketta must be a genius to know my exact size. Then I note the bra straps and panty lines showing a bit, so I adjust my under-wear. *That should do it,* I decide after checking from a few different angles.

When I come out, she purses her lips and snaps her fingers. "We need something else."

Quickly, I'm given a strapless bra and thong that must've been made during an extreme fabric shortage. Guess I didn't hide the lines as well as I thought.

"The Dior is delicate, if you understand what I mean." Quirking an eyebrow, she gives me a sweet smile, then turns to an assistant. "And she needs shoes. Let's try Prada. Peep-toe." She turns back to me. "Do you have a clutch, dear?"

I don't think it's the time to tell her about the black purse I bought from Target on sale. Then I remember the one Grant's mom left for me. "I have a burgundy purse."

"Lemme see."

"It's upstairs. On the bed."

"It's a Hermes," Grant calls out from his part of the living room.

"Ah." Marketta nods. "Your mother's 'present'?"

"Yep," he says.

"Then it's a good thing I have my own selection."

"I think I'm good with this one," I say, feeling a bit nervous and anxious. It's obvious everything Marketta brought is expensive. I remember Suyen telling me how much Grant's watch costs. Although he said his mom would pay, I feel a little awkward about asking her to spend hundreds of dollars for clothes and shoes when she's already given me a purse and is letting me stay at her gorgeous home.

My distress must be apparent, because Marketta pats my back. "Don't worry, dear. We're going to make you look amazing."

"Um, that's not really—"

"But we can probably do better than the Dior. Let's try that Givenchy, shall we?" she says, gesturing at her assistant.

I give up. This time, I'm escorted back into the dressing room with not just the turquoise outfit but shoes and lingerie. I guess this dress is also too *delicate* for my current underwear.

"Don't worry. She's going to make you look like a star," one of the assistants says with a smile.

"Thanks." I smile back reflexively.

Once they're out, I change into everything Marketta picked out. The fabric is also lovely, and the shoes fit like a dream. Maybe this is why people wear expensive shoes. I feel like I could dance in them for hours.

Finger-combing my hair, I turn to the mirror, then cover my mouth, pressing my lips together hard, while I scream my head off inside. Oh my *God*! I can't *believe* this!

The dress shimmers like the warm Caribbean on a sunny day. It flows over my body like a wave. The skirt that reaches the middle of my thighs flares out, rendering an air of sophistication and sexiness. It lifts my breasts, giving me cleavage I didn't know I had. No wonder Marketta called this the one with a nice bustline. The nude stilettos look fabulous, making my legs look longer without taking any attention away from the gorgeous dress. The green-blue color brings out my eyes, and my hair looks even fierier by contrast.

Holy *shit*. I'm so excited, my legs are shaking.

Taking a deep, calming breath, I step outside, ready for Marketta's approval.

But her reaction fades away because Grant's standing by her. He's in a dove-gray shirt with a luxurious sheen over black slacks. He stares at me, his eyes wide. His mouth parts as he runs a hand along his jaw.

I can feel my cheeks heat. "What do you think?" I make a small turn.

"Oh my fuck," he mutters.

"That bad?" I tease, absolutely loving his response.

"No. I... Jesus." He drags his hand over his mouth. "You look perfect. Better than perfect."

"She needs a necklace," Marketta says.

Is there no end to this woman's nitpicking?

"Yes, she does." Grant puts his hand out and crooks a finger.

"Here." Marketta points at a dark velvet tray that one of her assistants then brings over.

He picks up a stunning platinum and diamond key pendant and comes closer. Light shatters as it hits the gemstones. My heart pounds, and he goes around, standing behind me.

"Your hair," he murmurs.

"Oh. Sorry." I loop my hair around my hand and lift it up.

His warm breath fans over my neck. It gives me goosebumps as his fingers brush over my bare skin as he positions the cool necklace, and the key settles between my breasts. His hands linger a bit longer than necessary. My heart is racing like I just ran a marathon, and something hot and achy pools between my legs.

He comes around and looks down at me. "You're beautiful."

"Thank you." I seem to be drowning in his eyes. If it weren't for all these people, I'd kiss him for making me feel so special.

"I brought you sweaters, too," Marketta says, breaking the moment. "Not the frumpy kind, but nice ones. It's supposed to be unseasonably cold tomorrow, and I didn't know what you two packed for the trip."

Grant's eyes are still on mine. "Thanks, Marketta."

"I'll invoice you." She laughs. "Now let's get the rest of the things she needs, shall we?"

––––––––

The restaurant we go to is in downtown L.A., which takes almost two hours from Malibu to reach. The traffic's pretty awful, especially around this time.

Still, the place is worth the long drive. The entryway has gorgeous flower arrangements, although it's sort of weird to call them that, since they don't have flowers, just pale branches. But they're designed to look like coral formations, especially when the blue-green lights are on them.

Grant gets out and gives his keys to a uniformed valet. A staff member comes over and opens my door for me.

Just as I'm about to step out of the Mercedes, Grant comes around and holds out a hand. I place mine in it, let his long, strong fingers wrap around me and feel my heart flutter like a newly blossoming flower.

He doesn't let go as we make our way to the entrance. I'm in the Givenchy and the nude stilettos from earlier. In addition to the necklace I'm wearing, a pair of diamond earrings dangle away from my hair, which I put up in a loose bun with some strands framing my face. I don't think I've ever looked this pretty in my life, not even for my prom. I feel like a princess about to attend her first ball.

Grant has changed into a crisp white shirt, charcoal jacket and black pants. He hasn't bothered with a tie, but on his wrist is a new watch—the one Marketta brought. I also note platinum and onyx cuff links with his initials. Although we're both too young to drink, he exudes the confidence and sophistication of a far older man. He could probably order a drink and no bartender would think to ask for an ID.

I don't know if I can match his self-assurance and attitude, but I'm happy to be in the fancy dress and shoes. They make me feel like I belong, although I'm probably a bit overdressed.

The hostess stands in front of a huge aquarium full of colorful tropical fish. She's in a gorgeous blue dress, and she smiles winsomely, flashing white teeth. "Welcome to La Mer. Do you have a reservation?"

"Party of two, Grant Lasker."

She checks her tablet. "This way."

We're led into the restaurant, and I can't stop myself from looking around like a small-town girl who's never been to a big city before. All the partitions and walls are actually aquariums with fish, sand and miniature coral inside. I'm not sure if the coral is real or fake, but it looks authentic.

I also get to see the guests already seated, and I realize it's a good thing we didn't try to drive all the way to my grandparents' house for my black dress. It's a nice enough outfit, but it wouldn't work here. Even to my ignorant eye, what people are wearing looks priceless and exquisite, like the racks and racks of clothes Marketta brought for me.

As a matter of fact, I could've gone fancier and I'd fit in just fine. And it's the same for Grant as well.

Our table is in a private section, almost entirely enclosed by the aquarium walls. In the center is a candle with a miniature wreath made with tiny white flowers.

"I love this." I smile. "Thank you."

Grant grins. "I'm glad. I wasn't sure about the place."

"How come?"

"It's my first time here too. I had to trust that the publicity and buzz were true."

"Isn't it normally? Or at least, don't you know somebody who could give you an honest opinion?"

He shrugs. "Not always, not when the restaurant owner poured the kind of money into it that this one did."

"I don't know how much he spent, but it was worth it." I look at the bright orange fish swishing away. "It's amazing."

And you are amazing, I think as I look across the table. The warm glow from the candle brings out his sharp cheekbones and strong chin. His full lips are smiling, and I swear, he has the most stunning mouth I've ever seen on any human being—soft and kissable.

Probably the only soft thing on his body. Despite the A/C blowing, I feel overly warm. I reach for my ice water to cool myself.

Just then, our server appears. He's impeccably dressed, like the hostess, and ridiculously good-looking. It's like being attractive is a job requirement here.

We order drinks—a pink lemonade for me and a Coke for Grant. The menu only has two options: five-course or seven-course. We opt for the latter. According to our waiter, it's the most sought-after choice at the moment and highly recommended, especially since it'll only be available during the opening month.

The drink is fabulous—the best pink lemonade I've ever had. As each course comes, I see the portions aren't huge, but are delightfully arranged and presented. I've never had anything this elegant or tasty. My experience with seafood is limited to shrimp fajitas, fried shrimp and fish sticks—maybe sushi if I want to get super fancy.

"I feel like a fairytale princess," I say after our waiter clears away the fourth course.

"Cinderella?" Grant says.

I shake my head. "Belle."

He frowns. "Who's that?"

"The one from *Beauty and the Beast*."

He cocks an eyebrow. "So if you're Belle, I'm..."

"The Beast."

"The Beast. Hmm." His expression says he's not sure about being a Beast when he could've been Prince Charming.

"Uh-huh." I grin, enjoying teasing him. "All roaring and gruffness. He doesn't make the best first impression."

"Ah." His eyes narrow a little. "Is he an irresponsible idiot? Or just an asshole?"

"Neither. He's a little grumpy and mean on the outside, but soft and sweet on the inside."

He quirks an eyebrow. "Go on."

"He also owns self-cleaning plates, self-lighting candles and the most amazing library."

"I have at least thirty boxes of books in storage. I'll show you," he says.

"And he throws the best balls and dances like the wonderful prince that he is."

"Just so you know, there are self-cleaning and -deodorizing toilets at Mom's place." He tilts his head back toward Malibu. "Bet the Beast didn't have those."

"I wouldn't know." I laugh. "The movie didn't say."

"Bet the movie didn't tell you he's also the best kisser in the entire fairytale world." His tone is light, his words are full of humor, but his eyes...

My laugh dies down as every nerve in my body prickles with awareness. He makes me laugh and long for him at the same time. I've never experienced that before. Actually, every time with him seems to lead to something new.

As my mouth dries, I realize I've had my head buried like an ostrich.

He's the one I've been waiting for all this time.

16

ASPEN

We're only a few yards from getting back to the beachfront mansion when a couple of drops of water land on the windshield. I look up and see a sky full of leaden clouds.

"Thank God this came after we got home," Grant says as he pulls into the garage and kills the engine.

"You can't drive in the rain?" I tease as we enter the house. A couple of recessed lights come on, casting a warm but dim glow over the living room.

"Are you kidding? I learned to drive in Europe. Rain, snow, everything. It's the people in this city. A couple of drops, and they act like it's some Biblical hail of locusts."

I laugh at his dramatic description. "Well, we aren't used to rain. But I like it as long as I'm not driving."

It starts to pour. I try to see the dark ocean through the window, but it's almost impossible to see anything clearly. The raindrops hit the house, filling the empty space with white noise.

I reach for my phone and pick out a playlist of tango music, including "La cumparsita." I extend my hands. "Dance with me."

His dark gaze collides with mine in the dimly lit living room. I swallow a little, since we both know it's an overture.

"What are we dancing?" he says.

"A tango, of course." I smile. "Unless you aren't in the mood."

"Oh, I'm in the mood. I've been wanting to do it properly with you after that class debacle."

Do it...with you. "Ah, yes. The moment when I decided there was more to your beastliness than met the eye." I hit play.

He puts one hand on my back and lays his knuckles on my shoulder. As the music starts, the backs of his fingers glide down my arm to my wrist, raising goosebumps.

I make a circle around him. When the music shifts, he pulls me closer, and we're moving. Now that I'm not in sneakers, it's so much easier. I can relax in his arms and let him lead me as the soulful voice sings of heartbreak.

"I love dancing when it rains," I say.

"Why?"

"It's like creating a little eye of order within chaos. Listen to the sound of the rain. The tempo, the volume—it's all at the whim of Mother Nature. But dancing is orderly. Structured. It makes me feel anchored." And Grant feels like a safe haven, except I'm too shy to tell him. So instead, I say, "Actually, I love rain, period."

"Then why didn't you go to school in Washington state? It rains all the time there."

"Because, silly, if I got it all the time, it wouldn't be special."

In the glow of the light, I can sense his confusion.

"Why do people think love is special?" I stop for a second, realizing maybe love isn't the best analogy. But it slipped out, and it's going to be weird if I try to take it back. "Why do we make thousands of movies and stories and books about it?"

"Because they're profitable," he says.

"*No.* Because love is rare, which makes it special. Some people never even get to experience it before they die."

"If they never do, how do they know they're missing anything?"

"I think part of their soul longs for it. They know, deep inside, the other half of their soul is out there."

He laughs, more surprised than amused. "I didn't expect this kind of romanticism from a girl who chased me down to the polo field."

"This girl can be many things."

He extends his arm, and I spin out, then make a circle around him. His fingertips skim my waist—setting my skin on fire—as I turn on the smooth floor. He catches me, abruptly stopping the motion, then pulls me tightly to him. I can feel his heart pulsing, and we're so close, our breaths mingle as we stare into each other's eyes.

He lowers his head until the tip of his nose brushes mine. I tilt my chin closer. He strokes my lips with his tongue like a gentle knock, seeking permission. I open my mouth, let him in, then meet his tongue with mine. He tastes so good, full of raw power and desire. My senses are full of him—the flavor of him, the smell of him and the heat of him.

He explores my mouth, drinking me in. I kiss him back just as eagerly. A tiny, cautious voice whispers I should give this more thought, but a long, hot stroke of his hand from my hip to the side of my breast snuffs it.

He's the one.

Everywhere he touches tingles. I fumble, unsure how much to touch him—*how* to touch him so he can feel the same heat I'm feeling. The flesh between my legs throbs. If I were alone, I might relieve the pressure building there, but right now, Grant's holding me tight and his rigid cock is pressing against my belly. My lungs fight for air, and I feel dizzy with a white-hot need I've never experienced before.

"You drive me crazy," I say, breaking the kiss to draw in more air.

Ragged breaths puff out of Grant. "Turn off the music."

"It's going to cut off soon." The playlist isn't set to play indefinitely.

"Brace your hands on my shoulders and wrap your legs around me."

My heart hammering with anticipation, I do as he asks. He puts his hands under my dress, on my bare butt to support me, and carries me up the stairs. One of his fingers slips under the thong strap between my ass cheeks and presses against the opening of my pussy.

Oh my God. I squirm at the shallow dipping in and out of his finger with each step. What I sometimes do with my finger is nothing compared to what he's doing with his. It's bigger, thicker and slightly callused. Not to mention it feels incredibly illicit. It sends shivers along my spine, makes my toes curl.

"Jesus, you're so wet for me."

His raw words leave me slightly shy, but also excited. He reclaims my lips, and I'm utterly lost as his tongue invades my mouth while his finger pushes deeper.

He takes me to the bedroom and we fall on the huge, soft bed. He props his weight on his forearms on either side of me.

I always thought my first time would be nerve-racking and maybe a little scary. But looking up at his hot gaze, fear is the last thing on my mind. There's lust in his eyes, but I can glimpse tenderness, too. I know he's going to make it good for me.

He unzips the side of my dress and pulls it up, and the silk rasps against my hypersensitive skin. He tosses it to the foot of the bed, and it falls over the burgundy bag on the bench. My bra and thong follow rapidly.

"Um, my heels...?"

"Leave 'em on." He stares down at my body, his chest rising high.

I'm slightly nervous. *This is really happening.* It's going to be nothing like a quick fingering at night under my sheet. I know about the mechanics of sex, but it's awkward to accept that I have no real clue as to how to make it good for both of us. Some of the girls talk about going down on their boyfriends, but just because I've heard about it doesn't mean I feel any confidence in the act.

Besides, being naked when he's not intensifies my vulnerability. "Take off your clothes." I try to say it with more control, but my voice comes out shaky.

Grant straightens, his burning eyes on mine. He doesn't hurry as he slips off his shoes and gets out of his clothes. It's like he's putting on a private strip show just for me.

My mouth dries, my heart pounding with excitement as more and more of his gorgeous body is bared. It's actually hard to breathe faced with the beauty of his physique. Suyen says that naked men look ridiculous. That's definitely *not* the case with Grant. His muscles seem larger and more powerful without clothes. There isn't an ounce of fat on his tall, broad frame. And his cock—oh my God.

It's so thick, long and stiff. Veins pulse on the shaft. The tip's glistening, almost brushing his ridged abs.

"It's huge," I blurt out.

He grins wickedly. "And it's going to feel great."

"Are you sure?"

He leans forward, his tender eyes on mine. "I'll make sure of it. Trust me."

I nod. I do trust him—unconditionally.

He gifts me with a sweet smile, then rains kisses on my bare breasts without touching their pointed tips. It feels incredible, and I move my legs restlessly, wanting more. He pulls a nipple into his mouth, sucking it, flicking his tongue.

I cry out at the shocking, intense, unfamiliar pleasure, and tunnel my fingers into his hair, gripping him tight. My spine curves, creating an arch as I press against his mouth. He plays with my other breast, kneading the soft flesh and teasing the nipple. I writhe under him, lost in erotic sensation.

He caresses my sides, my belly, his deep groan letting me know how much he loves my curves. He moves his mouth down, creating a hot trail along my body.

As he gets closer to the junction between my legs, my initial nervousness returns. I feel like a rank newbie in an advanced tango class, someone who's so ignorant she can't even follow the lead. I waited because I wanted to share my body only with somebody who was worth it. But I'm sure he's done it *a lot* before, and might not want a girl who fumbles around like an idiot. It's the twenty-first century, not some medieval era when men hang bloody sheets out their balconies to brag that they got to deflower a virgin.

Maybe I should fake it.

Or maybe you should've womaned up and told him the truth before you got swept up in the moment, that you're a virgin who's never seen a cock in real life before—

"Focus."

I blink up at Grant's hard voice. "What?"

"You weren't here." He lightly rests his chin on my belly.

"Of course I'm *here*," I say with a shaky laugh, praying I'm doing a good job of hiding my nerves.

"Your mind wasn't." His expression's stiff, and there's a tenseness to his forehead and eyebrows.

Shit. I've ruined the moment. "I wasn't thinking about something else. It's just that, um...*I'veneverdonethisbefore.*"

A shocked silence stretches. "What?"

"You heard me." I'm not saying it again.

"You've never done it before?" He straightens, lifting his head off my belly and running a hand across his jaw. "Like, *never*?"

"No." My voice is tiny.

"Why not?" He shakes his head. "Never mind. I—" His mouth moves mutely. Grant Lasker, the man who's never lacked for a comeback.

I wonder if I should roll away, give him some space to think things through. Except I don't know if I can dislodge him. He seems more solid than a sequoia. "Are you, you know, weirded out?"

"No. No, that's not it."

I look at him skeptically.

"You want proof?" He points to his penis, which I have to admit is also like a sequoia.

I squirm a little. He's steely against me.

"It's just that I've never been somebody's first before."

"Oh..."

He looks down at me. "We can be each other's first."

He comes up and cradles my face between his large, warm hands and kisses me deeply, sweetly, then runs his hands over the rest of my body, my neck, collarbones, breasts, fingertips and more. Everywhere he touches relaxes; anxiety burns away, replaced by desire and need. I've never felt so treasured before.

Finally, his fingers glide along my slick folds. I hold my breath.

"Easy," he murmurs, dipping one finger into me. It feels good, although my instinct says it's lacking something. He pushes another finger in, and I moan at the sensation. I love the way he fills me. I want more of him inside.

My pelvis moves to the rhythm of his fingers. He feeds another finger into me.

"Oh my God." My breathing is rough and jagged over building pleasure. I didn't know it could feel like this.

He moves his fingers with more speed and power. I can hear something that sounds like someone slapping a shallow puddle.

I feel the wetness trickle down the groove between my butt cheeks, and my tailbone grows slightly damp. He pulls out his fingers and pushes my knees wide open. Then he runs the flat of his tongue all the way up to my clit. I shiver at the unexpected caress, my face burning with shock and need at the illicitness of what he's done. He pulls my throbbing clit into his mouth and sucks hard as he pushes his fingers back into me, hitting a special spot inside my pussy that makes me see stars.

Tension that's been gathering bursts unexpectedly, and I can't even scream. I fight for breath as I climb down from the high, the intensity of which I've never experienced before.

Grant shoves his fingers deeper into me, in and out, harder and faster. His mouth stays on my clit, his tongue moving over the sensitive bundle of nerve endings.

I come again, digging my fingers into his hair. "Oh my God, I can't—"

He responds by sucking harder. Even as I scream, "I can't," I rock against his mouth and arch my body as another climax takes over me.

My whole body feels like a puddle of goo as I pant in the aftermath, stunned at the most incredible pleasure he's just given me. Grant is shaking, and I can tell he's barely clinging to control. I want him to feel the same thing I did. I start to squirm, wondering if I should try to go down on him, make him feel good.

But before I can fully recover from the shock of the three rapid orgasms, he pulls away and runs his hand over the glistening mess on his chin. He licks his lips and pulls out a condom from his pants pocket and puts it on, his movements sure but hurried. His eyes are hot as he positions himself between my thighs, which are still quivering.

Oh my God. This is happening.

I should be nervous. Or even anxious. But all I want is to have him come inside me, and share in the bliss. Biting my lip, I place my hands on his shoulders, silently urging him.

He claims my mouth with a low groan as he pushes in. I inhale and exhale deeply as I brace for pain. It could hurt, and maybe pain is another reason I was reluctant to do it with just anybody.

He breaks the kiss. "Are you okay?"

I nod, trying to breathe, despite my instinct to hold it.

He pushes in a little bit deeper each time until he's entirely in. The fullness of having his cock inside me is overwhelming. I'm stretched to the limit, and can't seem to draw another breath. But it doesn't hurt. It's just a little uncomfortable and unfamiliar. I clench and unclench my muscles to get used to him.

He places his forehead on mine. "Fuck."

His chest heaves. Veins stand out along his temples, and sweat rolls down his body as he struggles for the control to make this moment perfect for me—for us.

Something tender and sweet swells in my heart. I lay a hand on his cheek and kiss him softly. "Thank you."

I don't have to say more because I know from the way his eyes flare that he knows exactly what I mean.

Kissing me with desperation, he starts driving in and out, slowly and carefully at first, gauging my reaction, making sure I'm really okay, then his thrusts grow more powerful and faster as he realizes I'm loving what he's doing to me. His cock hits the spot that his fingers did, and I feel streaks of pleasure all the way to the tips of my toes.

When the fourth orgasm rips through me, I'm left trembling uncontrollably. It's like my veins are full of electric charge. I wrap my arms around Grant, holding on to him like my safe haven to ride out the incredible high.

He calls out my name like I'm a piece of his soul as he shudders in climax. And I realize something irrevocable and indelible has just been etched onto my heart.

17

GRANT

The unfamiliar feel of somebody in the bed with me wakes me up. The faint spear of light coming between the curtains tells me it's early—maybe a little before six.

I turn over and see Aspen curled into a ball. She's so warm and soft. I have to stop myself from stroking her, lest I wake her up too.

Instead, I watch her sleep in the slowly strengthening light. Her long lashes make fan-shaped shadows on her cheeks, and her plump mouth is relaxed. There's a vulnerable rosiness to her that I like. And she smells so good in the morning without the shampoo and body wash masking her scent. I inhale the heady perfume of her smooth skin, feel my cock respond.

She stirs a little, placing a hand on my chest, curling her fingers over my heart, like she's staking a claim. For once, the notion doesn't bring a surge of annoyance and oh-shit-time-to-end-it-now agitation. It actually might not be too bad to let her hold on to my heart, which beats a little faster at the idea.

She presses closer, like she wants that as well. I carefully lift a bit of her silky hair and thread it through my fingers, then kiss the smooth strands. Everything about her is feminine and beautiful. The artists of the old era missed out. If they'd seen this woman, they could've created hundreds of gorgeous masterpieces. On the other hand, the possessive part of me is happy they never got to see her. She's too special to be replicated over and over again, displayed everywhere so just anyone can gaze at her.

She makes a soft sound deep in her throat, her eyebrows pinching. I hold my breath, waiting to see if she'll slide back into slumber. Instead, her fingers over my heart clench and her nails dig into my chest. Her lips purse, like she's unhappy about getting pulled out of her sleep.

Unable to help myself, I place a soft kiss on her mouth. Her face instantly takes on a surprised look, which is funny and adorable with her eyes still closed. Laughing quietly, I kiss her again.

She blinks slowly, her green eyes hazy with lingering sleep. Then they focus on me, and a tender smile breaks over her, unguarded and lovely.

It's the coolest thing in the universe that I'm the first thing she sees—and that I bring a smile to her face.

"Hey," she says, her voice husky.

"Morning."

She glances down and realizes she's half lying on me. "Uh. Have you been up for long?"

She starts to pull away, but I wrap an arm around her waist to keep her exactly where she is, pressing her plump breasts against me. "No."

"Why am I getting a feeling you aren't going to tell me the truth?"

"Because you want me to say yes?"

"You just seem really alert."

"A cruel thing to say to a man who hasn't had his coffee."

She laughs softly.

"How are you feeling?" I ask.

"Oh. Uh. Not too bad."

"Are you in pain?" I'm not sure how it works, but I've heard it can hurt.

"Um." She picks her words with care. "A little sore, but nothing I can't handle."

I search her face to make sure she isn't downplaying things to make me feel better. "I just can't believe you'd never done it with anybody before."

She clears her throat. "I didn't want to do it just to say I'd done it. I wanted it to mean something," she says, looking into my eyes.

And the fact that she chose me makes my heart swell with pride and tenderness that make my whole being ache. Wrapping my hand around the back of her neck, I pull her in for a kiss.

She kisses me back, parting her mouth softly. I run my hand down the smooth curve of her back, which ends in an ass that fills my palm perfectly. She squirms, moving her hips as she skims her small hands down my body.

Although I want to have her again, I don't want to hurt her, especially after she told me she was sore. But touching her is too good, feeling her growing excitement too addictive.

I graze my fingers over her ass and the sides of her hips, then brush them over the groove between the cheeks. Her breathing shallows, and her tongue moves more desperately against mine. She brings her hand down and grips my dick.

I groan against her lips. Her fingers feel amazing around my shaft. To reward her, I dip my finger slowly into her, making sure she's okay. Holy shit, she's already wet for me. She moans, wordlessly encouraging me. She moves her hand along my cock, her grip a bit too soft and her motions tentative, like she's afraid of doing too much and hurting me.

Smiling a little, I wrap my hand around hers, then show her exactly how much pressure I like and how fast and hard she can move it. It feels incredible to fist myself with her hand against my bare dick. I slide in another finger into her, then curl it to hit the spot she loved so much last night.

Her back arches, every muscle in her body tensing. She throws her head back, and her hair pours down her shoulders and back like a fiery waterfall. She grips me harder, probably just out of reflex, but *Jesus*. My eyes roll back in my head at the pleasure.

"Like that," I say, then continue to touch her sensitive spot while I pump into her fist.

She labors to drag in air, the sound ragged and uneven. Her mouth is parted, her eyes closed tight as she chases her orgasm. I want to see her face when she climaxes, but I also don't want to end the moment too soon, so I increase the tempo of my fingers without touching her clit.

Her grip on me tightens as she moves faster along my cock. I grit my teeth as an orgasm starts to swell.

I'm not coming before her.

Before I can rub the pad of my thumb against her clit, she pants out a taut "Oh my God" and shudders, spasming around my fingers.

Her peak is my undoing. As pleasure twists her gorgeous face, I can't hold back. My cum hits her hand and belly, marking her. The sight is so hot, I shake, my spent dick twitching again and again.

I wrap my arms around her and make a half-turn, so she's underneath, and kiss her hard. She puts her clean hand on my cheek and responds eagerly. After a moment, she pulls back with an amused grin.

"What's so funny?" I say, memorizing every beautiful line of her face.

"Aren't you supposed to be, like, tired and all?" she says, still smiling. "I read about sex, and you're supposed to roll over and sleep."

"Forget what you read about sex. I'm not your average guy. Besides, I already slept, and I'd rather kiss you." Just then, my belly decides to let out an embarrassingly loud growl.

"Sounds like the only kisses you need are made of chocolate. Come on. I'm actually getting hungry, too." She frowns slightly. "This sex stuff gives you an appetite."

I raise myself. "We can't have that. Why don't we take a shower and get some breakfast at the Waldorf Astoria? We should be able to get a table at Jean-Georges."

"We don't have to go out that far."

"It'll be nice. I like their breakfast." And I want to spoil her. And show her off. Marketta left three dresses, and accessories for all of them. In addition, she gave me some dress shirts and slacks, too. It'd be a shame to let them go to waste.

"Okay," Aspen says brightly.

I get off the bed and start toward the bathroom, only to stop when she lets out a yelp. "Oh my God!"

"What?" I turn around.

"Your back!" She comes over and looks at my back more closely.

I twist around to see what's wrong, then catch scratch marks on the mirror on the vanity. I put a hand on her shoulder and shift so I can see them better. She ran her fingers down my back last night, but I didn't feel anything in particular. But the vivid red marks are stark on my skin.

She covers her mouth with her hands. "Oh my *God*. Did I do that?"

"Well, I'm not flexible enough to reach my own back."

She looks even more devastated. "Did it hurt? Why didn't you say something?"

"Because I didn't notice? They look scary, but they don't hurt. I promise." I brush a couple strands of hair from her cheek as her wide eyes stare up at me. "Besides, I sort of like them. Now everyone's going to know I got them making you come."

Her face turns bright red. "How's anybody going to see them?"

"Maybe we'll go to the beach today." I wink.

She rolls her eyes, then laughs a little. "You'll catch cold. It's going to be chilly today after that rain."

"Then you can warm me up and nurse me back to health."

"By getting you enough cold meds and cough drops to open a small pharmacy."

I laugh and drop a kiss on the crown of her head. "Why don't you go ahead? It's going to take you longer." I want to go in with her, but I know my limits. If I see her body glistening under hot water, I'm not going to be able to stop myself, and we aren't going to be having brunch today. In fact, we probably won't leave the house until dinner. If then.

"Okay. I'll try to hurry."

"Take your time. I can use a different bathroom."

When I'm done with my shower, I get dressed in a white dress shirt and black slacks. Marketta sent a pair of onyx cuff links, so I put those on, too. Then I make a call to be sure that (a) we can get seated and (b) Dad isn't going to be there. He's a great manipulator of emotions—which is why he's such a successful movie producer, but in real life he excels at arousing rage and shame, exactly fifty percent each, in everyone around him, especially his kids. Which I guess is a talent.

Once I'm reassured that we will be seated *and* my father doesn't have a reservation, I go to the room, thinking Aspen's probably done and ready.

And she is done—in the pretty purple Dior, which makes her ass stand out. She smells like the body wash and shampoo I used. And I like it that we both share the scent. Makes us seem more like a couple.

But she's staring at the bed. Her eyebrows are pulled together, and she has a hand resting on her hip, like something is a problem.

"Everything okay?"

"No." She bites her lip. "I need to do laundry." Her tone's urgent.

"Now?"

She nods, not looking at me.

"I'll call the housekeeping service Mom uses. They'll handle it." I start to pull out my phone.

"No!" She takes a hasty step toward me. "No. *I* have to do it."

"No guest does laundry while they're staying here." *Where is this abrupt desire to do laundry coming from?* Then I finally see it. A small reddish spot, barely the size of a quarter. "You're going to wash this sheet for *that?*"

She nods without looking at me. "I can't believe it. It didn't hurt enough to leave a bloodstain."

This unexpected shyness makes me want to laugh, but I know better. "There are other sheets. And Mom's not going to care."

Aspen covers her face with her hands. "Oh my God."

"She doesn't do the laundry," I add, placing a hand on her shoulder.

"But she's going to hear about—"

"Nope. Housekeeping will send it out to the laundry service, and they won't tell. Trust me."

"How can you be so sure?" Even as she questions me, she radiates a strong please-convince-me vibe.

"They all sign nondisclosure agreements. If they violate it, they pay for the transgression with a kidney. Or worse." I have no idea whether Mom makes anybody sign an NDA, but given her paranoia…

"Really?" Aspen looks slightly hopeful.

"Yeah. You don't know the kind of lawyers Mom hires. They're assholes. But if it'll make you feel better, I'll pour a bucket of red paint over it so nobody can tell. I can get some that looks just like blood."

She chokes out a laugh. "It's going to look like we murdered somebody."

"Exactly. But nobody's going to know about that tiny thing."

"No." She giggles. "That's ridiculous."

I put both hands on Aspen's shoulders and start herding her out. "Okay, then. Let's go get fed, and let our NDAed housekeeping deal with the sheets."

———

The service at Jean-Georges is as expected: attentive and polished. The bright interior is perfect for breakfast, and we're dressed just right for the venue. This isn't just a place you go to fill your belly; you also go to be *seen*. Make a statement without uttering a word.

I recognize a few people. A couple of overprocessed and silicone-enhanced girls start to get up as if they want to come over to our table to talk, but I shake my head subtly, tilting my chin at Aspen. They just want to discuss what Dad's up to, and I'd rather not ruin a perfectly fine morning with one of my least favorite subjects.

"Oh my God," Aspen whispers. "Is that…Brad Pitt?"

"Looks like it."

"Wait. There are other actors here."

"Uh-huh. Models, too."

Her eyes are wide as she looks around. "I heard that celebrities eat here, but I didn't think I'd actually *see* any, you know?"

"Why not?"

"Because I've lived in L.A. all my life and never run into one."

"You want a couple autographs?" I won't interrupt them now, but I can probably arrange for something.

"No," she says quickly. "I don't want to disturb their breakfast. That'd be rude."

I find myself smiling at her consideration. When Aspen orders pancakes, I ask, "Do you like berries?"

She nods.

"Two bowls of fresh berries, whipped cream and powdered sugar on the side. And eggs benedict with smoked salmon for me."

The server also brings out coffee and other juices we asked for. Aspen looks around and whispers, "Wow. It's so gorgeous. I've driven past it a few times, but…"

"But now you're here."

Just then the light hits her, so it looks like she's glowing. I pull out my phone and take a snapshot.

"Wait, I didn't even pose!" she says.

"So?" I look at the screen. Aspen has a half-smile and her eyes are filled with dreamy wonder. I'm happy I got her exactly like this. Now I finally understand why Mom said photography is a compulsion she can't ignore. "You look perfect."

Aspen puts a hand on my forearm. "Lemme see."

"Here." I angle the phone toward her.

"Wow. Did you take photography lessons from your mom?"

I shudder. "No. She'd make a terrible teacher." Mom hates it when people don't understand her instantly. If she has to repeat herself, that makes you an idiot unworthy of her time and attention. The only exception, for some reason, is Noah. But he can be quite charming, and he knows exactly what to say to unruffle her feathers and flatter her ego.

Our food gets delivered to our table. The eggs benedict taste as great as I remember. Aspen bites into her pancakes, and her eyes go half-closed. "*Mm. So good.*"

The soft moan revs up my libido, and my dick is hard again. I shift subtly, thankful we're seated at a table. Aspen's entirely too pretty and scrumptious.

When we're done and just starting to get up from our seats, her phone rings. She reaches into her bag and checks it. "Sorry, I need to take this," she says. "Could be important."

"Go ahead."

She swipes the screen, biting her lip. "Hello, Grandma. Is everything okay?"

Ah. Her favorite people. She said she talks with her folks every weekend. Interesting, though—this isn't the weekend.

We start walking out, Aspen with her phone still glued to her face and me directly behind her. A couple of people wave, and I nod back discreetly. A model makes a phone sign with her hand and gives me a meaningful look. She's trying to get a movie role with Dad, but she'd be better off buttering up Joey than me.

"My address?" Aspen says, shooting a glance in my direction. "You don't really have to mail it... I mean, of course I love it, but I can wait until the summer."

Except I don't want her to wait until summer to get whatever that can make her happy enough that her grandmother wants to ship it right now. "Tell her we can stop by," I say, placing a hand on her shoulder. Her grandparents must live close by for Aspen to have suggested dropping by to grab a dress she could wear to dinner yesterday.

"Give me a second, Grandma." She pulls the phone away from her mouth. "Are you sure?"

"Why not? They don't live too far away, right?"

"If we go, they're going to want to feed us," Aspen says.

Normally, I avoid socializing with the families of girls I'm with. It isn't like the relationships are serious enough to go anywhere, and it's best to avoid awkward conversations with their parents. But I'd love to meet Aspen's grandparents, even if they ask some squirmy questions. Plus it'd be cool to see the house she grew up in, a glimpse of her childhood.

"So?" I say. "I love being fed."

"Okay." She turns her attention back to her phone. "Uh. Actually, a friend and I are in the area, so why don't we just stop by?" She listens, her gaze darting in my direction. "Well, it's a guy friend. Yeah. I guess? Dinner?" She lowers her phone. "Do you have any allergies? Things you don't like?"

"Nah. I'm easy."

She laughs and raises her phone again. "He's good with

anything. Uh-huh. Uh-huh. Okay. See you soon." Her eyes soften. "Love you too."

Although she isn't saying the words to me, they have an impact. Having her look at me with her eyes that tender... For once my brain might freeze and refuse to process the moment.

"Oh hey, I had no idea you were going to be in town."

My body tenses with dread. *Joey*. And if he's here, there's a good chance Dad's here too. *Fuck!* The hostess said he wouldn't be. I continue to look at Aspen, hoping Joey gets the hint.

There's a plant in his line of sight. Maybe he was speaking to somebody else.

But no such luck. He comes right over. *Damn it.*

"Jesus, look at you, Grant. It's been a while."

"Yeah." I force a bland smile, but only because Aspen's watching. Otherwise, I'd dispatch him with a cutting insult or two.

I don't know how a guy who works and lives in Southern California can stay so pale. Or have a forehead so high without a receding hairline. It's like he was born with an extra two inches above his eyes. And right now, those eyes are raking over Aspen speculatively, taking an inventory of her features and proportions along with her accessories and clothes. Something like approval flickers in his gaze, and it pisses me off. Nothing good has ever come from Joey's attention.

"Is my dad here?" I say, trying to turn him away from her.

"No. Do you need him to be?" His smug expression radiates petty power. In Hollywood, it's a big fucking deal to have direct access to my father.

"No."

"Fine, but your date might want to an introduction to the head executive assistant to *the* Ted Lasker." He looks at Aspen.

"Again, no." Aspen has started to extend a hand, but I pull it back gently. "She isn't interested in the movie business."

Joey lets out an incredulous laugh. "Oh, please. Everyone is, even when they say they aren't."

"Go away, Joey."

He rolls his eyes, then wags his fingers in a wave at Aspen.

"Anytime you change your mind, just say the word. Your boyfriend knows how to get in touch."

My free hand curls into a fist. Joey's Adam's apple bobs, and he moves away, toward the restaurant. Griffin hit him in the face once, and Joey knows we don't hold back. I'm glad it was Griffin who did the honors, since he knows how to deliver maximum pain. He didn't study kickboxing to have a punch like a block of tofu.

Aspen watches him disappear into the restaurant. "So...he's your dad's assistant or something?"

"He's nobody important. You don't need to know him." *Ever.* I'm certain that when Joey was born, his mom received condolence cards. As for Dad... Well, Grandma moved to Southern France, which says everything you need to know. I'm not subjecting Aspen to people not even their own families like.

However, I'll introduce her to my brothers at some point. They're great, and she'll love them. It's a little deceptive that I only want to show her a heavily edited aspect of my life, but I don't want to scare her away. I've seen how girls dumped Griffin after experiencing the kind of shitshow our dad can put on. I'm not going to risk losing Aspen when things are so good between us. Part of me feels guilty about withholding information, but hey, nobody discloses everything. I'm not an index fund; I'm a human being. She only has to see me, like me and want to keep me.

18

ASPEN

When Grant says we should hang out and do whatever after our leisurely breakfast, I assume he means something like a walk along the beach.

Instead, he charters a yacht and we sail up the California coast. The *Veronica* is a gorgeous white vessel. There's just the crew and us on the ship. On the deck is a hot tub and a huge setup of fresh fruit, finger food and drinks, together with comfy chairs and sunbeds.

"Too bad the weather's so chilly," I say, shivering despite a sweater. The air's cooler on the water. "I'd love to get a tan."

"Maybe this summer," he says, putting his arms around me to warm me—and probably to cop a feel, which is fine.

"I'd love that." I smile.

We share a large, cushy lounger. He pulls me into his lap, and I sit sideways with my arms wrapped around his neck. It feels like *this is exactly where I belong*, and my heart flutters as I inhale his scent along with the briny breeze.

The crew said we'd see some marine life, including seals, although I have my doubts. I've never seen any on coastal tours before. But I don't care. The endless horizon feels liberating, we're the only ones on deck at the moment and it feels like we're the only people in the world.

After spending some time watching the sky and the blue ocean, I start to feel something hard prodding at me. Smiling devilishly, I squirm.

"Vixen." Grant cups my chin and kisses me. Although the wind is chilly, I'm warm in his arms, and his mouth is searing. I kiss him back, sharing our moment in the ocean breeze, tasting him and a hint of salt. His hand travels down my back, leaving a hot trail. I press closer.

A huge splashing sound starts me out of the kiss. I look around to see a pod of dolphins jumping along the ship. I leap to my feet and rush to the side. "Oh my God!"

Laughing, Grant joins me. "Never seen dolphins jumping out of the water before?"

"Not in the wild." I stare at the gorgeous, sleek creatures. I wave, but don't know if they can see me. "Hey, do you think they have good eyesight?"

"Absolutely *no* idea."

"Holy shit," I whisper when one of them jumps so high, it almost comes close to where we are. "That's incredible!"

Grant puts his arm around my waist. "I'm glad you're enjoying yourself."

"I wasn't sure if we'd see anything other than the ocean," I say.

"Why not?"

"I've just never really been lucky." I smile at him. "Maybe things are changing now."

He presses a quick kiss on my temple, then looks into my eyes. "It's you who make me feel like the luckiest guy alive."

I wrap my arms around him tightly and press my cheek against his chest as we watch the dolphins. My heart never beat like this for anybody. And I know I made the right decision last night.

He's the one.

19

GRANT

We drive to Aspen's grandparents' house that evening, and I let my hand rest loosely on the steering wheel. The day's been fantastic, and I wish we could stay like this forever. *Maybe I'll buy a house in Malibu, too.*

I glance over at Aspen, who's wearing one of her pretty new dresses. I love seeing her in nice things I've provided. She deserves to be treated like a princess. "What does your grandmother want to give you?"

"Some organic strawberry jam from a local farm. I love the stuff, but they only make, like, a few hundred jars a year. Grandma managed to buy five this week."

I make a mental note to find out which farm it is so I can make sure Aspen's never out of their jam.

"So, what do you want to be when you grow up?" she asks.

"A beach bum in Spain."

"Seriously?"

I shrug. "I have money, Spain's pretty, and I speak the language... Why not? Play polo all day, and party on the beach all night. It's a great life."

She laughs. "Okay, I can see that. But if my grandpa asks, don't say that."

I stop the car at a red light and give her a look. "Is he going to ask?"

"He asks that to all the guys who come by." She rolls her eyes, although her mouth is curved into an affectionate smile. "He doesn't do it to my girlfriends."

An uncomfortable ball of acid burns in my gut. I hate it that she's had other guys come over to see her grandparents, although it isn't realistic to expect that she's never had any friends with dicks until now, even if she didn't sleep with any of them.

But maybe it's not that unrealistic—I've generally tried to avoid introducing my friends to my parents. "He probably wants to make sure you won't end up with some loser."

"Just saying. Forewarned is forearmed and all that." She smiles shyly. "I want him to like you."

My heart does a funky dance. I reach over, thread my fingers through hers and resume driving. She squeezes my hand and looks out the windshield, the smile still on her radiant face.

Her grandparents' home is a modest house with a red roof and a small yard. The place isn't very big. You couldn't fit a quarter of my dad's car collection onto the entire lot.

I park and help Aspen out. I'm dressed nicely—Marketta doesn't provide bad clothes—and have a bouquet of yellow daisies I picked up from a florist near Mom's place because Aspen told me they're her grandmother's favorite. Plus two bottles of premium Bordeaux that I filched from Mom's wine cellar. She won't miss them.

"Come on." Aspen takes my hand, and we step inside the house.

The place smells like meat and potatoes. It's a surprise, in a way —you never smell food when you walk into my parents' homes. But I like it. Very homey and welcoming.

There's smooth hardwood floor in the living room, and a small couch that looks more functional than decorative. The cushions are a bit squished, like people actually sit there. A modestly sized TV and three bookcases, mostly showcasing books but also some photos, are also there. The photos aren't anything like the ones Mom likes to hang in her home. Two of them show Aspen when she was just a little kid. She was amazingly cute with those wide green eyes and rosebud mouth and plump cheeks. There's one with her and an elderly couple, who I presume are her grandparents, at a park. She's fourteen or so in the picture, with long limbs and a gorgeous smile. One from a birthday—with a huge cake and numerous candles. Another one from high school graduation, her holding a huge bouquet of pink carnations, bracketed by her grandparents.

The couple from the photos walk out, arms open. The woman is lean, with graceful limbs, and her eyes and mouth look just like Aspen's. She's in a simple green and purple dress with a loose skirt, and she hugs Aspen hard. The man is tall, with ropey muscles, and the light, sure step of a dancer despite his age. He's in a long-sleeve V-neck shirt and jeans. He embraces her tightly.

"Welcome home, sweetie," he says.

"Hi, Grandpa! So good to see you." She hugs him back, then pulls away. "This is my friend Grant."

"Hello, sir." I paste on my best smile and extend a hand.

"Kenny. Nice to meet you, young man." He grips my hand firmly, enough to let me know he's still strong, but not so hard that it's painful.

"I'm Kat." The woman smiles warmly. "Always a pleasure to have Aspen's friends over."

"For you, ma'am." I hold out the daisies.

She takes them. "Oh, how lovely." She flushes as she buries her nose in the flowers. "Thank you, Grant."

"And the wine."

Kenny takes both bottles. "Aren't you underage?" His dark eyes say one wrong answer, I'm out.

"They're from the family collection," I say.

"Ah." He checks the labels and raises his eyebrows. "And your folks know you're giving us these?"

"They're fine with it." Each bottle costs less than the croc-skin purse Mom gave Aspen anyway.

"I see." Questions fleet through his gaze, but he nods. "Well, come on in. Dinner's ready." He turns to Aspen. "Your grandma made your favorite."

She grins. "Pot roast?"

"Yup." Kat smiles. "Do you like pot roast?" she asks me.

It's an effort to remember the last time I had any, but I put on my most sincere face. "Love it."

"Well, then. Perfect."

The meal's served in a cozy dining room with a small round table. I like it because I get to sit close to Aspen. Kat puts the daisies into a vase on the table, which adds to the festive mood. The food is simple: pot roast with potatoes, rolls and salad. Nothing like the fancy meals my family and their friends would serve to demonstrate how refined and sophisticated their palates are when they have guests over. But I like the simplicity and lack of pretension. Most importantly, I love how relaxed and happy Aspen is.

Kenny uncorks one of the Bordeaux and pours it into two glasses.

"Everything good, Grant?" Kat asks after I have a bite.

"Yes, ma'am. It's fantastic," I say with a smile.

Aspen beams at me, squeezing my hand under the table discreetly, although Kenny's sharpening eyes says he knows what she's doing. I squeeze her thigh then retake her hand. I can't blame him, though. If I were him, I'd hire the meanest female bodyguard and make sure nobody ever got near my granddaughter.

As the conversation unfolds, I brace for a comment. My parents would definitely say something nasty and cutting, designed to embarrass me or my date—or both. But Kenny just pours more lemonade for Aspen. He and Kat ask me what classes I have with Aspen, where I grew up and so on, probably to make sure I'm not a freak. It's obvious they love her, as they also ask her how she's doing, how her classes are. She laughs and basks in their loving attention. There's no shield or wall raised around them, not like at my family dinner—assuming a family dinner could even be arranged. Every time my family gets together, we all have an internal clock that ticks down the time until one of our parents makes a scene. Waiting for the drama, the insults and the tears.

Aspen is obviously in her grandparents' innermost circle, where she's not only safe but loved unconditionally, and they are in hers. To my shock, I find myself feeling easy as well, even though I'm just on the fringe of this warm family. And I want to belong to the special group of people who are closest with and most important to her. I want her to look at me with the same unguarded love. To know she can count on me—that I'll always be in her corner.

The logical part of me says I'm going too fast. People don't feel this way about others this quickly. But my heart says, *Fuck off, logical part.* Romeo and Juliet knew what they wanted in a fraction of a second. I don't need a lifetime to know what I want.

"So. How is Zack doing?" Kat asks.

Zack?

"He's doing great," Aspen responds.

"Still working at the restaurant?"

"Yup."

Wait. Are they talking about that annoying waiter from the Italian restaurant?

"Such a sweet boy. I miss him," Kat says.

He's an asshole who just wants to screw your granddaughter!

"We should invite him over when he's in town for the holidays," Kenny adds.

"We'll see," Aspen says. "He might want to visit his uncles and aunts in Denver."

Better yet, I'll buy him a one-way ticket to Shanghai.

"We'll ask him later," Kat says.

"So, Grant. How exactly did you meet Aspen?" Kenny asks. "It isn't every day she brings somebody from school."

The question feels kind of sudden. But I get it. He wanted me to relax, be lulled into a false sense of security, so I'd blurt out whatever came to mind. Thank God my parents trained me for this sort of ambush. I know better than to tell the truth—that I left Aspen to do the paper by herself—but I also don't want to lie. Before I can cobble a good story together, Aspen puts down her lemonade glass.

"He and I did a project together," she says. "You remember how I told you one of my professors jerked me around when he forced me to tango with him? Grant put an end to that, and the two of us did the tango for the class instead, which is how I found out he's a fabulous dancer, and... You know." Smiling, she winks.

"Oh." Kat blinks. "You're *him.*"

I spread my hands. "What can I say?" I give them an innocent smile, relieved that Aspen came up with a version edited to make me look like a hero. I'm going to treat her like the goddess that she is, so her grandparents will never find out I was a dick to her at the beginning.

"So you can dance." Kenny nods with approval. "What are you studying?"

"I haven't declared a major yet."

"Anything look interesting to you?"

He's as persistent as Mom when it comes to my academic situation. "Almost all of it, to be honest. But I'm leaning toward accounting." That sounds nice and dependable. The kind of stuff a non-troublemaker would get into.

"Accounting is great. Stable, with a more or less guaranteed future," Kat says.

Kenny makes a vague noise in his throat. Maybe he wanted me to pick a more exciting subject, but it doesn't really matter. Even if I were to get that particular degree, I'm not going to process other people's taxes. I need something more challenging and interesting to do with my life.

The dinner ends with Kat's apple pie, which is incredible. It isn't anything fancy, but there's something to it that's topnotch.

"You make the best apple pie," Aspen says between bites, almost moaning. "I've missed this."

"I gave you my recipe," Kat says.

"And I tried to follow it, but it isn't the same."

Kenny gives Kat an affectionate grin and kisses her on the cheek. "It's my girl's magic touch."

"I agree," I say. "Not even a Parisian pastry chef could match this."

Kat flushes, and Kenny looks at me with another nod of approval.

There's more conversation. Kat asks if I'd like another helping of pie, but I decline. I hate feeling stuffed. And from the way the others are eating, they don't make pigs of themselves either.

Kenny finishes his glass of wine. We clear the table—another new experience, because my parents have staff to deal with that sort of thing. But I like how everyone's helping. It makes the family feel more like a unit.

We move to the living room. After chatting for a bit, Kat puts on a tango. A strain from "Por una Cabeza" floats from the stereo. "Dance with me." She extends her hands.

Kenny takes them as he stands. "Of course."

Aspen leans over and whispers, "They always dance after dinner, which is why they don't eat a lot in the evening. It's like a ritual."

The two may be old, but they're superb, moving like they know exactly what the other is thinking. I'd never believe they're somebody's grandparents from their agility and control.

It isn't just the technique that's impressive, but the connection they have. The way they gaze at each other, the way they touch, the subtle, sensual movements of their feet, the smiles. You can watch them and know they're soul mates.

When they're done, Kat beams, and Kenny holds out a hand to Aspen. "Dance with your grandpa."

"Of course." She jumps up as a different tango tune fills the house, and Kat sits next to me and stretches out her legs and rolls her ankles.

Aspen's amazing, and their dance is different. It's more paternal and sweeter.

"She's great, isn't she? We taught her since she was a little girl. She has such a talent for it," Kat says.

"She's the most incredible woman I've ever met."

She laughs softly. "I like you. I think you're good for her."

Although I smile, I'm also slightly confused. She isn't just saying that to be polite, like my parents might.

She must sense my bemusement, because her grin broadens. "You make her act her age. Have fun. Laugh. She can be a bit too serious and intense." Wistfulness crosses her face. "She always tries so hard. Maybe too hard."

I smile, happy that I've won over at least one grandparent by doing what I naturally want to do—be good to Aspen. "Ma'am, I'll try to make sure she's always happy and having fun."

Kat nods. "Thank you. You're very sweet."

"By the way, Aspen told me you have some specialty jam for

her. Can you tell me where you get them? I want to surprise her later."

She beams. "It's from a place called Sun Valley Farms. Nice local people. Aspen absolutely *adores* their strawberry jam. The blueberry, too. Nothing like what you can buy in a supermarket." She gets up from her seat. "Let me get you their number. She'll be thrilled."

20

GRANT

The next day we land in Napa, our perfect time in Malibu having come to an end. Normally, I don't resent the wine country, but I wish we didn't have to come back. What wouldn't I do to whisk Aspen away to Spain right now?

As we deplane, Aspen sighs. "I wish I could call in sick."

"Why don't you?" If she's willing, I'll have the jet turn around and take off for L.A. again. We can always get a suite at the Waldorf or the Ritz for a night and come back late Sunday.

She scrunches her face. "I need the hours."

I want to tell her I can give her all the money she needs, but it would come across the wrong way. Money is a touchy topic for most people. They hate it, love it, disdain it and want it.

We bought two additional suitcases for all the stuff Marketta brought us. I want Aspen to continue to wear some of the nice things—the accessories, shoes and purses—so Sadie and her bitchy friends will quit giving her crap. They aren't worth anything without their daddies' money. Those girls are so helpless, they wouldn't know how to fill out a job application if their parents cut them off.

I load our bags in the Maserati while she takes the passenger seat. I start to go toward the driver's side.

"Yo, man!"

I stop and glance at Will sauntering my way. He's in a loud Hawaiian shirt and shorts, his huge feet in flip-flops. Sunglasses cover more than half his face, and he's grinning so hard, the tips of his mouth almost reach his ears.

I glance at the car to make sure Aspen's settled inside before I turn to my roommate. "What are you doing here?"

"Spent some time in Hawaii, but then got bored and decided to come back early to go to that wine mixer tonight." He winks. Everyone knows it's going to be more like a wine orgy. "You heard about it, right?"

"I guess." I probably got invited too, except I wasn't interested in anything that didn't involve Aspen.

"You coming?"

"Nah." Aspen won't be there, and I'm not crazy about wasting time with people I don't care about. I'd rather hang out at the library or café and watch her work.

"Come on! It's gonna be fun! You can bring that girl with you too." He bends sideways, trying to peer into my car.

I move to block his view, but not before he gets a good look, damn it.

He straightens, his eyes wide. "Oh shit. That's Aspen Hughes!" he hisses, his voice going squeaky with excitement.

"So?" His reaction is annoying the hell out of me. Why does he care who I'm with?

"You fucked her?" He runs a hand down his face. "Of course you did."

"It's none of your business, Will."

"You won the damn bet."

"What?"

"The bet between me, you and Heath! Remember?"

Oh... *Shit*. I vaguely recall something along those lines. The whole thing was so idiotic... But no matter how stupid I thought it was, I should've made it clear I wasn't interested.

"I know Heath didn't win. Otherwise he would've said something already and made us streak."

Fuck...

"So." He leans closer with a smarmy smile. "Was she really a virgin?"

I shove him away from the car, hoping Aspen doesn't notice any of this. "Dude! It's none of your business. Jesus. Just shut the fuck up."

"Oh, come on! Don't tell me you actually have feelings for her or something?" He spreads his hands out. "It's just... She's just a bet."

I steal a glance in Aspen's direction, praying she hasn't heard. "I'm warning you. *Shut. Up.* Now, I gotta go."

Confusion clouds his face. "Hey, I'm just trying to be cool about it. It isn't like you're the one who has to streak."

"We'll talk about it *later*." *Away from Aspen.* "Just zip it, okay?"

"Fine. If you want to be nice about it and spare her feelings, I get it." He gives me a conspiratorial grin. "But how about an introduction? I never even got to really meet her. Saying hi at the café doesn't count, right?" He steps forward, using a hand to rake his hair into slightly better order.

"No." I push him away firmly. "I need to go."

I get into the car and slam the door fast as Will shouts, "Why're you acting like some friggin' virgin?"

He says something more and gestures wildly, but I peel out of the airport, the tires squealing.

Aspen cannot know about that idiotic bet. Ever.

——————

Aspen

"Are you okay?" I ask as Grant speeds out of the lot and down the long stretch of the road, his jaw tight.

"What?"

"That guy at the airport. Who was it?" Grant's been tense since running into him. What did they talk about?

"Oh." Grant's mouth tightens for a second, his eyebrows pulling together, which means he's thinking. "That was Will. Nobody important." He smiles, but the tension in his neck betrays his agitation.

"But important enough that you said hi." I'm dying of curiosity since I heard him say something about acting like a virgin before Grant shut the door. I don't want to be stupid and jump to conclusions, but I want to know if that virgin refers to me. I don't think he would brag to his friends or anything—it just doesn't fit my image of him—but...not knowing is making me crazy.

"He's just my roommate."

"You could've introduced us. It looked like he wanted to say hi."

"Trust me, I did you a massive favor. It isn't like we're going to hang out," Grant says.

That hurts. "Why don't you want me to meet your friends?"

"Because he *isn't* a friend. He's nothing."

These evasive responses are triggering my bullshit radar. He wasn't like this in Malibu, and I don't know why he is now. "Do you room with people you don't like?"

"When I don't have any choice, yeah. I'll be moving as soon as I get something better. He was just a means to an end, and this topic is closed."

I sit back in my seat, stunned at his autocratic attitude. It's like a wall's slammed down between us. I understood how he might not want to introduce me to the guy who works for his dad. People have their differences. But Grant also doesn't seem to want me to meet his father, either. I didn't think too much of it because he was more than happy to meet my grandparents and charm them. But now his reluctance is making me wonder...

"Are you embarrassed about being seen with me in public?" I ask.

He lets out a shocked laugh. "Are you kidding? That's the most ridiculous thing I've ever heard."

"But you're acting like you want to hide me from your friends. And your father, too."

"That..." He huffs roughly. "My dad isn't a person I'd want to introduce to anyone, especially someone I like. As for Will... Like I said, just because we're rooming together doesn't mean we're friends."

Grant's explanation sounds like the truth—and is what I want to hear, like how he regards me as somebody he likes. But I still don't know why that means he doesn't want me to meet his dad. I loved introducing Grant—i.e., somebody special—to my grandparents. And I agree that being roommates doesn't make you friends. Just look at me and Sadie. But Sadie has what she considers to be legitimate grievances against me, including my refusal to swap rooms with Bronte. Will actually seems to like Grant. People aren't generally friendly with those who overtly dislike them.

Before I can open my mouth to voice my concerns, Grant threads his warm fingers through mine and brings my hand up to kiss the fingertips.

"Trust me," he says between tender kisses that make me feel like the most precious thing in his life.

21

GRANT

When I step into the dorm room after taking Aspen to Howell Hall, Will jumps up from his couch. "Okay, so what was that all about?"

"What?" I say curtly. He's the last person I want to talk to when I'm trying to figure out how to gracefully bury the stupid bet. Aspen was still looking at me funny when I carried her suitcase up the stairs to her room. All because I was short with her in the car. I don't think I was snapping at her, but that kind of tone isn't what I want to use when I speak with her. I just panicked when Will brought up the stupid wager.

"You treated me like shit back there. Were you showing off for her or something?"

I wave away his outrage. "No. Look, I didn't want you blabbing about the bet in front of her."

He looks confused. "Why? You think she's going to take a sledgehammer to your car?" He laughs. "Don't worry about it. Remember Becky Malone? She tried to trash her boyfriend's car for cheating on her, but couldn't even lift the damn hammer."

"Yeah, but then she got her new boyfriend to do the honors."

"Ah, come on. That's what insurance is for. And the police. Toss her in jail."

Heath comes out of the shower with a towel around his hips. "Is it true you won?" he demands.

"I told you I saw," Will says.

I rake my hair. I can't lie about having slept with her, not when I want to continue seeing Aspen. Time for Plan B. "Okay, look. Number one, yes, I slept with her. Number two, the bet was stupid. So let's call it off. You guys don't have to streak or do anything dumb."

"No," Heath says, pointing a finger in my direction. "My word means something. I'm doing it."

What the hell? He thought nothing of grabbing Aspen before, and now he wants to be honorable?

"I've got integrity," he adds.

Will nods. "Exactly. Bros before hos."

You've gotta be kidding me. "It isn't about integrity. I have something good going on, so stop trying to fuck it up."

"You're *dating* her?" Will's eyes are huge.

"Yes. Perhaps you've heard of the concept?"

Heath says, "So what? Us doing what's right won't fuck anything up."

What's his deal? Does he have an exhibitionist fetish? "You can keep your integrity and do the right thing because I'm telling you—as the winner—that *I'm okay with you not streaking.*"

Heath looks at Will. "No. We're paying up."

"Exactly." Will doesn't sound convinced, though. He's just going along with Heath for some reason.

This is...weird. And infuriating.

"Why are you looking at us like we're trying to screw with you?" Heath says.

"Because that's how it looks?" My mind is going three hundred miles an hour to figure out a way to stop these two morons. "Okay, look. If you absolutely *have* to do this, which—again—you *don't*, do it on Tuesday at ten." Aspen has a class that starts then, and even if Will and Heath move like slugs, they'll be done by the time she comes out. Hopefully, she won't notice them. And if somebody posts pictures of them online, she'll just laugh it off without realizing what it's about.

"But you have a class at that time, don't you?" Will asks.

"Yes, but I have no doubt that you two will do the right thing."

They both nod gravely, staunch men considering an important matter, while my sarcasm flies right over their heads.

Part of me says I need to come clean now, but the smarter part disagrees. There are girls who would just laugh and not care as long as they got to date me. But not Aspen. She has too much pride. She'd cut me out of her life and never speak to me again. I'd rather die.

What if she finds out on her own?

She won't. And even if she does, it will be after a lot of time has passed. After she gets to spend more time with me and know me better. By then, she'll know for sure I'm not an asshole and be able to laugh it off as some dumb thing I did when I was too immature to know any better.

I'll make sure of it.

22

ASPEN

Grant and I don't get to hang out after returning from Malibu. One of the baristas comes down with mono, and I end up taking her shifts. He comes by several times to buy coffee, but given that I'm supposed to be working, we don't get to chitchat much. But I'm happy to see him, and I decide I might've overreacted to what happened at the airport. Except for the first time we faced each other on the polo field, Grant hasn't done anything without a good reason—almost all to benefit me. It's possible his roommate is Sadie's secret admirer or something and would've gotten nasty with me. Besides, Grant is even more bummed than me that we can't spend all our free time together. I shouldn't ruin what's good between us.

My next paycheck's going to be sweet. I want to treat Grant to something nice, even if it's not as fancy as what he's used to. It's the thought that counts, and he'll probably like whatever I come up with. Despite his background, he isn't a snob. The way he interacted with my grandparents proved that.

–Grant: Please tell me your coworker's fully recovered. It's already Tuesday.

–Me: I haven't heard anything yet. Make it up to you later?

–Grant: How? Tell me more.

–Me: Haha! Use your imagination.

—Grant: Are we doing whatever my imagination comes up with? *wink emoji*

—Me: Maybe. *suggestive emoji* I gotta get to class now. Talk to you later.

Smiling, I slip my phone into the gorgeous burgundy bag Grant gave me in Malibu and head to Native Myths and Legends. It's an elective I'm taking to fill a humanities requirement. But as I near the class, it seems like there are a bunch of students walking toward me and away from the class. A piece of paper is taped to the classroom door.

Native Myths and Legends is canceled until next week.

No reason given, but then, Dr. Mazen isn't the type to explain himself. The man looks like a goat, with tufts of white hair and a pointed Van Dyke, and he's as stubborn as the animal, too.

Nice, making everyone walk all the way over here. Of course, there was no email notice or anything. He's as anti-tech as you can get. I actually saw him using a clamshell phone a few weeks ago.

Well, nothing to be done about now. I turn around and go back outside. Too bad Grant has a class right now. We could've hung out. But I really should go over to the library and spend some time with my notes from econometrics. It's amazing how much more enjoyable the class is now that I understand it better.

As I walk across the huge lawn in the center of the campus, I see people turning and looking at something, pointing and laughing. Almost everyone has their phone out.

I start to go over to see what the deal is—and then I can't help but see it. Two guys, nude except for sneakers, dash right past me.

Oh my God! What the heck? I heard that streaking was a thing on some campuses, but I've never seen or heard of anybody streaking *here*.

On their chests and backs is written in a bright scarlet red: *Grant Lasker is the bigger man.*

What the...? My head swivels. They're running, but not too fast. Probably pacing themselves a bit. Everyone's laughing and yelling encouragement and other stuff I can't make out in the noise.

I recognize both of them—Heath the dickhead who tried to grab me and Grant's roommate from the airport. The latter is doing a better job at maintaining his speed than the former, who's falling behind.

Ugh. I never liked Heath, and don't want see to see his bare butt. But why are they doing this? What did Grant do to them?

I sense somebody stopping next to me. Without looking away from the streaking duo, I say, "What's that about?"

A loud snort. "You don't know?"

Sigh. Just my luck it's Sadie who's standing next to me. "Never mind," I say, and start to move away.

"Don't you want to know what's going on?" she demands snidely.

I turn enough to face her, but my feet keep moving. "Look, if I'd known it was you, I wouldn't have asked."

"But I don't mind telling you. Because that"—she points at the duo streaking past the library now—"is about *you.*"

"Um, I'm pretty sure it's about Grant."

She smirks. "Yeah, but you're the whore who spread her legs for him."

Feeling like I just got punched in the belly, I suck in air. Since Grant and I have been spending a lot of time together, maybe some people guessed we're sleeping together. But...

I shake my head. I shouldn't let what Sadie's saying get to me. It's just her being a bitch. "First of all, I'm not a whore. And yes, Grant and I are together. So what?"

Sadie laughs. "Oh my God. You don't know anything, do you?" She looks around, like she can't believe it, then turns back to me. "Grant, Heath and Will made a bet—to see which one of them would get to sleep with you first. The losers had to streak the campus with their bodies painted. Why do you think it says, *Grant Lasker is the bigger man?*"

I stare at her. A swift denial surges, ready to roll of my tongue, but the memory of Grant's weird behavior at the airport when we returned from Malibu kills it.

"Did you really think he'd bother with you otherwise?" Sadie continues. "Treating you to a trip and some nice things? He does that for *all* the girls he sleeps with. They don't mean anything."

Ugly tremors start in my heart, then spread until my fingertips and toes seem to shake as well. My brain can't seem to process what she's saying. Everything that happened between me and Grant...it can't be fake. The sweetness, the consideration—

"Are you *crying*?" Sadie laughs.

I realize my cheeks are wet, and I wipe them impatiently. I'm not crying in front of her.

"Aww. Don't be so sad." Her gaze drops to the purse I'm carrying. "You got a seventy-thousand-dollar bag out of it."

"What?" The whisper's barely audible. *Seventy thousand dollars.* I let that number sink into my shock-numbed brain. He gave me something that expensive so he could win a stupid bet? It doesn't make sense, but then I realize I'm thinking like a poor girl. He spent lavishly during our time in Malibu. The private jet, the Mercedes, the yacht, the clothes, glitzy restaurants... Seventy grand is pocket change to him.

"Not bad for a whore," Sadie adds.

"Shut up." To my humiliation and horror, my voice is shaking. More tears fall.

"I know you thought you were special, but you aren't. If you were, he wouldn't be applying to transfer to Harvard next year."

He's transferring to Harvard?

Whatever she's seeing on my face is making her lips twist smugly. "Oh my God, he didn't tell you?" She laughs. "This is hilarious."

She's lying! She has to be. There's no way that everything Grant did was fake. Besides, he promised we'd be in the Investment Society together next year. He wouldn't have done that if he was transferring.

But would Sadie lie about something that could be cleared up with a simple conversation? She's mean, but she's not stupid.

Several people around me laugh. Heart in my throat, I look around. Some of them point and whisper. Oh my God. Is everyone laughing at me? They all know? And nobody thought to tell me?

I spot Clara in the crowd. She and I trade class notes. She couldn't bother either...?

The sound of my breathing grows deafening in my ears. My chest tightens. And the purse I'm carrying feels like a snake looped around my forearm.

I need to get out of here.

I turn around and start running away because that's the only thing I can think to do at the moment. Every stare, every whisper, every laugh slices at me. But the worst of it is that it was Grant who betrayed me. I can't believe I thought he was the one. How stupid could I have been?

But you didn't do anything wrong. He's the bad one. He's the one who betrayed your trust. Don't blame yourself for his actions. My grandmother's voice rings in my head. Even though I recognize the truth of it, the pain doesn't lessen. And my shame only swells.

Part of me says I should give him a chance to explain. But I can't imagine what his excuse would be.

Come on, girl. Sadie could've lied. She hates you, remember? Grant deserves ten minutes of your time.

Okay, fine. He does. I'll talk with him after his class is over. I'm not optimistic, but I'm going to do the mature thing and listen to both sides.

I round the corner of the English department building. Behind it is the field that I cut across to reach my dorm. But I literally crash right into Heath, who comes running the other way. I manage to catch myself before falling.

"Watch where you're going!" he says, wheezing. He starts to resume the run, but then looks more closely at me. "Wait. Aspen?"

I turn my face away, not wanting him to witness my humiliation.

"Jesus. What the fuck," he mutters.

"Shut up and keep running," I say, looking up at the sky because I am *not* looking at his dick.

"In a minute. Since we, like, literally just ran into each other, tell me something. Just what does Grant have that I don't?"

My fragile resolve to speak to Grant cracks. I turn to face Heath, needing to see his expression and gauge how truthful he is. "So there really was a bet?"

"Well, yeah." He looks at me like I'm stupid. "You think Will and I are doing this just for the hell of it?"

So everything Sadie said is true. Heath is an asshole, but I don't think he's lying. He knows I can check with Grant, and there'd be an ass kicking over a lie this egregious.

I start walking through the field.

"You didn't answer my question!" Heath shouts. "What's he got that I don't?"

Ignoring him, I pick up speed. More tears fall, and I sniffle. I can't believe Grant did this to me. I can't believe everything's been a lie. My first time—which I thought was so special—now feels *dirty. I feel dirty.*

My phone rings. I fumble it out with numb fingers. Is this Grant calling to gloat? He must've known I'd see the spectacle. Actually... He knows I have a class...

I shake my head. Who the hell cares what he knows or thinks? He might've found out that Dr. Mazen planned to cancel the class this week.

But the call's actually from Grandpa. I take a couple of breaths, trying to calm my racing heart. I can't sound upset over the phone. He'll know, and I don't want to worry him. Grant is something I'll have to deal with later, once I figure out what I'm going to do.

After clearing my throat, I answer. "Hi, Grandpa." There's nothing for a moment. "Grandpa?"

"Aspen." His voice cracks.

"What's wrong?" My heart starts racing again, this time with dread. He's never sounded like this before.

"It's your grandmother." Then he breaks down in sobs.

The rest of what he manages to say between shaking breaths leaves me reeling. Life just delivered a KO.

23

GRANT

Aspen doesn't answer my texts for the rest of the day. I stop by the library, but she isn't at the information counter. The librarian tells me she doesn't have a shift today. I go over to the café, but she isn't there, either.

Is she okay?

I know she didn't see Will and Heath streaking. She isn't the type to skip class. But then again, she isn't the type to miss work, either.

Maybe she caught mono from her coworker. I should check up on her before she takes some expired meds or something.

I head over to Howell Hall. On the way, I run into George from the polo club.

He gives me an amused grin. "Hey, what did you do to get those two morons to streak like that?" He isn't the only one who's curious. A few others, who feel they're close enough to ask, have already gotten nosy.

"Ah, they just lost a bet. Nothing serious," I say, relieved that Will and Heath satisfied their honor without telling everyone why.

"Must've been some bet. It was hilarious." George laughs. "You shoulda seen them."

"I had class." Not to mention that two guys running around in the buff isn't something I'd go out of my way to watch. "Anyway, I gotta go."

"Yeah, me too. See you this weekend?"

"For sure," I say. We have a game.

Howell Hall comes into view. I slow down when I see that the window to her dorm is dark. It's disappointing, but she could be taking a nap. She slept a lot when she was sick before. And she's been working extra shifts since we came back.

I go inside and knock on Aspen's door. No response.

Come on. I knock again, but still nothing. I look for Suyen, who seems to be in the lounge every time I bring takeout to share with Aspen. But she isn't there. I blow out a frustrated breath.

–Me: Hey, are you okay? Where are you? I'm getting worried.

I wait a couple of minutes, then call again. My phone log makes me look like a stalker. But until I know how she is, I can't stop.

Aspen still doesn't answer. This isn't like her. She said she wanted to hang out. Maybe something came up, although I can't imagine what.

I go back to the lounge and end up waiting for hours. Reading the news on my phone passes the time, but it doesn't make Aspen show up.

My worry is turning into alarm. Too restless and freaked out to sit still, I go out and walk around campus looking for her. I wish I knew where she usually parks so I could look for her car. After spending over an hour wandering the campus, I go back to my dorm, shut myself in my room and call her and text her for the rest of the night. I wish I'd asked for Kat's number when I was at their home. Aspen hates worrying her grandparents, but this is an emergency!

The next day, I go to Culture and Music in History and sit in the seat next to the one she normally takes.

"You don't have to sit there by yourself," Sadie calls out. Bronte and Tanya giggle.

I ignore them and stare at my phone, willing a text from Aspen to appear. She doesn't have to say much. Just a simple "I'm fine" would suffice.

Actually, that isn't true. I want to know where she is, what she's doing and why she isn't talking to me. I want to know if she's okay, if she needs my help, if there's anything I can do to make her feel better. My gut says something's gone very wrong, and my gut is always correct.

Sadie takes Aspen's seat. "Hi," she says perkily. She flutters her lashes, but instead of looking sexy, she looks like somebody desperate to get rid of something stuck in her eyes. Maybe she's the female version of Joey, because she's really irritating the shit out of me.

"Go back to your friends." I hate that she's in Aspen's seat. It makes it feel like Aspen's not coming...and her place is taken.

"Why? She isn't here."

"She will be."

Sadie snorts. "Look. She probably ditched you after you gave her the Hermes."

Jealous bitch. "She isn't like you."

"True. She isn't that special."

I ignore her and send Aspen another text.

–Me: Tell me you're okay. Please?

"I had to room with her for a year. I know exactly how she is."

I don't look at her, but I can feel her glare on my cheek.

"And soon you're going to know I'm right."

I block her out, and after a few minutes she flounces back to her friends. Just what the hell is going on?

Taylor's gaze rests briefly on Aspen's empty seat, and then he starts the lecture. Huh. Bet he knows something.

After the class, I walk up to him. "Professor Taylor."

"Ah, yes, Grant." He smiles like a sycophant. But then, he's probably harboring the hopeless dream of seeing "Twenty-Seven." "What can I help you with?"

"Do you know what's up with Aspen?"

"Why? Did she do something?"

Why the hell is he assuming she did something wrong? "I borrowed some money from her, and I need to pay her back. But I can't get in touch with her."

He laughs. "Oh, she can be odd about such inconsequential things. But I'm afraid she won't be on campus for a while."

"Why not?"

"Some sort of personal issue. I'm sure she'll be back when she has it sorted out," he says, waving a hand dismissively. "By the way—"

"I have to go." I'm not wasting any more time in his smarmy presence. It's suffocating, and I need space to process what he said.

The relief that she's okay is short-lived. Now that I know she's okay, I'm pretty fucking irritated that she hasn't spared a second to text me back. Doesn't she know I was worried sick?

—Me: I heard from Taylor you have something to sort out. Hope it's nothing serious. By the way, I'd love to talk to you. Text or call when you get a chance.

But she still doesn't reply.

By Sunday, I'm beyond irritated and worried. Just what the hell kind of problem could keep her away from her phone for so long? It doesn't take long to text back a few words! Did I do something? Or are her problems more serious than Taylor made them sound?

My play on the polo field is shit. George asks if everything's okay, and I tell him yeah. He can't do anything about Aspen.

I mull my options over in the shower after the game. I should find her grandparents' number and give them a call. I have no idea how many Kenny Hugheses are in L.A., but once I cross-reference the name with somebody who owns a dance studio, I should be able to find him. I know it's going to make me furious and relieved, but I hope she's okay. And maybe she couldn't call me back for some reason as silly as her phone breaking and she hasn't replaced it yet—

My phone rings. I dash out of the shower, water flying, and snatch the phone from the top of my locker, where I left so I don't miss Aspen's call—and swipe the green button.

"Aspen?"

"Ah, no. This is Marketta."

"Oh." My whole body deflates like a popped balloon. I rest a hand against the locker to keep myself upright. "Hey."

"I wanted to call in case you didn't know."

Her tone of voice is uncharacteristically somber. "What?"

"I don't know how to put this delicately, but I don't want you to get hurt."

"Is this about Mom?"

"Your mother's fine. It's that girl you brought to Malibu."

I stand straight up. "You know something about Aspen?"

Marketta lets out a soft sigh. "Everything you bought for her is on an auction site. Along with the bag your mother gave her."

I run my fingers through my sopping-wet hair, trying to compute all this, as the seed of dread Sadie dropped earlier starts to sprout. "What? An auction site?"

"She's selling what you gave her. The shoes. The clothes. Jewelry. Everything. I know they're the same. I checked the sizes and colors to be sure." She sighs again. "I think she's just using you."

My body grows icy. What she's saying is logical, but there has to be another explanation. *Using me?* Aspen isn't like that. "If that's the case, why didn't she wait until I gave her more?"

"Maybe she didn't realize you could be more generous? She's young. It could be her first time."

But would she have given me her virginity for some lousy stuff?

You know people who'd suck a guy off for far less, a voice that sounds just like my dad points out.

Guess this is what needed sorting out so urgently that Aspen couldn't text me back. She was too busy counting her money.

Marketta clears her throat. "Look, I've seen this before. She could have gotten enough, or she could be intending to come back later for more. Anyway, I hate seeing my clients get taken advantage of, and you're a good kid, Grant. I don't want you to start having feelings for her and get hurt. Better to nip it early."

"Right," I say numbly. "Okay, um..." My brain doesn't seem to be working. "Thanks."

"No problem. You take care." She hangs up.

I stare at the phone, then at the puddle of water under my feet. *Aspen was just using me?* But why did she stop so soon? She's a smart girl. She has to know she could string me along...

I don't know what's worse—that she's been using me or that I'm mad I found out about it. Fuck it. It might make me a pussy-whipped simp, but part of me says I don't care. I...I love her that much.

Fucking pathetic loser.

Hating myself and hating Aspen for making me feel this way, I let out a shuddering breath, then slowly lift my head. My teammates are all staring at me. Guess they witnessed the humiliating scene. How much did they hear? How much can they piece together?

Enough from the pity and sympathy in their gazes.

Fuck!

I want to storm out, but I'm still wet and naked. I grab a towel, run it over my body and get dressed without making eye contact with anyone. Then I walk out. The sky's endlessly blue, not a cloud in sight. The sun is gorgeous, the light generous and strong.

But I still feel cold. Marketta's warning came too late. I'm gutted.

I don't think I'll ever be okay again.

24

ASPEN

Grandpa always says nothing is certain except death and taxes.

But death didn't have to come so early. So abruptly.

Grandma didn't make it out of surgery after she was rushed to the hospital for an aneurysm that suddenly burst. By the time I arrived in L.A., she was gone. My knees gave out, and I landed on my butt in one of the hospital's ugly plastic chairs. Grandpa sat crumpled like his world had just ended.

My legs still weak, I dragged myself over and held him while he sobbed, my own tears staining the back of his shirt. I stared at the doctor as he spoke to us, like I should be able to process anything when I could barely cope with the fact that I was never going to feel her arms go around me in that tight hug that always felt like home. The dinner with Grant was the final time I saw her alive. And she'd looked so healthy, so bright. She'd danced with the same dexterity as always. People like her didn't die of aneurysms.

They shouldn't. It wasn't fair.

The doc seemed sad, but I didn't know if it was because he wasn't good enough to save her or if he was just worried about his surgical record. Learning that I was just a bet to Grant must've tainted my view of humanity, because it was impossible to think kind thoughts.

Fuck you, world. Fuck you, universe! She deserved better than this! Grandpa didn't even get to say goodbye!

The rage died as quickly as it surged, overwhelmed by endless waves of bitter grief. All the things I had wanted to do with her... The splurge trip to Buenos Aires after I graduated. The great-grand-children I wanted to give her—she so loved children. Now, I'm never going to get to do any of that. Death was faster than me.

When I finally took out my phone, there were hundreds of texts from Grant. I ignored them and texted Suyen.

She called me. "Oh my God, I'm so sorry," she said.

I couldn't speak. I sniffled as tears poured down my cheeks.

"What do you need? Anything. I'm your girl."

"I don't know," I managed, my voice cracking. "I just want her back."

"Oh, honey. You just... You just do what you need to do there. Leave everything up here to me."

I don't know how she managed to get into my room, but she packed my meager belongings from the college and brought every-thing down the next day. When I saw the things Grant gave me, my first instinct was to burn them in a bonfire. But I caught myself. Sadie said the bag alone was worth seventy thousand dollars. If the other stuff could also fetch that kind of money, it'd help pay the sky-high hospital bills. *Even when they can't save your loved ones, they want your money,* I think bitterly. I don't want to burden Grandpa with that when he just lost the love of his life.

"I want to sell these," I told Suyen, laying out the items.

"No problem. I'll take care of it," she said.

"Thank you."

Her mom also came from San Jose. She gave me a tight hug and cooked for us. "You poor child. You leave everything to me and Suyen, okay?"

I nodded. "Thank you."

She tsked and dabbed a Kleenex on my cheeks.

Everything passed by in a blur, filtered through a thick layer of grief. "Am I ever going to be okay?" I whispered before sipping the hot jasmine tea Suyen's mom made.

"You will." She squeezed my hand.

"How am I going to know? When does it happen?"

"When I lost my father..." she began gingerly, and I realized I too had lost my parents, except I'd been too young to understand what that meant. "I was devastated. Just so sad. Cried for days. But then...one day, I wasn't sad. Just numb. And then...one day, I wasn't even numb anymore. The living go on living."

I looked at Grandpa, who shed endless tears while staring at nothing.

Is he ever going to just...get over it?

Can any of us really reach that stage? It doesn't seem possible.

On the day we bury Grandma, Suyen, her mom and everyone who loved Grandma come. Grandpa sits silently next to me, his eyes red. I stand on the sunny green cemetery field in my black suit and stare at the coffin in the hole in the ground. I'm thankful that at least she isn't in the cheapest casket. Guess my time with Grant was good for something.

Shame threatens to overwhelm me at the thought of him, but I squash it. I'm not going to feel ashamed for somebody's else's wrong-doing. Grandma wouldn't want that.

Tears burn in my eyes, and I reach over and clasp Grandpa's hand. I have to be strong for him because now...there are just the two of us left.

I'm not just consigning my grandmother to the earth today. I'm scooping up all the pieces of my own broken heart and putting them into that wretched hole as well. Burying them so deep that they will never have the power to hurt me again.

PART II

THE PRESENT

25

ASPEN

I open the envelope with a sense of dread, and sure enough, it's another spirit-crushing bill from the Orange Care Center. *Four thousand and change.* My bank account says I don't have enough to cover it right now. Not if I want to pay the rent on my ratty studio apartment and have something other than water and stale discounted bread at the end of the day.

Three jobs, and I still can't make enough money. I suppose I should count myself lucky there's no credit card debt. That would've pushed me into bankruptcy, and then how would I take care of Grandpa?

There is the option of putting him into a cheaper nursing home, but I don't want to do that. We tried a few, and the Orange Care Center was the clear winner. The staff there treat him with kindness and respect, even when he continues to lose more of himself with every passing week.

Maybe I should talk to Jenna and ask for more hours, especially on weekends. They're the most lucrative. I'll also offer to work holidays. It isn't like I have anything better to do.

At five to six, I step into the bar for my shift. Today's Wednesday, so the money won't be that great. Still, it'll be a few bucks more than I had before.

Jenna bustles by. She's short and wiry and always bristling with excessive energy. The red shirt makes her face appear ruddy. She pulls up short when she notices me and throws her small hands up in the air. "Hallelujah! You're here!"

I pause on my way to the employee locker room. "What?"

"Satoshi and Mick both called in sick, and I've been going crazy. We're doing happy hour with the VC folks." She jerks her chin at a huge throng of people in business casual pouring into the place. They crowd around the bar and tables like thirsty locusts.

Now I understand the true magnitude of her panic. The people from the venture capital firm drink like fish, and they want their drinks *now*. Alcohol is apparently their preferred way of relieving work stress, especially when the company's footing the bill. Although they're demanding, they're fantastic tippers. Or at least the guy in charge of paying the bill is. They come in twice a month on average, and never tip under thirty percent.

Satoshi's not being here is unfortunate because that means whoever's manning the bar has to work even harder. But it comes with a huge tip—the kind of money I can't normally make on a Wednesday. And I badly need the extra.

"Anyway, I want you to help at the bar and cover the tables with the VC folks, since they're just going to want to drink," Jenna says. "They won't eat anything, except maybe some of the pretzels. So you focus on serving their slosh."

"Got it." The margin on drinks is huge, and of course, Jenna wants them to have as much as they want. The last time they were here, they only ate a couple of chicken wing platters, but put away enough alcohol that Jenna had to place an extra order with our suppliers afterward.

I dump my purse into a metal locker and pull my hair back in a tight ponytail, ready to rock and roll in my black shirt and skirt. The management said black pants are fine, but a skirt always gets me better tips.

Zack waves. "It's gonna be a gooood night!" He knows about Grandpa, and the crazy bills I'm dealing with. His own grandparents were in an assisted living center in Colorado until they passed away a couple of years ago.

"Yeah." I grin. "Thanks." He's the one who told me about the opening at this bar last month. It's more upscale than the one I worked at before, and the customers tip better. The area is safer, too.

After grabbing a few baskets of complimentary pretzels, I hurry over to the huge table where at least thirty financial types are milling around. Suits, loosened ties and expensive haircuts dominate. I paste on a big smile as I distribute the appetizers.

Before I can utter a word, one of the guys waves. "Hey, you ready to take our order?"

"Of course. How's everyone tonight?"

"Awesome!" he says.

I get my pad out and start writing. Most of them want hard liquor. A few ask for wine and cocktails. I note everything—more for Jenna so she can tally up everything at the end of the happy hour than for myself, because I already have it memorized—then reconfirm each drink, mainly so that if they've changed their mind, they can tell me now.

They chat and laugh at volume, creating an uproar. I go back to the bar, fill their order and bring everything back over. Then I hand everyone their drink.

"Here you go." I smile as I give out the last glass—two fingers of whiskey to a dark-haired man about my age who smiles back politely. Something about him seems vaguely familiar, but I can't place it.

I must've seen him before. This is my second time working happy hour.

The venture capitalists at the bar demand my attention too, shouting out their orders. I keep track, making sure everyone's happy.

"I love you," Jenna says after she hands a glass of chardonnay to a blonde.

"I love you too," I say with a grin. She's feeling grateful, so maybe it'll be easier to get her to agree to give me more hours on Friday and Saturday evenings. When I tried to bring it up last week, she said she wanted to see how I did first.

Hours later, when my neck and shoulders are tight from pouring and serving more drinks than I have in the last two evenings combined, the group finally calls it a night.

Zack goes to the register to settle their bill, then frowns. I serve a Stoli vanilla and Coke—the last order from the VC people—and go over to him. He lets out an uncharacteristic curse under his breath.

"What's wrong?" I ask.

"The machine's acting up." He shakes his head. "It was working fine just a minute ago."

I look at the all the things they've ordered. The machine has some items down, but it won't total the amount. And I realize it's missing more than half the drink orders from the tables I covered.

Jenna comes over and fusses with the machine, but can't seem to fix it either. It still refuses to add up some of the orders from the table I served, as well as a few from the bar.

She huffs out a breath, not bothering to hide her frustration. Math isn't her forte, and all the numbers and money have to match at the end of the day to prevent theft. The bar also handles quite a bit of cash.

"Is there a problem?" It's the familiar-looking guy.

"The machine's a little slow tonight." I give him a polite smile tinged with apology. I'm sure he's anxious to go make another billion. I turn to Zack and Jenna, who are whispering to each other but don't seem to be making much progress. "Why don't you let me do this?"

I pull out the stack of order sheets with all the drinks the VC people consumed and start adding them up in my head. It isn't that difficult. Once I get a total, I add the tax as well.

"There," I tell Jenna, handing her the paper with the final number circled.

"Is this right?" she asks, looking at the numbers like they're alien monsters. She's probably thinking she should run it through a calculator, except there are over twenty order sheets with tons of drinks on each for her to go through, which would take a while. And the VC folks are waiting.

"Let me see it." The man extends his hand.

Jenna hands it to him. I'm confident of my math. And my memory. I just hope his is as good.

He skims the list. "Your math is fine. And the drinks look about right, too. But let's check. What'd you serve that guy in the yellow shirt over there?"

"Three JD and Cokes, a boilermaker and a Stoli rocks with a lime wedge."

The guy motions with a hand. "Hey, Brian. Come over here for a sec." Brian walks over. "What'd you drink tonight?"

Brian frowns. "Uh... Not a lot. Couple of JD and Cokes and a boilermaker." There's a pause. "Oh, and a vodka."

"A couple?" the man says. "Two?"

Brian squints at the ceiling. "Think it was three."

The man looks at me. "Impressive. Okay, I'll trust your numbers."

"Thanks," I say.

"Thank *you*," he says, handing Jenna a sleek corporate card.

While Jenna wrestles with the machine to accept his credit card, he turns to me. "I don't see you here a lot. You work part-time?"

"Yeah. Although hopefully you'll see more of me in the future." I realize abruptly he has a wedding band on his finger, and I might be coming across as flirty. "You know, when I get more hours."

"You seem pretty on top of things."

"Just a have a head for numbers, I guess."

His gaze slides to Jenna briefly, then returns to me. "Ever thought about doing something else?"

"Like what?" *Careful, Aspen...* I've had some asshole propositions before, although not usually this openly.

"We're looking to hire an assistant. Why don't you come in for an interview?" He pulls out a business card and a pen and jots down something on the back before handing it to me.

The thick rectangular paper feels expensive in my hand. On the front it reads:

Emmett Lasker
Director
GrantEm Capital

The name Lasker makes me pause for a second as an old pain

pokes at me. It isn't exactly a common name, but it isn't super rare, either. Besides, Grant said if he could, he'd be a beach bum in Spain. Even if he ended up staying in the States, I can't picture him in L.A. He probably graduated from Harvard so he could have the piece of paper that said he'd done it and then went off to God only knows where.

I jerk myself out of the reverie. Grant means nothing to me. It's been fourteen years.

I flip the card and see a phone number.

"My direct number if you decide you're interested," Emmett says.

It's flattering to have somebody recognize me for a hard worker, but don't assistants get paid very little? Even less than bartenders? "Thank you. I'd love to, but I didn't finish college." Most people round-file my résumé when they see that I dropped out. I wish I could've finished my education, but too many things happened.

"Not a problem," Emmett says. "We hire people who can do the job, not people with a certain degree. Can you use a computer and draft a memo?"

"Sure, but..." I sigh, then gather myself. It may be TMI, but I don't want to waste our time. "To be frank, I need a job that can pay well enough for me to keep my grandfather in a nursing home. He needs help that I can't give."

"We have a benefit that pays something like two grand a month toward eldercare for our full-time employees. HR will have the details."

The rest of his explanation fades away as my mind latches on to the fact that his company pays two thousand dollars a month for nursing homes. *That's almost half the bill I get every month.*

Even if the regular pay is crappy, that benefit would make up for it. And I can work at the bar on weekends for extra cash, and I might —might—just be able to keep Grandpa in the Orange Care Center, where he feels most at home.

Jenna finally brings two credit card transaction slips for Emmett to sign.

As he scrawls his name on the sheets, I say, "When and where do I need to go?"

———

I have nothing to lose, I tell myself as I get dressed for the interview the next day. Emmett is clearly a man of action—he asked me to come in immediately. He actually looked like he wanted to conduct the interview at the bar.

My wardrobe is rather lacking. Hell, everything about my situation is lacking, and it'd be weird to see a closet full of fancy office outfits in my drab studio apartment with its dingy brown carpet—a carpet that's probably older than I am. But I manage to put together something that looks acceptable. A white button-down top and black pants. A pair of black Mary Janes with two-inch heels. I pull my hair back and put on mascara and lipstick, something I almost never bother with unless I'm working at the bar. But I want to look as presentable as possible, even if I'm not going to have the polished swagger of the venture capitalists at his firm. It's almost enough to make me laugh. Mascara and lipstick won't improve my situation if Emmett's changed his mind since last night. And he might well have, once he's really absorbed the fact that I'm a college dropout.

I fold my hands together and close my eyes in a quick prayer.

I drive to the address, which turns out to be a glossy high-rise. My twenty-four-year-old Mazda3 still runs, and please God let that continue, because I can't afford to replace it. Every time I look at the car, I tell myself I'm lucky. It could've died an ignoble death any time, leaving me stuck and SOL.

The lobby is glitzy, all smooth marble and chrome and a tall ceiling that begs you to crane your neck as you enter. Lots of tinted glass. Underneath the slick gloss is a confidence that only wealth and success can bring about.

I stamp down on the sadness welling inside me. Belonging at a place like this used to be my dream when I was younger and more naïve. But real life has a way of swatting you down until your vision fades away.

At the security desk, I sign in. One of the guards in a dark navy uniform makes a call, then gives me a visitor's pass.

"GrantEm Capital, thirty-fifth floor," he says with a small grunt.

He runs a hand over his head, which is covered with platinum fuzz like a summer peach.

"Got it." I smile, noting his name on his uniform. "Thanks, Otto."

He looks slightly surprised, then smiles back.

I slip into a waiting elevator, then exhale softly. My heart hammers, and sweat slickens my palms. *It's no big deal if I blow it,* I tell myself to settle my nerves, but that's a lie. Of course it's a big effing deal. It's going to allow me to keep Grandpa in the Orange Care Center. And that means everything. I'd sell a kidney if it were possible.

When I step out onto the work floor, the bustle and hustle slam into me like a physical force. The people who were cheerfully relaxed and having fun yesterday are gone. In their place are VC sharks, on their phones, on their computers, rifling through papers. Asking for clarifications and information. They throw out numbers like *a hundred million* as if it were something they could dig up by sticking their hands into their pants pockets. A steady stream of people marches out of a breakroom like ants, everyone holding energy drinks or coffee.

A pretty blonde coming out with a fresh mug pauses and turns to me. I remember seeing her at the bar a few times. Her intelligent blue eyes and kindness toward the staff were always noticed.

"Hey, you're the bartender from yesterday, right?" she says, all friendly.

"Yeah. Hi. I'm Aspen."

"Amy." She smiles.

"Nice to meet you. Um, I'm actually here to talk with Emmett Lasker. He's expecting me."

"He is?"

"Yeah. He wanted me to interview for an assistant position...?"

"Oh." Her face lights up. "Perfect! Right this way."

I follow her, wondering what it takes to work as a venture capitalist here. I know they move a lot of money—the kind of sums most people can't imagine. She probably has a really impressive résumé...

Oh, *shoot! My résumé!* I should've brought it with me! I totally spaced because I've never had an employer ask to see me without my having applied for a position first.

I can't believe I've already blown the interview, and I haven't even said hello to Emmett yet! Even if *he* doesn't want one, the HR people most definitely will. GrantEm Capital smells like the kind of place that will demand one.

"Don't be nervous," Amy says, peering at me.

I cringe inwardly. *Great going, Aspen. Forgot the résumé and now showing panic to everyone.* "Is it that obvious?"

"Everyone gets nervous when they interview with Emmett. But you'll be fine. He doesn't bite. And if he asked you to come in, he must really like you for some reason."

That's reassuring...a little. I manage a smile for her. "Okay."

She walks past a desk with a perky brunette in her late twenties. She watches us with keen interest. "Is that Emmett's eleven o'clock?" she says, checking me out.

"Yes. Apparently, nobody was there to meet her at the elevator," Amy says, nicely enough, but there's a subtle censure in her tone.

"I didn't know she was coming."

"Really? Security didn't call?"

"Yeah, but that doesn't mean she'd come up, like, immediately." Amy sighs.

The brunette turns to me. "Well, you're here. So, no harm, no foul, right?" Her eyes demand an agreement.

I shrug, wondering why she thinks I'll agree with her.

"Anyway, Marjorie, let Emmett know Aspen's here for the interview."

"Is she going to be Renée's replacement?" Marjorie asks.

Amy smiles thinly. "You'll have to ask your boss."

Marjorie hits the intercom. "Emmett, your eleven o'clock is here."

"Send her in."

After a long exhale, I walk inside his office. It's sizable, with a huge desk and a couple of couches and a table. There are two laptops—one on his desk and one on the table between the couches. At the bar he looked more casual, but here he is clearly master of his domain, exuding an easy confidence.

"Please, take a seat."

"Thank you." I perch my butt on the edge of a couch cushion.

"Thanks for coming in. I wasn't sure if you would. You seemed a bit reluctant."

"Well..." The name Lasker gave me pause when I first saw his card, but I didn't realize he'd caught that. *Okay, so he's perceptive. File that away.* I should probably admit my screwup before he broaches the subject himself. "I don't have a résumé."

"You don't need one if I ask you to come in. Résumés are for people who *want* me to ask them to come in." He speaks the words like it's natural for him to make an exception whenever he feels like it. "You can think on your feet and come up with a solution rather than wringing your hands over a problem. Furthermore, you went straight to implementation, which I like. Nobody wants to micromanage you here, and we expect you to proactively do your job. You can also do math on the spot without a calculator, which is good. Might come in handy from time to time, depending." His gaze flicks briefly in Marjorie's direction. "I do need to make sure you can do a business memo, though. It's easy to teach you how to use apps to manage appointments and agendas, but it's hard to teach someone how to write well."

"Okay," I say, relieved he thinks of me positively. I'm sure I can swing a decent memo.

He nods and hits the intercom. "Marjorie, can you bring in the folder I asked you to prep this morning?"

The brunette walks in. Her chartreuse dress is fashionably short, but not so short that it'd be unprofessional. Her shoes are shiny and new, and she walks with the assertiveness of someone who knows where she belongs. She hands me a brown leather folio. "Here you go."

Emmett points at the laptop on the table. "You can use that."

"Thank you," I say, grateful he has everything I need.

"Let me know if you have any questions." Emmett returns to his desk and starts working on his laptop. I'm glad, because it would've been awkward if he'd hovered and watched me like a test proctor.

I Google the general format for a business memo, then familiarize myself with the contents of the folio and start typing one up. It doesn't take long before I'm done. After making sure there aren't any typos or errors, I save the document again. "I'm finished," I say.

"Already?" He comes over and turns the laptop so he can read what I've written. His eyebrows rise. "Not bad at all."

Oh, thank God. "Thank you."

He closes the laptop. "There needs to be a background check. It takes twenty-four hours or less, unless we see something concerning. Provided you're clear, you can start immediately, unless you need to give notice to your current employer. HR can give you more detailed information about benefits, but we have the typical—medical, dental, vision—along with the eldercare I told you about yesterday. We pay bimonthly, and because you're in admin, your pay will be calculated on an hourly basis. You'll be expected to put in at least forty hours a week. If you go over, you'll be paid time and a half. We try not to make the admin staff work too many hours because you don't get bonuses like our associates. Any questions?"

Forty hours a week is good. That'll guarantee a steady paycheck. I run the numbers in my head. Unless their hourly rate is a joke, I can probably make it work. "Yeah. How much am I getting paid?" The most important question.

He throws out a number that makes my heart stop for a second. My hand flies to my mouth. He's offering a freakin' fortune! More than triple what I make anywhere else! I've *never* made that kind of money before. If I can stick it out here for a year and be really careful, I might even be able to replace my Mazda3!

"All good?" The twinkle in his eye says he knows I'm more than happy.

"Yes!"

"Then let's have HR do the paperwork."

————

I still can't believe what happened as I drive home. If this is a dream...

Well, it's a damn good one. The kind I never want to wake up from.

I park and go up to my unit on the second floor. No elevators in this old building. My next-door neighbor, Mrs. Yang, is just heading into her apartment. She stops when she notices me.

"Hello, Aspen." Her words are somewhat accented. She immigrated from Korea fifteen years ago, then moved here after her husband died. She looks shorter than she really is because her upper back is bent. She said it's from a car accident—"American drivers too fast." Not even surgery could straighten her out.

But that doesn't seem to slow her down. She's always busy, cooking, cleaning and chatting with her grownup sons on the phone. She keeps her short, permed hair a dark brown with whatever dye is on sale at Walmart, shops for loose, flower-patterned clothes from discount racks and splurges on comfy shoes, claiming that when you're her age, you need good footwear.

"Hi, Mrs. Yang!" I say with a bright smile.

"Something good happened to you?" she asks.

"I got a new job!"

"Oh, congratulations! It's a good job, yes?"

"Very! I'm so excited!"

"Me too!" As her bright eyes sweep over me, the corners of her mouth tilt downward in disapproval. "But you should take care of yourself, too. If you don't stay healthy, who will take care of your grandfather?"

I smile. When I first met her, I thought she was a busybody, but now I know she says what she does out of good intentions. She says I'm like the daughter she always wanted to have but couldn't because her womb was only capable of making boys.

"I'm okay," I tell her. "Just a little tired because I couldn't sleep well last night." I came in late from the bar, and I was thinking about the eldercare benefits the entire time—and what that would mean for me and Grandpa.

"No, no. You are losing your weight. Come. I just made some noodles. You can take them with you. They keep." She gestures for me to come into her place.

Although she doesn't move with the grace my grandmother had, her concern and sweetness remind me of Grandma and Suyen's mom. The latter in particular always worried her child was starving herself.

I follow Mrs. Yang into a unit almost identical to mine. Her carpet is pale gray and newer, which is good. Nobody should have to put up with threadbare flooring.

She takes off her shoes and walks inside. I slip off my heels and follow her into the kitchen. She opens a plain white fridge with a small dent in the door and pulls out a sizable Tupperware full of pan-fried noodles and veggies.

"Young women diet too much. They get weak bones," she says, placing the tub on the counter.

"Right." I nod, even though she's wrong about me dieting. I eat whenever I can, but when you're working so many hours and shifts, it's hard to eat regularly.

"But don't worry. My food doesn't make you big. Jabchae don't do that. Look at all the vegetable! You don't get fat from eating spinach, onion, mushrooms and carrots."

"Probably not," I say, noting that she conveniently didn't mention the noodles. She's convinced everything she makes is calorie-free, and I nod because it makes her happy.

"You take this. I think you like it before."

"I did. Thank you!"

She pats my arm gently. "You're such a good girl, Aspen. Always taking care of your grandpa. It isn't easy." She sighs a sad sigh. "You're so young to be working your life away. Enjoy yourself, too, okay?" Her tone says she knows that won't be happening anytime soon.

"I will." I smile and take the food. "Thanks again."

I make a mental note to buy her some flowers next time. I'm not the best cook, especially compared to her. She doesn't seem to drink—the wine I got her last Christmas is still sitting on a shelf—but she flushes like a young girl when I bring her roses.

Every woman needs a reason to be happy.

26

GRANT

.

At last. I roll my shoulders as I walk out of LAX, the mind-numbing business meeting finally done and dusted. It was made worse by the fact that I had to travel out of town. Hotels aren't awful—not when you're willing to pay a premium. But I prefer my own bed if I'm going to be suffering during waking hours.

The worst thing wasn't even the idiotic waste of time with the new management, who supposedly got their education from Ivy League schools but don't understand anything. It was that my ever-efficient assistant Renée had to quit suddenly three weeks ago. *Why did the military have to send her husband overseas?*

She was the best assistant I ever had. Emmett offered to share his assistant with me until we find a replacement, but that's sort of like someone offering to stab you in the eye so that you'll forget about the pain in your foot. Dealing with Marjorie is like having a hot poker up your butt.

I knew Marjorie was slow-moving and not particularly bright. I just didn't know *how* dim she was until I started giving her assignments.

My phone rings as I'm walking out to my car. *Emmett. Oh, good.* Now I can vent my spleen a little.

"Your assistant booked a fucking non-direct flight when I told

206

her three times to make sure it was direct! It added three hours to the trip!"

"Which you spent working at the airport," he says soothingly.

"I just want bare minimum competence from Marjorie," I say. "*Bare minimum.*"

"No. You want a Spectre," he says, referring to the Rolls-Royce coupe I ordered.

"I want the best car. With Marjorie, it's clear that 'the best' isn't an available option."

"Well, yeah, okay. True enough." Emmett sounds slightly dolorous.

"So I'll take minimum—"

"But that's why I hired you a new assistant!" he says, perking up again.

"You did?" There was no time to interview candidates while I was out of town, so I let Emmett handle it. "I thought you said the candidate sucked."

"No, that was the one on Tuesday. And yeah, she did. But this one's good. Calm. Levelheaded. Proactive. Doesn't wait for people to tell her what to do."

"That's good, as long as she's smarter than Marjorie."

"She can do math faster than Don, all in her head."

"Seriously?" Don is one of the quicker associates, excellent with numbers.

"Yup. Dropped out of college, but who cares? Her memos are good, too."

"Marjorie-good or Amy-good?"

"Hey, nobody's as good as Amy." He's still unhappy we had to swap associates, and he ended up with Sasha and I got Amy. But now that Amy's his wife, it would be awkward for him to do performance evaluations on her. Not to mention, if he gave her a glowing eval, nobody would believe it wasn't biased. "But she's good. Much better than Marjorie."

Emmett's laying it on thick. He knows I've been frazzled without Renée, and Marjorie doesn't cut it for me. I don't know how he puts up with her.

"All right. I'll see how good she is on Monday."

"Trust me. I have the hiring instincts of a god!"

"Uh-huh. One of those tiny little plaster cherub gods that pee into fountains." I snort a laugh, then hang up.

Emmett wouldn't be praising the new hire if she sucked, so a bit of optimism starts to well up. I have so many admin tasks to unload. I realize as I climb into my Maybach that he didn't mention her name. Oh well. I'll meet her soon enough.

I maneuver through the late Friday afternoon traffic, heading to Ink Art. I visit that tattoo studio every year on this day. I connect my phone to the car via Bluetooth and call Dani, the owner and lead tattoo artist at the place.

"Ink Art. How can I help you?" Her voice is raspy and low from years of smoking.

"This is Grant."

"Hey. I was just thinking about you."

"Likewise."

She laughs softly. "You stopping by today?"

"Uh-huh. I know it's last minute, but can you fit me in? I couldn't make an appointment because I was out of town and wasn't sure if I could make it." No Renée to manage that for me, and Marjorie would've forgotten.

"Of course. It won't be a problem. It isn't like it's going to take long, Quickie."

I chuckle at her nickname for me. "Okay. See you soon."

Half an hour later, I pull in in front of a pleasant tat studio. The textured tile floor is black and white, and the white walls are covered with Dani's original designs. Some of them are marked with a small red star in the upper-right corner to show that they're taken—and turned into tattoos on her clients' bodies—but some are still available. There are also some by her other artists.

Dani comes out around the counter. She's paler than last year, but she'd been in Hawaii for a week before I saw her back then. Her hair's dyed blue and cut short with a sloping bang that covers almost all of her right eye. Black kohl lines her eyes, and a blood-red shade glints on her thin lips. Intricates tattoos consisting of swirly lines and poetry quotes cover her long, lean arms. There is a thin black band around her ring finger. She said only an exceptionally worthy man will be allowed to put a ring there and cover the ink.

"Kinda slow today," I say.

"A customer just left. He'll be back later to finish it up." She cocks her head. "You're the only person who doesn't want anything fancy."

"I don't need fancy."

I get ready, unbuttoning my shirt and revealing my shoulder. She looks at the smooth expanse of skin, then runs an antiseptic swab over it, since the tat's going to be tiny.

"So why do you get just one at a time?" she asks, picking up the tiny needle.

"Because doing them all at once wouldn't be the same."

She adds a short black dash to my shoulder. Now there are fourteen. I look at them dispassionately.

"You add a dash on your shoulder every time you make another billion?" She knows I'm a venture capitalist.

"No. I don't need tats to keep track of how much I'm worth." I keep my response light and playful. The black dashes mean another year has gone by with my head screwed on tight.

"I'd feel guilty if you were anybody else. I charge a minimum of a Benji and a half." She shakes her head.

"Aren't you lucky I'm a billionaire?"

She laughs. "Yeah. Well, you ever want something fancy, lemme know."

"Will do," I say, although I know I won't.

I pay her two hundred. She shakes her head again.

"No need for a tip," she says.

"I want to." It's the same argument we always have. Dani was new and practically starving when I met her. People make assumptions because of her ink and loud makeup, but she's one of the hardest-working entrepreneurs around. She built Ink Art with sweat and blood, never taking a shortcut. I admire her for it.

"All right. Thanks, Grant. See you next year?"

"Yup. Have a good weekend." I smile and leave the studio.

One more year of my not falling for the romantic bullshit people like Huxley push to sell things—and I'll deserve another dash. The thought should fill me with smug satisfaction, but somehow I'm gloomy.

Must be the days spent in Boston. The weather was terrible out there, all those gray clouds hanging low, heavy with rain or snow. There's no telling in a city that can have a massive blizzard as late as April.

I stop by the office briefly to pick up the gift Marjorie said she left with security. They hand it over, and I grind my teeth.

What the hell am I going to do with a diamond necklace? I told her I needed flowers, something big and expensive, not jewelry. I don't give things that people can sell anymore.

I take a snapshot of the necklace and text her.

–Me: Does this look like a flower arrangement to you?

–Marjorie: You're welcome. Every girl likes jewelry.

I close my eyes for a long moment. She's *so* lucky she works for Emmett. I would've fired her a long time ago and bad-mouthed her shitty performance to everyone so that she could never find another job in the city.

I throw the jewelry box unceremoniously on the passenger seat of my Maybach and glare at the mess Marjorie's made. Normally I wouldn't bother with anything. Girls are happy with a fancy dinner and some sex. But it's Yvette's birthday, so I have to make an effort. I stop by a florist on the way to the restaurant and grab three dozen long-stemmed roses. They're clichéd, but then, Yvette is a clichéd kind of girlfriend—pretty, slightly self-absorbed and not overly bright. She doesn't challenge me, she doesn't bother me much and she doesn't make too many annoying demands. We can spend a pleasant, inoffensive time together, and she doesn't make me do or feel anything out of the ordinary.

I toss my fob to the valet at Éternité, one of the most popular and exclusive restaurants in the city. Yvette said she wanted to eat at La Mer, but I told her no. I haven't been there in almost a decade and a half, and I don't plan to change that, birthday or no birthday.

Besides, Éternité is just as good as La Mer. Owned by the same guy, too. The French-Japanese fusion restaurant has a long waiting list, but I can always get a table. *Assuming Marjorie hasn't screwed that up as well.* My gut tightens at the possibility. Thankfully, the hostess finds my reservation.

"Your party's already here and seated," she says with a smile.

I nod and follow an impeccably dressed staff member to my table. The interior is an interesting mélange of East and West. It's airy, with intricately embroidered hangings and unique flower arrangements. I scan the place for Yvette's familiar brunette locks, but don't see her.

"Here you are, sir."

I stop, then stare at Yvette, reeling. She beams at me like she's just been crowned Miss USA.

"Grant!" she says in her thin, high-pitched voice.

I stay standing. "What the hell happened to your hair?"

"Oh, this?" She swivels her head this way and that. "I dyed it yesterday. Don't worry, I didn't cut it. I know you like long hair."

"Why?" I say, staring at the red curls around her flawlessly made-up face.

"I saw you staring at a redhead when we were out last week." She shrugs.

I think back... I saw a woman with hair in the exact same shade as...

Fuck, I'm not going to go there. I haven't thought about her in years, and I'm not going to now. I wasn't really thinking about her last week, either. The hair was overly bright and caught my attention, that's all.

Yvette continues, "I thought you liked the color since, you know, aside from the hair, she wasn't anything special." She rolls her eyes. "So I thought I'd change." She smiles. "Do you like it?"

"No. You look like you're drenched in pig's blood."

Her jaw drops. "What?"

I start to leave, then realize I'm still carrying the roses. I shove them into her face. "Here. Happy birthday."

"Um. Okay." She takes them. "Thank you." Her voice is uncertain, but it says she's willing to forgive me if I apologize.

"We're done."

She gasps. "Are you dumping me?"

"Yes."

"Over my *hair color*?" She says it loudly enough that other diners stare.

I turn and walk away. I should've known the evening wouldn't end well when Marjorie screwed up my flight reservation and bought the wrong present.

I can't get rid of her fast enough.

27

ASPEN

On Monday at seven thirty sharp, I step out of the elevator and onto the thirty-fifth floor. I can't believe I'm working here!

I look down at the employee badge hanging around my neck, which I received from security on Friday. My photo shows me doing my best not to grin like a fool. But it was difficult to contain myself.

Once that was done, Emmett had IT set up a laptop for me and instructed me to learn the apps the company uses to manage schedules and meetings and so on. Marjorie showed me how for an hour, and then I used Google and the employee training to master the rest.

Emmett clearly expects me to hit the ground running, and I plan to do exactly that. HR told me my benefits will start from the first of the month, so I'll be without coverage for a couple of weeks. I can deal with that, especially since the position came with a two-thousand-dollar signing bonus I didn't know about. Leah, the HR rep who was helping me, told me Emmett probably forgot to mention it.

"He knows the general rules and policies, but not the small stuff. Not that it's his job to know," she said, tapping beautifully manicured black and red nails on her desk.

I merely nodded at the idea of two thousand dollars being "small." Also, I was too happy to argue.

"You need to stay with the firm for at least six months, or you'll have to give the money back. Prorated, of course."

"That won't be an issue. I plan to stay a while." I already told my two other part-time jobs that I was quitting, and my bosses said that was fine. I'm going to continue to work at the bar on weekends because Jenna's amendable to adjusting my schedule, and the money's good.

"Great!" Leah took all my paperwork and smiled. "We don't need the boss freakin' out over not having an assistant so soon again."

Doesn't Emmett *have* an assistant? But maybe Marjorie's a temp, and he's looking for a permanent hire.

I smooth my black skirt with slightly trembling hands and walk toward Emmett's office. I thought I'd be one of the first to arrive, but there are at least fifteen people as I walk by all the desks, including Amy, who's scowling at her computer.

Marjorie isn't here yet. I pull out my shiny new laptop and boot it up. While it's whirring to life, I go over to Emmett's office. The door is ajar, so I stick my head inside. He's at his desk, tapping on his tablet.

"Good morning, Emmett." I smile.

He looks up. "Hi, Aspen. You're in early. What's up?"

"Wanted to know if you needed anything before we discuss your agenda for the week."

"Actually, no. I'm fine." He stands and comes around his desk. "Let me introduce you to your boss." He starts leading me out to the hall, past all the desks.

I trot after him. "Aren't I working for you?"

"No. I have Marjorie. It's my brother who needs a new assistant. His had to quit three weeks ago, and it's been, ah, a little rough since then."

"He didn't want to interview me himself?" I wonder if the firm's going to rescind the offer if Emmett's brother doesn't like me. I can't have that.

"Nope. He left the hiring to me, and I'm great at detecting talent."

It'll be fine, I tell myself. Emmett seems to like his brother.

There's warmth is his eyes, and even though I don't know him very well, I trust his judgment.

We reach a corner office. From its location, it's going to be a mirror image of Emmett's in layout. Emmett stands by the door, blocking the plaque on the wall with the name of my real boss. He knocks a couple of times.

"Come in!" comes a slightly distracted voice.

Emmett opens the door and gestures at me. "After you."

"Okay." I start to walk inside, with him following closely behind.

My new boss is standing behind his desk, poring over some documents. He lifts his head.

For an instant it's like there's a human-sized snake in the suit. I stop cold, right in my tracks. All the blood in my skull seems to drain, and I feel lightheaded. I blink to clear the spots in my vision, praying I'm seeing things.

Emmett bumps into my back hard enough to knock me forward, but catches me fast, thank God. It'd be humiliating to end up on my knees, looking up at *Grant fucking Lasker*, the asshole I was dumb enough to fall in love with.

He looks good. More than good. His body has filled out with more lean muscle, and his shoulders are broader than I remember. The V of his back muscles is also wider on top and narrower as it slopes down. Meanwhile, his face is even more chiseled and refined, his clean-shaven jaw stubborn, the high cheekbones sharp enough to cut. His dark eyebrows slant furiously as his aquamarine eyes flare with old resentment and anger.

That reaction, more than anything else, stiffens my spine. What the hell does *he* have to be mad about? I'm the one who was used and betrayed. He lied to me to take my virginity, chortled behind my back with his rich friends and turned me into a campus laughing-stock. I wanted my first time to be with somebody special, somebody who cared. I thought I had found that in him. What a fool I was.

I hate it that he isn't a beach bum like I thought he'd become. He's the epitome of success in a slick suit and a watch that costs more than what most people make in a year, while I'm a mess in cheap clothes I bought on clearance years ago, and my shoes are so old the soles are too thin to provide any arch support.

Our difference in status couldn't be starker. The world is truly unfair, and everything about the situation slips underneath my armor and leaves a deep cut.

Since I left Napa Aquinas College, I thought I'd rebuilt that armor. Guess it isn't as strong as it used to be. But then, it was broken before. It might never give me the protection it once did. It's up to me to be a little bit tougher, paste on a smile like I'm not hurt.

Grant stares at me for a moment, then glares at Emmett. "Is this some kind of joke?"

"Uh...no." Emmett walks around me to face Grant. "This is Aspen. The new hire I told you about."

Grant opens his mouth, then closes it, placing a fist over his lips. Tendons stand out on the back of his hand, while his eyes are shooting death at me.

Fuck you very much. I'm not happy to see you, either.

But I keep the words inside. Not because Grant deserves my consideration, but because I need the money for Grandpa.

In addition, I'm beginning to feel sorry for Emmett. He obviously doesn't know what kind of asshole his brother is. Grant's been fooling him just like he did me.

"We need to talk," Grant says to Emmett.

"Okay."

"You." Grant points at me. "Out."

Emmett's eyes widen with shock.

I, on the other hand, am not fazed. I should've expected this. *How rude.* But I guess he doesn't need to hide his true nature from me. He doesn't have another bet to win. The memory makes my blood boil again.

Grant gives me a look. "If you don't like it, quit."

"I don't think so." Now that I know it's Grant, I'm even more determined to stay. He took everything from me, and now he can damn well pay for my grandfather's care. He owes me that much.

Emmett clears his throat. "What's going on here?"

"I don't need an assistant who's going to ghost me in a couple of weeks," Grant says.

"Don't worry, I plan to stay here as long as possible. As a matter of fact, maybe I'll work here for the rest of my life," I shoot back.

Grandpa will be with me forever. Of course, proclaiming the possibility of lifetime employment is absurd, but no more than Grant's idea that I'm going to ghost this job. I'm not the irresponsible asshole here.

"Okay, uh... I'm getting the impression that you guys know each other," Emmett says.

"Yes," Grant says at the same time I say, "No."

Emmett looks from one of us to the other. "Why don't you give us a minute, Aspen?" he says finally.

"Sure." I give him a sweet smile full of the respect he deserves as my superior. "I'll be right outside. Just holler if you need me." Then I give Grant a fuck-you glance and leave.

But once I'm out, I lean against the wall next to the door and let out a sigh. *Fucking Grant.* I thought I had most of my money problems sorted, but I know he's going to fire me, which means I'm back to square one.

Shit. Is it too late for me to call my managers and ask for my jobs back? I should've known better than to think a good thing could happen to me. Ever since I found out about Grant's bet, my life's taken one bad turn after another.

A few people walk past. I try not to burn with envy and sadness for myself. If none of those things had happened fourteen years ago, I could've had a job like them. Not at this firm, of course, but somewhere. And maybe I wouldn't have had to worry so much about my finances.

But there are things you just can't recover from, and life dealt me three powerful punches, back to back to back.

So I continue to stand here, mentally composing what I'm going to say when Grant's annoyingly smug face tells me I'm fired.

28

GRANT

The second the door closes behind Aspen, Emmett takes one of the couches. "What the hell was that about?"

"She can't work here," I say, sitting on the other couch. I'm shaking with the need to strangle her as I scream at her for betraying me. I clench my hands to hide the tremor.

"Why not?"

"She's an unreliable, money-grubbing bitch!" I'd rather die than tell Emmett what happened in college. It's so damn humiliating. I still can't believe how naïve and stupid I was.

"For a money-grubbing bitch, she doesn't dress like she has any money."

Because she auctioned the good stuff off, I think bitterly.

"Look. If you have a history with her, that's fine." Emmett raises his hands, palms out. "I'll take her."

"What?"

"I don't want to fire her. She's good."

"How do you know?" I almost ask if she let him fuck her, but Emmett's crazy about Amy, and he'd never betray her.

"What do you think I was doing after I hired her? I had Marjorie train her, and she did some work for me. She's quick, does everything I ask and more. She's getting up to speed and sometimes knows what needs to be done even before I tell her. Great attention to detail."

Emmett is picky, so if he liked her work, she did pretty well. "You just think she's amazing because nobody's as bad as Marjorie."

"Fine. I'll have Aspen replace Marjorie. *You* can take Marjorie. Or hire somebody else. Whatever works."

Except I don't want that. I don't want Aspen working for Emmett. She'll do whatever it takes to latch on to him—he's young and rich. She's not going to care that he's married. People like her don't worry about anything or anyone other than themselves. "No."

Emmett gives me a look. "No? You can't tell me who I can or can't have as my assistant."

"She's going to wreck your marriage."

He goes still. "Do you know something I don't?" His face slowly collapses into suspicion. "Oh, no. Did she fuck Dad? Because that's really gross."

Ugh. Now he's making me want to throw up. "No. She didn't do Dad." At least, I don't think she did. But who knows what she's been up to over the last fourteen years? "But I just know the kind of thing she'd do, okay? Trust me."

Emmett nods reluctantly, but I take comfort in the fact that he's on my side.

"I'll have her work for me." I need to protect him from unnecessary drama. And I like Amy. "But I promise you she's going to quit within three months."

Emmett shakes his head. "I doubt that. She's got more spine and gumption than you think."

"Wanna make a little bet?"

Emmett cocks an eyebrow. "Sure. What are we betting?"

I think for a moment. Maybe the Spectre...? It's a cool car.

"I don't want the Spectre," Emmett says before I can suggest it. "We have a kid."

"Fine. I'll get you a minivan," I say, mostly to mess with him. "Okay, how about: whoever loses gives the winner a handwritten, letter-sized note. It will read, *I'm wrong. You're right.* And it will be signed and framed."

"You're going to lose," Emmett says with a laugh.

"Don't cry when you have to give me the note. I'm going to hang it in my office so everyone can see it."

"Fine. But you can't do anything illegal."

"I'm going to get her to quit, not sue me. Not that a lawsuit would be a bad thing. I could hire Huxley & Webber and drag her through the court system for a decade or two."

Emmett squints at me. "What did she do to unleash your inner asshole?"

"I don't have an inner asshole."

"Yeah, you do. You're laid-back and nice until somebody fucks you over. Then you turn into a giant, raging pucker monster."

"Come on. Everyone does that, not just me."

"Yeah, but you're an extreme case. Scorched earth. Nuclear winter." Emmett makes a bomb explosion noise, raising his hands into the air like a mushroom cloud. Then he grows serious. "Did Aspen fuck you over?"

If I tell him everything, he'll side with me. My brothers and I... We've all got each other's backs. But I don't want to rehash my past. It happened fourteen years ago, damn it, and I'd rather drink a shot of Drano than tell him how stupid I was. "I just don't like how she looks."

He smirks. "Ohhh... You like her."

"How the hell did you jump to that conclusion?"

"Because I had issues with the way Amy looked when I hired her."

"What was wrong with the way she looked?" Amy has always looked the same—professional and pretty.

"Too sexy."

I roll my eyes. "Out. I have things I have to do today. And send Aspen back in."

"So the three months starts now?"

I smile grimly. "Yes. Three months from now, she'll be gone." I stand and return to my desk. "Have HR continue to look for a replacement for Renée."

———

After Emmett leaves, Aspen walks back in and stands in front of my desk. I leave her on her feet and lean back in my chair.

She hasn't changed much since college. She's still beautiful—that long, fiery hair framing the heart-shaped face, the moss-green eyes and the small, straight nose. Her cheekbones are so perfectly sculpted that they look like something out of Greek antiquity. And her lips... They appear fuller and plumper now. I want to chalk it up to fillers, but I know how that looks, and she hasn't had any work done on her face.

She's just naturally gorgeous. And her body is, too. All those curves from the full breasts that slope down into the cinched waist and flaring hips. Her legs are long and still shapely. The practical black pumps she's wearing should look boring. But on her, they're actually hot.

I hate it that I notice. I squint and study her harder to look for flaws, anything that will turn me off. Her cream blouse and black skirt are drab and cheap-looking. Two pearls on her ears—again, modest but nothing special. No other jewelry. No rings, which brings an odd sense of relief—probably because I want to see her poor. Her nails are neatly trimmed, but without any polish.

Everything about her betrays financial hardship. Resentment bubbles inside me. If she ghosted me like that, she should've found herself a rich and stupid guy to leech off. She should've reappeared in my life covered in shiny silk and glittering jewelry. There should be a two-yard-radius cloud of priceless perfume, and...

Fuck. She should be some old asshole's trophy. And when I ask her if it was worth it, she should look at me with misery in her eyes, as the diamonds on her ears and throat sparkle like tears. So I could laugh at her for being stupid. And laugh at myself for having been so blind.

She doesn't glow like she used to. Guess she found out the hard way that it isn't so easy to snag a sucker after ditching me the way she did. She's too old now to play the it's-my-first-time game. Emmett made it sound like it was some opportune coincidence that got him to hire her, but I don't believe that. She must've discovered somehow that I'm at GrantEm, and engineered events while I was out of town to get this job. She's nothing if not persistent and manipulative.

She should know I'm not the idiot I used to be.

"Put on something else when you come tomorrow," I say.

Her eyes narrow. "What's wrong with my outfit?"

"There's no need to play at being poor." I give her a fake smile. "You can put on something better. I won't treat you any different."

Her lips thin. "I didn't see anything in the employee manual that specified I have to wear something expensive to suit you."

"Things would go a lot better if you just learned to say, 'Yes, sir.'"

"And I'll be more than happy to say that—if the request is reasonable," she says in a dulcet tone.

"I'm your boss, not your friend. When I tell you to do something, it's not a request."

"Oh?" She raises an eyebrow. "Would you like me to get on my knees while I'm at it?"

The image of her on her knees before me, while looking up at me and whispering, "Yes, sir," makes my blood heat.

She continues to regard me with a challenge in her eyes. She knows exactly what she's doing. *Bitch.* "Why not? Getting on your knees might earn you some points."

"Is that an order, too?"

"It's a suggestion, since you seem so eager for this job. Employees with shitty evals get fired."

Her jaw flexes. "I'll make a note of that."

"Good."

"Would you like me to bring you a morning coffee too?"

I start to say yes, then stop. She could put rat poison in it. Or worse. "No. You don't go anywhere near my coffee, morning or otherwise."

"Scared I might spit in it?"

"You haven't earned the right."

Her face turns a dull red.

"But you can make yourself useful and return this." I pull out the necklace Marjorie bought for Yvette's birthday. I was going to make Emmett's lazy assistant handle it, but this will be better. "I want a full return, not credit or a replacement."

"What's wrong with it?" Aspen asks.

I open the lid and reveal the row of diamonds. I want her to feel a deep, lacerating despair and regret. If she hadn't betrayed me, she could've had stuff like this...and more. "It looks too cheap on my girlfriend. She deserves better."

I watch her for a sign of disappointment that I'm not single anymore. Or a hint of determination to break me and my nonexistent girlfriend up so she can take her place.

But nope. She immediately looks down, her long lashes hiding her eyes. Damn it.

I shut the lid with a controlled snap of my wrist.

"Got it," she says, taking the jewelry box. Her fingers move carefully, to avoid touching me.

"I need it refunded within an hour," I say. That will be virtually impossible. The jeweler is at least half an hour away, and they won't issue a refund without a receipt. I'm not telling her where she can find it. I hope Marjorie burned it.

"Can I have the credit card you used to buy this?" Aspen asks disdainfully. Her eyes glitter with something petty and sneaky.

"I don't think so. I'm not letting you anywhere near my credit cards."

"Let me guess. I haven't earned the right."

"Correct." I smile. "And on your way, stop by Bobbi's Sweet Things and get some pastries."

She flinches a little.

Guess she didn't like that, huh? I fire off a long list of different types of pastries that my team likes. "I don't need to repeat myself, do I?" *Say yes. I have a great response ready to go.*

"No," she says coolly.

I deflate just a little. Damn it, I really wanted to cut her down. I want to see her scream, "I quit," in a temper and flounce out of the building.

Still, I doubt she's got everything. I even spoke faster than usual. I can cut her down when she gets back.

Anticipating her screwup, I gesture at the door. "Now go. Do your job."

29

ASPEN

What an *asshole*.

I stalk out of Grant's office, gripping the jewelry box hard and trying not to look daggers at everyone else on the floor. He undoubtedly thinks he's winning. *Yes, sir? On my knees?*

And I haven't earned the *right* to be near his coffee or credit card?

Ha! Maybe I'll just kick him in the balls and get arrested for assault. Or break a window and help him jump out. My contribution to the betterment of humanity.

But the rage dies quickly. They're nice fantasies, but I have to think about Grandpa. If I lose this job and the benefits...I don't know how long I can keep him in the center.

I can suck it up for Grandpa. He's the only one I have left. If the situation were reversed, he'd do the same for me.

I sling my purse over my shoulder and head out to return the necklace. It's a pretty item, and it costs well over twenty thousand dollars. I know because I bought it when Marjorie asked me to on Friday morning. At the time, I had no idea what it was about. Actually, I wondered if it was a test to see if I was honest, because she gave me a paper with a long string of numbers on it and said all I had to do was show them the paper and they'd bill accordingly. The number must've been some kind of line of credit for Grant. Guess he still hands out lavish gifts to the women he sleeps with.

See? You weren't that special, a bitter voice says.

Yeah, yeah, yeah, I KNOW. No need to remind me again.

I wonder if this woman was a bet, too. Why not? To Grant, sex is a sport. Women a source of amusement.

Misogynistic pig. *Yes, sir,* indeed.

He's doing this to screw me over. When I asked him about the credit card—faux innocently, as a test—he didn't tell me the bill was on a separate charge account because he wants to see me fumble and fail. That dickhead behind the desk is the *real* him. Not the sweet guy who made me feel like a princess.

The thought is vindicating, enraging and saddening all at the same time. Maybe because I wish deep down that he wasn't such an asshole... That maybe...just maybe he felt something genuine for me so I wouldn't feel so dirty and cheap every time I remember my first time.

When I reach the jewelry store, the clerk who helped me on Friday comes over. "Hello, Ms. Hughes. What can I do for you?"

I look at him in surprise. He remembers me?

He gives me a professional smile. "We remember all our significant accounts."

"Ah. Well." I clear my throat. Let's see how long Grant stays *significant.* "I'm here to return the necklace I bought on Friday."

He blinks. "I beg your pardon?"

"My boss hates it. Says it isn't good enough for his girlfriend."

His frown deepens. "Are you sure that's what he said?"

"Quite sure."

"That would be a first."

"He specializes in first times."

"Pardon?"

"Nothing." I smile. "So. Can you refund the amount? I'm pretty sure it's never been worn."

He gives me a strange look. "One moment. Excuse me." He takes the necklace in the back, probably to use those funky magnifying glasses to examine it. Wouldn't it be amusing if Grant tried to swap the real diamonds with fake? Not that I think that's likely. They aren't worth it.

Soon, he returns with a white sheet of paper stamped with the jeweler's logo. "Here you are, Ms. Hughes."

"Oh? That's it?"

"Yes. Please sign here."

I scrawl my name.

"Thank you." He folds the paper and slides it into a white envelope made with thick, expensive paper and hands it to me.

I shove it into my purse and head to the bakery Grant mentioned. I know exactly where it is because that's where my grandparents' dance studio used to be. I stop out front and spend a moment just staring. Seeing the change is hard, but at the same time I'm glad it's a bakery rather than some bank or pawn shop.

Bobbi's Sweet Things smells amazing, and just walking into the place makes you happy. On top of that, the owner is a nice, no-nonsense woman.

I push the door and step inside then grab a basket and load it up with everything Grant asked for. It's a lot of stuff, and I hope he intends to eat all of it. Because then he'll blow up like a pig and get diarrhea. It'll be best if it happens when he's in the middle of some vitally important presentation.

When it's time to pay, I realize I don't have the money for all this. Grant didn't give me anything, either. He better not expect me to pay for his snacks.

—Me: Hey, what do I do if my boss didn't give me a credit card or anything and asks me to buy something for him?

—Marjorie: What store?

—Me: Bobbi's Sweet Things.

—Marjorie: No prob. We have a contract with them. Just tell them it's for us. Lemme send you our account # with them.

—Me: Thanks.

I sigh with relief. I should've gotten the information about all this before leaving. If Marjorie wasn't the type to check her phone every time it pinged, I'd be screwed.

When I return to GrantEm, almost ninety minutes have gone by. I enter Grant's office with the pastries.

"Here. Everything you asked for." I place the boxes on the table between two couches.

He comes over and starts opening the boxes, inspecting the pastries closely. Does he think I spat on them? I wouldn't do that, not even to him. Unlike some people, I have standards of decency.

He folds his arms and scowls at a chocolate scone.

"Any problem?" I ask, knowing I have everything he asked for. Of course, he could pull another dick move and insist that I forgot something and make me go back.

"No," he says finally. "And the jewelry? Were you able to return it?"

"Of course." I hand him the envelope from the store. "It's all in there."

He snatches it from my hand and tears it open, then glares at the paper. "You didn't fake this, did you?"

I roll my eyes. "Feel free to call them and ask."

He doesn't, though. He crumples the paper and throws it into the trash can by his desk. From the tic in his chin, I guess he's upset I accomplished all my tasks successfully. *Heh-heh-heh.*

He leans back, resting a hip against the edge of his desk. "You need to create seven memos before you go home. It's in the assistant's folder under my name in the intranet."

Finally, a reasonable request. Maybe he's given up for the moment after the two childish, bullshit assignments.

He grabs a scone, then waves me off. "Take the boxes and hand them out to the team."

As I follow his instructions, I realize I bought just enough for everyone but me. Wow. What a dick move. It's petty, but just pointed enough to make me feel excluded, especially as the area is replete with the scent of baked yummies.

Amy glances at my empty hands. "Wanna split this croissant?"

"No, thank you." I smile. "I'm not really hungry." In fact, I'm dying for a bite because I didn't have breakfast. But for all I know, Grant could be spying on me and do something asshole-worthy if I eat anything. Like make me run a mile, just because.

"It's actually too big for me, and I normally throw out about half," she says. "I'd hate to do that." She tears it down the middle and offers half with a warm smile.

"In that case, thanks." I take it and start nibbling.

"And next time, grab one for yourself," Amy says.

"And have Grant have an apoplectic fit?"

She frowns. "He won't notice."

"He will." He's out to get me. I can feel in in my bones.

She shrugs. "Just tell him Amy said it was fine."

"Isn't he your boss?" Even if he hasn't told her to get on her knees and call him "sir," he probably treats her like dirt.

"Yeah, but he won't say anything. He's been behind since Renée quit. Give him a few days, and he'll get caught up, and things will be fantastic." Amy grins reassuringly.

I smile back, but there's absolutely nothing that could make what's between me and Grant "fantastic."

And Grant makes sure my prediction comes true. He dumps a mountain of to-dos on me, and I work through lunch to get them finished.

"I don't like the summary section on the memo," he says, glancing at the executive memo I drafted.

"What about it is an issue?" I ask calmly, since he might have legitimate objections to my work.

"Everything." He smiles. "Perhaps you should consider redoing it."

I see. I smile back, while fantasizing about punching his face until his nose is bloody. "Sure."

Every memo is rejected with some vague notes of dissatisfaction. He never says thanks and never says he's satisfied.

On my fourth revision, he sighs. "Guess this is the best I can expect. Tragic."

It's really hard to smile when you're grinding your teeth, but I manage.

"I should've told Emmett I preferred someone with a degree in English or something."

The reminder of what I gave up sucker-punches me. I inhale sharply, praying he doesn't notice, but a satisfied look appears on his face.

Asshole.

"It's too bad none of the degree holders could satisfy your brother. He seems like a sharp guy. It's really unfortunate that he's married."

Grant scowls. "What does that mean?"

I infuse enough sugar into my voice to cause diabetes. "I'm just saying it must've broken a *lot* of female hearts. A sweet man with discerning taste and intelligence? Really rare. One of a kind, really. I certainly never thought such a life form existed until last Wednesday. And to discover that he's related to *you*? It was like finding teeth in a hen."

He snorts a laugh, but his eyes remain cold. "You think you're so clever."

"I *know* I am."

"Then why don't you join me for a team-building event and wow me with your cleverness?"

What's his plan? Make me scrub toilets with a tiny, toddler-sized toothbrush? He should know better than to expect me to give in.

I paste on my bring-it-on smile. "I'd be happy to."

He gives me an address. "Be there by four thirty—"

"No problem."

"—a.m."

I start. "What?"

He smirks. "I thought clever people would know such a simple thing."

Dickhead. "You want me to be there by four thirty in the morning?"

"That's what *a.m.* means."

This has to be some kind of hazing. "Is this part of my job?"

"Of course."

"Do all assistants do this?"

"Mine does. If you don't like it, you can simply quit. Nobody's stopping you."

I see what this is about. He doesn't even want me collecting unemployment. What an ass. He hasn't changed. Not even a little. "I'll be there. So what are we doing for team building?"

"Dress comfortably," he says cryptically.

He won't give me any further information, so I redo all my memos *again*, since he doesn't like any of them. Eventually he instructs me to send the first version of each memo to the relevant company director and partner. My blood boils, but I control my temper. It's just the first day. I knew he was going to be an ass.

When it's five, I straighten my desk and check off all my to-dos for the day. Zack wants to buy me a drink to celebrate my first day after work, and I'm meeting him at the bar where we both work.

I head over to Grant's office. "Do you have any last-minute tasks for me before I head out?"

He looks up from his desk and gives me a blank look. But it doesn't fool me. I can see his mind whirring. "It's not even six."

"Emmett said assistants work forty hours a week."

Grant scoffs. "Nobody on my team works forty hours. What do you think this is?"

What is he? Stupid? "A full-time job? So that means forty hours?"

"No. You work as long as necessary, until I say I'm satisfied."

"You gotta be kidding me."

"If you can't handle it, you can just turn in your resignation."

I want to strangle him. I do, really.

"This is a career, not a *job*. If you want a *job*, you go elsewhere. And since this is a career, you put in the hours necessary. Understood?" he says, addressing me like I'm intellectually challenged.

"Yes," I say with a fake smile. The only consolation here is that I get paid overtime. Actually, that may work out pretty nicely. I might even have some money left to save at the end of the month.

"Then get back to work. I'm not paying you to stand there like a tree."

30

GRANT

I roll out of bed at four, then let out a yawn. I was up until midnight working. Every associate did too, because we're that busy these days. As for Aspen...

Well, she stayed until midnight too. To be honest, there isn't much for assistants to do that late, but I made her write fifty additional memos. They are pointless tasks because Renée already did them before she quit.

But Aspen doesn't need to know that. And I like telling her she did everything wrong. Her eyes flashed murder, and I'm just dying for her to do something to get herself justifiably terminated. Or make her so mad she throws her resignation in my face.

I also enjoyed watching her march out of my office, while steam was coming out of her ears. When she's mad, there's an extra swing to her hips.

Not that I'm attracted to her, of course. I do *not* want to fuck her. Once was enough.

You did her more than once, a little voice whispers.

Stop being so technical.

I don't know why she's trying to continue her employment at GrantEm, but I'm not letting her get whatever she wants out of the firm. Most importantly, I'm not letting her near Emmett, especially after she spoke so admiringly about him. I don't need her wrecking his marriage. He's happy with Amy, and I'm not letting some gold-digging bitch ruin it. Little Monique won't grow up in a broken home.

I brush my teeth and put on a running shirt, shorts and shoes. Aspen should be here soon.

Ding-dong.

There she is. Four thirty a.m. on the dot.

I look at the intercom. She's in a car. It looks like a piece of junk...

Wait, is that the same one she had in college? It can't be. There's no way that thing would still be running.

Do not think about college. I buzz her in and watch her disappear into the well-lit driveway and the landscape. I hope she sees the enormous garden and the lavish mansion—all the marble and stone and crystal. I want her to weep and gnash her teeth that this could've been hers if only she hadn't betrayed me.

She knocks on the door. I let her into the glitzy foyer. It has a soaring cathedral ceiling and a giant chandelier made with Swedish crystal. Three François originals stand in the small nooks for *objets d'art.* Every inch of my home drips with wealth. Even Huxley admires it, and he doesn't impress easily. He's asked to host a few events here, but I've always turned him down. I don't like having people over. Other than my brothers—and staff—nobody's seen the inside.

Aspen is in a loose T-shirt and denim shorts. Her feet are encased in walking shoes that aren't ideal for running.

Well, she should've dressed better, I tell myself, although technically it isn't her fault, since I didn't tell her exactly what we'd be doing.

She glances around a bit, and I let her soak it all in.

Finally, she looks at me. "So where is everyone?"

Her eyes betray nothing. She might as well be in a typical middle-class home for all the reaction she has. And it's *very* annoying. She should be impressed. She should be sorry as hell. As a matter of fact, she *should* be so regretful that she's tearing up. "This is everyone. You and me. The team."

"Are you kidding?"

I hold her eyes. "Do I look like I'm joking?"

"Did you ask your other assistants to do this, too? The one who was with you before me?" Her tone says no wonder Renée quit.

"No," I answer with faux sweetness. "She had other responsibilities. Family. A child."

Aspen flinches. Does she have a kid? There's no ring on her finger, but that doesn't mean she hasn't been with other men or that she hasn't had some douchebag's baby. Surely she's gotten herself a new meal ticket after that disaster in college...when she must've realized she could've wrung me much drier.

The notion slides into me like a blade. It's a struggle to maintain a glib façade. "Are you going to tell me you have a kid too, like Renée?" I ask, my tone infused with mockery.

Aspen pales like I just pushed an ice pick into her heart. She looks at me like she can't believe I could be so cruel, and it makes me feel like an utter douchebag. The fact that she has the power to make me feel like shit only intensifies my fury. How can I react like this when I know she's faking it? Everything about her is a lie, designed to manipulate me.

Steeling myself, I stare back at her. *Your reaction means nothing to me.*

Finally, she says, "No."

"Then there shouldn't be any problem."

"So what are we doing?"

"Running for an hour."

"Running?" she repeats.

"Yes. That's how I build my team." *That's how I plan to punish you.*

"By forcing people to run at four thirty in the morning."

"Correct. A little cardio wakes you up better than coffee, it's healthy and it provides a great bonding moment."

"*And* it's an exercise to turn your people into homicidal maniacs."

"Mm. Well, if anything happens to me, my lawyer will contact the police and let them know who the last person to see me alive was."

"You want to put me in jail?"

"If it's deserved." But Aspen in jail *isn't* what I want. I want her to be defeated, to feel the pain I felt when I found out about her selling off all the nice things I'd given her because I cared for her. And that means I'm going to do everything in my power to ensure she quits.

"Fine," she says. "Well, no time like the present."

"I'll set the pace, and you'll follow."

"How come?"

"I'm the boss. You don't expect me to follow you, do you?"

"Oh, no. Not at all. Your ego probably couldn't handle it."

"Ego, schmego. I know I'm the best." I usher her outside.

The garden is huge and well lit, and making a circle around the periphery of the property will do. Besides, the view is nice—there's the water lily garden that looks like it popped straight out of a Monet, the tennis court, the colorful flowers, currently in full bloom, and the impeccably trimmed trees. The lime trees in particular smell fabulous this time of year.

I start at one of my faster paces. Although I work like a dog, I also keep up with my exercise regimen, and I run three times a week. Most people aren't that diligent, and Aspen probably isn't either. I expect her to cry uncle. Beg for mercy. If she says she'll do anything, I'll tell her the only way to end this is to quit.

She keeps up for about ten minutes, but after that, she starts wheezing. Part of me wants to slow down a bit, but I steel myself. Jesus, I'm trying to make her so miserable she surrenders and gets the hell out of the firm. Who cares if she pukes in the middle of the run? I'll make her clean it up, or it's going into her performance eval.

Assuming she lasts long enough for one.

When I realize she's falling behind, I make a half-circle and run back. "Faster! We don't have all morning!"

She glares at me. If she could, she'd strike me with lightning.

Lucky for me, she doesn't have that kind of power. I turn forward and pick up speed. I hear her feet slapping the ground faster. She's breathing like she's dying.

She might pass out, a concerned voice says.

I grit my teeth. I'm not going to care if she passes out. And I'm not going to do anything about it if she does. God damn it. I want her to suffer.

An hour later, I'm standing in front of the mansion's main entrance. She reaches me about ten minutes later, arms flailing like a broken marionette's, then folds over, a hand on her left side. Sweat runs down her body in rivulets, and her face is so red, it looks like an overripe tomato.

Part of me says I should give her a moment to recover. And maybe something to drink. Since she doesn't have a towel, I should bring one out.

But I force myself to stand there, my hands clenched and legs rooted to the spot, so I don't do anything stupid to ruin what I'm trying to achieve. After all, I wouldn't have to do this if she wasn't so stubborn. Just what does she think she can gain by insisting on working at GrantEm?

"I'm going to grab a shower and go to the office. I suggest you do the same."

She can't even straighten herself long enough to look at me. "You want me—to shower—here?" she manages between wheezing breaths.

An image of her nude pops into my head—covered in slippery suds in my shower as water sprays the slopes of her lush tits, down her belly and into the V of her thighs...

Now my blood is hot for reasons that have nothing to do with the run. *Fuck.*

"You want me to provide you with a shower?" I scoff more harshly than necessary to hide my physical reaction. Then I slam the door in her face and go straight to my bathroom. My dick's so swollen, it's painful to walk up the steps.

I hope she didn't notice, because it'll be annoying as hell if she realizes she has any sort of power over me, even if it's something as dumb as causing me an unwilling erection. She'll find a way to screw with me.

I rip off my clothes and hop into the gigantic glass stall. Five showerheads pummel me with water while I wash myself more roughly than necessary. My dick doesn't care about my mood.

Down, motherfucker.

It bobs instead, its head touching my belly. Son of a bitch. I throb, and I have to do something about this before going to the office. I refuse to walk around with a hard-on, especially around Aspen.

Dammit. I grip my penis and pump it, closing my eyes and thinking about something filthy to speed up the process. Some porn I saw a while ago with the girl sucking a guy off and getting sprayed in the face. It was hot.

But it doesn't work.

I think of Yvette—before she dyed her hair. She wasn't so bad. Our time was satisfying, like a champagne brunch at Nieve is satisfying.

Still not happening. It's like my dick is saying, *You can do better, man.*

Shit. Why can't I just ejaculate? I have work to do!

An image of Aspen during that first time arises. The shyness in her voice, the unschooled but eager stroke of her hands. The desperate way she clung to me as I pushed her higher and higher. Her sharp cries. All the ways my body burned for her.

No, no, no. I try to shake off the memory. *That was all fake.* I've done everything in my power to scrub it from my thoughts. I even transferred so I could be away from the places we went together.

But it's too late. My whole body tightens, all the way to my scalp. My cum shoots out hard and hits the wall, leaving white streaks. I glare at it, breathing roughly. *Traitor.* Fucking traitor dick! This is unacceptable.

The endorphins from the run vanish. All I'm left with is fury and self-recrimination. The only sliver of comfort is that Aspen's never going to know what just happened.

31

ASPEN

I rush through a shower. I don't have time to dry my hair, so I just squeeze out the water and towel it semi-dry, then twist it up into a knot. It feels sort of gross, but I have no choice. I put on a white button-down shirt, black slacks and the same boring black shoes I wore yesterday and hurry out of my apartment.

My muscles protest. My side still burns, and I swear, I'm never going to be the same if Grant continues to make me run. The problem is I don't know how I'm going to get out of it. The only exception he said was if I have other responsibilities...like family or a kid.

He sure knows how to twist the knife, I think as the familiar pain lingers in my chest. It's an old pain, and it no longer has the sharp edge it used to. But that doesn't mean the wound doesn't hurt. Or that it hasn't left a scar.

The family that used to include my grandmother is now down to just me and Grandpa. And I don't know how long I'm going to have him before there's nothing but me left.

I give myself a mental shake as I climb into my car. Grant doesn't care about that sort of thing. He's a cold, calculating asshole who only cares about himself. I've given some thought as to why he's acting like

I'm the one who backstabbed him, but once I consider his ego, the explanation is simple: he's angry he didn't get to end the farce the way he wanted. I'm sure my disappearing like that wasn't part of his script. He was dying to see me on the day Heath and Will streaked. Grant probably wanted to see my reaction for himself and gloat over his win.

Holding a grudge over that for fourteen years seems petty and mean. But then, only a petty asshole would have made a bet like that in the first place. I won't excuse his behavior or even imagine he had a good explanation. My first time should've been special, but instead it's been tainted forever. Because of *him*.

By the time I trot—or limp quickly—into GrantEm, I'm ten minutes late. Crap. I brace myself for some nasty comments.

But thankfully, Grant doesn't seem to notice. He's at his desk, looking cool and collected as he goes over some files on his laptop.

Life really isn't fair. Grant's gorgeous, his dark hair perfectly styled and the expensive clothes fitting his lean, muscular body like the proverbial glove. It's perverse that, even knowing how toxic he is, butterflies flutter in my belly anyway. My sense of self-preservation seems to fail every time I'm around him.

Maybe he's like a predator that releases some airborne toxin to confuse and mesmerize its pray. I remember seeing on a documentary that some toads can do that. It's the only explanation for my thinking he looks this hot.

Don't let him know you still feel that old attraction.

I jerk my gaze from him and turn on my laptop. While it's booting, I go to the breakroom to grab some coffee. I'm going to need lots of it to stay awake.

"Late start?"

I turn at Amy's friendly voice. She's grinning as she grabs a coffee. Unlike me, she looks well put together in a blue dress that's perfect for the office, and her long golden hair is cascading down her slim back.

"How did you know?" I ask with an embarrassed smile.

"Your hair. It's wet."

"Oh." I tell her what happened this morning, sticking just to the facts.

"Oh my God, *what*?" She shakes her head. "That's so unlike Grant."

I give her a vague smile. She obviously doesn't know what a snake he really is.

"I mean, he likes to exercise, but he's never asked anybody to join him," she says.

Of course, I'm the *special* one. "He said it was work."

"Super weird. Anyway, he should've told you that you didn't have to go back home. We have showers here."

I grind my teeth. He never told me because he's a dick. Thank God for Amy.

She continues, "And a few rooms with small beds to snooze on. Some of us use them when the hours get too crazy."

"Do you work crazy hours all the time?" I ask, despairing that I might be stuck working until midnight every day. Thank God I only have the part-time gig at the bar now, but I'd like *some* sleep.

"Not all the time, but a lot. If you're looking for nine-to-five, you're in the wrong industry."

I swallow a sigh. I should've known this job as Emmett described it was too good to be true. *At least I get overtime,* although it's a small, sad consolation. I always try to get at least six hours of sleep. Grant cut that by nearly half. Maybe he's a vampire who doesn't need to sleep.

When I return to my desk, Grant is looking for me. I grab a legal pad and walk into his office.

"If you're going to be late, at least be at your desk so I don't have to waste time searching for you," he says, leaning back in his seat.

Guess he noticed after all. "If you'd told me I could shower here, I wouldn't have been late," I point out.

"I thought you'd read about it in the employee manual you love so much." His gaze rakes over me. "By the way, you're still dressed in Salvation Army rejects."

"Actually, they're from Macy's," I lie. They're from a thrift store.

His face twists derisively, then he fires out instructions. He wants me to make twenty photocopies of the documents on the table next to me and send faxes to some people in Japan. Then he asks me to work on a PowerPoint presentation from Bradley, one of the associates. Grant doesn't care for the color scheme, font or anything else, but he says Bradley has more important things to do than mess with the details. And he makes sure to use a tone that lets me know it's my job to do inconsequential and idiotic tasks for the people who matter.

If he thinks that's going to make me break down and cry, he has another think coming. I'm never shedding a tear over him.

"Do you have any specific template in mind I should reference?" I ask, all professional.

"No. It's up to you to figure it out." A corner of his mouth quirks up.

"It could go faster and more efficiently if you'd just tell me what colors you'd like." *Especially since whatever I pick won't be good enough for the jerk-face.*

"This isn't kindergarten. You don't change PowerPoint to reflect your boss's color preference. Pick colors that are appropriate for the meeting."

I start to purse my lips, but catch myself and paste on a bright smile. I'd rather defecate in the lobby at eight thirty a.m. than let him know I'm bothered by what he's doing. "Got it."

"Like I said yesterday, you need to work on your 'yes, sir.'"

"I'll get right on that after I'm done with all my other tasks." I raise my legal pad and flip him the bird behind it. When I can quit this job, I'm going to shove my middle finger into his face—

Wait, what on earth am I thinking? The only way I could quit this job is if Grandpa didn't need to be at the Orange Care Center anymore. Suddenly I feel sick to my stomach that the thought of being able to quit ever crossed my mind. What's *wrong* with me?

Grant's eyes narrow, and he's looking at me closely.

Although I'm feeling shaky, I paste on an even bigger smile and leave his office. He's never going to know why I can't quit this job. If he knows how desperate I am, he'll hold it over me and abuse me further. He's the worst kind of bully.

I start to cross off everything he asked me to do. Regardless of my personal feelings, he *is* still my boss here, and I gotta suck it up for Grandpa.

Of course, Grant is a supreme *dick*-tator, because he makes me spend over four hours redoing Bradley's PowerPoint.

Finally, I throw my hands up in the air. "Exactly what are you looking for?"

"A professional look that will inspire trust. But I suppose that's not something you're capable of pulling off." He makes an isn't-that-sad face.

"Inspiring *undeserved* trust isn't something I'm good at. But I guess that's why you're the boss."

He leans forward in his seat. "What's that supposed to mean?" he asks in an awful voice.

"Whatever you want it to, I imagine. Again, you're the boss."

"I've never done anything to deceive people."

"We can agree to disagree." I'm not bringing up what happened fourteen years ago. That'd betray how deeply I was hurt, and I'm not giving him the satisfaction.

"If you think I'm that terrible, you should quit. I won't stop you."

"The pay here is good enough to make me overlook your short-comings."

"Oh, that's right. I forgot. You can be had cheaply."

It feels like he just backhanded me. A tremor starts to run through my body, and I tense every muscle I can to prevent myself from trembling in front of him. Suyen was able to get almost two hundred thousand dollars after selling the stuff he gave me in Malibu. To me and Grandpa, that was a fortune that paid for the hospital bills, funeral costs and some of my college loans. But to Grant, I'm just a whore who sold herself cheap.

I breathe in slowly and count to ten. I'm not letting him know what effect his words have. He's confirming everything I already knew about him.

"I guess it looks that way to a man who only understands price. Not value."

"What does that mean?" he snaps.

"I'm sure you can figure it out. And while you do, let me just get right on the PowerPoint," I say, turning around. "Again."

As I open the office door and step out, I bump into Larry. He's a brown-haired, brown-eyed second-year associate of average height and a highly forgettable face. He apparently worked at Morgan Stanley and got a degree from Harvard, the school Grant must've transferred to, because who turns down Harvard? Larry looks at me oddly, and I realize he heard the preceding conversation.

Humiliation burns through me. Hopefully he'll keep his mouth shut, but what are the odds? I've never been that lucky.

Then again, who cares? I'm not here to make friends or get along. People can gossip and say whatever crap they want. None of that matters as long as I can get enough money to take care of Grandpa.

Grant makes me tinker with the slides until midnight, then says, "See you at four thirty."

"Of course." *I hope you get diarrhea.*

———

Unfortunately, he's healthy as a horse the next morning. Runs like a horse, too. Who knew a polo player could run so well? Polo outsources running to the horses!

I follow him, feeling like I'm dying. My body just isn't designed to run, especially not so early in the morning, and most especially when it only had three hours of sleep in two days.

I'm not late for work, since I shower at the office, but Grant still nitpicks and makes me redo everything over and over. I run into Larry again outside Grant's office. He gives me a weird smirk, which I don't appreciate.

But he isn't the only one. There's Jesse as well. He graduated from Harvard, too—a fact that's impossible to forget because he talks about his Harvard years all the time. He sure clings to his stint there, like a security blanket. He should just have "I went to Harvard" tattooed to his forehead instead of constantly talking about it.

If Grant is trying to use overeducated associates to annoy me, he's failing. But the attempt doesn't surprise me. I've seen how bright-eyed frat boys can unite against a cause, no matter how idiotic, because one of them asked. Although Grant is their boss, I'm sure he's more like them than me.

Is he going to make them streak across the office, like he did with Heath and Will, to humiliate me in front of everyone at GrantEm?

If so, I'm not going to freak out and run like I did back when I didn't know any better. I'll record the entire thing and use it to sue his ass. Paying me millions in damages might not make a dent in his fortune, but I'd be able to quit this shitty job and flip him the bird as many times as I wanted.

But that's just a nice fantasy, because Larry and Jesse don't streak. And I'm stuck working until midnight, just like the associates and analysts, and getting up at the crack of dawn to run.

On Friday, Jesse comes over to my desk while I'm making yet another small and unreasonable tweak to my memo that Grant demanded.

"So. Like, what are you doing that you can't leave until midnight?" he asks, an insipid smile on his face.

If he thinks I'm going to be circumspect with him... "Work." He doesn't respond, so I add, "I'm sure you're familiar with the concept."

He flinches a little, and his cheeks turn bright red. But then he scoffs. "Sure. But I've never been dumb enough to redo the same memo until midnight."

"Did you just call me stupid?"

"Of course not. But if you feel the word applies..."

"For your information, I'm redoing the memo on *your* model. So ask yourself why Grant feels that he has to assign the task to me, rather than you." *Who's the stupid one now?*

"You—"

"Jesse, did you finish the due diligence I asked for?" Amy calls out from her desk.

He blanches, then hurries back to his seat.

I feel my lips twist with derision. He struts like an adolescent peacock, but he always gets subservient around Grant and Amy. I can understand Grant—Jesse wants to advance, and Grant is some-body who can move him up—but Amy? She's one of the smartest people I've ever met, and she has some seniority, but is that all? Jesse reminds me a lot of Heath, who thought that, because he was rich, I should've thanked him for groping me. Although Jesse probably doesn't have a trust fund like Heath, he's definitely the type to look down on anybody he thinks is less than him.

Amy tells Larry something, and he nods hard. I could've been like her, I think wistfully. If things hadn't gone so wrong fourteen years ago...

Because finding out about the bet and losing my grandmother wasn't everything. I would've gone back to school in the fall if that had been all. But...

Depression starts to well up, and I shake it off. I can't do anything about the past. I can only play the cards I've been dealt, even if the hand is so awful I'd be better off folding.

At least I can sleep in tomorrow. Saturday... Ah... It's the sweetest word in English language.

At midnight, I give Grant all the memos and the corrections he asked for. "See you on Monday." *I'm free, free, whee!*

"Monday?" he says, looking up from his laptop.

"Yeah. Today is Friday." Maybe he forgot—

"Just because tomorrow's Saturday doesn't mean we skip our team building."

I blink slowly as I struggle to process what he's saying. "There's no way I'm working tomorrow." I have a shift at the bar, and I'm not telling Jenna I'm not coming in. I *like* her, and I'm not leaving her short-handed on Saturday night.

He raises an eyebrow. "I have work to do until noon. And I expect you to be here."

Choke him with my own hands or stab him with the letter opener next to his laptop? The former is laborious and takes too much time, but the latter is messy.

I concentrate on Grandpa and the overtime pay, desperately clinging to control. "I see. Yeah, fine. We can do that."

32

ASPEN

Grant wasn't kidding about people working on Saturday. A bunch of associates are in, including Larry and Jesse. Amy is missing, but then maybe she finished everything already or is working from home.

My head feels like it's full of wet cotton balls, but I drink two cups of coffee to get the gears turning. I don't know how Grant can function.

He spends most of the time in his office after telling me to do "whatever tasks need to be done." I have no idea what that even means, but I'd rather die than ask.

So I tinker on my laptop and do some admin stuff, like filling out my time sheet, which is due next Friday. I also organize his calendar, making sure everything looks great.

I see a lunch appointment with Yvette on Monday. I almost do a double take at the two red hearts next to "Yvette." That doesn't seem like something Grant would do. But his previous assistant was apparently a no-nonsense woman. She also didn't work until midnight because she was that efficient—and because Grant didn't hate her and make her redo everything two million times just for the hell of it. So...I kinda doubt the hearts were her doing.

Guess the double hearts are Grant's thing. And this Yvette must be somebody he's dating.

The weirdest feeling comes over me. Of course he's been with other women after fucking a girl who was just a bet to him. I just wonder how he labeled me on his phone. Bet-sy? The Idiot? Easy Lay?

If he's putting hearts next to her name, maybe she's the one he's going to marry. My gut churns harder, and I realize I'm angry and sad and resentful. He's won—moved on and is leading a fulfilling life with money and respect and power. Whereas I lost and am going fast down a one-way street that ends in a brick wall.

It's so unfair. Why couldn't I have just one win? Something I could look at and be happy about?

The lunch appointment also has a note underneath: *Send a bouquet of white lilies to Yvette's home before lunch.*

They must be Yvette's favorite, I think bitterly, and make sure to order the biggest and most expensive one to be delivered on Monday, while praying Grant develops gout before then. It would serve him right.

I leave at noon without telling Grant. He said the work was ending at noon, and I don't want to give him an opportunity to dump more bullshit busywork on me. I always visit Grandpa on Saturdays, and I want to do that before the evening shift at the bar. Although the Orange Care Center is a great place, I want everyone to know he's loved, and that I'm keeping an eye on him.

I'm the only one he has. And he's the only one I have. I've grown apart from my friends, even Suyen. We just aren't in the same place anymore. She graduated Napa Aquinas College, found a job at a vineyard like she always wanted and now is married with two gorgeous children. Last I heard, she was busy with work and her local PTA, which doesn't surprise me, but we haven't seen each other in ages. We only know what we're up to when we see each other's posts on social media. Zack's the only one from my college years who's still in my orbit, but he'll move on soon enough when he falls in love with the right girl and realizes he needs to do something more with his life than bartending.

The only constant in my life now is Grandpa. I don't know what I'll do without him, even as I lose a little more of him each day.

The center is a bright yellow building, like someone squeezed the sun into a large square box. Sunflowers grow in the left section of the garden. Last year, they had red and purple morning glories there. They change every year, based on the residents' votes.

"Hey, Aspen," Gi-Hoon says. He's one of the center's weekend receptionists, a father of three, and his mother lives at the center. The fact that he chose to put his own mom here is one of the things that weighed most heavily in my decision to pick this place over the others.

"Hi." I sign in.

"You look tired. Long week?"

"Yeah. I started a new job."

"Good for you." He smiles. "Kenny's in the activity room."

I smile back, then head to the memory unit on the third floor and go into the huge activity room. Other seniors are watching some kind of standup comedy on TV and hollering lines that don't make any sense. But it doesn't matter as long as they're enjoying themselves.

I find Grandpa sitting by the window. The tan, robust man who seemed as solid as a thousand-year-old oak is gone. Now he's frail, with almost translucent skin. He doesn't seem as tall as he used to, but he still stands with his back straight and shoulders spread like a dancer.

"Hi, Grandpa," I say softly, praying he's having one of his better days.

He turns around and smiles. "Kat."

I hold my breath, wondering if it's going to be one of *those* days, then quickly paste on a smile, not wanting to distress him. His eyes are clear, but he isn't quite with me today. He confuses me with Grandma often. His mind refuses to accept she's gone.

He takes my hand in his and tugs me closer. "Look at the sunflowers. Aren't they pretty? They almost look like your favorites."

"Yes, they do," I whisper, not wanting to tell him the love of his life is gone and I'm his granddaughter. I tried correcting him the first few times, and it only led to confusion, denial and anger. I honestly don't know how much time we have left together. Every time I come over he seems to have grown visibly older, and I don't want to waste our visits.

"I voted for yellow daisies." Mild annoyance crackles in his reedy voice. "But some bastards outvoted me." He studies my expression, like a child trying to gauge his parents' reaction to his excuse as to why he didn't do well on a test.

I give him my best smile. "It's okay. Sunflowers are beautiful."

He grins with relief. "I think so, too. Next year I'll definitely get those daisies."

"I'm going to hold you to that promise."

He nods. "Don't worry, Kat. You'll love them." He turns away from the garden. "By the way, shouldn't we be practicing? The competition's only three weeks away."

"Is it?" He must be back in time when he used to compete in dance contests with Grandma. He likes to slip into happier memories, and I try not to pull him out of them.

"Yeah. You should've dressed in a skirt."

I look down. I'm in my slacks. "But I'm in the right shoes." I show him my Mary Janes.

"And you look gorgeous no matter what you wear." He looks at me, his eyes shining with endless love.

My throat tightens. How happy Grandma must've been to receive this kind of deep devotion. He's been true to her all his life, even after her death. At that point he was still lucid, still dashing. But he wasn't interested in anyone else. Once Grandma was gone, it was like whatever love he could give drained out of his heart.

He hums some tango beats, and I dance with him. Despite his age, he moves pretty well. It's as though his body hasn't lost its memory. I keep up with him, doing all the fancy steps I saw Grandma do, trying to bite back the tears over how frail he feels, how he's retreated into his memories to escape from pain. I tell myself it's great he can still dance so well. That means he's healthy. He's going to be with me as long as possible, and I'm not going to be alone in this gargantuan city that cares about no one.

"I missed you so much, Kat," he says, his voice breaking.

Wait... Does he...?

"I'm so lonely. Don't leave me." His hold on me tightens as we reach the climax of the tango. Instead of finishing the dance, he hugs me tightly. "Kat, I'll do better. Don't go." He sounds like a lost boy.

I pat his back, unsure how to console him. When he's like this, I'm overcome with helplessness. I hate it that I can't make it better for him. I hate it that I can't bring Grandma back from the dead. I hate it that I have to leave because I know he'll be inconsolable when I walk out.

"I'm not going anywhere," I say finally. I sound shakier than I want, and I inhale to steady myself. "Let's just keep dancing, okay?"

"Are you going to stay?"

I force a smile. "I'm here, aren't I? Let's dance."

He nods. "Okay. Let's tango."

By the time I leave Grandpa and come in for my shift at the bar, I feel like I'm a hundred years old. He was inconsolable when it came time for me to leave. Even when I promised to be back, he screamed, "Liar! You lying bitch!"

It shocked me to my core. I've never heard my grandfather curse like that. His face red with rage, he glared at me like I'd betrayed him. When I continued to stare in shock, he crumpled to the floor. "I don't wanna be alone. I don't wanna be alone. Kat... Kat..." He began to sob, rocking back and forth. I didn't know what to do. The outburst and the immediate breakdown weren't something I've seen before, and I didn't want to hurt him.

I squeeze my eyes shut. The doctors warned me he's not going to get better. They also said that Grandpa may exhibit a side of himself I've never seen before. That's apparently "normal."

But nothing about "lying bitch" coming out of Grandpa's mouth is normal. It breaks my heart that he's morphing into someone I don't recognize.

He's still the same person, I tell myself. *He's in pain, is all.* I put a hand over my mouth to swallow a small sob because I can't let it out. If I do, I'm going to break down, and grieving freely is a luxury I can't afford. I have responsibilities—somebody to provide for. I have to do my shift at the bar.

Composing myself, I check my phone for messages from the center, just in case. But there is only a text from Grant.

–Grant: Where are you?

He sent that at 1:23 p.m. The question stiffens my spine. It must be nice to be able to spend his time harassing a girl he screwed over, whose dreams he crushed, because I've never been the same after that awful incident. I've lost so much more than just my grandmother.

I pull myself together. Stewing in old anger isn't going to solve anything.

–Me: In a place called "not the office." It's the weekend, and you specifically said we'd work until noon.

–Grant: That doesn't mean you can walk out without telling me.

–Me: I followed your directive from yesterday.

–Grant: Irrelevant.

–Me: Would you like me to announce when I need to go to the bathroom as well?

–Grant: Yes.

Petty shitbag. I know he wants to get rid of me. For some reason he's decided what happened during our sophomore year was terrible, and *I'm to blame*. I don't know how. Maybe there was another part of the bet that I inadvertently ruined by leaving the campus. Because of that, he might've had to streak too. His pride wouldn't have been able to handle it.

I don't give a damn what his deal is, but I'm not going to waste more of my precious free time answering his ridiculous texts.

I put my phone into my purse and go into the bar. When I store my belongings in the employee locker and come out to the front, Zack waves. "Hey."

"Hi. I didn't know you're working Saturday evening too." He normally covers weekdays and Sundays.

"Mick quit, and so I'm picking up this shift."

"He quit? How come?" There are some dirty glasses in the sink, and I start washing them before it gets too busy. They need to be hand-washed so they look crystal clear. "I thought he liked it here."

"He eloped. And moved."

"Seriously?"

"Yeah." Zack begins to dry the glasses I lay on the rack next to the sink and place them up on the shelves. "Some chick he met in Vegas."

That sounds even more unbelievable. "How long have they been together? He never said anything about dating someone."

"No, they just met. He said it was love at first sight."

"Wow."

"Brave, huh?" Zack says. "I wouldn't have the guts."

"More like reckless. This is why people get divorced so much."

He gives me a vaguely disappointed look. "Kinda negative thinking there."

"Not negative, practical. You can be cautious and still get screwed over." Just like what Grant did to me. And I thought I was so careful back then. Obviously, I wasn't vigilant enough.

"Yeah, but sometimes things work out if you just give them a chance," Zack says. "There's a reason so many fairytale couples fall in love at first sight."

"Sure, in fairytales." I laugh. "You're such a romantic. But your girlfriend's lucky to have a boyfriend like you." I met the pretty redhead a few times when she came to the bar.

He concentrates on wiping a glass. "We broke up."

"Oh, no." I look at him with concern. "The instalove didn't work out?"

He shrugs. "She, um...couldn't be the princess I need."

"You're just picky." He hasn't been able to stay with the same girl for more than half a year. It's weird, because he's a really nice guy, and the girls he's been involved with seem so sweet.

"I think it's more like, I know what I want, and they're not it."

"Then why don't you go get it? Or, you know, her." If I were him, I would. Although he works at the bar, he doesn't have to. His grandfather left him a modest trust, which is enough to keep him comfortable as long as he isn't crazy with his spending. He says he likes bartending, but he never seems that thrilled to be dealing with customers. There has to be something else he wants to do with his life.

He shrugs again. "She doesn't see me the way I see her."

I finish washing the last of the glasses and dry my hands. "Have you made a move?"

"No."

"How come?" I twist around to see him. "Nothing ventured, nothing gained, right?"

"It's just... I don't want to ruin the friendship. I'm afraid if I screw it up, she won't even want to be friends anymore."

"Hey, don't look at me. I don't have the answer."

Zack gives a short laugh and turns away, arranging more glasses on the shelves. "Right."

I'd like to help, but my life is a complete mess. It's just that most people don't know because I try to avoid talking about it. Maybe my experience with Grant made me become even more private, but I don't want to turn into a source of somebody's entertainment. I have so little that I can't afford to lose anything.

Still, nothing ventured really *is* nothing gained. You don't get anywhere waiting for life to give you stuff.

I pat Zack's shoulder. "Just remember—the brave shall inherit the earth."

A customer enters the bar and approaches. I paste on a bright smile and take his order.

Love and dreams are for fairytales, another luxury I can't afford. Reality requires that I make money.

33

GRANT

Aspen doesn't text me back. She must've decided to ignore me, like she did when she took the things I gave her and split. The memory still hurts, but I force it aside. I will not continue to give it the power to humiliate me.

I'm focusing on what matters: she's my assistant, and I expect her to respond. And not leave until I tell her it's okay to do so. I wouldn't have stayed and watched the news on YouTube until twelve thirty if I'd known she was already gone. I would've napped, because I don't really have any work to do over the weekend and I'm tired from the lack of sleep. Although I'm generally high-functioning on four to five hours of sleep, three and a half for five consecutive days is pushing it.

I grit my teeth. Small price to pay to get rid of her.

But after a long nap this afternoon, I'm feeling more rested. And I'm not going to waste Sunday either. I know this war's going to be hard, since she undoubtedly went home to make up for the lack of sleep.

–Me: Show up at 4:30 a.m. tomorrow for the team building. It doesn't stop on Sundays.

If she doesn't check that message, it's on her. I'll give her the most epic reaming of her life so she'll have no choice but to quit.

I know what everyone whispers at GrantEm when they think I'm not listening. Emmett is an outright dick because he says what he thinks without any softening. He's a firm believer in the unvarnished truth. I, on the other hand, don't swing the ax of truth at associates. That's why I'm the nice one...with one caveat. Don't cross me to the point where I'll release my inner demon. I've only done it twice at the firm, over the gross incompetence of one analyst and one associate. Both of their eyes turned red with unshed tears of humiliation, and they resigned because they knew their careers at GrantEm were over.

Imagining Aspen crying makes me... I can't decide what I'm feeling. Not satisfaction. I know what that's like. Not victorious. Angry, maybe? Petty... Just a little bit of fuck-you, but...

Maybe a trace of sadness. Like...why the hell did it have to be like this?

I shake myself mentally. What the fuck? *She* screwed *me*. Of course it has to be like this! There is no other outcome that would be fair and right. She could've just quit when she realized I was going to be her boss, but she didn't. So it's on her and no one else. I'll go dancing when she resigns in tears.

On Sunday, Aspen shows up on time. There are dark circles that look like bruises under her bloodshot eyes. Didn't she sleep after leaving the office? She presses her lips together to hide a yawn, like yawning overtly would be admitting defeat.

Damn it. She's a tough opponent. But I'm tougher. Meaner. And more determined.

Something Griffin's wife Sierra said crosses my mind. She mentioned that her ex used makeup to create fake bruises on his face to garner sympathy. It's possible that Aspen is doing the same. She's a girl, so she's gotta know what she needs to create convincing dark circles. There's no reason for her to *not* sleep like a lazy sloth all day long after she left the office yesterday.

God, how stupid am I? I almost got suckered *again*. I'm going to teach her I'm not the naïve idiot I used to be. Looking back on it, I was just pussy-whipped.

"Let's go," I say, my voice hard.

And we run. Actually, I'm running, and she's barely keeping up.

The back of my skull prickles constantly. Is she glaring at me? If we were in New Orleans, she would've visited a voodoo shop to buy a curse.

But she doesn't wheeze as hard as she did on the first day. She could be getting used to this, which won't do. Maybe I should pick up the pace a bit.

When we're done, she puts her hand on her back but doesn't double over. The arched-back pose is difficult to ignore. Her breasts are fuller, and I itch to free them from their sports bra and run my thumbs over the tips. My dick perks up at the thought.

Damn it. I absolutely *refuse* to jerk off to her again!

My jaw tight, I stalk into my house and slam the door in her face. I take three long, steadying breaths. My dick doesn't drop down. No, the fucker's rising higher.

Traitor! Quisling! There's a reason Benedict Arnold had *dick* in his name.

I march to the shower. The only—minor—consolation is that Aspen's never going to know I've been blowing loads thinking of her.

———

"You didn't go to the office yesterday," Aspen says accusingly in the Monday morning darkness. She's still sporting those bruise-colored circles under her eyes, which have to be from makeup because she had all day to get caught up on sleep. "You also didn't answer any of my texts." She rolls her ankles. The movements show off her long, shapely legs.

I give her a thin smile. Whatever come-hither move she's going to pull today isn't going to work. I got up extra early to jerk off before she showed up. I pictured her naked body again while I gripped my dick, but I'm not going to think about that now. "I never said we were working on Sunday. It's your fault for not asking."

The smile on her face stays, but her eyes scream, *Fuck you, asshole.*

"And as for texting... Need I remind you I'm the boss?"

"So?"

"That means I don't answer to you."

Her face scrunches. It must be hard to purse her lips and smile at the same time.

"If you don't like it, you can go elsewhere, where *you* can be the boss." I put so much condescension in my tone that it's impossible to miss the skepticism that she could be a boss anywhere.

Today, I set a faster pace. She does her damnedest to keep up. I have to admit she's got more resolve than most of my associates. She hasn't said a single word of complaint, which is also something. Larry would've been on his knees begging for mercy—but then, he's soft.

When the run's over, I go into my house before she can stick her tits out again. But my dick's already hard at the mere thought of her in a sexy pose. I glare at it. *What the hell is wrong with you?*

The fact that my dick isn't cooperating puts me in a foul mood. Maybe I should just get laid. Sex with Yvette was getting stale, and I suspect that not having decent sex in a while is what's making me have dirty thoughts about Aspen. She isn't *that* special. My libido keeps insisting that sex with her was the best I've ever had, but it's because my libido has the IQ of a turkey that was dropped on its head when it hatched. It was hot, but not *that* hot. It certainly wasn't the best. It couldn't be. Life can't be that cruel.

Still erect, I thumb through my contacts for a woman I can see later today or tomorrow for quick, no-strings-attached sex.

Damn it. None of them interest me. They're all pretty, but...

Shit. I feel like a guy who just wants a nice steak, but is surrounded by over-fried fish sticks. I toss the phone on the bed and get in the shower. *I will not touch my dick.* It's gotten into a bad habit. It got to come once, and I won't do it again.

Who's in charge now, dick?

I leave the house smug, but the feeling doesn't last long. Not because my penis stays up the entire time—it eventually gets the hint and behaves. The problem is I feel like there's a needle tip sliding across my nerves like a plectrum. Everything seems irritating. Even the sound of Bradley's voice annoys me as he goes over some numbers.

I glare at Aspen working on some bullshit task I gave her. Just look at her. Cool and collected, her eyes focused on the monitor. She occasionally tucks her hair behind her ear, a mannerism she had when she studied in the library for midterms. I hate it that I remember. And I loathe recalling how hot it was when her arm brushed mine, how felt like I was the king of the world when she looked at me with shining eyes as I explained econometrics to her. How exuberantly she kissed me.

There must be something seriously wrong with my brain. It hangs on to things I want to scrub from memory, then pulls those events out for me to relive like they're something precious.

With a great deal of pettiness, I focus on finding flaws in her. Other than the fact that she's a shitty gold digger who can't even latch on to a sugar daddy correctly... No, that thought isn't doing the job. Her clothes are...bad, as usual. Where is she finding them? They don't fit her as well as they should—she should have them altered—and they sort of make her look frumpy and boring.

Do you want her hot and exciting?

I scowl. Of course not, but it doesn't add up. She should be in her sexiest outfit and doing her best to sleep with me again. As a matter of fact, she should've been on her knees the moment she saw me, her lips around my dick. Or maybe she doesn't want to do that until I buy her a nice outfit, like I did before?

If that's the case, she's in for a severe disappointment.

After Bradley leaves, my phone pings.

–Unknown: Is this Grant?

Who is this? The next text comes fast, like the other person has anticipated that I'll be confused.

–Unknown: It's me. Sadie!

Sadie who? How presumptuous of this freak to assume I know her? I start to block the number.

–Unknown: Sadie Woodward. From college! Remember? We went to Napa Aquinas together.

Oh...*her*. That annoying stalker. How did she get my number? I changed it after I transferred. I didn't want anybody from college to contact me, and I most certainly didn't want Aspen to try to get in touch, to ply me with bullshit. As furious as I was, deep inside I knew I was too soft for her. If she'd given me just the right sob story back then, I might've cracked. Because I was that crazy about her.

Thankfully, the years have hardened me.

–Unknown: I got your number from Heath.

How the hell did *he* get my number? I haven't spoken to him or Will since I left Napa.

–Unknown: I heard you were in VC and wanted to pitch something. I have this amazing idea that can change the world.

Ha. Everyone says that, but most of the ideas are so unworkable it's mind-boggling that anyone would think a VC firm would be seriously interested. I start to resume blocking the number, but in my peripheral vision, Aspen looks up from her laptop and *bam*, my dick's excited. Again.

I hate this uncontrollable reaction. But then inspiration strikes. I'm trying to get her to quit, and what better way than to bring her college nemesis into the office as my guest? It'll be amusing to watch her choke as she's forced to be polite to Sadie.

–Me: Fine. I'll give you ten minutes.

–Unknown: When?

–Me: Arrange that with my assistant.

I give her Aspen's number and email.

–Unknown: Awesome. I knew you'd come through. You're the best! I knew you'd see the potential, unlike my boring father.

My lips twist. If her own dad doesn't want to touch it, it must be complete crap. He always overindulged his daughter, to her detriment. That's why she thinks everything that pops into her head is golden.

Larry comes in next, and I give him a cold look over the sloppy work he's done. He thinks he's special because he spent two years at Morgan Stanley and got his MBA from Harvard. He could've gotten his degree from God Almighty, and I'd still think he was a pretentious dumbass.

So I tell him exactly what I think about his poor deliverables. His face turns white, red, then back to white. He looks at me like I just called his dick small. Well, if he's using his penis to do the work, it must be damn inferior.

"QA everything before you send it to me," I say firmly. "Unless you're of the opinion that there are better VC firms out there for you."

"No. Of course not, sir." He snivels. If the door weren't open, he'd collapse on his knees. He's so spineless, he makes jellyfish appear rigid.

"Out," I say, turning my attention back to the chart I've been looking at on my computer.

"Yes, sir."

He shuffles his feet, moving like a slug, while making as much noise as possible. Does he think I'm going to stop him and take back anything I just said? "Faster," I say without looking at him. "Unless you want to stay here until well after three."

His feet slap the floor rapidly. He knows I can make his life hell for the next few weeks. Perhaps I should see if I can make him quit, too.

I hear a thump and something hitting the ground.

"Watch where you're going!" Larry shouts.

I grind my teeth. I open my mouth to tell him to shut the door and keep it down—

"You're the one who ran out of the office without looking," Aspen says.

My head snaps up before I can stop myself. Sheets of paper are spread around her. She's still holding some in her arms—it must be the copies I asked her to make.

From the angle of their bodies, it's obvious Larry ran into her. Other associates are craning their necks to watch the show.

Aspen crouches down to pick up the documents. When she reaches for a sheet in front of her, Larry kicks it away.

"Hey! What's your problem?" she says.

"What kind of idiot does busywork until midnight?" he sneers, unleashing the humiliation he felt at my reprimand on Aspen.

All the irritation that's been simmering since the morning run explodes into searing anger. I get to my feet and stalk out.

"What's going on?" I ask in my calmest voice.

"She bumped into me and got rude about it." Larry looks smug, certain I'll side with him.

My gaze slides to Aspen. She doesn't say a word in her defense. Instead, she continues to gather the papers.

It should satisfy me to know she doesn't expect me to be on her side. I wanted this, didn't I? But the fact that she won't even try to make her case pisses me off.

I'm an asshole, but I'm not unfair. I can see who's at fault here.

"Rude? *She* didn't call *you* an idiot." I keep my tone deceptively reasonable.

"Well." He clears his throat. "Why else would she be here until midnight every day? Renée wasn't."

"So someone working long hours gives you the right to call them an idiot?"

His eyes shift as he struggles to come out with the right answer.

"Who does Aspen work for, Mr. Carr?" I say, running out of patience.

Beads of sweat pop along his hairline, which has started to recede. He knows I never call anybody at the firm Mr. or Ms. unless I'm furious enough to fire them.

"Well?" I cock an impatient eyebrow.

"You, sir."

"Precisely. Which means what?"

"Uh... I should've let it go when she bumped into me?" The end of his sentence goes up higher than a note from a medieval castrato.

"Is that all?" He's thinking so hard, I can hear the gears in his head turning. "Are you me?" I demand.

"I'm sorry?"

"Do you think you are me?"

He swallows. "No, sir."

"Then you have no right to criticize my assistant." There's a vague voice in the back of my head that says if I want her to quit, I shouldn't be yelling at him. I should embrace people in the office being abusive to her. But the notion pisses me off. Nobody else gets to fuck with her. They don't have grievances with her the way I do.

Who the hell does Larry think he is? He can get in line to mess with her after she fucks him over, not before!

"I-I'm so-sorry," he says.

"Why are you apologizing to me? Did you call *me* an idiot?"

He almost jumps. "Of course not! Never!"

His protest feels flimsy because I've overheard him say shit about me, but I don't bring that up. He doesn't have to like me, just do his job.

He turns to Aspen, then glances at me again. His gaze says, *Are you sure you want me to do this?* It's as though he presumes that he ranks higher than her in the firm's hierarchy. He wants a way out without humiliating himself, since apologizing to her would be intolerable in his condescending, elitist worldview.

I glance down. Aspen's almost done gathering the papers. She doesn't even look at me. I don't know why that upsets me even more. She knows I'm not fond of her. As a matter of fact, I made it clear I want her gone. So why isn't she acting grateful that I'm verbally beating Larry up on her behalf?

And why do I care that she isn't looking up at me like I'm her hero? She won't quit if she thinks that. I need to get my head screwed on tighter, because I'm being stupid here.

Larry must sense my mounting fury, and he's smart enough to understand that it isn't all directed at him. He bites his lip, stalling.

Fuck this.

This entire scene is due to his being an obnoxious idiot who can't say he's sorry. For that, I'm going to make him pay.

"Guess the team is in worse shape than I thought. All of you will be joining me and Aspen for the team-building exercise."

Larry starts. "What's that?" Maybe he's finally realized he's misjudged everything—that he isn't very important to me or GrantEm. People with his qualifications are dime a dozen in the industry. Most of them are smarter, too.

"Be at my place at four thirty tomorrow morning. We'll be running for an hour, so dress accordingly. Afterward, I expect you to show up here—*on time*—fresh and ready to go."

Amy stands up, incredulous. "How long are we going to be doing that?"

Shit, I curse inwardly. I didn't mean to include her, but I can't exclude her now. It would make me look like I was unfairly favoring her, and she'd kill me if I did anything that could negatively impact her professional reputation. My irritation jumps up another notch. *Fucking Larry.*

"Until I'm satisfied that we're all on the same page." My tone is harsher than I intend. I don't explain what the "same page" means. These are smart people. They can figure it out.

Everyone glares at Larry, who can't meet anybody's eyes.

Amy breathes deep and clenches and unclenches her hands. She's probably fantasizing about strangling Larry. "Thanks, Larry." The words drip with sarcasm.

He turns paler than milk, his legs shaking. Serves him right. Emmett will never forgive him for depriving him of his wife so early in the morning. Unlike Amy, Emmett has no problem complaining —subtly, of course, so Amy doesn't find out—when I give her "too much work." Ironic, since he made her work past midnight every day when she was reporting to him.

Aspen stands with the papers clutched to her chest. She's studying me, and I can't figure out what's going on in her head.

Why should I care what she thinks? I'm the boss. "Aspen, email everyone my address. No excuses if anybody misses the exercise."

34

ASPEN

Grant goes back into the office and slams his door. Everyone flinches at the sound, then buries their heads back into work. Except Larry. He just stands in the same spot, staring wide-eyed at the door.

Maybe he's never been reprimanded publicly. Ah well, not my problem.

I place the papers I picked up on my desk and neaten the stack. Then I start drafting the email Grant asked me for. Given his mood, if I go into the office to give him the documents right now, he'll snarl about the email status.

I can't figure out what to make of his outburst against Larry. If I were a naïve college kid from fourteen year ago, I might've thought Grant was defending me, but he should've been holding a tub of popcorn and egging Larry on. Maybe even recording the incident so he could relive it.

Did Larry get on Grant's bad side? Or maybe he's just being crabby. He's been in a bad mood since he walked into the office this morning. Not sure why. He's usually happily satisfied after tormenting me with a ridiculous morning run.

I draft the email with Grant's address and read it over to make sure there aren't any mistakes or grammatical errors. He'd jump on them immediately—and maybe ask me to come in an hour earlier to run for *two* hours. I shudder.

Larry turns to me. "What are you doing?" he says, his voice low.

"My job," I answer without looking at him. I have nothing to say to a guy who treated me with such disrespect.

"You can't," he says shakily.

I turn my head in his direction. "I can't do my job?" Desperation is pouring out of him. He's actually sweating. "Says who?"

He struggles to say something, but every time he opens his mouth, nothing comes out. Finally, he runs a hand over his face, smearing the sweat. "Don't be difficult. You know why."

Do I look like I'm playing dumb? "No, I don't."

"Come on."

"You can say, 'Come on,' a billion times and I'll still have no idea what you're talking about."

He stares at me hard. I hold his eyes. His face crumbles, and he drops to his knees.

I gasp. I can feel others' gazes on us, although nobody's staring overtly, not after that verbal ass-kicking from Grant. Nobody wants to be next. "What are you doing?" I hiss. "Get up."

Larry's not listening. "Okay. I'm sorry I bumped into you and made you drop the papers. I should've helped you pick them up. I'm an asshole. I admit it."

Maybe he's lost his mind over having to run for an hour with Grant tomorrow morning.

"So be a good girl and say you're cool."

I raise both my eyebrows. "A *good*—?"

"And can you please talk him out of it?"

"No." If I had that kind of persuasive power over Grant, *I* wouldn't be doing the "team-building exercise."

Larry's brow furrows. "Look, I said I'm sorry."

"Yeah, but you didn't mean it. You only said it to get me to do something for you."

"Not for me. Just make sure that Amy doesn't have to go running."

I give him a look. Why does he care so much about her? "Do you have a crush on her or something?"

Amy has a ring on her finger, and it's probably not something Larry can afford. It looks ridiculously expensive.

Larry chokes. "Are you trying to get me fired?"

"Just asking."

"If Amy has to do this, I'm dead."

"How come?" She's so nice that I can't visualize her resorting to violence.

"Are you fucking stupid?" he hisses.

"No. But you are."

His jaw drops.

"Calling somebody 'fucking stupid' doesn't make them want to do something on your behalf. Didn't they teach you that at Harvard?"

His hands clench and unclench. He's probably fantasizing about choking me. I check my desk, noting the position of my letter opener.

"Amy is married to Emmett."

She is? I would've never guessed from her friendly attitude. And the number of hours she puts in.

"If he finds out what happened, he'll *murder* me. Amy just had a baby not too long ago."

My eyes swing in her direction. She doesn't look like somebody who had a baby recently. She's so energetic, so bright, without the dark circles and exhaustion I associate with new moms.

Or maybe people who had a normal pregnancy and labor don't feel anything but happiness and blessing. Emmett probably spoiled her rotten. He seems like such a nice guy.

Larry continues, "Apparently, she didn't have an easy time of it. Emmett's not going to forgive someone who makes her life more difficult than it has to be."

That explains Larry's panic, and everyone else's reaction earlier. I'm still not sure why *I* have to fix the situation, though. If Amy doesn't want to show up at Grant's house tomorrow, she can talk to him directly.

I turn to my laptop and hit "send."

Larry gasps. "Did you send it to Amy too?"

"Yep. She reports to Grant."

"You bitch!" He jumps to his feet. "I can't believe this! I even begged you on my knees!"

I shrug. "Your choice."

He turns purple. I didn't know people could actually be that kind of color.

"If you're going to have a tantrum, the bathroom's over there." I pick up the stack of documents, hugging it to my chest. "Now if you'll excuse me, I have to see Grant. Try not to bump me again."

The fight drains from Larry, and he moves away from my desk. I walk to Grant's office and knock.

"Come in."

I step inside. He's reclining on one of the couches, reviewing something on his tablet. Three furrows are etched between his pinched eyebrows.

"What?" he says, starting to sit up.

I put the documents on his table. "Here's what you asked for this morning."

He grunts a sound that's somewhere between *thanks* and *fuck off*—it's hard to tell with him—and glares at me like he's pissed.

I remain standing—which gives me the advantage of towering over him—and stare back. He's mad when I'm working; he's mad when I'm not working. The fact that I breathe seems to irritate him. There's no pleasing this man.

"Why were you taking that kind of shit from Larry?" he says finally. "You don't take anything from me."

"I didn't want to make a scene." I keep my tone mild. One of us has to be rational.

"So you're gonna let him stomp all over you?"

"He's taking his cues from you. So I don't know why you're upset," I reply, and Grant flinches. "You never respected me in any way," I elaborate, in case I wasn't clear.

"*That's* your excuse?" he says.

It's all I can do to not roll my eyes, only because I need this job for Grandpa. "Fine. Next time something like this happens, I'll make a scene so awful we'll have to get HR involved."

"You'd better."

This man is crazy. I should quit trying to understand his logic because there is none. He does whatever he wants and doesn't care about consequences. It's like he hasn't changed even one bit since college.

I want to flip him the bird—mentally, of course—and leave. But a tiny part of me hates owing anybody. I'm not an unmannered, uncivilized jerk like him. "Anyway, thank you."

He looks at me like I just threw acid at him. "For what?"

"For what you did out there. You didn't have to defend me."

"How others treat you is a reflection on me."

Of course. I should've realized it wasn't about me. Why did I bother to thank him in the first place? Still, I have one more thing I need to get off my chest. "By the way, I think maybe you should not have Amy run."

"Why not?"

"Didn't she just have a baby? She probably wants to spend some time with it."

Grant squints at me. "She told you that?"

"No. Larry did."

"Apparently Larry doesn't have enough things to do."

I say nothing. Knowing Grant's vindictive pettiness, Larry won't be going home until three for a while.

"I couldn't do that even if I wanted to. Amy specifically does not want any special treatment."

Amy's a better woman than me, because I would've used whatever I could to avoid running. But then, I know how awful it is. She probably doesn't.

"Also, it isn't your job to speak to me on Larry's behalf. You work for me," he says.

"Sure." I say it to humor him. Who knows what's going to trigger his next explosion?

"Besides, if you dressed better, maybe Larry wouldn't have been such a dick. He is shallow and judges people by the way they dress."

Oh, this again.

"You look like shit. Frumpy. Just awful."

Wow. He's extra grouchy today. "Thank you, Grant. That's exactly what every employee wants to hear from their boss. When HR updates its manual to indicate how much I ought to spend on my wardrobe, I'll get right on clothes shopping. Until then..." *Fuck you, fuck you, fuck you.*

"We've never *had* to make it a policy because people here just don't dress the way you do. Homeless people wear better clothes."

"I'm impressed you're such an expert on homeless fashion. Who would've known, given the billions in your bank account?"

My sarcasm flies right over his head. "I don't keep my money in a bank account. That would be stupid," he says.

"So is stuffing your mattress. Anyway, if you're done being a snob, I have real work to do."

"You mean the work *I've* assigned you?"

What wouldn't I do to wipe that superior expression off his face! But before I can fire off a response, the door to his office bursts open and a lithe redhead barges in. She's in a skintight white dress that leaves *nothing* to the imagination—I think I can see her nipples—and her bright hair swirls like flames around her stunning face. A cloud of expensive perfume follows her as she comes in.

"Yvette?" he mutters, rising to his feet.

Oh. So *this* is the woman with two hearts after her name? I take another look. She definitely has the body to deserve those hearts.

"I'm so glad we cleared up our misunderstanding," she says breathlessly. "I knew you'd realize you'd made a mistake if you gave yourself some time!"

Confusion clouds Grant's face, but the woman doesn't seem to care. She runs toward him, tottering dangerously on her stilettos, and opens her arms, ready to hug him like she'll never let him go.

He raises a hand, palm out like a shield. Her forehead smacks into it, and her body twists as one of her legs goes up high. Her other foot slides on the slick floor, and she lets out a yelp as she crashes butt-first into the ground. Something rips. She lies there a moment, her long limbs spread out. The dress is split on the side and back, revealing a generous expanse of smooth, tanned flesh.

I cover my mouth with both hands. *Oh my God.* Before I can ask if she's all right, she screeches.

"What the hell? That was *so mean!*"

"Not any more than your trying to assault me!" he says.

"Why are you acting like such a jerk? You sent me flowers!"

Oh no. She came here because of the flowers I sent...? I feel extra terrible. I should probably offer to help her get up.

Grant lets out a loud snort. "I did no such..." He trails off and swings his fiery gaze at me.

I feel like I'm being seared by the laser of death. I clear my throat. "It was on the calendar. There were two hearts next to her name."

"Only two? I'm worth more!" Yvette says.

"No, you aren't, because you weren't going to last more than two months," Grant says.

My jaw slackens. The hearts mean how many months he's planning on dating the person? Holy... What a dickhead rating system!

Part of me vaguely wonders how many were after my name, but I shake off the pointless curiosity. It doesn't matter, since I left him first.

"What's *wrong* with you?" Yvette says.

"Nothing. It's all you."

"Me? What's wrong with *me*?"

He looks at her like he can't believe it has to be said. "Everything!"

"Like *what*?" she yells, shaking with rage.

"Your face. Your voice. Your brain—or lack thereof!"

Yvette blinks. She looks at me as though she's expecting some backup, but I'm not getting involved in this.

"At least I have a nice body!" Yvette shouts.

Grant shrugs. "I've seen better."

Wow. His callousness is stunning, but not unexpected. He's just that kind of person. I lucked out when I discovered it back in college. If I'd stayed with him longer, I might've lost all pride and sanity—like Yvette—and ended up screaming about why he should still like me while sprawled on his office floor.

Grant turns his fury in my direction. "Check with me before you send any more gifts!"

Should've expected him to blame me. "Got it."

"And get her out of here. Permanently." He gestures at Yvette like she's trash soiling his office.

"Okay." I help her up gently. "Come on."

She barely resists. Actually, she's probably too stunned to do anything but meekly follow me out. "He is *such* a dick!"

I don't say anything, especially since everyone's holding their breath to hear my answer. Larry probably has his phone out to record me.

Silently agreeing with her, I merely gesture at the rips on her dress. "Do you need something to cover yourself up?"

She glances down. "Let 'em look. I have a toned body."

I escort her to the elevator bank. "Here you go. And sorry about the flowers. I didn't realize."

"No, honey, it's fine." She leans in. "When you're ready to fuck him over, you let me know, okay? I'll be there to record everything. Shit's gonna go viral."

I nod to placate her. "You'll be the first person I call."

35

GRANT

"Hey, bro, what the hell?"

I raise an eyebrow as Emmett comes into my office and closes the door behind him. It's twelve thirty p.m., and everyone's out for lunch, except me—because I have some stuff I need to go over while I munch on my beef and cheese burrito.

"Took you long enough." I expected him to barge in much earlier.

"Because Amy was at her desk until noon!" He sighs. "She works too hard."

"That's why she's the best. But I thought you'd be having lunch with her."

"I told her I had a call with some people in Hong Kong."

I laugh. I can't decide which is funnier, his terrible lie or her pretending to believe it. There's no way she bought that—it's three thirty a.m. in Hong Kong right now.

"So, what's up with making everyone on your team run at four thirty in the morning tomorrow?" Emmett says as he takes a seat, propping an ankle on the opposite knee.

"If you need me to explain it to you, you should give up your Stanford diploma."

"Oh, come on. You can't do that."

"Why not?"

"Amy's a new mom! She needs more sleep and time with Monique in the morning."

I'm not getting in the middle of this. "Fine. If she asks me, I'll make an exception for her. Considering her circumstances and all."

Emmett's face scrunches. "You know she's not going to do that."

"Exactly, and I'm not going to offer, since she'd murder me for treating her differently."

Frustrated resignation crosses his face.

"Why are you even here?" I ask. "You know it's going to piss her off, right? You should stop before she finds out. I'd hate it if you had to sleep on the couch."

"I never do that."

"It was a figure of speech. I expect you're smart enough to take one of the spare bedrooms."

He rolls his eyes. "When did you start running so early, anyway? You should quit that shit."

"Since we started the bet, which I plan to win."

"Wait..." His jaw hangs loose. "Are you making Aspen run with you?"

"Yup."

"She's going to hate you."

"Oh, I know." I smile, even as my chest starts to burn. I glance at the half-eaten burrito. The beef's probably bad.

Emmett shakes his head. "You are so going to lose."

"I don't think so. Unlike you, I don't care about anything except making Aspen quit. And she's going to, because I know all the buttons to push. And I will. Push. All of them. Hard. Repeatedly."

She fucked me over last time. It's my turn to fuck her over, with a lot of interest.

———

By Friday, everyone is dragging their feet like brain-deprived zombies. Aspen should be in the worst shape—she's been doing the runs for two weeks—but she's actually the most alert, other than Amy. What's her secret? The coffee in the breakroom? But we can't have anything special in there. If we did, the others would be fine too.

Annoyed, I get to my feet and stalk over to the breakroom. As I turn the corner and am about to enter it, I hear Jesse whining.

"This is *not* what I signed up for. Grant doesn't know the difference between team building and team punishing!"

"You gonna put that on the upward feedback?" It's Sasha's voice.

"Maybe," he grouses.

"Go ahead," I say as I enter the breakroom.

Jesse jumps half a foot in the air, spilling coffee all over his shirt. "Shit!"

"Are you okay?" Sasha says, handing him a fistful of paper towels.

"Yeah, I think so," he says, giving me a careful sidelong glance. He isn't looking at his shirt. He has a more pressing problem.

"Did you burn yourself?" I ask mildly.

"Not at all, sir." He slinks away, walking sideways like a wary crab with his eyes on me until he reaches the door, then dashes off.

"Wow. You put God's fear into him." Sasha smiles. She used to work for me and still knows everyone who reports to me. "What's up with that? You're supposed to be the nice guy."

If she thinks that'll persuade me to change my attitude, she thinks wrong. "I *am* nice, as long as they do their job."

"Mm." She checks her watch. "Gotta go. Have a meeting." She trots out fast.

She's probably trying not to cross me. I've heard Emmett's in a crummy mood these days as well, probably because Amy's running with everyone else in the morning.

I make myself a cup of extra-strong coffee, then return to my office.

Aspen walks in, carrying a legal pad like a shield. "I just wanted to confirm with you about the steakhouse dinner with your brothers on Saturday at seven."

I nod, looking at her with my eyes narrowed. She's still in the cheap clothes. I don't get it. Does she think it's going to inspire some pathetic urge for me to buy her new things, like I did before? People like her don't change. She has to have been hopping from man to man, milking them as dry as she could.

She's still beautiful enough to con men. The smooth skin. The wide moss-green eyes. The full lips. The perky breasts and long, shapely legs. As a matter of fact, her legs have gotten better over the years.

"Great. And I need you to sign off on this time sheet," she says.

I frown. I've never had to sign off on time sheets before. "For what?"

"If I put in more than fifty hours a week, I need your signature on it. And I've been putting in over eighty-five."

"What?" I tilt my head. "That's the most ridiculous thing I've ever heard."

"How so?" Aspen looks genuinely confused. "HR probably wants to keep us honest."

"I've never signed off on time sheets, and everyone puts in over fifty hours a—" A horrible possibility slams into me. "Do you get paid overtime?"

She nods serenely.

What the fuck? "Why didn't anybody tell me?"

"I thought you knew. It's your company."

Her answer shuts me up. But it doesn't quell my outrage. I'm even more furious she's right. But how the hell am I supposed to keep track of things like that? That's the job of HR!

Wait a minute... Emmett knew about this! When I told him I was making Aspen run with me, he only said I was going to lose.

Bastard!

I jump to my feet and stalk out of my office, leaving a stunned Aspen behind. I march to Emmett's office and barge right in. Marjorie doesn't stop me, but then, she rarely stops anyone from entering her boss's office.

"You asshole!" I say as I shut the door behind me.

He looks up from a thick pile of documents. A smile slowly splits his face. "You saw the time sheet?"

"You *knew*!"

"And...?"

"Why didn't you say something?"

"You didn't ask." He shrugs, but his attempt at nonchalance fails because the bastard can't quit smirking. "Also, it was more fun to watch you dig that hole." He puts the file he's working on to the side. "I thought you knew, but you were making her work insane hours anyway to force her into quitting."

I do the math. "She's going to get paid almost as much as an associate with an MBA! That's gotta be illegal!"

He shrugs. "Talk to Jeremiah."

Fuck. For Emmett to be this smug, he knows I'm stuck. He probably already spoke with her.

He continues, "But I'm pretty sure it's legal. Not paying Aspen for the hours she's worked would be illegal, though. She's not on salary."

"You're just pissed because I made Amy run, too."

"No. Actually, if you'd exempted her, I would've been in a lot of trouble. So thanks for that."

I return to my office. Aspen's at her desk, and I gesture for her to follow. She stands and enters my office and shuts the door behind her.

I sit at my desk and tap my fingers on the desk. Gotta cool down and figure out the next step. "You don't have to join the team-building exercise anymore."

"Are you sure?" Aspen says. "I don't mind."

She's giving me a neutral smile, but I know what's behind it. *Heh-heh-heh, fuck you.*

No wonder she didn't argue too hard to get out of it. I've been outmaneuvered and used. At my own fucking firm. That never happened until she popped back into my life.

What is it about her that does this to me? No other woman has ever been able to use me or fuck me over. Just her.

"*I do*," I say smoothly, fighting the urge to snarl. Showing how pissed I am would be admitting defeat. This is just one minor skirmish. The war isn't over yet. "And once you get paid, upgrade your wardrobe."

"What's up with your obsession with my clothes?"

"I don't like it when people dress to inspire pity." I hate it that she keeps trying to remind me of how she was when we first met.

She might not have the selection of men she used to. After all, she isn't as young as she used to be—although she's still annoyingly gorgeous—and might think this is her final opportunity to make a big play. She might assume I'll still be weak for her, if she can just remind me of the good times we had.

I won't be played. Never. It doesn't matter how carefully she's plotted everything. I don't believe for a second that she didn't know Emmett was my brother or that GrantEm was the firm we cofounded.

She needs to dress like the slick, money-grubbing bitch she is, in designer clothes, carrying purses that cost more than most people's rent. I'd wager my Maybach that she dresses fancy when she's at a bar to hook up with some rich guy.

The notion annoys me further. I don't want her all over some rich asshole, not because I have feelings for her, but because nobody should fall victim to her greedy ways.

In addition, the most indisputable proof of her duplicitous nature is the fact that even though she puts on shitty clothes, she makes sure they don't hide her curves. I've seen others at the firm checking out her ass. Fuckers. I should dump more work on them. If they have time to stare at her ass, they have time to do another financial model.

36

ASPEN

I actually feel human again after six days of decent sleep. Not only did Grant quit asking me to run with him at four thirty a.m., but he also started to let me go home before six.

As nice as extra free time is—and if this continues for another week, I plan to ask the bar for evening shifts during the week—I'm going to miss the overtime pay. My first paycheck will hit my bank account on Friday, and it's going to be epic. I've never made this much before, ever. I didn't even think it was possible.

I made a reservation at the fancy steakhouse Grant and his brothers go to, for myself and Grandpa. I want to celebrate my new job and treat him to something nice. Time is so finite. I'm not making the same mistake I did when I was in my twenties, thinking I can always spoil my grandparents with something nice later, when I have more money. I regret that I never got to do anything really nice for Grandma, and I don't know how much time is left with Grandpa. He's so frail now, his mind more lost in the past than lucid in the present. Not that I blame him. He's reliving his happy moments, when he and Grandma danced, competed and loved.

I just wish he could remember that I'm here, too...that *I* need him. There are times I'm terrified that I'll be alone. That I'll make the news because my landlord comes over to evict me for not paying the rent for weeks and they discover my body. Or maybe the neighbors call the police because they smell something decomposing. It's pretty depressing to read stories like that. And every time I do, I feel like I might be next.

The steakhouse said they could only accommodate me on Saturday at six fifteen, about forty-five minutes before Grant and his brothers' dinner reservation. They also confirmed they can seat us at a table far from the one set aside for the Lasker men—although the reservation clerk seemed to think it was an odd request. But I don't care. I don't want Grant to see Grandpa. Not out of any sense of shame, but because I don't want Grant to twist that into something he can use to hurt me. Back in college, I would've never dreamed he'd do such a thing, but now...I wouldn't trust him to not kick a puppy.

Just look at how he abuses the people working for him. He's still forcing that horrible morning torture on them. Everyone's miserable. Even Amy comes in looking half-dead.

I'm in the breakroom grabbing some afternoon coffee when Jesse approaches. He looks like warmed-over roadkill. The dark circles under his eyes reach halfway to his chin.

"Aspen." His eyes seem to glow with an almost religious fervor.

"Hi, Jesse," I say, taking a small step back.

"I just wanted to say..." He licks his lips, the flick of his tongue like a snake.

I brace myself for anything. Larry surprised me with his rudeness, and who knows what Jesse might do? "Yes...?"

"Do you think you could take one for the team?"

He's staring at me like I should know what he's talking about, but I don't. "Uh, what exactly would this 'taking one' entail?"

"Grant was a great, reasonable boss until you showed up."

"Okay." *I'll take your word for it, buddy.*

"But then he started to get weird."

He was always "weird," if by "weird" you mean a complete dick.

"I feel like you're the problem."

I fake a smile. "Well, we can agree to disagree." *Jerk.*

"It means only one thing."

"I'm not quitting," I say at the same time he says, "He wants your body."

I stop. Jesse does too. We stare at each other. I can't have heard him correctly. *Grant? Wants my body?* In what universe is that even a possibility?

"You're crazy, and that's putting it kindly."

"So are you. Why would I want you to quit?" He frowns. "Just... be open to him."

"I'm sorry?" Maybe there's another meaning for "be open to him." Some kind of super MBA lingo.

"He's not that bad. Supposed to be a great boyfriend. Never forgets an anniversary, all that."

Jesse must not know about Grant's heart-rating system. "I'm going to pretend we didn't have this conversation, not because I'm not offended, but because I feel marginally sorry for you that you have to go to Grant's place to run at four thirty a.m."

"But—"

"Unless you'd like me to take it up with HR?"

Jesse slinks away. But I wonder if others feel the same way about me and Grant. How ridiculous. There's nothing except bitter memories between us. Well, bitter for me, since I'm the one who was made a fool of. Grant just acts like he was the victim because he's delusional. He's undoubtedly edited how it happened back then to make himself the good guy.

Besides, if he *really* were a good guy, he wouldn't be making me deal with Sadie. She's been bugging me nonstop for an appointment so she can pitch him some supposedly great business idea. She's been polite so far, which has been a pleasant surprise, but it's hard for me to credit her with actually growing up. I just can't forget how cruel she was that morning when Heath and Will went streaking.

But for everyone's sake, I hope I'm wrong and Sadie surprises me.

37

GRANT

I'm a couple of minutes late for dinner with my brothers. It's a regular thing, although not all of us can always attend due to our busy careers. Sebastian is sometimes in Northern Virginia to deal with his jewelry business, and he might not be around this weekend because he had to fly there to deal with some financing issues.

I place my hand on the steakhouse door and notice Noah walking up. Well, it's more like shuffling like somebody put him in a ball and chain. On each leg.

"What's going on?" He's generally more upbeat. Or has his nose glued to his phone.

"Hey." He sighs, raking his dark hair.

"Somebody steal your camera?" Noah's a wildlife photographer who's working on his first novel. He is determined to win the Pulitzer with it—or so he claims, which is why it's taking him so long to finish. He probably hasn't even written the opening sentence. But given the amount of time he dedicates to photography, I suspect that that's his true passion, and he's just saying he's working on a book because that's what a lot of his "cool" colleagues are doing.

"No." He sighs again. "I just wanted a croissant."

"And...why is that a problem? You can grab one from anywhere."

"I don't want one from anywhere. I want one from Bobbi's."

This is weird. Noah loves all carbs equally. "What's so special about Bobbi's?"

He looks at me like I'm simple. "Bobbi made it."

I pat his shoulder, hoping he gets over this weird obsession with the bakery. The food is good, but not worth this kind of angst. "Try again tomorrow. Go early. Before they're sold out."

"She dropped the last one." He has the look of a man who's just been informed by his doctor that his erectile dysfunction's permanent and nothing can cure it. "The last croissant. On the floor." He shakes his head. "Still wanted to eat it."

"Dude." I lead him into the steakhouse. "Let's get you fed."

The hostess notices us and smiles. "Mr. Lasker. Mr. Lasker." She smiles at each of us in turn.

I stop at the sight of Aspen and her grandfather Kenny in front of the hostess. It looks like they were talking to her, but she's decided to ignore them.

Aspen's in a typically shabby outfit—a black dress made with cheap fabric. It also looks like it came out of a time capsule buried twenty years back. What's her motivation for wearing that when she's out with her grandfather?

Kenny isn't much better. He seems much frailer than I remember, but then, it's been fourteen years. The man's shoulders are rounded, and he seems smaller and more delicate. None of the force he exuded back then is evident. His suit doesn't fit, and he seems to be uncertain of his surroundings.

I look around, but don't see Kat. Is she here? It's hard to imagine Kenny without his wife. Whatever you can say about them, nobody could deny they're in love.

Aspen steps forward to shield her grandfather from my view. But she isn't big enough to hide him, and it only serves to annoy me. What the hell does she think I'm going to do to her grandfather, and why is he letting her do it? He was so protective of her during our dinner at their place. I haven't forgotten the way he gave me the third degree.

"What's going on?" I ask her.

"Nothing," the hostess says quickly. "Your table—"

"Aspen, what are you doing here?" I ask again.

She bites her lip, her cheeks reddening. "We had a reservation for six fifteen, but the restaurant apparently can't find it. Or a table."

"Well, it isn't easy to accommodate people without a reservation," the hostess says, addressing me directly. "Obviously, she made a mistake."

Her attitude is annoying. I'm not familiar with this particular hostess, but from the way Aspen's face is turning an even brighter red, I know this woman has been obnoxious and snotty. She seems more interested in convincing *me* that there's nothing wrong than figuring out how to make things right for Aspen.

I keep my gaze on the hostess. "Aspen here is my assistant. She made my reservation for tonight. Which you *do* have, correct?"

"Yes, of course. We—"

"Yes, of course you do. And I'm quite certain she didn't screw up her *own* reservation. So you're going to give her and her grandfather an apology, and a good one, and then give them the best table in the house. If that's too much for you to handle, perhaps you should look for another job that you're better qualified for."

Her jaw slackens. "You can't talk to me like that!"

"Oh, but I just did."

The manager on duty rushes out. "Mr. Lasker."

Did she somehow call for reinforcements? Annoyance surges, but Noah mutters, "You're welcome." Okay, fine. I don't need a manager to resolve this, but maybe it'll go faster.

I explain the situation, and the manager turns deathly pale. "I'm so sorry, sir."

"Your apology should be addressed to Aspen and her grandfather. They had to waste"—I glance at my Harry Winston—"over forty-five minutes of their time."

"Of course." He turns to them. "I'm terribly sorry, Ms. Hughes."

Her green gaze, full of distrust, darts between me and the manager. It's the same look she had when she was dealing with Sadie and her friends. The fact that it's directed at me pisses me off. I deserve better, especially when I just helped her out.

"To make up for the inconvenience, we'll be comping your full meal and drinks," the manager says.

Aspen blinks, her mouth parting. She looks at me like she's expecting a gotcha.

"They aren't going to spit in your food," I say dryly, too irritated to set her straight. It's like she's forgotten that *she's* the one who fucked *me* over. My revenge is reserved for her, not her grandfather.

The manager jumps. "Of course not!" He adds a nervous laugh like we're all joking.

I don't crack a smile. "Send them a bottle of 2008 Dom."

He flinches. "Of course, sir." Then he personally starts to lead them to their table.

"That hostess needs to apologize, too," I tell him as I follow to make sure he doesn't stick them at a shitty table in the back by the kitchen.

Aspen keeps her hand on her grandfather's elbow, but also shifts closer to me. She lowers her voice. "You can go now."

"Oh, no problem. You're more than welcome. Really, it was nothing."

She sighs. "Thank you. But—"

"I want to say hello to Kenny."

"Honestly, *that* isn't necessary."

"Of course it is."

When they're seated at one of the nicer tables and the manager has left, I turn to Kenny. "Hello, sir."

He looks up at me. There's a polite smile on his lips, but something about the way his eyes search my face feels off. "Oh, hi!" His eyes widen. "Zack."

Zack? That weasel waiter from Benedicto's who wouldn't quit hitting on Aspen when we were there? The donkey Kat was thinking of inviting over?

Squirming a little, Aspen refuses to meet my gaze. She puts her hand on Kenny's sleeve. "It's Grant, Grandpa." She flicks her eyes in my direction, then looks back at Kenny. "He just looks different from before."

That's bullshit. I'm older, of course, but I haven't changed that much. There's no way Kenny could've confused me with Zack.

"Grant?" Kenny's brow furrows. "Can't quite seem to... Which one was...?"

He doesn't remember?

Aspen clears her throat. "From when I was in college," she says, then turns to me. "You *really* should go join your brothers now, and let us have dinner in peace. We're here to celebrate my new job, and we can't have a good time with you hovering over us."

"Okay. I'm just surprised that your grandfather doesn't remember me."

Her lips tighten. "Maybe you didn't make much of an impression."

I doubt that. But she's full of wariness. It's as though she believes I'm going to hurt her and her grandpa, which bugs the hell out of me. Just what kind of dickhead does she think I am? I treated her well when we were together. Admittedly, I've been a difficult boss to please, but that's only because she deserves it.

"Maybe so." I drag out the words.

Kenny seems to rouse himself and blinks a few times. "Kat?"

Kat? Aspen's grandmother isn't around, but... Kenny's looking at Aspen. A possibility flashes through my head. *He thinks Aspen is Kat?*

"Your brothers are waving at you," she says.

She's lying. They aren't the type to wave. But now isn't the time to talk about what's up with Kenny. Not only would it be rude to do it in front of him, but I'm feeling too disquieted. "I'll leave you two to your dinner. See you on Monday, Aspen." *And we'll talk.*

She nods goodbye before reviving her smile and turning to her grandfather.

When I finally get to the table with my brothers, they all stare. Everyone's here, even Sebastian. Noah's holding his phone, but for once isn't looking at the screen. His eyes are glued to my face. If he's reacting like this, the rest of my brothers must be dying of curiosity, except possibly for Emmett, who already knows a big chunk of what's going on.

"Your new assistant's hot," Huxley says.

"I guess Emmett told you all who Aspen is," I say, taking my seat.

"Uh-huh." Huxley's gaze is appreciative as he glances at her again. He's in advertising, and he loves beautiful things, including women. He has the same look we all inherited from our father, Ted Lasker—the dark hair and square jaw—and he has the brain from his mom, too. He has no problem getting women, and the only ones he stays away from are the ones he'd have to marry if he slept with them. Namely, the women from the Webber family of Huxley & Webber.

"Shut up and stop eye-fucking her."

Hux doesn't seem bothered by my injunction. He'd be more scared if it had been Griffin, because Griff could kick all of our asses with both hands tied behind his back. "Don't just want to *eye*-fuck her," he says, giving Nicholas a significant look.

The idea of Huxley kissing and touching her makes my vision go red. "She's my assistant!"

"And? It isn't like she's your wife," he says, at the same time Emmett says, "Not for long, though, right?"

I give Emmett a hard stare.

"Hey, you're the one who swore he was going to get her to quit in less than three months," Emmett says. "Let's get up to speed here."

Sebastian shakes his head at me. "You know...a free meal probably isn't the way to drive her off."

I shoot him a fiery look.

He raises both hands. "Just sayin'."

"She also got free champagne," Noah puts in. "The 2008 Dom."

Nicholas whistles. "That's a great choice." He knows his vintages, and he loves them. I have no idea why he never added a vineyard to the collection of businesses he owns.

"Expensive, too," Griffin says.

"If you're serious about winning the bet, you should've tossed her out of the restaurant," Huxley says.

"I'm not that much of a bastard," I reply.

"Yeah, you are. You act nice, but we all know that inner asshole is just waiting to emerge." Emmett gives me a meaningful look.

"You're just pissed that Amy still has to do the team-building exercise," I say.

"Yeah, because you're still mad at me about the time sheet thing."

My brothers burst out laughing. Of course, Emmett told the others about that too.

But I'm too distracted to care because all my attention is devoted to Aspen. Something's very wrong, and for the first time since she walked into my office, I wonder if I've misjudged her situation. I didn't imagine the shadow of pain in her eyes when Kenny called her Kat. And he looked at her like she was the love of his life.

If she's taking care of him, and he's not quite with it, things have got to be difficult. A smidgeon of unwilling sympathy stirs, and I feel slightly guilty about making her work all those pointless hours simply out of spite. She might've needed time with Kenny more than the overtime pay.

Then I start to get annoyed over the fact that I'm feeling bad about it. How was I supposed to know? She never explained her circumstances. She just held her head high and acted like she was fine with the abuse I doled out.

Damn it, she was *asking* for escalation. Just because she's in a shitty place doesn't mean she's not the girl who fucked me over.

38

ASPEN

I yawn a little as I enter the office on Monday after a late night closing the bar. Zack and Satoshi were on the shift with me, but they said I could leave early, since they know I have to go to GrantEm first thing in the morning. But I didn't want to impose on them like that. Plus, I'm not running at the crack of dawn anymore.

Grant's already in his office. I try to come in before he does, since I don't want him labeling me as lazy or making snide comments, but it doesn't seem possible unless I arrive by five thirty in the morning. And he's made it crystal clear I'm not to do over-time. The time sheet probably stunned him.

Cheap bastard.

On the other hand, the work he had me on was bullshit. And we both knew it.

I boot my laptop and check Grant's agenda for the day. I see the name I still hate on today's calendar, then smile like it doesn't matter. He's paying me to do a job, not to have feelings about whom he has meetings with.

I enter his office. He must bathe in the blood of babies or some-thing, because he looks disgustingly refreshed and gorgeous, although he has to be sleeping less than five hours a day. Everything about him glows—from his dark hair to the tanned skin to the sharp eyes that never fail to pin me to the spot, like he used to when I was younger and dumber.

I go over the day's agenda and a few critical meetings for the rest of the day. He merely nods. I should leave, but I stay because I'm a decent human being—and I hate the fact that I owe him my gratitude. "Thank you for Saturday." *Wow, that sounded pretty begrudging.* I can fake better than this. So I say something I wasn't planning on. "It was nice of you to do that."

Grant waves a hand. "It was nothing."

His cavalier tone somehow makes me feel worse. Look at us—fourteen years later, I'm so pathetic that I can't even get a seat at a restaurant I reserved. Not only that, I had no way to force them to honor the reservation. Meanwhile, all he had to do was look at the hostess sharply and have a word with that manager who magically appeared, and things were immediately sorted out. Even if I hadn't had a reservation, if he wanted, the steakhouse would've come up with a table.

"By the way, is everything okay with your grandfather?" Grant asks.

I tense. Grandpa isn't somebody I want to talk about, especially with Grant. He's the only one I have left, and I feel like a lioness standing guard against a hostile intruder. "He's fine," I say firmly.

"He didn't seem to remember me at all," Grant says.

"It's been a long time, and he doesn't remember all my friends." Not true, of course. My grandfather hates Grant for what he did, but I'm not going to bring up the unpleasant history. Grant isn't going to admit he did anything wrong. If he was, he would've apologized when he saw me for the first time in the office. Instead, he acted like I spat on one of his polo horses.

All I want is get through the workday and have the firm help pay for Grandpa's care. My personal feelings don't matter. They can't.

"He kept calling me Zack. And he confused you with your grandmother."

"I don't know why that's pertinent. It won't impact my performance, and there's nothing in the policy that says I have to share my personal life with my employer."

A muscle in his jaw twitches as he narrows his eyes.

He can give me all the slit-eyed suspicion he wants—I'm not saying another word. "If that's all..."

"Yeah, that's all. Go." He makes a shooing motion.

I return to my desk with a soft sigh. Hopefully he'll keep his nose out of my business. Doesn't he realize he lost all right to ask personal questions when he turned me into a laughingstock on campus? Or maybe to him it was as trivially inconsequential as what he did at the steakhouse.

Maybe he wants to make amends...? What he did on Saturday could be an overture of sorts...

Ha! I cut myself off before it gets too ridiculous. The time to make amends was fourteen years ago. He probably decided to be nice on Saturday because his brothers were watching. *No, wait— that hostess refused to sleep with him and he's having his petty revenge.*

No matter what he does, I'll never forget that I can't take anything at face value. Time spent obsessing about him is better used rereading the memo to make sure it's perfect. I turn my attention to my laptop screen and glue my eyes to the document. No more frittering away my time and life. I've wasted enough on him already.

Half an hour later, the app on my computer alerts me to the first meeting of the week. And sure enough...

Sadie, the pain in the butt from my college years, walks in. She's in a teal jumpsuit that emphasizes her small waist and flaring hips. Her breasts are at least two cup sizes bigger than I remember. I wish I could say they look bad, but they're actually fantastic. Everything about her exudes expensive care, including her perfume and a stylish haircut that leaves her blonde tresses framing her expertly made-up face and cascading down her back.

Her eyes widen when she sees me. "Oh my God! I didn't realize Aspen Hughes was really *you!*" she says in a loud voice. The way she moves her head around to make note of people's reactions makes her delivery theatrical. "I thought it was someone else with the same name." She laughs. "Are you seriously back in Grant's orbit? Where's your pride? Just what does it take to keep you away?"

"Hello, Sadie," I say with a neutral smile. Getting into a sarcastic argument with a potential business partner would definitely be against the policy. Even if it weren't, it would give Grant the perfect excuse to fire me. I'll be damned if I lose this job over Sadie.

"I'm honestly shocked. I thought you'd be busy in some other industry that suited you better." Her tone is positively snide.

My hands tighten into fists. If she calls me a whore, I'm going to sue for sexual harassment and verbal abuse.

"But I guess you take what you can get, right?" Sadie lifts a shoulder.

"If you keep talking, you're going to be late for your appointment." *She's a guest. She's a guest...*

"Grant must've felt sorry for you." Her gaze rakes over me. "Not even a vagrant would wear what you're wearing."

Gasps go up around the office. I see a few associates staring at Sadie like she's grown an anus on her forehead.

Her eyes go extra bright. I know that look—she gets that gleam every time she's about to do something to cause me trouble.

She swings around hard. Her hand catches the strap of my purse on my desk and knocks my bag on the floor. The worn faux-vinyl of the strap breaks, and the contents of my purse scatter all over the floor, including a couple of tampons.

"Oh, oops!" She puts a hand over her mouth. "Sorry."

"It was an accident."

"Of course. Totally my fault. But maybe next time, buy a better purse? That strap came apart like a wet paper straw."

"Sadie." Grant's voice rings out like the crack of a gunshot.

She turns around and spreads her arms. "Grant, babe!"

I wonder for a second if she's going to run to him in her heels. It'd be hilarious if she fell down like Yvette did. On the other hand, since Grant is the one who had Sadie make this appointment, he might move himself to catch her.

The thought is depressing, although I'm not sure why. They deserve each other, given what horrible human beings they are.

I get up and begin picking my belongings up off the floor. Sadie takes a small step back, her heel landing among my things. Just an inch to the left and her stiletto would've pinned my hand to the floor. Instead, it cracks my compact.

Grant stalks toward us. "Get the fuck out."

Sadie glances down at me. "You heard him."

"Not her, *you!*" Grant points at Sadie.

She puts a hand over her chest. "Me?"

What? Why did he have her make an appointment, then?

"Yes, you! Out!" he says.

"But you haven't heard my proposal!" she whines.

"And I never will. I work with people who can handle themselves professionally."

"But—"

"Besides, I forgot about that voice of yours." His gaze on Sadie's red face, he says, "Aspen, make sure to block Sadie's number and email address."

"Sure," I say.

"You can't make me leave without hearing me out first!" Sadie's voice is shriller than a badly played violin.

"Wrong. And if you won't walk out on your own, I'll have security drag you out."

I jump to my feet. "Let me just call them right now."

Sadie's eyes go wide, and tears start to form. Grant cocks an eyebrow. She should know better. Tears won't move him. He has no heart.

He looks at his watch. "Call security. Tell them to be up here in one minute."

I pick up the phone.

"Fine! I *get* it!" Chest heaving, Sadie flips him the bird, then gives me a hateful look. "You're both disgusting. My God! You're letting a gold digger manage your life," she yells at Grant, then points at me. "And *you*. You're just...just...*trash!*"

Then she marches away. She isn't stupid. She has to know Grant has no qualms about throwing her out in the most humiliating manner possible.

I lower the phone. My eyes lock with Jesse's, who immediately ducks his head and scribbles something on a pile of documents in front of him. The area suddenly bustles with activity, and I sigh inwardly. I guess the office got quite a show.

"In my office," Grant says.

"Just let me pick these things up off—"

"*Now.*" Without waiting for a response, he stalks back into his office.

I gaze at my scattered stuff. Chapstick. A black wallet so old it's gray. The tampons. The broken compact. Pens and receipts...

"I'll get it for you," Amy offers. "Go ahead. You don't want him waiting, not when he's in that kind of mood."

"Thanks," I say. "Just dump it all on my desk or something."

"Got it."

Taking a steadying breath, I walk toward his office. I don't know what he's going to say to blame me for the spectacle, but I can handle it. I can take anything as long as I keep this job.

39

GRANT

I clench and unclench my shaking hands, feeling like the top of my skull's about to blow off. If Sadie weren't a woman, I would've beaten the shit out of her.

Hey, you knew what kind of snobbish bitch she is. You knew how she felt about Aspen, and you knew there was a strong possibility she was going to be an obnoxious cunt.

True enough, but I didn't expect Sadie to still be quite that crass. Or break Aspen's purse. Sadie was supposed to be a difficult client for Aspen to handle, not humiliate her in front of the entire office. It's hard to believe, but Sadie has actually gotten worse since college. Or maybe I just didn't notice how bad she was back then.

I should've canceled the meeting after running into Aspen and Kenny over the weekend. Aspen's probably struggling to take care of her grandfather, which explains why she seemed disappointed about being forbidden to work overtime. Nursing homes are pricey, and she doesn't need Sadie's brand of snobbish obnoxiousness.

Aspen walks in. "You wanted to talk to me?"

There's nothing but placid professionalism on her face. No anger. Nothing to indicate she wants to strangle me, which only fuels my irritation. She should be pissed about the purse, even demand that I have Sadie replace it or do that myself, since she was my guest. But from the look on Aspen's face, Sadie might as well have never visited.

You aren't even worth her anger.

The thought slices deeply, a hot blade into a soft block of Brie. "Make an appointment with Lola Court," I say. Aspen doesn't ask who she is. It's like she isn't even curious, which makes me want to punch something. "She's my personal shopper."

Aspen's eyebrow twitches. Is she thinking about Marketta? But she doesn't say anything to indicate she's curious. Or maybe she forgot about Mom's personal shopper, who retired a few years ago. Lola is one of Marketta's protégées.

"For when?" Aspen asks.

"In the next thirty minutes. Tell her I'll be coming by."

"Okay. What do you want to do about your ten o'clock?"

"Reschedule it. It isn't that urgent."

Aspen nods. "All right."

She starts to turn away. I stop her. "Is there something you want to say?"

There. I'm giving her an open opportunity to vent.

She blinks a couple of times. "No, I don't think so. But I'll let you know the new time for your ten o'clock."

She walks out, then closes the door behind her.

Fuck. She sure knows how to twist a knife. She has to know why I asked that question. And she knows I always sided with her when it came to her and Sadie. She could've—

But you didn't side with her today. You caused the whole incident.

A few minutes later, I get a message from Aspen through the firm's messaging app.

–Aspen: Lola Court says you can stop by anytime.

I jump to my feet and stride out of the office. Aspen's at her desk. Her purse with the broken strap is nowhere to be seen, and the floor is clear.

"Let's go," I say.

"Us? I'm going too?"

"Yes."

She frowns, but then her face clears. "Oh. Ms. Court mentioned that she could have everything delivered to the office or your place. Your choice."

What? I stare, wondering what she's talking about. Then it finally dawns on me that she thinks I'm taking her with me to carry my stuff. What's left of my patience vanishes. "Just get up and come with me."

Lola's probably wondering why I want to see her. She normally selects various options for me and sends them over to my place. I keep what I like and return the rest. After years of providing the service, she knows my taste and preferences.

But this isn't something I can handle using our usual method.

We reach the garage across the street from the office building. I lead Aspen to my Maybach and open the passenger-side door before I remember we aren't dating, and I don't have to be nice to her. As a matter of fact, I need to do everything in my power to get her to quit.

But it'd be ridiculous to slam the door shut now. Besides, I'm just trying to make up for the fact that Sadie is a destructive bitch.

"Get in," I say.

Aspen looks at me like I've lost my mind, and a layer of skin seems to peel off me under her scrutiny. Hating the vague sense of vulnerable uncertainty she's stirring within me, I let go of the handle and walk around to the driver's side.

I start the engine. The audio plays Paloma Faith's "Only Love Can Hurt Like This." The singer's voice reminds me of the time Aspen drove me to the Mexican restaurant the day I fell off Starfire during a polo match. Back then, it was "Do You Want the Truth or Something Beautiful?"

Does she remember that too? It's impossible to read her face, since she's looking out the window like she can't bear to be in an enclosed space with me.

Well, too fucking bad. She's here. And she's going to have to deal.

"Can we listen to something else?" Aspen asks after a few seconds.

"No."

She sighs and shrugs slightly, probably thinking that all she has to do is wait a couple of minutes for the sound system to play the next song.

I don't think so.

I hit a couple of buttons on the steering wheel. The song dies with the final note, as the singer says, "A deadly kiss."

Aspen's shoulders visibly relax, until the song starts again. She turns to me. "Why is it playing again?"

"I like to listen to the same song on repeat."

"No, you don't," she says.

"How would you know?"

"You never did."

"People change." *People like you and me.* "Or maybe you didn't know me as well as you thought." *Just like I never knew you that well. I still don't.*

I can feel her gaze on my cheek. Finally, she lets out a resigned sigh. "You're right." For some reason, her agreement sounds like she's saying, "You weren't the person I thought."

I unclench then clench my hand around the steering wheel. "You have no right to say that."

"Say what? That you're right?"

"I was an open book with you. What you saw was what you got."

"Oh, right. I'm sure the CIA thinks the same when they show you those documents with ninety percent of the content blacked out."

"I didn't hide anything from you."

"No, of course not. If you had, I never would have figured everything out."

Figured everything out? "What the hell does that mean?"

Aspen doesn't elaborate.

"Aspen—"

"You need to go into that garage over there." She points at a building to the right, behind Lola's place. "Lola said there's some construction that's blocking the parking lot in front of her boutique."

There is indeed some work going on that's blocking the entrance to the lot. It's obnoxiously loud, and I can see why Lola offered to send things when Aspen called. I want to continue the conversation, but there's no reason Aspen should have to walk all the way from the garage. We can talk later, on our way back to the office.

I pull over. "Go inside and wait for me." She gets out, and I go and park, then make my way to Lola's boutique.

I've only come here once or twice before, for urgent purchases, but Lola should have something Aspen can take. I'll buy her two purses. Griffin's mom said every woman needs at least two, although ideally she'd have a purse to go with every outfit. But she's a model, and Aspen's not. Two should be plenty—

But wait. If I buy her two, she'll be able to auction one off like the other things I gave her.

Just one, then.

I step into Lola's boutique, into the elegant Mozart and a pleasant wood and floral scent over shining marble and glittering mirrors.

"I'm so sorry, but we don't allow loitering," comes Lola's voice. Underneath the polished politeness is a hint of who-the-hell-do-you-think-you-are mockery.

I walk into the main section of the lobby. Aspen's standing there, her face bright red. A couple of Lola's people stand in the corner, watching and whispering. They sweep their eyes over Aspen's length, judging and pricing everything on her, even her haircut— assuming she's cut her hair in the last year.

I don't need to be able to read minds to know what's going on. They're looking at Aspen's clothes and realizing that the sum of everything she has on wouldn't even equal their underwear. People who come to places like this may appear to dress sloppily, but if you know what to look for, you can tell that the ostensibly grungy clothes are made with fancy hand-woven fabric from Europe and worth thousands of dollars.

"I'm going to have to ask you to leave," Lola adds.

"That's unfortunate," I say coldly.

Aspen lets out a soft sigh, but she doesn't look at me.

Lola turns to me. "Grant." She smiles. "Sorry about this... unpleasant situation. I'll have Gillian handle it and—"

"You're fired."

Aspen swivels her head in my direction. Lola lets out a nervous laugh.

"Aspen, let's go," I say, taking her wrist gently but firmly. Her skin's shockingly warm against mine, and I can feel my palm throb. Or maybe it's her pulse. But every nerve ending in my body prickles like it's overcharged. An urge to let go, so I can regain control over myself, overwhelms me. But I don't.

Aspen doesn't yank her wrist out of my grip, either. I can feel her gaze on me. She's probably looking at me like I'm crazy, but I don't care. My headspace is too jumbled, and I don't like what I'm feeling right now, because watching some bitch hurt Aspen is making me feel small and pathetic. A bully who picks on somebody defenseless, just because she can.

"I'm sorry? What's going on?" Lola says.

"Are you too intellectually challenged to understand a simple sentence? You. Are. Fired."

Her jaw drops. Her chin's so unnaturally pointed, she looks like a shocked praying mantis.

"But..." Her panicked blue eyes dart in Aspen's direction. Emmett also uses Lola's service, but if he hears I fired her—and why —he'll drop her too, and she knows it. "Grant, I apologize. I didn't realize she was your new girlfriend. If she'd told me that from the beginning, none of this would've happened."

What the fuck? Did she just victim-blame?

"I told you I was here for Grant Lasker." Aspen sounds mildly tired.

And Lola didn't believe her. My expression must've spiked Lola's fear, because she starts babbling. "You usually bring girls who are better dressed than this. If this is a test, obviously I failed, but give me another chance. I can do better. You know that—"

"Stop digging. You'll never be able to get out of the hole."

She shuts her mouth so hard and fast, her teeth click.

"I don't do second chances," I say. "If you can't do your job, you're done."

"You can't throw away a decade-long relationship like that!"

"Watch me."

When we're out of the boutique, Aspen pulls her wrist out of my grip. I look down at my empty hand, feeling bereft. I flex my fingers.

"Now where are you going to go to buy whatever you needed?" Aspen says as we walk toward the lot.

"There are a bazillion personal shoppers in this city." I pull out my phone. To be honest, I don't know any other than Lola. But my brothers should know some.

–Me: I just fired Lola Court. Need a replacement. Any suggestions?

Noah responds instantly.

–Noah: Whoa. What did she do?

–Me: Something worthy of termination. So. Any suggestions?

–Sebastian: Sorry. My shopper's in Virginia.

–Noah: You should just dress yourself.

–Me: Not all of us enjoy rolling around in the dirt to get a shot of some aardvark.

–Emmett: Is Amy going to be offended when she finds out why? Given my sister-in-law's personality...

–Me: Yes.

–Emmett: Then she's gotta go.

–Huxley: Mom likes Josephine Blackwood. But I'm not sure if she's taking new clients.

–Me: We'll see. Can you send me her info?

40

ASPEN

Grant must be on man-PMS or something. He's moody, temperamental and just plain weird.

He doesn't seem to want any thanks for helping me and my grandfather, but he wants to know about the situation Grandpa is in. He knows what Sadie's like, but brings her over anyway, only to kick her out unceremoniously. He cancels a meeting and goes shopping, only to fire his personal shopper for being rude to me.

I'm used to people being obnoxious to me. I've worked in retail, restaurants and bars. A lot of people assume you're an idiot who can't do any better when you hold those jobs.

And there's Grant, who's been the ultimate asshole of my life. He was impossible when we started working together, so I don't understand his sudden change in attitude... Unless he thinks he's the only one who should treat me like shit. But that doesn't make any sense. Why would he think that? There isn't a bet for him to win. He can do whatever he wants.

He didn't ask me to find a new personal shopper. He just called the replacement he found, and now we're at another boutique with a stunning Latina who positively glows, her dark eyes sparkling with good humor, her smile open and friendly. Her long brown hair is artfully curled around her face, and she struts like a model in her high heels. On her left hand is a ring with a diamond so large, you could probably pawn it for half the state of Delaware.

"So. What can I do for you?" she says with a warm smile at me and Grant.

"She needs a new purse," he says.

"Wait, what?" I shake my head. "I thought *you* needed something."

"I do. I need to replace your purse."

"Do you feel bad about what happened with Sadie?" I ask, lowering my voice.

"It happened during work."

I put my hand out. "I'll just take cash." Everything in this place looks expensive. I don't need a pricey purse, just something functional. He can give me seventy thousand—assuming he wants to get me a purse that outlandishly priced again—and I'll buy myself one from Target and keep the change as special compensation for a crappy work situation.

His eyes narrow. "No." He turns to Josephine, who's watching us with badly disguised interest. "Here." He hands her a black AmEx card.

"Thank you. So just a bag?"

"Yes," I say, at the same time he says, "No."

Josephine raises a well-plucked eyebrow and shifts her gaze between us.

"The works. She needs new clothes. Shoes. Accessories." His gaze flicks to my head. "Maybe even a decent haircut. It looks like she hasn't been inside a hair salon in a decade."

"*What?*" I run my fingers through my hair, feeling defensive—mainly because he's correct. I cut my own hair when it gets too long. "My hair's fine."

"It looks like a rat's nest," he retorts.

Jerk. "Josephine, please use that card to prepay for an appointment with his ophthalmologist. Clearly, Grant needs his eyes checked."

Josephine clears her throat. "We can do something different with the hair. No problem. So. Budget?"

"I didn't know we discuss things like that," he says stiffly.

"Everyone talks about budget," I say. What's he trying to pull here? I can—maybe, sort of—understand he wants to buy me a Prada or something to replace the bag Sadie broke, since she was only at GrantEm with his blessing. But she didn't rip my clothes or set my hair on fire!

"Not me," he counters with a smile that doesn't reach his eyes.

It has to be a trap, some creative way to torment me. It's just that he expects me to put up with it because it's *him* doing it. I've seen what passes for "high fashion." I'd rather die before putting on clothes that make me look like a walking tree or something. "I don't want your charity."

"It's not charity. First, *I'm* buying them, so they're *my* clothes. I'm just *loaning* them to you for the time you work for me. And second, how you look reflects on both me and the company."

I finally understand why people sell their soul to the devil. It would be tempting—*so* tempting—if I could just wipe that superior look on his face. And kick his ass.

"I need to go to a meeting, but you'll get this done with Josephine," he says.

"I have work to do too!" I protest.

"This is part of your work. I expect a memo on it."

Then he's out the door, leaving me with a personal shopper holding his shiny black AmEx.

I turn to her. "This really isn't necessary."

"Yes, it is, because now it's my job. Besides, you heard the man. You're going to get *paid to shop*!" She winks.

"He didn't mean it." *He only said that to put me in a bad situation later.*

"He seemed pretty sincere, and you have a witness if there's ever a question." Josephine loops her arm around mine. "I'd be ecstatic if I had a boss who paid me to go shopping."

"Your job *is* shopping."

"True. I love working for myself." She smiles. "And I *love* to shop. Don't you?"

I say nothing, since I don't want to crap on her enthusiasm. Shopping isn't fun if you're on a tight budget. It's morale-killing to find a pretty dress and shoes, only to realize you can't afford them.

"Do you know what the best kind of shopping is?" she asks, obviously having sensed my not-so-sunny mood.

"When you get to do it with your boss's blessing during business hours?"

She laughs. "No, although that isn't bad. The *best* is when somebody else is paying for everything." She flashes the black AmEx. "The sky's the limit!"

But that's the problem. I don't want a sky-limit spree because it's going to come with a destructive caveat or two. The naïve girl who got excited over gorgeous dresses that made her feel like a fairytale princess is dead and gone. Grant knows that—he killed her—which is why he hasn't bothered to stay here and do the things he did back then—like look at me like I'm the most beautiful thing he's ever seen, or place a necklace around my neck, brushing his fingers on my bare flesh and making me tremble.

That moment is never going to come back. All the sweetness and trust that existed between us is forever shattered. But, of course, it wasn't real to begin with—it only existed in my imagination.

But it isn't Josephine's fault that I can't enjoy this. So I try to go along with her excitement. After all, she's just doing her job.

"Want something to drink? We have Dom, which is amazing."

"No, thank you. I have to go back to the office. But I'll take some water if that's okay."

"Flat or sparkling?"

"Flat."

A clerk brings out a bottle of water for me. I take a sip, wishing it was one of Satoshi's or Zack's dirty martinis.

"So what are we looking at here?" she asks. "It didn't sound like he's taking you on a date."

I almost choke on the water. "We don't have that kind of relationship." I cough to clear my throat.

"No need to be shocked. You'd be amazed how many bosses date their employees," she says. "So. Office clothes?"

"Office clothes." Grant emphasized that how I look reflects on him, and we're only together at work.

"No problem. Let's start with ten sets."

"*Ten?*" I repeat numbly. "Why do I need that many?"

"How else are you going to look fabulous? You'll be able to mix and match what I pick out for you, which should stretch your outfit options to twenty. That way you won't look like you're wearing the same thing all the time. But you need a minimum number of items to work with to be able to do that successfully. It's obvious that he wants you to look the part."

She doesn't sound judgmental like Sadie or Lola, but maybe she's seeing something I'm not. "I honestly don't think I look that bad."

"You don't. But the suit that your boss is wearing is worth, mmm, thirty or forty thousand dollars."

Holy *shit*! There are suits that cost that much?

"And the cuff links? Those are custom, so probably around six, seven thousand?"

Oh my God.

"I think he wants you to elevate your wardrobe, so you don't look so, ah...economically modest next to him."

She doesn't have to be so delicate. I probably look like a hobo next to him. It didn't seem to bother him when we were younger, but maybe it does now. Or maybe it always did, which is why he spent such an extravagant sum to dress me in Malibu.

"Besides," Josephine says, waving a hand, "he's probably going to expense the whole thing, so don't worry about it."

"You aren't going to put me in things that cost that much, are you?" Grant said they were loaners. I don't want him to demand I pay for potential damage when I return them. I'm going to have to blame standard wear and tear, but my stomach hurts already from the possible battle to come. I wonder if I can get him to sign a legal document saying I'm not responsible for the condition they're in when I give them back.

The things I do to keep my job. But I think of Grandpa. It'll be worth it. Everything's worth it to keep him in a nice, safe place where the staff treats him with the dignity he deserves.

Josephine gestures at a few people, and they start bringing out racks of clothes. The experience reminds me a little bit of how things were with Marketta, but of course we're not at Grant's mother's place in Malibu.

"I want you to try *these* skirts and tops"—Josephine says, tapping her lip—"and *those* dresses." She plucks the items off the racks with impressive speed.

"Are we going to do any pants?" I eye her selections with a bit of suspicion. The things she's holding are vibrant jewel tones. Given her taste and confidence, they're likely to fit like a dream, but skirts and dresses seem... I don't know. Too flirty? Too feminine?

Or maybe I'm reluctant because they remind me too much of the first set of clothes Grant bought me—those stunning dresses I only got to wear once before I asked Suyen to get rid of them for me.

"Honey, you have amazing legs. The kind that every woman in this town would kill for. You ever wait tables?"

"Yes," I say slowly.

"Uh-huh. And all guys tipped double when you wore a skirt?"

"Well...yeah."

She beams. "I knew it! So why hide them with pants? Unless the firm allows you to wear shorts...?" She looks at me expectantly.

"No. I've never seen anyone wearing shorts in the office."

"That's what I thought. Anyway, that's why I'm picking these out. You don't seem interested in buying everything in sight, so we have to maximize your potential."

"Can we make this as efficient as possible?" I ask. Grant will probably complain if I take too much time here.

"Sure. Do you mind if I go into the dressing room with you?"

"If it'll make things go faster? Not at all."

I put on the first set of items that she picks out. She watches me put on some of the clothes and shakes her head.

"I just wanted you to know that you can't wear underwear with that."

Awkward. "I'm not taking off my panties in front of you," I say with extra friendliness.

"Believe me, I don't want you to." She laughs. "But when you wear that at work, you just can't."

I pause. "Is this the kind of 'delicate item' that I can't wear with lingerie?"

"Basically. These"—she gestures at several skirts—"mold to your body and emphasize your line, which, by the way, is fabulous. So you can't put on anything underneath because it will show."

I cross my arms across my chest. "We have to pick something else. I am *not* going to work commando."

"Why not?" She looks genuinely confused.

"Because it's unprofessional." She probably works for Hollywood celebrities who go commando everywhere, including Catholic mass. It's likely she doesn't know you don't do that at an office.

She laughs, the sound full of rich humor. "Honey, it's not unprofessional if nobody knows."

"But *I'm* going to know that I'm not wearing underwear."

She snaps her fingers. "Exactly! Unless you tell, nobody's going to know. I'm so glad we agree on this."

I'm beginning to realize she's not going to see things from my perspective. What is up with personal shoppers and their intense dislike for clothes you can wear with lingerie? It's almost like their archenemies own all the lingerie stores in the country.

"But you didn't only pick out no-underwear clothes, did you?" I ask.

"Of course not." She gestures at a separate pile. "You can wear lingerie with those. And we'll just pick these out." She plucks a few lacy undergarments from a neat pile.

"I don't think that's necessary."

"Of course it is. Nothing boosts a girl's confidence like sexy lingerie. Trust me. Aaaand...let's see... We'll throw in a couple corsets just because they're hot."

"I thought underwear didn't matter because nobody can see it."

Josephine makes a finger gun and points at me with a small click of her tongue. "But *you* know what you're wearing underneath. I'm going to get you garter belts and fishnet stockings, too. Every woman should have some, just in case." She then shamelessly tosses in a few pairs of silky stockings too.

It's tiring to wonder what Grant's motive is for doing this, and trying to estimate how much everything costs, since Josephine isn't giving me a chance to check any of the price tags. He made it clear they were loaners, and since he can't repurpose these and gift them to his girlfriends or next assistant, my head hurts from trying to figure out how he plans to screw me over with them later. Not only that, I have to watch Josephine closely to ensure she doesn't add more accessories and shoes. She's convinced I need a different purse for each day of the week. And something like twenty pairs of earrings and ten watches. I only need one on my wrist. Not even Grant wears ten watches!

The entire time she's brushing off my objections, she vibrates with vitality. It's like she's a money vampire. The more of Grant's money she spends, the more energized she becomes.

She even forces a haircut on me, insisting it's what Grant wants, although I can't imagine why he'd want my hair cut. Maybe to make a better trophy when he mounts my head on his office wall.

I ask to have it lopped off into a bob, but she gasps in horror. "I'd prefer to work for your boss a bit longer."

"He won't notice." He only cares about how others might perceive him. He wouldn't care if I showed up bald.

"He most definitely will. Trust me on this, Aspen. I'm the expert, remember? Besides, I'm not asking you to do anything extra here. Just what you have to."

I give her a skeptical look. "You forced twenty pairs of shoes on me."

"Exactly. If I had it my way, you'd be leaving with at least forty. You have such fabulous feet, and we have so many pretty shoes. They complete your look for the day, you know."

I mentally throw my hands up in the air. Why even try?

She continues, "Normally, I'd suggest highlighting it too, but your hair's already so perfect the way it is. I love the mix of copper and gold. Very classy. You're lucky your hair's naturally perfect."

"Thank you." I'm surprised at her praise. She's demonstrated that she doesn't give out empty compliments. She was pretty brutal about some of my selections—mainly because I wanted to pick out black for easy coordination. She said if I want to look like a drab, colorless bore, I'm welcome to it, but as long as she's dressing me, I'm going to pop like a finely cut diamond in a pile of coal.

"Where do you live?" Josephine asks.

"Why?"

"I'll have everything delivered to your place. Obviously, you can't carry all this." She gestures at the mountain of bags and boxes.

It's after five and I'm mentally exhausted. And I absolutely do *not* want to make multiple two-hour trips between my place and here to get everything. So I scribble my address for her, then check the list of inventory carefully before signing the paper she gives me.

I start to call for a car pickup, but Josephine checks her phone and smiles. "Your ride is here." She starts to walk me out.

"What? When did you arrange for that?"

"Earlier. Grant said you needed it."

If it were anybody but Grant, I'd be grateful for the thoughtfulness. But...Grant? Thoughtful? I'd have a better chance of finding a cuddly rattlesnake.

"I see."

"Just look at you. You're a star!" Josephine smiles, obviously pleased with herself.

I look over at the mirrored wall of the lobby. It takes a moment to recognize myself. In a mustard top and magenta skirt, I look *nothing* like earlier. The shoes are patent nude sling-back pumps, huge chandelier earrings dangle around my chin and my hair is expertly layered to frame my face.

"Amazing, right?" Josephine is buoyant with excitement. "Man, I'm good!"

I laugh. "Yes, you are." It's hard not to compliment her on a job well done, although part of me wonders what Grant will think of it. He might disapprove. After all, the man takes practically every opportunity to humiliate me.

The only car waiting outside is a black Mercedes, driven by a uniformed chauffeur. Splashy, but it's difficult for me to enjoy the smooth ride or the luxurious leather seat when I'm so unnerved. This experience is reminding me too much of Malibu. There has to be a gotcha.

I ask the driver to take me to the office. I need to get my car—and drop by a deli near my apartment for a sandwich. I'm too frazzled to cook.

By the time I grab a turkey and cheese sandwich and make it

back home, it's after seven. As I park my car and climb out, I spot Mrs. Yang carrying two huge bags of groceries.

"Hi, Mrs. Yang!" I call out.

She pauses for a second to smile at me. "Hi!" She'd wave if it weren't for the groceries she's carrying.

"Let me help you with those." I trot over.

"Oh, they're very heavy," she says with a concerned look.

"It's okay." I take them from her. They aren't too bad, but I can see why she might find them heavy. She acts tough, but she's a lot frailer than she lets on, which reminds me of Grandma. Nobody would've known she was in her sixties by observing her. So much energy, so much wit and humor. My heart aches as I remember her. If she hadn't died so early, Grandpa might've been better. He aged two decades when the doctor announced he couldn't save her. And he let himself go, too, like he no longer had any reason to live.

"You look fabulous. I love your new hair," Mrs. Yang says, looking up at me.

"Thank you."

"And your clothes. So stylish. That bag is Hermes, isn't it?"

I start. I have no clue, to be honest. I just accepted whatever Josephine pushed in my direction. "Uh, yeah. I think."

"It's so fashionable. My son said he's going to buy me one when he becomes a K-pop idol." She snorts. "I tell him it'll be easier and faster to be a doctor, but he's not so smart. Doesn't study." She tsks.

"He might surprise you. Aren't K-pop stars popular everywhere these days?"

She makes a displeased noise. "I doubt it. He's too lazy to learn to dance. Not everyone can dance, you know? And even if he practiced, he has my mother-in-law's face. He's never going to be a star with a face like that."

It's good I'm not taking a drink at the moment. Since I don't even know how to respond, I just smile and nod.

When we arrive in our hall, there are a couple of delivery men with boxes and boxes of things standing outside my apartment. One checks his phone, then the number on my door.

"Can I help you?" I ask.

"I'd be obliged. You know when the lady who lives here is

coming home? We were told she should be here, but she isn't answering the door. Or her phone." The fellow is large and rawboned, and his nametag says *Chuck*.

I reach into my new purse and see a couple of texts and missed calls. *Oops.* "This is my unit. And you are...?"

"Chuck. And this here's Norman. Josephine Blackwood sent us."

"Already?" I squeak. When she said she was going to have the items delivered, I thought she meant maybe tomorrow or the day after. Not within a couple of hours, especially since we weren't finished until the end of the business day.

"We're actually running a mite late."

"Did you order something special from Amazon?" Mrs. Yang says, her eyes bright and eager. She has to know whatever I'm getting is unusual—most of the time nobody cares to text or call you to make sure you're home when they deliver.

"No. Why don't I put these in your kitchen for you?" I turn to Chuck and Norman. "Can you give me a second?"

"Yeah, sure."

I nod my thanks and take the grocery bags into Mrs. Yang's kitchen. I put them on the counter, then head back out to the hall.

Mrs. Yang follows. I let everyone into my small apartment. If the delivery men are shocked at how shabby it is, they don't show it. But the boxes take up more than half the space. I make sure everything matches the inventory sheet Norman hands me, and sign off on it. There's no way I'm letting anything fall through a crack when I have no clue how much it's going to cost me. Grant will make sure I pay.

After they're gone, Mrs. Yang turns to me, her eyes wide. "You bought all this stuff?" She gestures at the Mt. Everest of...things.

"Not me. A...guy."

"Oooh, he must have done something very bad, yes? Are you going to forgive him?"

"These aren't really about anything he did." They're more about what he's planning to do to me.

"You don't know because you're so young," Mrs. Yang says. "When men want to say sorry to their friends, they punch each other, you know? But they can't punch women, so they give us gifts.

My husband did. And my sons. They bring flowers. The bigger and more expensive the flowers, the badder they were, you know?" She gauges the sheer volume of stuff before us. "It must have been terrible. Maybe he hit you?"

I don't offer the humiliating details. What he did was just as bad. He stomped on my innocence, my dreams. He killed something inside me fourteen years ago.

She frowns. "Well, whatever it was, don't forgive him. Men who hit women are bad news." She wags a finger, just in case I miss her disapproval.

"Don't worry. I won't."

41

GRANT

It's early in the morning, and I lie in bed, thinking about the proposal I received. It looked okay, but something about the way the potential market size was calculated bothers me. It seems overly pessimistic, which is odd. Most pitches *over*state what's possible in order to get the maximum amount of funding.

I should take another look, just to make sure. And it should be with some coffee in my system, but I don't feel like getting out of bed. It's quiet and peaceful and—

My bedroom door crashes open. Aspen saunters in. She's in an emerald-green dress that fits her like it was designed for her and shows entirely too much cleavage and leg. The color brings out her eyes, and she moves with the confidence she used to exude when we were in college.

"What are you doing here?" I say, half sitting up. I don't recall giving her the security code for my place. And she doesn't have the keys.

She ignores me and walks toward my closet. I jump to my feet to stop her. I don't want her anywhere near my personal space, especially my closet.

But it's too late. She slides the doors open with a loud bang, then starts laughing at what's hanging inside.

"Oh my God, this is so ridiculous!" She looks at me over a shoulder, her eyes blazing with scorn. "You're just so pathetic, thinking I could ever be the girl you thought you knew."

Her words cut, each deeper than the one before.

She turns to face me full on. "I'm aspiring to more. *Much* more, while you're living in the past. Grow the fuck up."

I struggle to come up with something just as hurtful to say to her. I want her to know the pain I'm feeling—

She turns and loops her arms around... *Dad?*

How and when did he come into my bedroom? I've *never* let him inside my home. And most importantly, why the hell is she pressing her body against *him?*

An urge to tear her from him burns through me. I start to move toward them, but my limbs feel sluggish.

He puts his hands around her waist, and she rises on her toes and kisses him. My belly roils, and I feel like projectile-vomiting on them. I throw a punch at his face because that's what he deserves for touching her. Once I knock his teeth out, I'm going to grab her and—

I miss. Dad smirks and Aspen giggles. An alarm blares next to my head, making me wince.

I flinch, then open my eyes and stare at the ceiling, while my heartbeat thunders in my ears and my lungs suck air. What the hell...? That was just a dream?

Groaning, I swat my phone until the alarm quits and run a hand down my face. What a sickening nightmare. And why Dad? He's never been in a dream before. Ever. As for Aspen... I've had a few dreams, but they've been sexual in nature—with *me.*

If she's going to kiss Dad, she should do it in *her* dream. Actually, *no*, she shouldn't kiss him at all. That's disgusting.

I know why I had that dream. It's because Yvette sent me a picture of her kissing Dad in the Bahamas, her hair still bright red. I responded that he was welcome to my sloppy seconds.

I get up and start toward the bathroom, then pause and make a quick detour to the closet. When I spot the things inside, I let out a small sigh. I should throw them away, but I haven't been able to. I don't know exactly why I bought them, or why I'm still holding on to them. My brothers would say I'm acting like a kid who won't give up his childhood teddy bear. But these things aren't teddy bears. They're more like...reminders. Like the fourteen neat lines tattooed on my shoulder.

After the run with my associates—which I plan to stop after today, since they've learned their lesson—I shower and have two strong coffees, then go to work. Endorphins from my morning exercise linger, but I'm still grumpy from the nightmare. The image of Aspen and my dad just won't go away. Why couldn't it have been about Yvette and Dad? I wouldn't have cared at all.

There's an email from Josephine Blackwood with an invoice attached. I glance at it to see what she bought for Aspen, and nod with approval. The woman has good taste and judgment. Then I wonder what "miscellaneous lingerie" means. Like...thongs? Demi-bras? Lace? No lace?

Stop thinking about Aspen's underwear!

I shake myself mentally. Just as I close the email, my senses go on full alert like they always do whenever Aspen's around. I see her walking toward her desk near my office through the open door, and everything in my gut tightens. She's in an emerald-green dress, like the one I saw in my dream, except in reality, the dress stops an inch above her knees, and it doesn't show any cleavage. But my mind's already filling in the blanks, and my palms tingle like they're tracing her curves.

The thin material of the dress swirls and clings to her thighs. I narrow my eyes. Unless I'm mistaken, it's one of those fabrics that you can't wear with underwear. *And there's no line.*

My blood boils at the thought of Aspen's hidden nudity. And that *she's in the office like this.* Matthias smiles at her and says something, to which she replies with an even prettier smile. She hasn't smiled like that at me.

Wait... Did that cocksucker just check her ass out? Oh, *yes he did.* And she's still smiling at him, like she enjoys the attention! He's just some former Goldman Sachs investment banker with a lousy Harvard MBA. Nothing special! Maybe I should continue the morning run one more day and invite her too, so she can see he runs like there's a cattle prod stuck up his ass. That should kill whatever attraction she's feeling for him.

A tight knot starts to burn in my gut. Don comes over to says something to her too. He hands her a granola bar, and she beams! What the hell? He got that from the breakroom. And *I* pay for everything in there, not him! If she's going to say thanks and smile, it should be to me, not him.

She finally sits down and opens her laptop. I glare at her, my teeth clenched so tight my jaw aches, then glance at the green crystal Mt. Everest clock from Noah. She wasted five minutes flirting with those jerks. She's never done that before.

It's that dress—and the way it clings to her ass. I pull up the intercompany messenger and fire off a shit-ton of due diligence to Matthias and Don. If they have the time to eyeball the curvature of her butt, they can take on this massive project.

She shifts a little and the dress rides up, showing a taut expanse of mid-thigh. My mouth dries. I reach for my coffee and realize the mug's empty. Damn it.

She smooths her clothes and stands up, grabbing her legal pad. The dress falls over her, clinging to her high breasts and waist and hips like a lover's kiss. My blood is so hot, my skin feels like it's burning.

Finally, she's going to go over the day's agenda with me. I rein in all the snide comments popping into my head about her flirting with other guys in the office, because they would make it sound like I cared.

She walks in and closes the door. The shoes are stilettos that emphasize the stunning length of her shapely legs. The sight reminds me of how she looked back in Malibu, when she stood in nothing but lingerie and heels. My dick starts to perk up, and I resist the urge to shift in my seat. Can't let her see my physical reaction.

What she's wearing and doing has to be calculated. She knows the impact she has on men. I shouldn't have bought her anything except the bag. This is what happens when I let my emotions guide me, because she still does something volatile and dangerous to me.

Her hips swing as she walks closer. I find myself running my tongue along my lip and immediately stop. *No. Just no.*

"You're late," I say.

"I am not." She looks at a slim Harry Winston on her wrist.

Josephine must've noticed mine and got her a matching one, like we're a couple or something. "It's nine right now."

"Nine-oh-three," I correct her. "You should reset yours so it's accurate."

"I'll make sure all my watches and clocks are set to the Grant Time Zone." She shifts, and the fabric moves with her.

I look closely. No line. Not even a string showing.

"Are you staring at my crotch?" she asks.

"I'm wondering why you're in that dress." I wasn't staring at her crotch. I was trying to figure out what could be underneath.

"Because you asked me to upgrade my wardrobe and paid for it?" Her hair's unbound today, framing her face perfectly. Very irritating.

"It's unprofessional."

"How so? I picked the dress this morning based on your feedback." She deepens her voice and raises her index finger. "'You look like shit. Frumpy.'" Then the middle finger. "'Homeless people wear better clothes.'" The ring finger. "'I don't like it when people dress to inspire pity.'" A corner of her lips twists as she raises the pinky. "'How you look reflects on both me and the company.' So I picked out the most fabulous outfit from the ones your personal shopper sent me. And you're right." She gives me an insincere smile. "People *do* treat me differently now that I'm not dressed like a hobo."

She hasn't forgotten my other dig. *If you dressed better, maybe Larry wouldn't have been such a dick. He's shallow and judges people by the way they dress.*

"Even Matthias and Don said hi, and they're never that friendly."

That spikes my blood pressure again. "That doesn't mean you should dress like a"—I struggle with a suitable word, since I'd rather get trampled by a horse than admit she's hot or that I'm affected—"hussy!"

Her eyebrows climb a couple of stories. "A *hussy*?"

Not the word I was looking for, but it's too late to take it back. I opt for offense. "I wanted you to look and act professional, not flirt with every male on the floor."

"Matthias and Don hardly constitute 'every male.'"

"Don gave you a granola bar he *filched* from the breakroom."

"So? At least he's nice enough to bring me things without expecting anything in return. That's called 'altruism,'" she says, overpronouncing the word.

"It's easy to be altruistic with something somebody else paid for. In case you didn't know, *I* pay for the snacks in there." Technically it's the firm, but I'm the cofounder and co-owner, so it's really me.

She taps her lip. "Hmm. You know, you're right."

I open my mouth to say something, but this sudden agreement leaves me momentarily mute.

"I'll take him up on his offer to go out for a coffee break later. His treat, he says. I'm sure he'll pay for it with his own money."

She's doing this on purpose. She has to know she still has the power to arouse fury and other frustratingly intense feelings I'd rather not name, no matter how much I try to hide her effect on me. Although our time together was short back then, we knew each other pretty well—easily well enough to know which buttons to push.

"He won't have time for a coffee break because I just put him on the Levine due diligence," I say, rather pleased with myself for my foresight. Over my dead body is she going to be having coffee with Don.

She cocks an eyebrow. "And if you hadn't, you would now."

"I'm the boss. If you don't like it, quit and be your own boss."

She shakes her head. "The others were right," she mutters, more to herself than to me.

"About what?" I demand.

"You being grouchy. If you're going to be difficult and moody, why don't you just call Yvette and relieve yourself? She'd welcome the opportunity."

The mention of Yvette doesn't inspire anything except a recollection of my nightmare. My mood darkens. Aspen can't possibly know about my awful dream, but that doesn't mean she didn't push my button. Again. "What the hell does that mean?"

"You're the boss. Use your boss brain and figure it out," she says as she holds her legal pad higher on her chest to flip me the bird. She thinks she's so clever, but I can see her reflection on the minibar fridge door to her left. "The word around here is that you need to get laid." She probably didn't mean for me to hear that, because she muttered it quietly. But I hear it anyway, and what little patience I've been holding on to frays, like a sweater when you tug at the loose thread.

Does she think that I haven't tried to get laid? None of the women on my phone look good. And I never experienced that until she reappeared in my life. It's all her fucking fault that I am impossible and I can't get laid. Or that I'm plagued by erotic nightmares. Or that I keep thinking about her, wondering about her, and stew in pain, anger and resentment, old and new.

And jealousy, too. Because God knows I got jealous as hell when she smiled at Matthias and Don. And I hate it that she makes me feel this way.

Her I-didn't-do-anything expression snaps something inside me.

I jump to my feet and stride toward her. Apprehension flares in her eyes. Her tongue darts out and licks her lips. On a different woman, I might call it a nervous gesture, but never her. When she does it, it's a temptation. A dare.

She holds her ground, her chin held high. I snake my hand out, wrap it around her wrist and pull her to me. She loses her balance in those heels. The legal pad clatters on the floor, and her body collides against mine.

Christ. She's not wearing a bra. I tunnel my fingers into her hair, holding her tight. The visible pulsing in her delicate neck drives me crazy. I want to bury my face there and inhale her scent, suck, letting her feel my teeth against her skin, until I leave my mark on her, so everyone else in the damn office knows to stay away.

Her eyes on mine, she doesn't push me away. Something that looks like *you wouldn't dare* crosses her gaze as her breathing roughens and her cheeks turn rosier.

I gave you a chance to stop this, I think savagely before my mouth crashes down on hers. My head starts to spin, and I can't get enough. I drink her up like a man who hasn't had water in weeks. She's so sweet, so delicious. What's even hotter is that she's kissing me back, aggressively—like she wants to devour me and hurt me at the same time.

I know the feeling.

I slip my free hand under her dress and run it along the smooth expanse of her skin, which is taut and warm under my palm. I reach her ass, let my fingertips graze her waist and the dip by the tailbone and feel nothing. She's most definitely not wearing any underwear. My cock is so hard it's agonizing. I want to punish her for coming to work like this, but I also want to reward her. The contradictory desires only add to my maddening lust. She's the only woman who can drive me crazy like this.

I turn us and push her backward until she's perched on the edge of my desk. All the while, our mouths stay fused, our tongues warring. I tug at the zipper behind her back, pulling it down, until her gorgeous tits are revealed to my hungry gaze. They're so pert and round. My mouth waters, and I don't hold back like I did before, when it was her first time—when I wanted to make the moment so, so special for her.

We're too old for that, too jaded. I want to fuck her out of my system. I desperately want to prove to myself she isn't that exceptional, and I've over-romanticized what happened between us fourteen years ago.

I pull a nipple into my mouth, sucking, flicking my tongue over the hard tip. She makes a hot, ragged sound, then quickly places a hand over her mouth to muffle it.

"I want to hear you."

"No." Defiance mixes with the lust in her glittering eyes as she keeps the hand over her mouth.

"You'll let me hear it." I take her nipple back in my mouth and run my hands over her, rediscovering her sensitive spots, driving her as crazy as she's driving me.

Logic doesn't exist; the old resentment doesn't exist. The only thing that exists is the scent of her, the taste of her, the heat of her. She makes a sound in the back of her throat that her hand can't muffle, and satisfaction pours through me. I chuckle softly.

"Fuck you," she whispers, her voice unsteady.

Laughing, I pull her other nipple into my mouth and trace her every curve. But even as I do my best to dominate her senses, I'm lost in her, like an alcoholic lost in a bottle. When I touch the flesh between her legs and have her juices soak my fingers, I almost come in my pants.

She's panting hard, her breasts rising and falling rapidly, her thighs spread wide, her pink flesh glistening for me. *Me.* She can call me an asshole, cut me at every turn, but her body craves *me*—what *I* can give.

I manage to pull a condom out of my pants pocket and put it on, then fit my cock at her entrance. I dip my head to reclaim her mouth, but she turns her head, so my lips end up on her smooth cheek as I slide into her. *Holy shit.* She feels even better than I remembered. So tight. So hot.

All my nerve endings light up. The gods could offer me immortality to pull away, and I wouldn't. I drive inside her, pounding hard, making sure to hit the spot that she responded to the best all those years ago.

She throws her head back, her neck tight with tension. I wrap my fingers around her hair and try to kiss her. But she clenches her teeth and pulls away. In the back of my head, a small warning goes off, but I'm too lost to give it much notice.

The rough breathing and the tiny sobs that escape the hand over her mouth betray her excitement—how close she is to climax. I drive harder and faster, reaching down to rub her clit. I need to see her unravel, to go out of control like me.

Finally, she shudders in orgasm, and I let go. The pleasure hits with the force of a building collapsing—like an all-consuming, haze-inducing union with the universe.

I struggle to breathe and prop myself up so I don't crush her. Her breasts rise and fall, her nipples pointed and gorgeous in the sunlight. I lower my head and place a kiss between the soft, sweet mounds. She puts her index finger in the middle of my forehead and slowly pushes me up.

"Enough," she says, her voice husky.

"I don't think you're finished. You were always greedy for more." *Why is she rejecting me now?* Her lips purse, and I try to kiss her until she's pliant and soft again.

She turns away. "Stop."

"It's a little too late for games."

"It's not a game. I don't understand why we should kiss now."

What the hell? We kissed earlier, and she didn't object. My lower lip still stings a little from a scrape she gave me with her teeth —not that I'm complaining. The pain reminds me this is real.

"It isn't like you expected something sweet and naïve, did you? We aren't in college anymore," she adds.

The unsettling sensation I ignored earlier returns.

Before I can give it any consideration, she continues. "We were just scratching an itch. You wanted to get laid, and I haven't been with anyone in a while either. So. It doesn't mean anything."

What she's saying is exactly what I should be feeling too, but somehow her words make me feel cheap and used. A hot burn that has nothing to do with lust starts in my belly.

She shrugs. "I enjoy my vibrator, but I don't kiss it afterward."

There must be something really fucked up in my head, because that makes me not just furious but hard. I shove my dick back inside her almost violently, and smile with grim satisfaction when she lets out a startled gasp.

"Can your vibrator do this? Fuck you hard until you come again?" I ask.

She refuses to respond, even as sexual need colors her face.

I fuck her until my knees shake and she nearly passes out from a series of orgasms. But even then, I feel like I've lost.

42

ASPEN

By the time I leave Grant's office, it's almost noon. My legs are unsteady, and the flesh between my thighs feels swollen and slick, even though I cleaned myself up in his office.

Thankfully, everyone's too busy to look up from their laptops. Grant wasn't kidding about dumping work on Don and Matthias, and they must've grabbed a bunch of junior associates and analysts to assist.

Pasting on a neutral smile, I sit at my desk and take a long, calming breath. But it doesn't work to settle my nerves. *What got Grant so mad and weird?* Does he want to do it again? Is he going to be a jerk about it and make my job even more difficult? Or maybe fire me?

Well... If he tries to fire me, I'm suing him for wrongful termination.

I start to purse my mouth, then stop when my lips sting. He kissed me wildly, without any of the finesse I remember. What triggered him to kiss me like that in the first place?

But what was more disturbing was my reaction. I succumbed to the kiss, like it was the most natural thing in the world for him to claim my mouth. And I *burned* for him. It's humiliating how wet I got. How easily I climaxed.

The only consolation was that he couldn't seem to control himself either. And he kept trying to kiss me even though I turned my face away. The kisses remind me too much of the affection he used to shower me with. They clouded my judgment, until my heart fluttered, like the sex between us meant something.

I can't let him kiss me freely, not when his kisses have such power over me. And especially not when I know it's foolish to try to put any sort of meaning behind the act. He was probably just horny, and, to be honest, so was I. The last time I had sex was... God, I can't even remember.

Besides, he waited until I was better dressed before making his move. He's such a snob that he can't bring himself to touch me unless I'm in a designer dress.

I had more orgasms in his office than I have in...over a decade. But it was cleansing, in a way. Like a Grant detox. I'm completely, utterly done with him, and we won't ever do anything like that again.

43

GRANT

Aspen stays away from me as much as she can for the next few days, and I give her space because I need to figure out why I'm having trouble evicting her from my mind after that sex in the office. And why does my dick continue to get hard in the morning every time I see her? I came three times inside her, until my brain basically turned into oatmeal, so why do I continue to obsess about her?

Maybe because something about her bothers you? Something's puzzling you?

Maybe it's because there are things about her that I know nothing about. I hate not having complete information about the people I'm dealing with. I didn't care if I knew nothing about Yvette or the other women, but there are exceptions to rules. Aspen happens to be one at the moment. That doesn't mean she's special.

No woman will ever be special again.

But I don't have time for a detailed reading of her HR file. One of the companies we've invested in has a massive scandal that's impacting their reputation and the marketability of their product. Cutting off our funding is an option, but I prefer to avoid that, since I have to consider our investors' best interests. I have a fiduciary duty to maximize their return.

The mess would've been easier to clean up if the founder hadn't tried so hard to protect his daughter, who's not only their marketing VP but at the center of the scandal. If she was going to have an affair with one of the staff, she should've made sure he wasn't making a video of them playing out her fantasy of forcing him. And she should've at least made sure to fool around with someone smart enough not to make his phone passcode *123456*. He might as well have begged to be hacked. And the hackers accepted the challenge and posted the sex video everywhere.

The idiot privately blackmailed the company, saying he'd tell everyone he was forced. And the VP responded by denying it was her in the video, since she's married with four children, even though the video shows her face clearly.

My neck is tight from marathon phone calls and meetings. Terence is resentful that everything has to come out and his daughter's marriage is irrevocably damaged, but I really don't give a damn. Her inability to keep private things private isn't my problem. Her lack of common sense negatively impacting our investment is.

Larry and I leave together after our final meeting with the company at their headquarters.

"One more day and we can take time off and just forget all this," Larry says with a wan smile.

"A happy hour won't be out of order." Everyone has worked hard, and I want to reward them. As soon as we can get our money plus the returns we're expecting on this venture, I'm divesting fully. Life's too short to clean up somebody else's mess.

Larry perks up some more. He loves free booze even more than women. "Awesome."

My phone pings, and I glance at the screen, praying it's anyone but Terence and his daughter. But it's Leah from HR.

—Leah: Aspen's grandfather is at the Orange Care Center. It's a very nice place. A friend's mother-in-law was there. That place costs an arm and a leg, though. Which explains why Aspen was interested in this particular benefit.

Leah's not generally chatty, but if it's a topic she's an expert on, she grows more animated. Or maybe she's offering some extra information because she wants to cozy up to me. She got divorced last year, and has made it clear that she would love a quick fling. I pretend not to notice—it would complicate things for me to screw somebody from HR.

"I have another appointment," I tell Larry. "You can update the files and let Aspen know that I'm not coming back in. Make sure she leaves right at five."

"Of course." He nods and heads toward his car. He's been extra polite to the admin staff after the team-building exercise. It's too bad he couldn't learn to be decent on his own without having to put his entire team through that torture.

I look up the nursing home's address. The website indicates that visitors are welcome with a resident's approval.

Seeing Kenny sounds like a great idea, especially since Aspen wouldn't tell me anything about herself when I asked. Kenny didn't seem wholly together, but that might work to my advantage. He might say things that he shouldn't. Once I have my curiosity satisfied about Aspen, I won't be thinking about her all the time anymore. My dick certainly won't get hard at the thought of her, either.

Sex with her is a problem. She can use it against me, just like she used it to manipulate my feelings fourteen years ago.

You're wasting your time. Why do you care about her circumstances, anyway? HR already vetted her.

I ignored the small voice. I'm not doing this because I care about her. This is due diligence. Unless I have all the facts, I won't be able to do what is necessary. Namely, ensuring that she quits on her own. I want her gone before she does anything else to mess with what's left of my sanity.

The Orange Care Center is over two hours away from downtown in rush-hour traffic. It proves to be located on the outskirts of Los Angeles. It has a modest garden with average landscaping. The only really eye-catching things are the sunflowers, which are brilliantly yellow, and the fact that the building is painted the same bright hue. I thought it would be orange, like the name implies.

I walk inside and see a bottle blonde with a silver ring through her left eyebrow, and a middle-aged Asian behind the counter. "Hi," the man says with a smile. His nametag reads *Gi-Hoon Jung*. "How can I help you?"

I give him my most charming smile. It's the kind of smile that puts people at ease and inspires confidence and trust. It also helps that I'm in a Brioni suit, designed to exude power and authority. "Hello. My name is Grant Lasker, and I'm here to visit Kenny Hughes."

He beams. "Yes, of course. He's such a fabulous guy. Is it all right if I check your ID and scan you into our visitor system?"

"By all means." I give him my driver's license.

He looks at it, then uses his smartphone to take a photo. "I just need you to sign on the screen here."

The screen is pre-filled with an image of my ID, along with the date, time and person I'm visiting. I scrawl my name with my index finger in the rectangle at the bottom.

"Let me go check with the memory unit. Sometimes Kenny's in a great mood, but sometimes he's not interested in seeing anyone." Gi-Hoon makes an apologetic face. "Good days, bad days."

I try to hide my surprise. It never crossed my mind that I might not be able to see Kenny. Or that he could be having a "bad day." Just how awful is it that the center won't let him see anyone?

While Gi-Hoon checks, I look around the area. On the other side of the door behind the counter are some old people. They're watching TV and laughing. A few of them are playing cards. Kenny doesn't seem to be with them.

Gi-Hoon returns. "He says he would like to see you. He seems to be in a great mood."

"Thank you." *Thank God I didn't waste four hours coming out here.* "I'll call first next time."

"That would be fine, but it doesn't really guarantee anything. His mood changes quite rapidly sometimes." Gi-Hoon is apologetic again. "Anyway, the memory unit is on the third floor," he says. "Just take the elevator over there. Kenny's in the breakroom."

I take the elevator up and step out into the memory unit, which feels a little off. Not because there's anything wrong with the place. There's just something sad about a big room being so full of old people, all of whom are probably far from their families. Aspen has to be living closer to the office than here. Otherwise, her commute would be atrocious.

How often does she come by? Probably not every day. And even if she wanted to, she couldn't when I was making her work until midnight. Guilt needles me, and I take a steadying breath. *I didn't know, and she didn't tell me.* She never tells me anything. She just does whatever she wants, not caring about how I'm going to feel when I find out about it.

She couldn't have made clearer how little she cares about my feelings when she sold my gifts fourteen years ago. A lousy two hundred K was more important.

I walk through the double doors into the memory unit. An electric chime sounds. Somebody from the reception desk looks up, notes me and then looks down again, focusing on paperwork.

I walk down the hall. A woman wanders by, her eyes vague. A staff member is with her, talking in a low voice. It's not clear whether the woman hears him or not. I hope Kenny isn't that far gone—it'd be sad to see a man who used to be so vibrant reduced to that.

I reach the breakroom, which has a huge TV. Kenny is in a small plastic chair, his eyes on the screen. He laughs occasionally, although I'm not sure what's so funny. Nobody is joking with him, and the TV is showing a crime drama.

I walk up to him. "Kenny? Sir?"

Slowly, he turns to me. His eyes focus, and a smile splits his face. "Zack."

I frown, hating that he's smiling like that while thinking I'm Zack. This is the second time he's thought I was that guy. Just how close *was* he to Aspen and her family? And is Kenny lucid enough to tell me anything useful?

Still, most of what I'm feeling is sympathy. I don't look anything like Zack. Does Kenny confuse Aspen and Kat with other people, too? That would hurt. It might explain why Kat wasn't with him and Aspen at the steakhouse. She might not be able to bear being around a husband who doesn't recognize her anymore.

"I was just thinking about you," Kenny says. "Come, have a seat." He gestures.

I drag a plastic chair over and lower myself into it. The seat is unergonomic and uncomfortable.

"I was just thinking that you're the perfect person to take Aspen to the prom," Kenny says.

The prom?

"Don't be shy." He pats my hand. "Take charge of the situation. I know you have a crush on her. I don't like most of the boys that she hangs out with, but not you. You're solid."

Over the sympathy, hot jealousy burns through me. Zack probably did get to take Aspen to the prom. She wouldn't have gone with some other guy when her grandfather was rooting for the two of them. I wonder if he's still in her life, and if so, are they dating?

Probably not. If they were dating, she wouldn't have slept with me. Or maybe he sucks so awfully in bed that she just doesn't care.

I shake my head. *Focus on Kenny.*

"I'm afraid the prom's over," I tell him gently, hoping I don't confuse or upset him. I'm out of my element. "Aspen's thirty-four years old."

Kenny looks at me in bewilderment. "Thirty-four?"

I keep my voice soft and gentle. "Yes. All grown up. With a job."

He blinks a few times, then suddenly swings a hand out to smack me. I catch the hand and return it to his side. *What the hell?*

"You asshole!" he says.

"Excuse me?" How did I go from the nice guy who should take Aspen to the prom to some dick he should hit?

"You son of a bitch."

"You know who I am?"

"Yes. *Grant.*"

The sheer venom he puts into the word doesn't make sense. There has to be another Grant.

"She invited over once." Rage seethes underneath his shaking voice.

"I brought wine and flowers."

"I should've known you were too slick. You didn't just bring any flowers. You brought Kat's favorite."

He isn't confusing me with anybody else. But then, why is he so angry? "Yes. I wanted her to like me."

"Why? So she could bake you a pie? All her pies are mine!"

"Uh..." I raise my hands in surrender. "Yeah. Sure. Sorry."

"You ruined Aspen's life!"

"I didn't do anything," I protest, lowering my arms.

Kenny jumps to his feet, his hands clenched. I watch in mute fascination as he swings his fists and hits me on the shoulders. It doesn't hurt. He's too frail to hit very hard. But the ugliness on his face is paralyzing. He was such a gentleman fourteen years ago. I can't reconcile that image with this...person in front of me now. Can becoming old and losing memories change someone to this degree? Or is there more?

"*Ruined* it!" he shouts. "Because of you, she couldn't even finish college. It's all your fault!"

A staff member comes over, putting gentle but firm hands on Kenny's arms to stop him from hitting me again.

"You don't have to restrain him," I say. "I think I triggered bad memories somehow. I didn't mean to. I'm sorry."

"It's okay," the man says over Kenny's ranting. "It happens. I'm just surprised, because he doesn't usually get violent. Are you hurt?"

"No. I'm fine." I stand, while Kenny continues to froth and call me names.

"I think it's best if you leave," the guy says with an apologetic smile.

"Yes, I think so."

As I walk away, I can't tear my eyes from Kenny's fury. His mind isn't wholly there, but he truly believes that I'm the reason Aspen's life's ruined. Not only that, he blames me for her not finishing college. But that doesn't make sense. She was desperate to get her diploma and studied harder than anybody I knew at Napa Aquinas to keep her scholarship.

I walk back out into the parking lot with more questions than answers. It's hard to tell how much of what Kenny said I should take at face value. And does he get violent with Kat? Is that why they put him in the center?

Just what the hell happened to Aspen and her family?

44

ASPEN

The nice thing about the whole team being in chaos over a scandal is that Grant's been too busy to see me for our morning briefings. I did all my work through email and the company messenger. However, now that things have settled down, we're going back to the standard routine.

But at least it's Friday, and I'll have the weekend to get some space and process. I still don't know what to make of the fact that I had sex with him. Or the fact that my reaction when I think of him no longer includes just annoyance or distaste. It was *totally* uncharacteristic of me to succumb to him...or still be reliving those endless orgasms. It's like he's even better now than he was before, which is probably due to more experience.

But I know that isn't all. His being my first did something weird to my psyche that makes me feel this crazy attraction all the more keenly. It's just different with him versus other men. Different and *better*.

I take an extra-deep breath as I glance at Grant's agenda again. *It's just a job.* He's paying me to do the briefing, so I should do it. *Think of Grandpa.*

I can do anything for him, including sucking up and pretending the sex with Grant never happened.

And it *won't* happen again.

I gather my notes and walk into Grant's office. He studies me, his gaze unreadable. He doesn't look like a man who wants to devour me, although my idiot hormones start to heat up under his penetrating scrutiny.

At least I'm wearing underwear! I made sure of that since the green dress incident, although Josephine hasn't sent a single pair of slacks. Intellectually I understand that one extra layer of flimsy fabric isn't much, but it feels like a shield nonetheless.

Keeping my voice level to hide how he's affecting me, I start to go over his agenda for the day. When I'm done, I look at him with the neutral smile I've perfected over the years to give bar customers who are a little too friendly.

"Any instructions?" I ask.

"Why didn't you finish college?"

"What?"

"You heard me."

Why is he asking that, especially now? Will he try to fire me, claiming I'm unqualified for the assistant position? No—if that's what he wanted, he would've asked earlier. And if he tries now, I'll sue for wrongful termination. I was crystal clear on being a college dropout when Emmett tried to hire me, and he said it wasn't a problem.

"Which version do you want?" I ask.

Confusion crosses his face, which is annoying. What's so puzzling to him? He knows why I had to leave the campus. Even if it hadn't been for Grandma's death, it would've been excruciating to continue at the college. It's a small school, and the constant stream of whispered mockery would've worn me down.

"The honest version," he says finally.

Now I understand what this is about. He wants to hear me describe my humiliation in detail for his amusement. *Asshole.* Too bad; I have no intention of humoring him. "The tuition was unaffordable."

"You had scholarships." His eyes narrow with displeasure, which gives me immense satisfaction.

"Not enough."

"You cleared at least two hundred K from that auction."

"What are you talking about?"

"Don't act stupid. I know you sold the things I gave you."

He knows?

"Don't even think about denying it. I saw the listings."

He actually sounds like he's upset about that. Why didn't he reach out if it mattered that much to him? Or maybe he didn't want to bother because they were really just a payment for my virginity like Sadie said, but now he's unhappy because... Is this because he had to buy me things again, so I look "nice enough" for him?

"What did you do with all that money?" he demands.

"It's none of your business what I did with the money. It was mine. I earned it." The bitterness I tried to hide spills into my voice anyway. But it's hard to hold back when he's acting like I'm in the wrong.

"You *earned* it? I gave you those dresses and so on as gifts, and you turned them into barter items."

I let out a cynical laugh. Of *course* he's one of those people who revises the past to make himself come out to be the good guy. He's conveniently forgotten about the bet and the streaking and the humiliation I suffered. Whenever the memory of other students laughing at me surfaces, I feel like throwing up.

"If you don't have any further instructions, I'll leave," I say. "I do have real work to do."

"The work *I* have assigned you." His jaw flexes. "Don't act like we're nothing."

"I wouldn't dream of it. Of course we're *some*thing. You're the boss, and I'm the assistant. Thank you for pointing that out, because I would've never known otherwise." And I walk out of the office before Grant can say anything else.

45

GRANT

I glare at the door. Unlike before, Aspen shut it after slipping out.

It's none of my business what she did with the money? It was something she earned?

She should've just admitted that she used me. I would at least have some respect for her honesty. But now the fury that's been simmering in my blood is at a full boil. I only kept my mouth shut because I didn't want to say something too revealing—like how much her betrayal hurt me. That'd be too humiliating.

Regardless, having her confirm that I was an idiot all those years ago makes me want to kick something. The fact that sex in the office didn't do a thing to lessen my appetite for her worsens my mood. Now every time I look at my desk, my mind conjures up the image of her sitting on the edge of it, legs spread and ready...

And—of course—now my dick is hard again.

Fuck. Me.

Stewing about what she's done to me would be letting her win, and I'm not going to give her that much power. I wrench my attention back to work, spending the rest of the day in one meeting after another. Aspen wisely keeps her distance. Perhaps she can sense I'm ready to bite her head off.

Still, as the day goes by, my temper starts to cool and my mind

335

clears. I realize that some things about Aspen just don't add up, and I didn't get the answers I needed earlier because she distracted me by pissing me off.

Those answers are still important. With them, I won't have to second-guess myself or wonder if I've misjudged her. Although Kenny's outburst was shocking, he knew exactly whom he was talking to. I doubt someone with memory problems would generate so much anger over nothing. Something's triggered it, and his resentment isn't just old—it's genuine.

Did Aspen blame me? Why? To distract Kenny from asking about why she wasn't finishing her degree? Given how much she loves her grandparents, she must've used some of the money on Kenny and Kat. And they must've questioned her about it, and she probably lied to them.

But why is she secretive about it with me? She doesn't care what I think about her, and has to know my opinion of her couldn't sink any lower. Lusting after her body is a separate issue. Actually, she should've used my curiosity as an opportunity to manipulate me into giving her more—whether it was money or something she could sell.

Larry sticks his head into the office. "Are you coming to happy hour?"

"No." I have a couple of things to clear on my agenda, items I've had to push back because I was dealing with the scandal.

His face falls a little—he's probably wondering who's going to foot the bill, since Emmett is out of town at the moment.

"Here." I pull out my corporate card. "Give that to Amy and have her expense everything."

He immediately brightens. "Thanks!" He leaves with alacrity.

I sigh. Why isn't Aspen as easy to read as Larry? She's shrouded in a thick fog I can't seem to cut through. Every time I think I have her figured out, something new pops up to throw me off.

Eight o'clock comes and goes, and I decide to pack it in for the evening. The floor is deserted, completely silent, and as I make my way to the elevator, I notice the framed photos of Emmett and Monique on Amy's desk.

I turn around, go back to Aspen's desk and stand there, staring at it. It's completely clear. Not a pen, not a stapler... Nobody would know from a casual glance that the desk was being used at all.

Earlier, the lack of personal touches made sense. She knew I was dying to fire her, and she didn't know if she'd have a job. But now she's been here long enough to bring some things to liven up her desk, like she did when she was in that godawful dorm.

But there's nothing. Not even a photo of her grandparents.

If I were naïve, I'd say she's just a deeply private person. But I doubt she's suddenly developed an overwhelming urge to maintain her privacy. She's hiding something. I need to know what that is, so I can end this unnatural obsession with her.

―――――

I walk the long hallway of the Orange Care Center. The memory unit is dimly lit. I'm looking for Kenny, but all I see are random old people who stare and whisper.

The words are unintelligible, but my gut says they're talking about me, and nothing out of their mouths is complimentary.

Who cares? I don't give a damn about what people think of me, unless it's somebody who I decide matters. And these people don't.

Every time I take a step, there's a crunching sound. Something hard and sparkling covers the floor. I glance around; it covers the entire memory unit. I kneel and look at the glittering stuff more closely. Jagged pieces of something. Broken glass, maybe.

Except it doesn't look like glass. More like diamonds.

Kenny's on the other side of the hall. He glares and points his finger. "You!"

"Hello," I say.

"Grant Lasker," he says. "You killed my girl."

What?

"You killed her. *Killed her.*"

He's confused. Again. "Aspen is fine."

"She's not fine! You killed her! You killed her!" He grows louder with each word, until every syllable is thundering in my head. Everyone's staring at me, their eyes judgmental. Instead of coming to soothe Kenny, the staff stares at me as well.

"Sir, you're just confusing things," I explain. "I didn't kill anybody."

"You have her blood on your hands!"

"I don't—" Something feels weird about my hands. I look down and see sticky red liquid flowing down my hands, from wrists to fingertips. Chills shiver down my spine, and I shake my hands. Liquid is flung, but the droplets land only on me.

A loud ringing comes from the doorway. I turn back, but as I do, Kenny lunges across the hall, moving as fast as a teenager, his fingers curled like talons. Then he's on me, the fingers digging into my neck, and—

The ringing blares again, and I open my eyes, breathing hard. It's dark and...

Shit. I check the time—it's barely six. I sit up and rest my throbbing head in my hands for a moment. *It's just a dream,* I tell myself, trying to calm my racing heart. What was up with that vivid nightmare, though? Maybe it's the whiskey I had, although I've never had weird dreams after a nightcap. Maybe my interaction with Kenny bothered me more than I thought.

The ringing comes again. What the... It's the doorbell. *Who could be visiting this early?* My brothers all know better.

I pull up the security app on my phone and squint at the screen. A woman with huge sunglasses is standing at the door, her mouth set in flat disapproval.

Mom...?

What's she doing here? She's supposed to be in Greece with her new boyfriend. If this were anybody else, I might assume he dumped her the day before the trip, and she needs moral support. But Athena Grant doesn't need that kind of feather-unruffling.

I pull on shorts and a T-shirt, then go down to the foyer to open the door. She lets out a long-suffering sigh. "Took you long enough," she says as she enters. She drags two huge suitcases inside.

"It's six a.m. What's going on?" I take her in. She's in a loose gray tunic, skinny jeans and fashionably scuffed cowboy boots. Huge golden chandelier earrings hang from her ears, and her strawberry-blonde hair is long and loose around her face. Her skin, as usual, is glowing.

Marching past the foyer to the living room, she takes off her sunglasses and sticks them in the front pocket of her tunic. She loathes being recognized. According to her, being recognized means she might have to interact with "stupid people"—i.e., ninety-nine percent of the population, as far as she's concerned.

"Last time we spoke, you were going on vacation with your boyfriend," I say, following her.

"Yes, well, that was before he splattered the walls of my home with goat blood," she says, like things like that happen all the time.

"*Goat* blood?" It's way too early for this shit.

She sits in one of the plush armchairs and crosses her legs. The motion is smooth and practiced, like she's a model. "Yes."

I park myself in an armchair set perpendicular to hers. "Okay. I know I'm going to regret asking, but why did he splatter goat blood all over your home?" Mom's dated outrageous men before, but none this insane.

"Some sort of voodoo love spell. Apparently, he's decided that I don't care for him enough."

The man is more perceptive than most of Mom's boyfriends. They all think that she's in love with them. But she never is, not really. And even if she were, she wouldn't love them the way most people think of "loving" someone.

In her worldview, the fact that she's deigning to interact with you at all means she loves you. Expecting more is unreasonable.

"So I dumped him," Mom says. "I plan to sue him for damage to my home, wasting my time and causing me immense discomfort and inconvenience."

"Are you going to ask Jeremiah to take the case?"

"Yes." She sighs. "Which is why I'm suing him for discomfort as well. But I intend to win, so there's really no choice."

Figures. Mom hates losing more than having to work with Jeremiah. Losing means being proven wrong, and Athena Grant can never be wrong.

"He dropped to his knees—literally, not metaphorically—and begged me to take him back, but I told him I couldn't. He's simply too dumb. He makes donkeys look like nuclear physicists. A *love* spell? It's as if the Enlightenment never happened. Who believes in such sheer idiocy now?"

I'm not surprised by her reaction. You can't persuade her by appealing to her emotions, because she has less than most. Not that most women would take back a guy who splattered their home with goat blood, even in the name of love. "So why are you here instead of managing the cleaning crew at Malibu?" This is now the most critical question.

She stretches her fingers, studying her immaculately lacquered nails. "I'm not just having it cleaned. I'm also remodeling and putting in better security. I obviously don't have enough security cameras and alarms. Otherwise, I would've known that he was bringing in animal blood."

I don't know what kind of security system could detect animal blood, but...okay. Whatever makes her happy.

"It's disgusting, although I suppose I should be grateful it wasn't fish blood. The stench would *never* come out."

My stomach is sinking. "So...you want to stay here?" *No, no, please no.*

"Of course," she says, like it's a foregone conclusion.

"I don't think that's a good idea." No way. There's no way I can let her stay here for however long it takes to install the security of her choice. I love her, but I can't live with somebody who can never, ever be wrong. "Let me have the concierge arrange for a hotel. It'll be more comfortable and convenient."

"You don't have to be so cold."

I almost choke. Cold is a word invented for her!

She continues, "And rude. I already checked, and no one has anything I like. Just be agreeable, sweetie."

Uh-oh. She only calls me "sweetie" when she knows she's about to ask for something unreasonable and has nothing to trade for it.

"I let you use my house when you were in college to impress a girl," she adds.

"That was fourteen years ago!"

"So?"

I shake my head. "Don't you think it's revealing you can't think of a favor you've done for me since?"

"Blame yourself for being an independent child." She shrugs. "Regardless, the house was really nice, you must admit. I had the place deep-cleaned before you showed up."

"Right. And you removed the mattress from every bedroom."

"I left *one*, which was all you needed. I looked at the security feed, sweetie. You only had one girl over. And even if you had had a couple more, that bed would've been more than adequate."

"*Mother*."

"Don't you 'mother' me. I'm merely pointing out you got exactly what you wanted." She smiles smugly. "You wouldn't have had your fun without me."

"Fun? It was a disaster." It's irritating that she's so happy when, every time I think about the episode, I inwardly writhe with shame.

"Why?" Her brow furrows. "Did you get her pregnant?"

"That would've been preferable to what happened." An unplanned pregnancy would've been a shock, but nothing I couldn't handle. Unlike Aspen's betrayal.

Mom looks at me like I took a dive into a tar pit.

"She was using me!" I say, losing patience with both her and the fact that Aspen can still affect me. "She took all the things I gave her and auctioned them off for money soon afterward."

"Count yourself lucky. You managed to escape the clutches of a stupid woman."

"She's not stupid, just manipulative!"

"Of course she is. What did I tell you about people who don't add up?"

"Figure out why they aren't adding up?"

"You weren't listening." She sighs. "When people don't add up, it means one of three things—they're lying, they're stupid, or they're crazy. She could've hung on to you until you naturally grew tired of her, instead of hurrying the process along. What an idiotic gold digger. Isn't it common sense for those types to leech as much out of their men for as long as possible?"

I grind my teeth as Mom lectures me like I haven't thought of all that already. I might've been gullible with Aspen, but I haven't been lobotomized.

Mom continues, "Or are they too lazy to do even that? Young

people these days have the work ethic of a gnat. No patience, no perseverance. Always wanting instant results."

I block out her tirade about the younger generation. I've heard it all before. And it's the same complaints she has with everyone else she disapproves of.

At least my mother is consistent.

But she's wrong about Aspen. She doesn't add up, but she isn't stupid or lazy or crazy. It's something else much more complicated. She's a thousand-piece puzzle, and I haven't even put together the edges.

I go to the kitchen to make some coffee—I'm going to need it. I'm pretty sure I can get Mom to leave by exaggerating the number of hours my housekeeping staff spends here cleaning my place, and lay it on thick about how chatty they are. Interacting with people is her idea of hell, and having chatty housekeeping staff around will fit the bill.

I just have to be sure that my concierge can get the best suite at whichever luxury hotel in the city she finds acceptable, since she hates slumming even more than people.

46

ASPEN

Bright sunlight pierces my eyes as I step outside the hall. I blink and squint as my vision adjusts. Before me is a huge green field. Countless college students are milling around. I scan the crowd to see if there's anybody I know, and realize everyone is someone I went to college with. What are they doing here?

I look down at myself and see denim shorts and a sage-colored Napa Aquinas College T-shirt. I haven't dressed like this in forever.

A warm hand holds mine, threading its fingers through my own. I look up and see Grant standing next to me, gorgeous in designer clothes and with a Harry Winston watch around his thick wrist. He presses his palm against mine, steady and calming.

"It's starting," Grant whispers, his breath fanning my earlobe and sending shivers down my spine.

"What is?" Whatever he's planning is going to be amazing. I can feel it in my bones.

"Something awesome. You'll like it. It's all about you."

Holding my hand more tightly, he walks with me, matching my steps. The students part like the Red Sea for Moses. They look at our linked hands, then raise their eyes to look at me. Their lips are curved in smiles so identical that they feel artificial.

Unease slithers underneath my skin. "You're really not going to

343

tell me what this is about?" I say it playfully, to hide my anxiety. I don't want to ruin the moment.

"It's a surprise." He places a kiss on top of my head.

I'm being nervous for nothing. I should trust him to make whatever this is good. He's never given me a surprise that wasn't delightful.

"It's starting!" shouts Sadie. Why does she sound so excited? She should be huffing and marching off in a fit of pique.

Grant takes a step sideways and stands behind me. He wraps his arms around my shoulders and leans his chin on my head. I can feel his body heat all along my back. The pose is protective and cocooning, but for some reason, claustrophobia clutches my throat.

"Just watch," he says sweetly.

Instead of reassuring me, his words make me feel doubly trapped. Something is *wrong*. I start to tell him to let go, but two naked guys burst out and start running along the field. I squint to see who they are. Heath and Will. They're shouting, too. I try to take a step back, but I can't, not with Grant holding me.

"I don't want to see this," I say over the hammering of my heart.

"Yes, you do." His voice is so calm, like the lull of the peaceful ocean at night.

Before I can sink into his hypnotic pull, I jerk myself back to the reality of what's happening in front of me.

"You're the star, baby."

"I'm not dressed like a star," I say stupidly.

"Sure you are." He laughs softly. "The Dior fits you perfectly."

What? I look down to check what I'm wearing. I'm in that dress Marketta picked out. When did that happen?

"Grant Lasker is a better man than us!" the boys shout in unison. "He deflowered her like a pro."

Grant laughs. I feel the shaking rumble against my back. Hot humiliation bursts inside me, and I can't breathe. Muffled giggles and outright laughter come from everyone.

"Let me *go*!" I struggle against Grant's grip.

But he tightens his hold. "You're going to watch this. This is the price you pay for stealing."

"You can have it back!" I shout, struggling to break free. But he's too strong.

"How? You sold it all, remember?"

"You can have it back! You can have it back," I repeat in an endless loop. I'll do anything to make this moment stop.

"No, I can't. Nothing you do can change the fact that you *took my things and sold them*. You owe me."

"I don't owe you anything! Everything ended when you used me. You did it for *amusement*."

"If I'd just wanted to have fun, I could've done it a lot cheaper," he hisses into my ear.

"The money was nothing to you. Just like I was nothing to you!" Tears pour down my cheeks. I twist and turn left and right. Desperation builds. Everyone is watching; I have to get away. Escape. Never let anybody see how much this hurts—

Suddenly Grant lets go. The momentum of my struggle throws me off balance. I fall to my side.

My face smacks against something rough and unpleasant. Pain blossoms. I blink a few times and lift my arms, relieved that I can move freely now.

I'm not back in college anymore. I'm on my apartment floor, with sheets tangled around my sweat-soaked body.

I take a shaky breath, both relieved and annoyed. It was just a bad dream, nothing more. I haven't dreamed of the streaking incident in years, but I guess the conversation about the auction triggered the memory.

I push myself up, sit and press my forehead, which throbs with tension, against the heels of my hands. Something wet falls on my thigh, and I realize I was crying in my sleep.

Pull yourself together, girl. Grant isn't worth another tear. You've hurt enough already.

I wipe my face with my fingers. This is so damn embarrassing. I straighten the sheets, then hop into the shower to wash away the film of sweat, along with the remnants of the nightmare. It's Saturday, a precious day away from Grant.

After the shower, I have a bowl of dry cereal, do a load of laundry and vacuum the place. I hit the grocery store last night after work, which means I have more time than usual. I should visit Grandpa earlier than normal. It'll be nice to have lunch with him. We haven't done that in a while.

I put on a cute black tango dress Grandma bought me. It still fits, and I want to be ready in case Grandpa confuses me for Grandma and wants to practice for another upcoming competition. Every time he calls me Kat, my heart aches because we both miss her so much. When he wants to dance, I'm grateful I'm good enough to pretend and let him get lost in happy memories. It's one of a few things I can still do for him.

When I arrive at the Orange Care Center, Gi-Hoon smiles warmly. "Hi, Aspen. Great day to visit. Kenny's been in a fabulous mood since he got up."

"Ooh, good news!" At least Grandpa didn't have a nasty dream like me. He might've had some of his favorites, like the one about when he met Grandma. He said a couple of years ago that he's the happiest when he dreams of that moment.

When I arrive on the third floor, Grandpa is laughing and clapping at what somebody said. Tears glint in his eyes, and he dabs away at them. It buoys my heart to see him having such a fabulous time. It validates every sacrifice I've made to keep him here.

"Hi, Grandpa." I kiss his cheek. "Don't you look dashing today?"

"Hello, baby. Kat picked these out. Aren't they wonderful?" He gestures at his white dress shirt and slacks with a smile. "How's school?"

He's back in time again, when Grandma was still alive. But it's still a relative win because he knows who I am. "Fine. I got an A on my pre-calculus pop quiz," I say, waggling my eyebrows mischievously.

"Good for you," he says, giving the air a small punch. "I told you that you could do it."

A hot lump forms so suddenly in my throat that I can't speak. I draw in a trembling breath before I can manage a smile. "Yes, you're right. All I needed was to study a little harder."

"I'm going to tell your grandma. Maybe it will get her to bake us one of her delicious apple pies." Bright affection glitters in his eyes.

He always loved her pies. "By the way, your boyfriend came by last night."

"My boyfriend?" Who is he talking about now? I had a couple of boys I hung out with when I was in high school, but I wouldn't call any one of them a "boyfriend."

"The bad one." His lips tighten, and I still have no clue who he's talking about. I never hung out with any guy he'd deem "bad" when I was in high school. "Infuriating, as usual. Infuriating! He acted all innocent, but I know better. I can just tell with a glance."

"I know you can," I say soothingly, rubbing his tense shoulders.

"It wasn't Zack. But that was fine, because Zack came by too. He drove the jerk away."

Grandpa thinks that every guy my age is Zack, so I smile. "That was nice of him."

"Zack was just the fellow to show that other kid." Grandpa shakes his head. "Cocky. All talk."

I nod, curious whom he's confusing Zack with. What he's saying about a bad guy and Zack coming over and all that never happened. If I didn't know better, I might think Zack really did come by to see him, but I've never told him where Grandpa is.

"So what did that other guy say?" I ask, trying to humor him. It makes him happy to carry on a conversation. Even if it's about a fake event, I play along. It doesn't hurt anybody.

"Said he *didn't do anything*. So I told him bringing me some fancy wine and bribing your grandmother with her favorite flowers wouldn't cut it."

I fold my hands together so they won't shake. There's only one person that could be. "Grant? Grant came to see you?"

"Yes. *Grant*." He nods decisively. "A terrible boy, that one."

He harrumphs, but doesn't rage like he did when he found out about Grant's betrayal. It eventually became impossible to hide. I kept delaying going back to school, and Grandpa kept insisting that I go back as soon as possible because that was what Grandma would've wanted. When I finally came clean, he erupted with such fury that I was scared he might do something violent.

They say that strong emotion and memories are connected. We remember what impacts us. So even though much of Grandpa's life since Grandma died is gone now, he might well still recall that Grant was too slick for his taste, even if the details of why are missing.

"Do you know that Kat wants to expand the dance studio?" Grandpa says suddenly. "I told her I was open to anything she wants, but I'm worried we may not find good instructors. I want to maintain a certain level of quality, and..." He fades off. "It's difficult to find people who can do what your grandmother can."

"I know exactly what you mean," I respond without missing a beat.

We have lunch at the cafeteria, and I let him go on about his plan to take Grandma to Buenos Aires for her birthday. "It's a secret," he says with a conspiratorial wink.

I force a smile, praying he doesn't notice the tears forming in my eyes. Taking my grandparents to Buenos Aires was my dream, all those years ago. And that dream is dead, never to come true. "My lips are sealed."

He tells me all the things he'd like to do for Grandma, and I nod and offer suggestions, smiling until my cheeks hurt. He careens from one subject to another in a random pattern as his mind shifts, like a butterfly that can't decide which flower it wants to land on. I follow as best I can, wanting to preserve his good mood. But in the back of my mind there's a question that won't go away: what triggered Grant to come up after all these years?

"Tell him if he's going to visit again, he better bring me a real good burgundy," Grandpa says suddenly.

"Who?"

"Grant," he says. "He didn't bring anything when he came."

"Okay. I'll make sure." I kiss Grandpa on the cheek, making a mental note to see if I can bring some for him instead.

He yawns. "Boy, I'm tired. Kat and I danced all night yesterday. We're trying to perfect this move, but she sprained her ankle, I'm afraid."

I nod silently. I don't have the heart to tell him they couldn't have danced all night if Grandma had an injured ankle.

"Think I'll nap a little. How about you?"

"I have to go grocery shopping," I say, hoping this will get him to accept my departure without a scene. Sometimes everything can go smoothly, then he'll freak out over my needing to end our visit. Telling him I have to work doesn't penetrate when he's in that kind of mood.

"Good idea. See what Kat wants before you go. She was saying something about needing tomatoes."

"I'll be sure to check." *Seems like today will be okay.*

I walk with him to his bedroom. He doesn't seem to take in his environment and realize that we're not really home. The room he has is large, but doesn't have the pale paisley curtains Grandma picked out when they moved into the house where I eventually grew up. The walls are industrial white, rather than the cheery, creamy yellow with stenciled daisies.

Still, I'm glad he doesn't notice those details or remember them, because he's happier this way.

He slips under the sheets and curls up like a child on his side, his hands folded together as though in prayer. I kiss his temple, then shut the light off and close the door.

When I reach the lobby, I stop in front of Gi-Hoon. "Can I ask you something?"

"Sure. Everything okay?"

"Yeah, fine. I just wanted to know if anybody came to visit my grandfather in the last few days."

"Yeah. Some guy came by. I think he might've been one of your grandfather's dance students."

Not a bad guess on Gi-Hoon's part, but Grandpa's students have no idea where he is. On top of that, they haven't visited since he first entered a nursing home. Why would they start now?

"Do you remember his name?"

"No, but since he isn't family, I asked him to sign in. Here's the visitors' log." He pulls out his phone and flips through. "Lemme see... Here it is. Grant Lasker."

What the *hell*? A furious sense of violation explodes in my chest, leaving my whole body trembling. I lean over to look at Gi-Hoon's screen. And there it is. Grant's ID and signature.

Bastard. Fucking *bastard*. He took my virginity, turned me into a joke and now he needs to rip into my private life? Nothing good can possibly come from this.

Is this why Grant asked me about the auction and what I did with the money? Did he make snide comments about Grandpa's clothes like he did with me? Grandpa takes great pride in how he looks, so that would cut him deeply. Or...did Grant manage to get Grandpa to say something he didn't mean or understand while he was confused?

I don't care if Grant wants to hurt me. But Grandpa is off-limits!

"Is everything okay?" Gi-Hoon asks, searching my face.

"Yes. Fine. I've just got a migraine at the moment. Thanks." I flash him a smile. It's tighter than I want, but it's the best I can do.

Shaking with rage, I walk out to my car, get in and start the drive to Grant's place. It's time I set some ground rules.

47

ASPEN

As I make my way down the interstate, I go over all the things I want to say when I see Grant's smug face. Number one on the list: *stay away from my grandfather*. If I have to, I'll get a restraining order so he can never go near Grandpa again. I'm sure there's some reason a judge would side with me. Maybe causing emotional distress to Grandpa or something. After all, Grant is at the top of Grandpa's shit list.

Grant doesn't care about your wishes, a cynical voice inside me points out. *Just like he didn't care about what you wanted or needed back then.*

Images from the dream flood my mind—how he forced me to watch the spectacle, how everyone laughed. It's like he wanted to cement his victory with my humiliation.

He doesn't—he *can't*—respect me, I think with a bitterness that leaves me shivering. He didn't before, and that clearly hasn't changed. He should've gotten the hint I don't want him anywhere near my grandfather based on our interaction at the steakhouse and how I refuse to bring him up or talk about him.

Even if I want to give Grant the benefit of the doubt, I can't imagine what altruistic motive he could have for visiting Grandpa behind my back. If he didn't mean any harm, he didn't have to sneak around.

I hit the security pad by the gates and wait. Grant's going to see I'm here, and he's probably going to know why, too.

He can choose to ignore me or not let me in. Or...

He might not be home at all. I have no idea what he does on weekends—that falls outside the work schedule I manage. But he doesn't have anything to do in the office today. And he doesn't go in unless he needs to.

Crap. I clench the steering wheel. Should I confront him on Monday instead?

Before I can figure out what to do, the gates open. Maybe he wants to have this discussion on his turf, where he has an edge.

He should've known something like that won't deter me. If I worried about stuff like that, I'd still be holed up somewhere, unable to leave my home, much less get a job with a boss who hates my very existence.

I park my car and climb out, then smooth my dress and push my shoulders back. My chin's held high, and I walk up to the main entrance and hit the bell.

The door opens, revealing a tall, voluptuous strawberry blonde. I freeze. I didn't expect to find a woman with him. Acid burns away my stomach lining. I hate it that she's gorgeous and in an outfit that looks both casual and extremely expensive.

"Oh. You." The woman's voice betrays only mild interest. "I didn't realize you were still in my son's life."

It takes me a moment to put things together. "You're Grant's mother?"

"I am. Athena Grant."

"You look so young," I blurt out. My cheeks heat at the assumption that she was sleeping with Grant. *Thank God I didn't say it.* That would've been embarrassing.

"You're pretty for an idiot. Or maybe you can afford to be an idiot because you're pretty."

"What?" *Is this woman insulting me?* The words are cutting, but she's speaking as though she's reciting a line from a Buddhist scripture.

"You should've milked Grant until he ran dry. You left too soon. Coming back now is a little late."

I can barely process her words through the blood roaring in my head. *How* dare *she talk to me like this?* She knows nothing about me, yet here she is, making all sorts of outlandish assumptions about my motives. "Because I didn't want his money!"

"Everyone wants his money." She says it like it's a foregone conclusion, and she won't consider any argument to the contrary. "They just don't want to admit it out loud because it's crass. But honesty is good for the soul, and regrets are acid that eats away at you. I bet it's killing you to know you could've had more. After all, Grant is quite generous with people he cares about. It's really unfortunate that he hides his ambitions and generosity so well."

"You don't know your son very well. Grant's only generous when he wants something. He cares about no one."

"I don't have time for this." She waves her hand dismissively, then checks the security intercom when it beeps and hits the green button. "If you're here to complain, you'll need to wait. Grant's on the phone with someone with more interesting things to say."

I knew this confrontation was going to be difficult, but I didn't expect to battle his mother, too. On the other hand, when did I ever have a fair fight with him?

"Who are you talking to, Mom?" Grant comes out, shoving his phone into his pants pocket.

I glare at him. He must've been bad-mouthing me to everyone, including his mother. He must've had a good laugh about my situation. And Grandpa, too.

"This person," Athena says.

"Aspen?" Grant sounds surprised, but I'm too angry to buy it.

"My limo's here," she says as a white stretch limo pulls up.

"I can see that." Grant escorts her toward the sparkling car while holding up a finger and mouthing, *Give me a second.* Like I have a choice if I want to talk to him. "They'll take care of everything so you won't have to a lift a finger."

"I hope so." Athena sighs. "Last time, they absolutely *wrecked* my breakfast. *Twice.*"

353

"And they're thrilled to have a chance to redeem themselves," Grant says soothingly.

Guess he cares about his mom. I haven't seen him this solicitous with anyone else. Well, he was with me, but that was only to get laid. I doubt Athena has anything Grant can want...

He might want the photos she's taken.

True, but if that's the case, he's even worse than I thought. I'd prefer that he isn't quite that awful. I'd like to think that the guy I gave my virginity to has at least one teeny redeeming quality, like being nice to his mom.

A uniformed chauffeur steps out and opens the door for her. She air-kisses Grant's cheek, then slips inside the car. The chauffeur puts her suitcases into the trunk and gets behind the wheel. Soon the engine starts, and the car's gone.

Finally. My turn.

Grant turns to me and gestures to come inside.

I follow him into the foyer and stop. I'm not here to sit down in his huge living room, likely furnished to impress, and hold a conversation. I just want to lay down the ground rules, like I should have when Grant first asked me about Grandpa.

Grant stops and turns around. He isn't stupid. He can sense something's up. "What are you doing here?" He sounds genuinely confused and maybe even concerned.

Why is he faking it? There's no audience to impress. "Stay away from my grandfather. We're not some misery porn for you to enjoy."

"What?" He looks at me like I just slapped him. "You think I visited your grandfather for some kind of sick emotional kick?"

"Why else? It isn't like you have anything to talk to him about." Even if Grandpa weren't suffering from dementia, there wouldn't be anything for them to talk about. Not civilly, anyway.

Grant's jaw slackens, then his cheeks turn red. "What kind of an asshole do you think I am?"

"The absolute worst kind." *The kind that betrayed me.* The kind that I'm still having trouble getting over. Which is what makes it even worse. I've never had difficulty ignoring people who don't add anything positive to my life. Why can't I do it with him?

He couldn't look more awful if I'd buried a knife in his gut. "If you think I'm such an asshole, why did you pick me to be your first?"

His question cuts deep, reopening the wound I'm trying to heal. He wants to force me to admit how badly I misjudged him, doesn't he? Does he want me to break down and cry too? He'd like that, the way he would've enjoyed torturing me by making me work late and run at the crack of dawn. If he didn't have to pay me overtime, he'd still be harassing me.

I put on a brave front because pride is all I have left. I'll be damned if I let him take that away from me, too. "Like you said, it was my first time. I didn't know any better."

His jaw tightens and his eyes flash. "You still don't seem to know any better, because fourteen years later you let me fuck you in the office."

I bite my lip, my face burning with embarrassment and self-loathing. I should've known better than to have sex with him—that it would inevitably come back to haunt me. "I was taking one for the team," I mutter finally.

"What?"

"Everyone was wondering if you should just get laid because you've been impossible! The prevailing opinion was that I should sleep with you or find somebody who would."

His face turns beet red; a tendon stands out in his neck. He clenches his hands, likely fantasizing about strangling me. That's fine. I dare him to try. I'll kick his balls up into his teeth and call 911. It'll be satisfying to see him in cuffs.

"Are you finished?" The softness of his tone makes his voice awful.

"No. I forgot to add that I couldn't find anybody who'd sleep with you without getting paid." *That's right—feel the same pain you've caused me.*

He grabs my face between his hands, crashing his mouth down in a punishing kiss. I bite his lip and taste a coppery tang of his blood. Instead of pulling back at the pain, he kisses me harder. I clutch his shirt, then kiss him back—if what I'm doing can be called that, since there's more teeth than lips and tongue. I want him to be as frustrated, hurt, confused and crazy as I am. I want him off his equilibrium. I want him to be as helpless as I am, as guilt-laden and conflicted.

It's so wrong that I can want him with the intensity of a billion burning suns, while still hating him so much I want to chop his limbs off with a machete. My body's already responding to the shiver-inducing sensation of having his tongue gliding against mine, and the air is thick and hot in my lungs. The trace of blood doesn't lessen the addictive flavor of him. And the feel of his erection pushing against my belly is driving me wild.

I honestly need therapy more than sex. But my body and hormones disagree as his hand glides down and slips under my dress. Before I can stop him, he's already touched the V between my legs.

"You're wet," he mutters against my mouth.

"So? You're hard."

"Some sacrifice you're making for the team."

"Asshole."

He laughs, the sound like a devil's whisper. He dips his head to reclaim my mouth, but I jerk away. He grabs my hair, looping it around his fist, and then his mouth is back on mine and he's kissing me like I'm more important than breathing.

Nobody can fake this kind of desperation. My head spins as I struggle to draw in air. The fact that he reacts to me like a horny teenager is driving me crazy. And a small part of me despairs over the fact that no matter how much I hate him, I'm always going to crave him like a drug.

He pushes me against the wall, then rips my underwear apart with ease, his arm muscles flexing. He undoes the zipper on the side and tugs my dress down, exposing my breasts. The cool air in the foyer feels good against my overheated flesh. Pushing the bra out of his way with his nose, he buries his face in the mound, his mouth on the hardened tip. He inhales my scent and groans around my nipple. Lust sparks along my spine, and I grow wetter. He seems to know exactly how to push me, and I'm embarrassed at how soaked I am between my legs.

I want to hide my reaction, stay quiet and unresponsive, but I can't. He sucks my nipple harder, and my back arches before I can regain control. He laughs softly, but there's no trace of mockery, just an odd sense of resignation and heat. I feel like a kid who can't quit pushing her finger into a live socket, even though it's going to shock me. I'm overcome with this weird thrill—dangerous, self-destructive and fucked up.

After disposing of his shorts and boxers in one rough gesture, he positions me until I'm cradling his cock between my bare folds. I bite back a curse at how good it feels to have him pulsing against my most sensitive flesh.

"Holy fuck," he mutters.

I take that moment to look at him, wishing there was something that would turn me off. But all I see is the need blazing in his darkened gaze, his cheeks flushed and mouth wet. He's absolutely stunning in the throes of desire, and my hormones go wild. A soft whimper tears from my tight throat.

Cursing, he drives into me. The position leaves me vulnerable, pinned against the wall, helpless and needy. He feels like hot steel inside, and the power of his thrusts is pushing me closer to a delicious edge. It feels like my entire body is on fire, and my nerve endings burn with pleasure.

There's no self-loathing, guilt, resentment or recrimination as he's pounding into me. It's just the heat, the bliss, the raw need. I'm obscenely wet, and he's impossibly perfect inside me.

I hang on to him tighter with my thighs, digging my finger into his shoulders as I climax faster and harder than I've ever done before. "Oh my God," I sob, out of my mind with pleasure.

Shudders go through him, and he pulls out fast, although his arms are still wrapped around me. His hot cum hits my thighs, and, a moment later, it's on the pristine floor and my panties. It's lewd, but hot at the same time. Proof that we're nothing but animals acting on instinct when we let our urges take control.

I loosen my grip and lower my legs until my feet are touching the floor. I move carefully so as not to step in the fluid. Now that sanity is slowly returning, I don't know what to do. I came here to warn Grant to stay away from Grandpa, and I don't know if I got to do that.

"Aspen," Grant says.

Suddenly, apprehension clutches my chest, and I don't want to hear whatever he plans to say. All I want from him is to leave me alone. He's going to want more than I ever want to give, just like he did all those years ago. I yank the bodice of my dress up, covering my chest. I need to re-shield myself, *now*.

"Listen—"

My phone rings. *Thank God for the distraction.* I hurriedly reach into my purse, dropped on the floor earlier, and answer.

"Hey, Aspen," comes Zack's voice.

"Hey, Zack." *Yes.* Warm affection and gratitude wash over me for his impeccable timing.

Grant puts a hand on my shoulder. I shrug it off, turning my back to him. From this angle, I can see the vast expanse of tile and marble that leads to the other side of this gigantic mansion. "What's up?" I say.

"I was just calling to see if you can cover my lunch shift next Saturday. No, wait, I mean the one after that."

Normally I'd love to help Zack out, but a lunch shift means being at the bar by ten. Added to my regular evening shift, I might not have the time to visit with Grandpa.

"Hang up now." Grant is directly behind me, his voice low and tight.

I turn my head away, hoping Zack didn't hear him.

Grant says, "We aren't finished."

He's right, but I need a moment to recover and pull my thoughts together. And this call is the perfect opportunity.

"I know you usually have things to do on Saturday," Zack says. "Satoshi and Jenna said you wouldn't have to come in until eleven thirty."

"I'm warning you, Aspen."

Like he cared about my warning to stay away from Grandpa! Resentment lances me, and I'm more determined than ever to ignore Grant. My call with Zack doesn't concern him, and he needs to shut up and wait until I'm ready, just like I did with him when he was dealing with his mother.

"I'm sorry. Are you busy? It sounds like you're with someone," Zack says.

"No, it's fine," I say blithely, hiding my annoyance that Grant's being loud enough to be heard. But what I'm really upset about is that I can't seem to ignore his presence behind me because even though I'm speaking to Zack, most of my focus is on Grant—and what he might be doing to get my attention. "Just the TV."

Grant grips my hips and drives into me in one swift stroke. I gasp, stunned that he's already rock-hard again—and that having him back inside me feels even better than before.

"Are you okay?" Zack asks.

"Yeah," I gasp, my voice choked.

Grant pulls back and drives into me again, harder and deeper. He grinds against me, his hands on my breasts. He nips the side of my neck, then sucks hard, like he's branding me with his kiss. Hot streaks race through me all the way to the tips of my toes. I should tell him to stop, but I can't. Nothing right now could make me tell him to stop. Not when I want more of him.

"Tell him who you're with, Aspen," Grant rumbles, his voice seething.

I'll be damned if I do what he wants. "My phone's out of battery. Bye," I say, and hang up.

From the tight flexing of his fingers on my flesh, I know my disobedience pissed him off. Sure enough, there is a swift, stinging slap on my ass as he begins thrusting. It should feel punishing, but it feels incredible instead.

Another orgasm rises hot and fast, then shatters over me, just as powerful as the one before. I scream as I ride the wave, furiously conflicted that I can come in a situation like this. But in a moment the languid postcoital bliss threatens to extinguish that anger.

He pulls out and comes all over my ass. His large hands smear the liquid on my butt like he's marking his territory. I push him away, turning around. My knees are weak and shaky, and I lock them tightly so I don't stumble and embarrass myself. I grab his pants off the floor and try to clean my butt, but he takes my wrist.

From the stubborn set of his mouth, he isn't going to be reasonable. Fine. I'll just pretend I don't have anything of him on me.

I drop his pants. He lets go of my wrist.

"What's wrong with you?" My attempt at sounding firm is ruined because my voice is raspy from the back-to-back orgasms.

"Are you working at some bar with Zack?" he demands, his chest rising and falling. Thank God he didn't get a chance to rip off his shirt, because his bare torso at eye level would be a distraction I can't afford.

"What if I am?"

"You need to quit."

I scoff. "No, I don't."

"Yes, you do. Because I just told you to."

"Oh, you *told* me to." If arrogance were a credit card, his would be a black AmEx. "Well, I hate to *tell* you, but you don't have that kind of authority over me."

His eyes narrow. "It's against the firm's policy."

"Yeah, for your fancy MBAs. Not the admin staff." He opens his mouth, but I raise a finger. "Don't even. I already checked with HR. It's fine as long as the part-time work doesn't interfere with my duties."

"Fucking HR," he mutters, his aquamarine eyes flashing. "So you'll continue to work with that asshole?"

If I didn't know better, I might think he was jealous. But you can't feel jealous over somebody you don't care about. I steel myself against any more ridiculous notions. I refuse to delude myself that Grant is capable of being a decent human being—because that would allow him to slip behind my shield.

"When did you start caring whether or not I work with an asshole? I've been working for one for weeks now at *Grant*Em." I give him a pointed smile. "Surely I can work with another, although calling Zack an asshole is totally unfair. He's one of the nicest guys I know. Unlike *you*."

Fury burns in Grant's eyes. It's a bit intimidating, but I'm not backing down. If I do, I'll have to give in to him, and I'd rather lick the foyer floor.

"Mind your own business, Grant. You're my boss, not my friend. You don't get to stick your nose into my personal life, my family or who I spend my off-time with."

Then I snatch my purse and panties up off the floor and flee to my car before Grant and I end up doing something stupid again. Like more sex. But even though it's a cowardly escape, at least I got to unload what I came here to say. And if he ignores my warning to stay away from Grandpa, I swear to God I'll get that restraining order.

48

GRANT

By the time I drag on my shorts, Aspen's car is gone. Damn, that was fast. And we left everything unresolved because her telling me to stay away from her private life doesn't mean I'm going to do as she says. In fact, it makes me want to do it more.

I should figure out which bar she works at and stop by later—just to mess with her some more and have a look at Zack for myself so I can understand what she sees in him. I'm 99.99 percent convinced I'm not going to notice anything special. The only reason he made an impression at all fourteen years ago was because he was hitting on her in front of me.

But my plan goes awry that afternoon. Mom calls, rather annoyed, which I don't understand because the hotel hasn't had a chance to screw up her breakfast yet. But what happened is quite a bit worse.

Her ex-boyfriend stalked her to the hotel, distracted the front desk clerk to get Mom's room number from the key-card sleeve, then broke into Mom's suite because he decided he needed her blood *and* fingernail clippings in order to cast another love spell—one that's more potent and targeted than just dumping a bunch of goat blood in her home. Mom coolly blames me for sending her to the hotel when she didn't really want to go—*fuck me*—while I blame the front desk clerk for leaving the sleeve on the counter where anybody could see it! Why the hell do they think I agreed to pay them five figures a night?

So Mom returns to my place, while the hotel's general manager apologizes profusely, probably to stave off a lawsuit. They know who I am—and more importantly, who my mother is.

I settle her in one of the guest bedrooms, while having the concierge service look for another place—somewhere with rock-solid security *and* an excellent breakfast that can be cooked to her specifications. I love my mother, but I can't live with her, especially when she complains endlessly about the "injustice" of having to deal with an insane ex and subpar respect for her privacy.

By Sunday evening, I finally find a place to move her and hire a private security team to doubly reassure her, since she wouldn't go otherwise. They come with Nicholas's stamp of approval, so I know they're going to be competent. Nicholas despises incompetence as much as outright malice.

On Monday, I go to work at my regular time. I'm here before most, even Emmett, who these days can't bear to leave his new baby Monique.

I boot my laptop, my body buzzing with anticipation. Aspen gave me a piece of her mind, and it's time for me to give her a piece of mine.

And she *will* hear me out.

But first, I need to check our HR policy book. It's been so long since I had to look at it that I don't remember much. Plus, I signed off on the whole document after skimming it, since Jeremiah Huxley had gone over it and made sure we were in compliance with the law and nothing was going to screw us over.

I scan the policy book until I reach the section on support staff, then slow down to read closely. God dammit. Aspen is correct. How could we have overlooked this? What was I thinking when I approved it? More importantly, what was Jeremiah thinking?

Shaking my head, I pull up Aspen's personnel file and spot a small section at the very end where she listed her part-time job at a bar near our office where we often have happy hour. She indicated she works there on Saturdays and Sundays, evening shifts only, to reassure HR it wouldn't interfere with her duties at the firm.

How rich! Her part-time job is already interfering, since she won't obey my simple instruction to quit! Her responsibilities at GrantEm include carrying out my orders, and I don't give a shit if she thinks I'm being unfair. She thinks me breathing is unfair.

I send a quick text to the only person who can advise me on how to correct this oversight in our HR policy. There's no loophole Jeremiah can't find.

–Me: We need to talk.

–Jeremiah: Billable?

I roll my eyes. Of course she wants to confirm that first. If I say yes, I'll be her priority. If I say no, she'll ignore me.

–Me: It's about our HR policy.

–Jeremiah: Billable, then. However, I'm out of the country until next week. If it's urgent, get in touch with Andreas. He'll take care of it.

Andreas is another senior partner at the firm. But I don't want to talk to him. I doubt he knows our HR policies as well as Jeremiah.

—Me: It's fine, I'll wait.

–Jeremiah: Suit yourself. I'll let you know when I get back.

She's probably feeling smug that I'd rather wait for her to return than talk to Andreas.

As soon as I'm done texting, the fine hair on my body bristles and my blood jumps twenty degrees. I don't have to look up to see that Aspen's arrived. She shoots me a quick, unreadable look through the open door and boots her laptop. She's in a magenta dress that I've never seen before. Given the cut and the material, it's undoubtedly something Josephine picked out. What happened to the green dress? Aspen hasn't worn that one again.

She clicks around on her laptop, reading her screen, then walks into my office. I lean back in my seat, trying to project the image of a man in control. *Nothing to worry about here.* The image is more important than the reality. My mouth is dry, and I want to taste her again. But he who masters himself masters the situation.

Part of me is still mad about her accusations. I didn't do

anything to hurt her grandfather. I don't know why she thinks I'm a first-rank asshole, but I don't kick puppies or hurt the elderly.

Then there's another part that's furious over the fact that, even though her pussy had to still be shaking with the aftershocks of the explosive orgasm I gave her, she *smiled as she was talking to another man on the phone.*

She holds her legal pad like a shield, and she's careful not to move her head too fast, ensuring her unbound hair covers her neck to hide the huge hickey I left there. If she's going to smile and do things for that asshole Zack, the least I can do is leave my mark on her.

The intensity of my own possessiveness and jealousy is shocking, but I'm not going to deny my feelings.

She does a quick briefing, giving me an overview of the day's agenda and what's coming up during the week. I listen only vaguely —my phone's going to alert me to all the meetings anyway. Her mouth moves, and I can't tear my eyes from it. Her lips are painted reddish pink, and they look soft and pliant.

When she's done, she smiles. This smile's nothing like the one she gave Zack, a piece of quartz to a diamond. Annoyance from the weekend combines with the irritation with her you're-nothing treatment. I deserve a diamond.

"Do you have any instructions?" she asks, still with that subpar, soulless smile.

"Did you quit your job?"

The tip of her left eyebrow twitches. "No. I'm here."

"Don't be obtuse. You know what I mean."

"I already told you what I plan to do, and that plan does not include quitting my job at the bar."

"It reflects poorly on me," I say, since I can't throw the firm's policy in her face.

"It reflects on you not at all. And in any case, HR disagrees."

I've never hated HR before. But now it seems as about as necessary as toe fungus. "What if I give you a raise? To offset the money you're making at the bar?"

"I don't feel comfortable taking money I don't earn. Also, I don't think it's a good idea to give you that much power over my finances.

After all, you are a capricious man." She adds the last part like it's a universally accepted truth.

Except that's bullshit. I know what I want, and I don't change. Why else would I be twisting myself into a pretzel around her? Even though I know she used me, my idiot self still wants her.

"I'm not capricious."

She shrugs. "Agree to disagree." Her tone says, *Fuck off*. "Now, if you don't have anything other than my part-time employment to discuss, I'll go back to my desk and work on the executive memo that's due today."

"So you aren't going to quit?"

"No. I. Am. Not." She says it like she's speaking to a child.

"Fine. You're dismissed." I'm not going to change her mind this way. Clearly, a different strategy is required.

There's always more than one way to skin a cat. I need to have a conversation with Andreas, since Jeremiah's still out of the country. He can help me with my next move.

I send Aspen a quick instruction through the company messenger.

–Me: Call Huxley & Webber and make an appointment with Andreas Webber as soon as possible.

–Aspen: If they ask, what's this about?

–Me: An M&A.

–Aspen: As in merger and acquisition?

–Me: Yes. He'll know what I mean.

–Aspen: Okay. But you know you don't really have any free time until next week.

–Me: You'll have to move my meetings if that's what it takes. I need to see him, ideally today. Tomorrow at the latest.

———

On Tuesday after six, I go to the bar near the office where Aspen works part-time. Andreas fit me in at the end of his day, then told me everything I want can be done on my timeline.

I've been here a few times for happy hour with the people at GrantEm, but this time is different. I want to see what's so special about the place that she won't quit. Surely, she can't be enjoying the bartending work. You're on your feet the entire time and—worse—have to pretend you like listening to people's drunken ramblings. Most people aren't that bright to begin with, and alcohol only magnifies the effect.

Since it's a Tuesday evening, the bar's relatively quiet. I take an empty stool and look around for Zack. He wasn't anything exceptional fourteen years ago, and I don't see how he could've become someone worthy of Aspen's consideration since. But regardless, I love a challenge and competition as long as the prize is worth it—

Wait a minute. Aspen is "the prize"?

Before I can dig deeper into that, Satoshi greets me with raised eyebrows. "Happy hour? On a Tuesday?"

"No. Just me today."

"Okay. Whatcha in the mood for?"

"Pick me a beer," I say, not caring.

"Coming right up." He hands me a bottle of blackberry beer from a local microbrewery.

I take a sip. It tastes vaguely like the fruity beer I had in Germany.

"Good?" he asks.

"Yeah. It's fine." I don't see anyone except Satoshi and another bartender whose name I don't remember. "Zack coming in today?"

"No," Satoshi says, wiping down the counter. "He generally works on weekends. Sometimes on Wednesdays and Thursdays."

Damn it, I missed him by a day. But I can't come by tomorrow or Thursday. I have business dinners on both days. "Does he work a lot with Aspen?"

"They're both in here on weekends."

I bet that isn't by accident. He must've engineered it—he's always wanted her. Even now, he's probably thinking of a way to sleep with her. *Over my dead body.*

"Grant?"

I turn and see Huxley taking the empty stool next to me. "What are you doing in this part of town?" I ask.

"Had a meeting with a pharma client." He jerks a thumb outside. "And I need a drink before heading home."

"That kind of a meeting?"

"Yeah." He asks for a finger of whiskey. Satoshi places a glass in front of him and pours the liquor. Huxley swirls the amber liquid, takes a sip and looks at me over the rim of the glass. "What's wrong?"

"What do you mean?"

"You go for a beer when you need to think. And you're in a bar, which means you're having a problem serious enough that you don't remember you don't think well in bars."

I sigh. "I'm having an HR issue, and your mom's out of the country."

"She's on vacation. Andreas made her because she won't use up her PTOs, and HR doesn't want to cash her out. She's very expensive." Huxley shrugs. "Who are you trying to sue?"

"No one. I'm trying to get my assistant to quit her second job."

"What's she doing? Dealing drugs on the side?"

Normally Huxley's joke would be funny. Right now, the only thing it elicits is a sigh. "No. She's a bartender."

"Offer her a pay raise. Problem solved."

I shoot him a dry look. "I tried that, and she said no."

"Did you make an offer she couldn't refuse?" His tone says, *I don't think you did.*

"It was a fair offer."

"Maybe she's hoping for more." He shrugs. "Besides, why do you care if your assistant has another job? Is she planning to quit?" He pauses abruptly. "Wait. Didn't you make a bet with Emmett to *get* her to quit?"

I nod, but I'm now ambivalent about that bet. Do I really want her to quit? She needs money for that assisted-living facility. Hell, the reason she gritted her teeth and put up with my earlier bullshit was probably for the two-thousand-dollar eldercare benefit the firm offers.

"So why are you trying to get her to quit her second job? If she quits bartending, she may never quit the job at the firm."

"That's a separate issue."

Huxley looks at me. "Oh shit. You have feelings for her. Or, at least, you want her body."

Since I don't want to admit anything, I grunt. Huxley doesn't gossip like Noah, but he'll talk if the topic's juicy enough. And my having feelings for Aspen definitely qualifies.

"Son of a bitch." He chuckles, which adds to my annoyance. "For a super-smart guy, you're pretty stupid about these things."

"Really, Einstein? Why don't you tell me what to do, then?"

"Be like Nike. Just do her." His expression states, *Do I have to tell you everything?*

"We already had sex. Didn't solve my problem." Just the opposite—I'm constantly hyperaware of her now. And she's even more delicious and irresistible than I remember.

"Fine. I'll help you out, since your overdeveloped brain's incapable of helping itself." Huxley gestures for another finger of whiskey. "You're overcomplicating this. Imagine her as one of your other girlfriends, someone you had a good time with."

That doesn't work. Aspen isn't like any other women I've been with.

He continues, "They all ended when it was time. So have sex with her until your body says, 'I'm done.' Knowing your history, it won't take long."

He's so wrong that it isn't funny. "She does things to me."

"Which is why you need to screw her out of your system."

"That's not going to work. Trust me."

He squints. "So she's, like, what? Some kind of super bacteria?"

"What the hell are you talking about? What does that even mean?"

"You know, the kind of bug that you can't kill with your standard mode of treatment. You basically said she's a disease that won't die."

The analogy is ridiculous, but I'm too tired to come up with a better one. Plus, Huxley would laugh his ass off. "I guess."

"Grant, nobody's that special. You even said it yourself. Love doesn't exist, remember?"

"Of course I do." It's been my motto for the last fourteen years.

"All so-called superbugs are squashable. You just aren't trying hard enough."

"I am. But every time I see her, my chest hurts." Actually, it's more like my heart, but I'm not telling him that.

Hux looks alarmed. "For real?"

"Real as I'm sitting here."

"Wow. And I thought you were better at managing stress. Forget sex. What you need is a cardiologist. Here." He pulls out his phone and sends me a number. "Call this guy. He's my grandmom's cardiologist. He's fantastic..."

Huxley goes off on some tangent. I tune him out and look around the bar. Several guys are drinking beer and laughing and talking. A bartender whose name I don't know smiles at them, her eyes crinkling. Since it's a slow day, she lavishes them with attention —most likely to increase her tips—and I hate it. It reminds me of what Aspen likely does here to earn tips. But she shouldn't have to smile at anybody for money. Ever.

Her smile's too lovely. Beyond price. Most importantly, she's a prize worth fighting for—

The realization bursts like a bomb inside my head. But instead of stunning me, it leaves me crystal clear for the first time since she reappeared in my life. It's the truth I've been denying all this time because I didn't want to accept it, even though subconsciously, I knew.

Just the idea of her being with another guy makes me sick. Fourteen years apart, and I still feel this way. And it isn't going to change. She left an indelible mark on my heart all those years ago, and it's only gotten deeper.

But in order for me to embrace that, I have to forgive her for what she's done.

Do I want to do that?

Yes. I'm sick of denying myself. I'm sick of trying to hurt her because it doesn't give me satisfaction, just pain and guilt. She did what she did when we were in college. Everyone makes mistakes when they're young. All she's been trying to do is take care of her grandfather by working her ass off. She could've latched on to some rich asshole, but she didn't. Surely that means she's changed, just like I've changed.

If I forgive her, we can start over. And I'll be able to let go of this anger and resentment.

Let it go. Give yourself another chance—let yourself explore this possibility with her.

Yes, forgiving her is the right thing to do. I don't know why I've clung to my pride for so long. My heart feels lighter, and I'm almost giddy.

I sleep like a baby that night, knowing that I've made the right decision.

49

ASPEN

Something's very wrong.

Grant demanded that I quit my job at the bar three times on Monday and another three on Tuesday. Now, it's Wednesday morning. I give him the day's agenda and brace myself for the same insistence.

"Great. Thanks." He smiles.

"Any other instructions?" I ask, wary.

"No." The smile stays pleasant, and there doesn't seem to be any devious intent in his gaze, either. "You go on and do whatever you need to do."

Ooo-kay. That's...creepy. Did he get a terminal cancer diagnosis yesterday? I've heard news like that can alter a person's personality overnight. On the other hand, his meeting was with a lawyer, not a doctor. What's going on?

But I'm the only one unsettled, because everyone else on the team is thrilled.

"We finally have our good boss back." Larry is practically weeping into his morning coffee, all because Grant told him he did a good job on the latest deliverable.

"Thank God." Jesse runs a hand down his face.

"He's probably happy he has the perfect assistant," Amy adds. "He's been lost since Renée left."

I give her an uneasy smile. I'd wager my right hand that I'm not the reason for the change in Grant's mood.

"Thank you," Jesse says to me. "Seriously."

My smile grows even more awkward. "You're welcome...?"

"Oh wow, that's a big mosquito bite. Does it itch?" Larry says, pointing.

"What?" I realize he's pointing at my neck, and my hair's tossed back, which means the hickey Grant left is visible.

Crap. Larry must not have seen it well enough to realize no mosquito leaves a bite this large. "Actually, it was a wasp," I say, putting my hair over the spot.

The rest of the day, as Grant's attitude stays friendly, my alarm grows.

Maybe he decided to take your advice and leave you alone.

No. Sad to say, that wouldn't be like him at all. I wish he'd just stay an asshole. That way, I'd know how to properly respond. I don't know what to do with this nice Grant. Maybe he's plotting something. I hate it that I can't imagine what he could be doing to screw me over this time. Or how it will affect me and my grandfather. Grandpa is all I have left.

Furthering my anxiety is the fact that Grant is extraordinarily busy. He has meetings that aren't on the calendar I manage. And that only ups my anxiety. If he isn't trying to screw me over, why is he hiding them?

I spend the rest of the week feeling like I'm standing on a wafer-thin sheet of ice. But the precarious peace holds. Grant stays pleasant the whole time. It's like a nice, rational twin took over, except I know he doesn't have a twin. But I can't fathom why he's acting like he doesn't have a grudge or resentment over my being at the firm. At the same time, I'm afraid to ask him why he's being decent, in case that triggers his evil side again. As unnerving as it is, I prefer him being nice rather than nasty.

On Saturday, I visit with Grandpa. Unfortunately, he's having a bad day. His temper's all over the place, and he shouts nonsense, claiming "they" are going to get him because "they" are jealous of him and Grandma. I try to tell him there is no conspiracy, but that's no use. He can't name who "they" are, but that doesn't matter. At the end, he accuses me of being on "their" side.

"You're going to put them over your family? Your own flesh and blood? Is that what this is about?"

"Grandpa, no," I say, trying not to cry.

"Don't you call me that! You're no granddaughter of mine!"

His furious words stab into me, making me feel cast aside and unwanted—truly alone. He's confused. When he calms down, he'll hug me and smile, but right now he's not the grandpa I remember and love.

Fucking dementia, taking the only one I have left. It's a cruel disease that preserves a lookalike husk of the man I knew, while everything that made him who he was gets stripped away piece by piece.

"Maybe it's best if you come back later," one of the nurses on the floor tells me, her eyes full of empathy. "There's no reasoning with him when he's like this."

"I know." I draw in a steadying breath, trying not to give in to my own frustrated grief. It isn't Grandpa's fault, and I have to cope with his condition. Still, I resent it that we don't have a ton of time left—every day, dementia takes another sliver of him.

Having to cut the visit short puts me in a gloomy mood. But I listen to some music and clean my apartment, trying to pull myself out of the funk. I can't impose my crappy mood on the customers at the bar. It isn't professional, and I need the tips.

My phone buzzes on the kitchen counter where I left it. I pick up and see a text.

–Jenna: Can you come in about half an hour early?

–Me: Sure.

–Jenna: We have some changes at the bar. Can't text.

Changes at the bar? What does that mean, and why do I need to show up early?

Apprehension rears its ugly head. Jenna might want to let me go because she needs a bartender who can do more hours. Or maybe she has some issues with my recent performance. Although I got better after Grant quit forcing me to run in the morning with him, when I was sleep-deprived I made quite a few mistakes, the kind not even a new bartender would make.

But if that were it, why wait all this time to complain? I hate not knowing. Although she asked me to come in half an hour early, I go in almost forty-five minutes early to see what's going on.

When I arrive, Jenna bustles over. "You're already here."

"What's up?" I ask, scanning the bar area to gauge the bartenders' mood. Satoshi's stoic as usual. Zack is handing a huge margarita to a blonde woman and seems utterly relaxed.

"We need to talk." She gestures to Zack, who whispers something to Satoshi and leaves the bar to follow us into the employees' locker. "We have a new owner," she says as she shuts the door behind her.

Whew. So this isn't about my job performance, although the news is still surprising.

"Since when?" Zack says in shock.

"Since today."

"I thought Owen wasn't selling." I heard from Satoshi that Owen had offers, but he didn't want to give up the bar. "This place is a cash cow."

"I know, but he decided to sell it on Wednesday."

"And we already have a new owner? Isn't that kind of fast?" I know nothing about buying and selling bars, but wouldn't it take longer than three days? It isn't like buying an umbrella.

"The new owner paid cash," Jenna says in a hushed tone. "Apparently, it was a generous amount, far more than the bar's worth."

"Are they going to close it down or something?" Zack asks.

I think his concern is misplaced. This area is already gentrified, and the bar's swimming in cash.

"No, no. He just wants to downsize," Jenna says.

Oh shit.

"He thinks we have too many bartenders."

And there are only two bartenders having this chat. My shoulders start to sag.

"Anyway..." She sighs. "That basically means one of you, because you're the newest."

I take a moment to process the news. I don't want Zack to be forced out. He's been trying to find a purpose in his life after his father's death a few years ago, and he hasn't done it yet. He's working at bars and retail only because his grandfather would disapprove of idling. Not only that, he started at the bar a couple of weeks before I did. So he has seniority over me.

"You should stay," Zack says.

What? I stare, unsure how to respond. Part of me wants to be selfish, but that would be wrong. I can't do that to him.

"You need the money more than me," he says.

"But how about you? I don't want to take this from you when you need it to sort yourself out after your father's death."

He looks at Jenna. "Could you give us a couple of minutes alone? Please?"

"I'll be out at the bar with Satoshi." She gestures for us to go on and leaves.

Zack checks the door to make sure it's shut firmly. "I'm not working here to sort myself out."

"You're not...?"

"No. Look, um..." He lets out a long breath.

"What? What is it? You can tell me anything."

He lets out a short, nervous laugh. "Okay, then..." He shakes his head, looks up at the ceiling for a moment and then brings his eyes down to stare directly into mine. "I have feelings for you."

It takes a moment for the meaning to percolate through. But when it does, I don't know what to think.

"I'm not asking you to make a decision or anything. I just want you to think about giving us a chance. We've been friends for so long, Aspen. I know I can make you happy, and your grandfather would like me to be there for you."

Oh, no. I squirm, hating that I'm going to end up hurting him. I've never seen him as boyfriend material, and he'll be miserable if he's with a woman who can't reciprocate his feelings.

The door bursts open. "Well, that was touching."

Grant? What's he doing here?

He walks in. He's in a suit, like he's just had a business meeting. His dark eyebrows slant upward, three lines forming between them in disapproval. The firm, flat line of his mouth twists as he looks at Zack. A hint of superiority fleets through his gaze.

He stops next to Zack, creating a stark comparison. Grant is taller and broader, his shoulders wide, his muscled chest thick. The suit he's wearing cost tens of thousands of dollars. He radiates a natural authority and assurance—*of course* he should always get what he wants.

I can't tear my eyes from him. Even when he's overbearing, he's magnetic. I've never met any other man who could do this to me. It's unfair that evolution did a number on me, so I'm only interested in an alpha-hole rather than a sweet guy who might be a little lacking in some areas.

"What are you doing back here? Employees only." Zack bristles with hostility.

"A rule that the owner made, right? Well, that's me now."

That yanks me out of my reverie. "*You're* the new owner?"

"Lock, stock and barrel," Grant says.

What? Jenna said the sale was sudden, and I'm certain he didn't develop an unnaturally abrupt desire to own a bar in the last few days.

"You can't just buy the bar like this!" Zack says, gesticulating into the air.

Grant raises an arrogant eyebrow. "I could buy ten thousand bars like this."

Now—finally—I see what's been going on. I turn to Zack. "Can you give us a moment?"

"Are you sure?" Zack glares at Grant like he's a roach that made his girl scream.

"Positive," I say firmly.

Zack looks like he wants to argue, but accepts my decision and walks out.

Once we're alone, I inhale deeply. "Is this why you haven't been asking me to quit my job here?"

"One of the reasons, yes."

"Are you going to do this every time I get a part-time job—? No, don't answer that. My blood pressure's too high as it is."

"At least you have great health insurance coverage." He smiles.

377

I can't decide if he's joking or mocking. Maybe it's a bit of both. It's impossible to tell when my head is throbbing with rage. "This isn't funny."

The smile disappears. "I don't like my assistant grinning like a brainless baboon at every asshole who wants a drink." His eyes flash with something I don't want to understand or identify. It's too volatile. Scary. Like lightning splitting the night sky.

But then, my mood isn't much calmer. I need this money to survive. Without overtime, I don't make enough from GrantEm to get by without tips from the bar. The Orange Care Center costs more than the two-thousand-dollar-a-month eldercare benefit, and Grandpa is in their memory unit, which is the most expensive. Without my part-time job, I can't afford groceries, unless I eat nothing but beans and rice. "It's called doing my job. I'm getting paid to be nice to them."

"Then you can smile for me. You're getting paid to be nice to me."

"No, I'm getting paid to do your admin duties. They don't include smiling like a brainless baboon!"

He pulls out his phone and taps the screen a few times. "There. I just updated your duties on the personnel file."

I feel like there's steam coming out of every opening in my head. "I want to murder you."

"Go ahead." He spreads his arms. "Take your shot."

"So you can toss me in jail?"

"Nope. If you want, I'll sign something saying I asked for it."

"You're just so... Arrgh!" I have no idea why he's doing this. He was out of his mind for my body last weekend, then got nasty, then got nice, and now this! The whiplash is too much for me to process.

"I don't want us to fight. I don't want to be bitter about what happened."

About what happened? What's he talking about? And why does he sound so sincere?

"I want to forgive you for what you did."

For a stunned moment, I just stare. My brain is working overtime, but it can't compute what just came out of his mouth.

Grant is looking at me expectantly and a bit proudly, like he's done something extraordinarily magnanimous. And maybe with a little self-congratulation, like he's proven himself generous by bestowing a great favor on a poor peasant. His gaze says he's ready to see me melt and collapse in gratitude.

Finally, the meaning of his words really penetrates and my head explodes. There's probably a mushroom cloud rising from my scalp. "Forgive *me*?!"

"I want us to start over." He speaks calmly, but a small frown betrays his confusion and slight disapproval. He thinks I'm being unreasonable, like a child kicking and screaming in a temper tantrum.

"Unless you hit me hard enough to give me amnesia, no! And if you try to brain me, I *will* press charges!"

He looks at me like I've just grown feet out of my ears. I'd laugh if I weren't so furious. But forgive *me*? How dare he!

"If you want me gone from the bar, fire me!" I shout, pointing a finger in his face. "But until then, *I'm staying*!"

50

GRANT

Aspen storms out of the locker room, leaving me watching the door swing shut behind her.

Okay, that isn't how I thought the talk would go. I expected her to be a little peeved that I bought the bar. It wasn't that difficult to convince Owen, and it doesn't take long to run a transaction through when you have enough cash on hand to close the deal. But when I told her I wanted to forgive her and start over, I thought she'd be relieved. Even happy.

Aren't people supposed to feel like a weight has been lifted off their shoulders when they're forgiven?

She reacted like I insulted her, and it's pissing me off. She won't accept my forgiveness unless she gets amnesia? What the hell kind of gratitude is that?

I stalk out of the locker room. She's trying to get behind the bar to work with Satoshi. I take her arm firmly—without hurting her—so that she knows I'm serious. She's shockingly warm. If I didn't know better, I'd think she was feverish. But I know it's from her unreasonable anger.

"We need to talk," I say.

"I'm done." She keeps her eyes on a spot between two vodka

bottles, refusing to look at me. Her cheeks are flushed unnaturally red on her otherwise pale face.

"No, you're not. *We're* not." I tilt my head in the crowd's direction. "You want to do this in front of all of these people?"

Her eyes flick toward them, then return to me. Stubbornness sets in her chin, and she nods jerkily. "Fine. Two minutes. I'm on the clock."

"You forget I'm the one paying you."

Her lips flatten until they look like angry dashes. "You want to talk in the back?"

I gesture at her to follow and take her to the owner's office. It's a sad little space with a tiny window that overlooks the employee parking lot, a metal desk, an ancient desktop computer that probably doesn't boot anymore and piles and piles of disorganized documents and receipts. When I pointed out the mess, Owen said he throws them in boxes and passes them on to his accountant when he gets tired of looking at them.

I don't offer Aspen a seat, and she doesn't take the folding metal chair. I stay standing as well, towering over her.

"You're being unfair," I say.

"Why? Because I didn't kiss your feet for your grand act of *forgiveness*?"

"If you're going to kiss me, I prefer you kiss my mouth. And it wasn't an act. I want us to move on. I don't understand why you're angry about that. I'm letting go of what happened between us, when you're the one who used me."

She lets out an impatient breath. "Is this about the things I auctioned off? Because I don't know why you're hung up about that. You didn't tell me they were 'loaners.'"

God, she's frustrating! *She's* the one hung up about the auction.

I rein my temper in. If I lose it, this conversation won't go anywhere productive. "You're twisting what happened. I only said that about the things Josephine picked out for you because I didn't want you to sell them online again."

"Why? Afraid I'd take my money and quit?"

The more she talks, the more slippery my grip on my temper

becomes. I do my best to modulate my tone. "No. I want you to keep them and wear them."

"Which I do now, so it shouldn't matter what I did with the things before, just like I don't harp on you about—" She shuts her mouth, her face going white, then red.

"About what?" I demand.

The bright fury in her vanishes as abruptly as a light bulb going off. Her shoulders sag a little, until she blinks and straightens them again, like she's realized she's letting her vulnerability show in front of somebody she can't trust.

My gut burns. Earlier I might've chalked it up to anger over being insulted, but it's not anger, it's pain. She didn't used to be so on guard with me. I was the one person she let in, trusted enough to be her first.

"You hurt me, Grant." Underneath her seemingly calm voice is a seething sea of emotion too confusing for me to fathom. "You took what I offered and cheapened it. What's worse is that by being 'generous,' you made sure almost everyone would turn against me. You were right—the things I auctioned off brought me almost two hundred thousand dollars. And people looked at me like I was insane to complain about it. But it can never make up for what I lost."

What's with this resentment? "What could you have possibly lost?"

"Stop playing dumb. Sadie and Heath told me everything."

"Told you what?" Sadie dropped by the office, but she didn't get a chance to spew any poison. And Heath probably hasn't seen Aspen once she left college. "What did they say?"

She says, "You turned me into the biggest joke on campus."

"What are you talking about? I defended you—"

"You were going to humiliate me, then transfer to Harvard!"

"*What?* That's ridiculous." I need to get on top of this fast. "I never told you about my transfer applications because I never planned to actually go anywhere. I wanted to stay at Napa Aquinas College. *With you.* Regardless, you can't possibly be upset about the transfer," I say. "I didn't even go to Harvard."

Her face twists. Her lower lip and chin tremble for a second before she clenches her jaw tightly. A sheen of moisture glistens in her eyes. Even the tip of her nose is flushed. She sniffles, then hides her eyes with a hand, but that can't hide the tears falling down her cheeks.

My frustration and exasperation dissolve, even as I tell myself I'm being stupid to be affected by something as clichéd as tears. But then, I've never been smart when it comes to Aspen.

I go over to the desk and pluck a couple of Kleenexes. When I turn around and start toward her to offer them, her hands hang loose at her sides, but she looks at me like I've just broken her heart.

"I know about the bet."

I freeze. *The bet...?* She can't possibly be reacting like this over the bet I had with Emmett...

My head empties of thought as though someone swung a mallet and hit me between the eyebrows. The most unbearable pain spreads in my heart. It feels like somebody stuck a knife in, pried my chest open and carved it out, so there's nothing left but a bloody crater. My pulse thunders in my ears, and I blink, struggling to focus in spite of my dimming vision.

"You only wanted to be my first to win." Her words are muffled by the deafening roaring of my blood.

Shock clenches around my lungs, and my skin feels hot and tight. Every cell in my body pulses with shock.

She knew...? *But why didn't she say something back then? Why didn't she kick my ass or—?* I think numbly, still frozen to the spot. Of all the reasons for her to hate me, this never entered my mind. I didn't think she'd ever found out.

"For God's sake." She wipes her face roughly, her eyelashes trembling like wounded butterflies. Her gaze is unsteady as more tears fall. "You can tend the bar yourself tonight."

Then she turns and runs out.

51

GRANT

The sound of a car door slamming jolts me. I flinch, and the gears in my head start to turn overtime to make up for being idiotically frozen just moments ago.

First things first, I have to talk to Aspen. I run out after her. But the roar of an engine from the parking lot says I'm too late.

A sedan swerves precariously along the road, heading away from me. Fear pours into my veins—*she's going to crash that car*. She shouldn't be driving if she's that upset!

But the car straightens out, and I rake shaking fingers through my hair. My mind is clear now, all cylinders finally firing.

With the clarity comes only one question: *What have I done?*

The damn *bet*... I specifically asked Will and Heath to keep that quiet when they insisted on streaking! She wasn't ever supposed to find out—and I thought she hadn't. Not when George, one of the most social and popular guys on campus, had no clue.

I pull out my phone and log into GrantEm's intranet, using my admin privilege to access Aspen's HR data and get her home address. Then I hop into my Maybach and plug it into the GPS.

The apartment complex she lives in is...*a dump*. Jesus. How can a building this awful still stand? It should be illegal to charge rent here.

There's nothing overtly dilapidated about it—you have to keep up appearances. But it's the small things—like cracks that haven't been repaired in the sidewalks and the lobby. A few of the steps on the stairs are missing anti-skid strips, and from the amount of dirt that's accumulated, they've been missing for a while. The security camera is bigger than my arm, and I don't know if it still works—or if it can actually get decent images if there's a crime. It's worse than that Howell Hall Aspen used to live in.

I check the phone again. Aspen lives on the second floor.

Since the building's so old it doesn't have an elevator, I take the stairs to the second floor, stepping around cigarette butts and fast-food taco wrappers. A couple of spider webs. Nobody cleans this area. Ever.

I knock on her door. I don't know what I'm going to say or how I'm going to fix this—my head's too jumbled—but *I have to see her*.

No response. I open my mouth to call her name, but end up making a pathetic croaking sound instead. I clear my throat. "Aspen." I knock, then pound. "Aspen! I know you're in there."

The more she gives me the silent treatment, the more desperate I become. I keep on banging on the door, louder and harder until my fist hurts.

The unit next to Aspen's opens. An old Asian lady sticks her head out and looks me up and down. Her disapproving eyes linger on the cut of my suit, then slide to my watch, belt and shoes, then up to my face.

"She's not here," she says. "She's working. I heard her leave."

"Did you hear her come back?"

She shakes her head. "No. I don't think she's home. I was in the living room. Heard nothing."

Where could Aspen have gone? She wouldn't have gone over to Zack's when he's at the bar tonight. She wouldn't have gone over to see her grandfather, not when she's this upset. Does she have other friends in town? I realize I know very little about her. My fault—I never made any effort to get to know her. I was too busy living in the past.

Idiot! Dumbass!

"Do you know where she might go if she's not working? Maybe a friend? It's important."

The neighbor lady shrugs again. "I don't know. I never seen her with friends. Anyway, maybe you can be quiet? I want to watch my drama."

"Yes, ma'am."

I head back downstairs, then walk around the parking spots around the building, looking for her car. The lot is as crappy as the building itself and poorly lit, so I use the flashlight on my phone and check every blue car. But nope. She isn't around. And the lot's full except for a couple of empty slots.

Okay, so Aspen's not home. I climb into my car and text her.

—Me: Where are you? I'm at your place. We need to talk.

I stare at the screen, while counting slowly. I reach ten, but it stays unread.

—Me: Aspen, we have to talk. Please.

Still unread. I call, but it goes unanswered.

Shit. I should've never let her run out like that. Now what? Don't women like to unload everything on their friends when they're upset? Who would she meet?

Suyen...

They were tight back in college, and Aspen might've gone over to Suyen's place. I try to look her up, but can't find anything useful.

Who would know everything about everything?

I mull it over for a second, then snap my fingers. George Harford. Even though he graduated from Napa Aquinas twelve years ago, he'd still keep up with everyone. He thrives on socializing.

I thumb through my contacts until I find him. He's one of a few people whose number I didn't purge from my phone when I left college.

—Me: George, it's me, Grant Lasker. Mind if I ask you something?

I don't have to wait long before a response pops up.

—George: Hey, long time no see! How are you, man?

—Me: Great. You?

I'm all amicable and social, even though my impatience is

mounting. George doesn't like to get to the point unless he feels he's done sufficient hi-how-are-yous first.

–George: Awesome as always. I hear you're a big shot now.

–Me: If you can call VC a big shot.

–George: Ha! My pop told me he'd die happy if I were as half as ambitious as you.

I smile a little. George works hard, but plays harder.

–George: So what's up?

–Me: You remember Suyen from college?

–George: That skinny Chinese girl?

–Me: Yeah. You know how to get in touch?

–George: She's still in Napa. Works at some vineyard. Why? Wanna buy some wine?

Disappointment ripples. I doubt George knows whom Aspen hangs out with these days. They were never that tight, and she obviously wouldn't have kept in touch with the people from school, not if she felt like she became the biggest joke on campus.

–Me: No. I was just curious.

–George: I didn't think you guys were that close. But you were dating her friend for a while, right? Aspen?

–Me: Yes. Do you know what she's up to these days?

I ask, praying he's heard something that could give me a clue as to where Aspen might've gone.

–George: Far as I know, she's working multiple jobs in L.A. Didn't sound like she was doing too well. Too bad she didn't finish her degree. She was always studying.

A huge boulder of guilt presses down upon me.

–Me: Since Suyen's not around, who does Aspen hang with?

–George: Beats me. She always liked to keep to herself. She was sort of private back in school too.

Damn it. If he doesn't know, I'm stuck.

I drum my fingers on the steering wheel.

Sadie and Heath told me everything.

It doesn't take much imagination to know Sadie's the one who hammered the final nail in the coffin. That bitch. But Heath... What did he say?

—Me: You know what Heath Harringer is up to these days?

—George: Actually, yeah. He moved to L.A. last month. He's looking for investors for some business idea. I told him I wasn't into it because that's my old man's thing. I'm actually supposed to play tennis with him tomorrow, but I have a date. He's gonna bitch, lol. Keeps saying he wants to get back into shape.

Here's my opening.

—Me: When are you supposed to see him?

—George: 10. He joined my tennis club.

—Me: Tilden Courts, right?

—George: Like always. My mom's probably going to be buried there, lol.

Figures. It's the same club his entire family goes to, and I've been there several times to play with Sebastian, who uses tennis to let off steam. He's really good, and I'm one of the few of us brothers who can keep up with him.

—Me: Look, why don't I play Heath tomorrow? You can go have your date guilt-free.

—George: Really? You don't mind?

—Me: I have some spare time in the morning.

I'm actually supposed to go to Emmett's place to see my brothers for brunch, but they can wait. This is more important.

—George: That'd be great. I owe you one, my man.

—Me: Not at all. It'll be good to catch up.

—George: I'll let him know you're coming.

—Me: Actually, don't do that. I want to make it a surprise. I haven't hung out with him in ages. It'll be fun to see his face.

—George: Got it. I won't say a word, then. Thanks!

—Me: No problem.

And thank *you*, George. I'll have the perfect opportunity to "run into" Heath and make that fucker talk.

———

The next morning, I arrive at the club before eight. Its brochure says everyone's welcome, but what it really means is "everyone who can fork over the five-figure membership fee every year." The place isn't just for playing tennis. It also has a huge track for horseback riding, and I keep my horse here. I don't get to ride her often—no time these days—but the staff ensures my baby gets sufficient exercise.

A lot of people come here to hang out and network. More than half the members don't really play or ride. They come to chat, while swinging their rackets a few times so it looks like they're getting some exercise.

There are also people like Sebastian, who comes here to play for real, but he's an exception. I change into my riding gear, take out Morning Star—a gorgeous Arabian mare I bought three years ago—and ride her hard, needing to vent some frustration.

Aspen hasn't responded to my texts. I tried calling again, but all my attempts got sucked into voicemail.

Damn it.

Although I couldn't sleep last night, my head is crystal clear. I rein in my frustration at her continued refusal to talk. Getting the silent treatment doesn't mean I'm going to sit around wringing my hands until Monday.

I can gather all the data I need before we see each other, so I can get a full picture of what the hell happened. Exactly what was it that Heath said that she didn't confront me fourteen years ago?

Half an hour before nine, I get off Morning Star, who settles down and stops prancing when I pull out a few apples. She munches happily, nostrils flaring.

I check the time and go into the locker room to grab a quick shower to get rid of the horse smell. Then it's into tennis whites for my "match" with Heath.

"Grant?"

Speak of the devil. I turn and take in my old roommate. He's the same—tall, with broad shoulders and mean eyes that assess every-thing and everyone around him for utility to benefit himself. Unlike in college, the end of his nose now has visible pores, looking like an unripe strawberry. Faint brackets are etched into either end of his thin lips, making him appear parsimonious. And I can see why George said Heath wants to get into shape. His belly is sporting a little paunch.

I fake a friendly frat-boy smile that would make my dad proud. "Heath! Just the man I'm here to see."

"Me?" He laughs. "For what?"

"George has a hot date, apparently. So I told him I'd play with you instead."

"That dog." He laughs harder. "I knew you guys were still tight. When I asked him about you, he was all like mysterious and shit."

I cock an eyebrow. "You wanted to talk to me?"

"Yeah. I got your info from another guy who got funding from you." He opens a locker and takes off his shirt, revealing an overly tanned chest. "I have a business idea I wanted to pitch. You're in VC now, right?"

"Uh-huh." *You fucked me over behind my back and now want money? I don't think so.* "But why didn't you call?"

"Well, I was gonna. But some assholes from Singapore said they were interested in putting up some money. I even flew out to meet them." He strips down to his boxers.

"How'd that go?"

"Ah, they weren't serious. Just jerked me around. Dicks."

Good for them. "Well, if you want me to take a look at your business plan, just contact my assistant for an appointment."

"We can't just have lunch or something?" Heath's tone says, *Come on.*

"Dude, I would, but I'm *really* busy. I don't even know what my days are like. Aspen handles my calendar."

He tilts his head, giving me a curious look.

It's an effort to smile, but I manage. "Aspen Hughes. Remember?"

"Yeah, of course." He shakes his head. "Can't believe it, is all. That girl has *no* pride."

My smile broadens as I fantasize about shoving his tennis racket up his ass. "I pay her well."

"Yeah, but..." He laughs. "Man, you should thank me."

"Yeah? What did you do?" *I need to know every drop of poison he poured on Aspen. After I get it out of him...he'll learn what happens to people who fuck me over.*

"Okay, so she saw me and Will streaking, right?"

Fuck. I knew it. I picked a time when she had a class, but she might've left early. Or Heath and Will could've started late enough that she caught them.

I hide my sinking feeling, though. I want Heath talking freely. "Uh-huh."

"And she ran into me."

"She did?" I feel sick.

"Yup. I mean, like, literally *ran into* me. And, you know Aspen, she was acting all superior and shit, as usual." He rolls his eyes, sticks his head through the neck of a pale gray shirt and pulls it down. "So I had to knock her down a peg or two, you know, show her where she belonged. I told her she was nothing—just a bet. Isn't it ridiculous that she thought she meant something because you happened to screw her?" He snorts and elbows me lightly.

"Didn't I ask you keep the bet secret?" I cling desperately to control. Breaking his face would be satisfying, but it won't give me all the answers.

"Did you? I can't remember." He shrugs. "But sometimes you just have to show bitches like her. She doesn't think she's so special anymore, does she?"

"No," I say flatly. And she should've thought she was special because she was everything to me. Jesus. I still want her enough that I wanted to pretend nothing happened. Except...

Fuck me. I told her *I'd* forgive *her*. And acted like she should be *happy* about it. No wonder she looked at me like I'd stuck a knife between her ribs.

My stomach churns. I feel sick as the full impact of what I did unfolds in my mind. I shouldn't have jumped to conclusions after Marketta's call. I should've driven to L.A. and forced a conversation with Aspen. Then we wouldn't have wasted so much time.

And then maybe she wouldn't have stayed away from Napa Aquinas College. Although she can be bold and brave, she's also careful not to make herself too vulnerable. She doesn't have a lot of friends, but the ones she lets in are loyal to her. And of all the people she's known, I'm the one who got to be the closest, to touch her and have her. I should've been the one to protect her.

It makes me sick to think that we could have had more than a decade together, and just...lost it. How arrogant I've been to think I was able to hide the bet from her. All because I was too embarrassed to face the truth—that I was a selfish, careless asshole until I met her. I never wanted her to find out what a shallow dick I could be. I didn't want to disappoint her or have her regret being with me.

"You okay?" Heath says.

"What?" I jerk my head up and realize he's fully dressed for the game.

"You're sweating."

I run a hand across my forehead and feel the cold, clammy sweat beading along my hairline. "It's from earlier. I did a little riding before you came in."

Heath gives me a skeptical look. "You going to be able to play? I need a good match."

"Oh, it'll be an excellent match, believe me." It's even harder now to keep my voice level. "I promise."

"Okay. But fair warning: I won't go easy on you."

"Wouldn't expect you to."

We go out to the court. The sky is cloudless and beautiful, even by SoCal standards. What a fabulous day for justice.

He goes to the other side of the net and points his racket at me. "Since you're tired, I'll give you first serve."

I narrow my eyes, studying his smug, confident posture, and squeeze the ball in my hand. The racket feels like an instrument of retribution.

"I'm ready!" he calls out with a smarmy grin. "Do your worst!"

Oh, I will. I toss the ball up and hit it hard. It shoots through the air, straight for him.

He doesn't get a chance to lift his hand to block it. It hits his face with a crunch. Blood spurts from his nose. His knees bend awkwardly, and he falls on his ass.

He covers his face. "Fuck!"

Or at least I think he said that, because the word was muffled and he was slurring a bit.

I look at him dispassionately. There's no satisfaction. I took my anger out on him, but the person I'm truly furious with is myself.

Still, Heath needs to pay for what he's done. And Sadie will too. But I'll have to pay the most—because all of this is my fault.

Heath says something to me, the words too garbled to understand.

"Stop whining," I tell him. "That's just the first course."

52

GRANT

I return to the locker room and shower again, feeling the urge to scrub myself clean. When I change back into my clothes and head to my car, one of the receptionists rushes toward me.

"Sir!" she says.

"Yes?" I'm impatient to get going, but this shouldn't take long.

"What happened on the tennis court—"

"Was an accident. I'm sure Heath told you that. Sometimes, you know, the ball just goes where it wants to go."

She looks uncertain. She has a crush on Seb and watched us play last time we were here.

"Sebastian is the ball whisperer, not me. Ask him if you like."

"Okay." She nods. "Sorry to bother you. I just needed to know to make a note for our incident report."

I turn away, go to the Maybach and dump my bag and racket in the back. My phone says Aspen still hasn't read my texts. But then, I wouldn't either if I were her. I'm surprised she didn't spit in my face the second she found out whom she was working for.

Fuck. I screwed up everything. Now all the terrible, snide things I said to her come rushing back. And I made her stay late at the office...come in on weekends...run at the crack of dawn...and acted like she was a gold digger because she sold the items I gave her...

Even if she was in a maybe-I-could-forgive-Grant mood after fourteen years, she wouldn't be after what I put her through.

But that doesn't mean I'm not going to do whatever it takes to let her know I'm sorry. As a matter of fact, I need to try harder to make up for being the Asshole of All Assholes.

—Me: Where are you? We need to talk. Please.

She's not going to respond. I know that, even as I send the text.

I head toward her place, rather than waiting for her to come to her shift at the bar later. And that's assuming that she'll even show up after walking out yesterday. Christ, I screwed up everything. I call myself every name in the book. How can I have this IQ and not even be able to keep the only woman I ever loved happy?

When I reach her apartment, I knock. Then bang when she doesn't respond.

"Aspen! I know you're in there!" I start pounding. "Come on! I have to talk to you! I spoke to Heath!" I'm hitting the door hard enough that it rattles.

The door next to hers opens again, and the same Asian lady sticks her head out. "Can you be quiet? I can't hear my drama." Then she stops. "Oh, it's you again."

"Yes. Do you have any information about Aspen?" Like why she's not answering her door or my texts.

"You're wasting your time. She's probably visiting her grandfather."

"Did you see her leave?" I ask, hopeful.

"No, but she always visits her grandfather on weekends. She's a good girl. Anyway, trust me. She's not home."

I squint at her. "Are you saying that to get rid of me so you can watch your drama?"

"I would never lie about her grandfather." She seems sincere.

Besides, if Aspen's at the Orange Care Center, it'll be easier to talk to her. She won't want to make a scene or run out, lest she upset Kenny. I hate to use that as leverage, but we *have* to talk.

"Okay," I say to the neighbor lady. "Thanks."

So I drive out to the Orange Care Center. Gi-Hoon greets me again.

"Is Aspen here to see Kenny?" I ask.

"No. Actually, she hasn't come by at all." Gi-Hoon frowns. "She's probably working."

"She does work a lot." Maybe I can get him talking. I suspect Gi-Hoon knows a great deal about Aspen's life.

"She does. That poor kid. She's been taking care of her grandfather all by herself."

"What about Kat?" I can't picture her letting Aspen shoulder everything, even if it hurts her to see her husband not remembering her.

Gi-Hoon gives me a blank look. "Kat?"

"Her grandmother. Kenny's wife."

"Oh." His expression clouds. "Didn't she tell you?"

My belly tightens instinctively to brace for pain, like it just knows whatever he's going to say is going to be bad.

"She passed away quite a while back. A brain aneurysm, I think? It was very sudden, from what I heard. Apparently, Kenny took it hard."

He would have. Kenny and Kat were so in love. But Aspen would've taken it just as hard. She was incredibly close to her grandparents. That explains why she's working so hard, why she took all sorts of abuse from me to keep her job. She's the only one who can provide for Kenny.

I squeeze my eyes shut for a moment. Every time I learn something new about Aspen's situation, I wonder if I can ever recover from all my blunders. Why couldn't I have been just a little bit nicer? Why couldn't I have at least treated her the way I treated Renée? But no. I did everything in my power to let her know how much I despised her, how little I think of her.

I got a second chance, and I blew it like an idiot.

"Anyway, why don't you sign in so you can see Kenny?" Gi-Hoon says, obviously assuming I'm here to see him.

I'm ashamed to face Aspen's grandfather, but I sign in anyway. I need to apologize, even if he doesn't understand. I should look into treatments that might delay the pace of his memory loss. There might be new and experimental therapies available, as long as you can afford them. I should also figure out a way to pay for his stay here without alerting Aspen that I'm the one paying. She'll never accept it if she knows, but I can't bear to see her continue to struggle.

I don't ever want her to take abuse from anybody because of money she needs to take care of her grandfather.

I go to the third floor. Many of the residents are watching TV, although there's a group playing bingo with a young aide.

Kenny isn't in the breakroom. I speak to one of the nurses, and she says he went to his room. We go over together.

"He's been a bit lethargic since this morning. Probably because he was overly energetic last night. They were showing an old episode from *Dancing with the Stars*, and that got him excited."

I smile. "That's like him. He loves to dance."

"He does." She beams. "It was so cute."

Kenny's door isn't closed. He's lying in bed, looking out the window, but turns his head before the nurse can say anything to him.

"Oh, hey." He smiles slowly.

She pats my shoulder. "I'll leave you two alone."

"Thanks." I approach him. Anxiety winds me tight. I'm not sure how he's going to react to my apology. Or how I should go about it so I don't end up making him violent, like last time. Actually, his getting violent with me was deserved, I decide. He can hit me all he wants if it makes him feel better. "Hello, sir."

"Hi," he says, his eyes searching my features with the quiet desperation of someone who's trying to put a name to the face.

"I'm Grant. I'm one of Aspen's...friends." My chest aches with regret and guilt at the lie. She and I could've been more. So much more.

He gives me a toothy grin. "Another one? She sure is popular, isn't she?"

"Yes, she is."

"I'm so glad she has so many friends." He gazes at me.

"Lots and lots," I reassure him.

He pats my hand. "I know." He pauses for a second, then blinks. "Every girl in my life is a marshmallow. Kat. Georgia. And Aspen."

"Who's Georgia?"

"Aspen's mom. You never met her. She died when Aspen was

just a baby. Aspen never knew her parents." Kenny looks sad. "That's why she's the softest marshmallow of us all. She's just so defenseless. Not knowing your parents' love does that to you."

"You gave her all the love," I remind him gently.

"But I'm not her dad. Kat's not her mom. Aspen knows we worry. She tries to pretend she's a prickly pear, but we can see she's just a marshmallow."

"She is." And I did everything in my power to crush her. I don't think I could feel worse.

"Can you be there for her when she's hurting? I can't always be there. I'm here. Trapped here." His eyes appear clear and lucid, although he can't be if he is asking me this favor. I can't imagine Aspen hiding the bet from him, especially when she had to leave school because of the fallout.

"Of course. I'll always be there for her." Whether he recognizes me or not, whether he remembers this or not, I'm keeping this promise.

He smiles. "You're such a good boy. I just knew when I saw you. You look at her the way I look at Kat. You want her happy, the way I want Kat to be happy."

"I do. And I'll make her happy."

He pats my hand. "Thank you. That's all I wanted." He blinks, and a change seems to come over him. "It's nap time." His tone is abruptly childish. "You should go. I don't like it when people look at me when I'm trying to sleep."

"Okay. Have a nice nap."

I stand to leave, but pause at the door. He's gazing out the window, at the garden with sunflowers, talking to himself about what he should get for his wife for their anniversary, lost in the past.

53

GRANT

On Monday, I enter the office at the usual time carrying a rectangular item wrapped in thick brown paper. Aspen's desk is empty. She still hasn't returned my texts or calls. I don't know if she was home, because when I went by again yesterday evening, all the lights were out in her apartment. She didn't show at the bar, either. Damn it. I shouldn't have bought it and acted like such a dick. She said she wouldn't quit, but given her pride, she might have. Jenna said Aspen hadn't called in sick, but the disapproving pursing of her mouth said she blamed me. And I take full responsibility.

After placing the wrapped item on the table between the two couches, I set up my laptop and roll my shoulders. My eyes feel dry from lack of sleep. I tossed and turned until it was time to get up and come to work.

Aspen will be here. She'd never jeopardize her grandfather's wellbeing, and she needs the monthly two thousand dollars GrantEm pays the Orange Care Center.

Emmett enters through the open door. His eyes are slightly bloodshot, although they're otherwise alert.

"You wanted to see me?" he says.

"Yeah." I gesture at one of the couches as I take the other. "How's Monique?" When I texted last night to see if we could meet up, he said he couldn't because Monique was running a fever and kept vomiting.

"Much better." Emmett yawns, sitting down. He's only showing how exhausted he really is because he's with me. He would never do that in front of others.

It's the same for me. You don't show vulnerability to people you can't count on to have your back.

He adds, "Amy's taking the day off, though, because she's refusing to be away from her mom."

"Poor Amy," I murmur. "Can't be easy to take care of a sick baby."

"The nanny's coming, so it should be okay. They can tag-team her." He crosses his legs. "Anyway, what's up?"

"It's about our bet."

"Our bet?" He looks confused.

"The one about Aspen. I lost." I've always been competitive, but right now, it feels great to admit defeat. The bet is immaterial. What's important is Aspen. And I need to resolve this if I want to start fresh.

He frowns. "I must be a lot more tired than I thought, because I could swear you just forfeited. Don't we still have time until the three-month mark?"

"We do, and I did."

"Weird. You hate losing more than anything." He cocks his head, scrutinizing me. "So you aren't going to get her to quit?"

"No."

"And you aren't going to try to back out of the bet?" His tone is somewhat wary.

I laugh humorlessly. "No." I take the package off the table. "Here. Hang it with pride."

He rips the wrapping off. It's a framed paper, on which I've handwritten my defeat.

To Emmett,

You were right, and I was wrong.

Grant

Emmett stares at the paper. "You're serious."

"Yeah."

"Why?"

"I want a clean slate with Aspen," I say.

"Ah." He raises his eyebrow with a knowing smile. "You like her."

I say nothing, since I'll be damned if he's the first one to hear me say it, especially when I haven't had a chance to tell her everything and ask for *her* forgiveness.

"Well." He grins. "Good luck." He places the framed paper on the table and stands.

I rise to my feet. "What are you doing?"

"I don't want it."

"What? Why not?"

"If I had a bet like that involving Amy, I'd forfeit too. Your happiness means more than having a piece of paper from you saying I'm right. Besides, paper or no paper, we'll both always know I was right." He grins and walks out.

Looking at the framed paper on the table, I rub the back of my neck with a small smile. It's surprising, but at the same time, so much like Emmett. But then, all my brothers are like that. Tight.

Optimism seeps through me. The bet's resolved, and I just need to talk to Aspen. I check the time. She should be here any moment.

I put the framed paper in one of the drawers at my desk and wait for her to come in to brief me on the day's agenda, mentally going over what I'm going to say. Nothing has ever mattered this much before in my life. Anxiety wells like a tsunami, but I master my nerves.

Failure is not an option.

54

ASPEN

I feel like a disaster.

I don't know what made me say what I've been bottling up all this time. But when I threw it in Grant's face Saturday evening, it was like something broke inside me, and I couldn't stop shaking. My body felt so cold, like somebody plunged me into icy water. I couldn't breathe, and I could feel my jaw trembling.

As surprised as he looked, I was more traumatized, like I'd dug into the old wound and wriggled my fingers around in it until the tissues that had finally begun to heal came apart again.

I had to leave before I did something humiliating. Like collapse. Or cry.

I'll never, ever give Grant anything to attack me with. And showing emotional weakness to him would be akin to a doe baring her throat to a wolf.

I somehow managed to drive home without crashing. Then parked in a lot attached to the building next door because ours was full, and huddled under a blanket in my apartment to get warm. I covered my ears when Grant banged on the door and called my name.

Even if I'd wanted to answer, I couldn't have, not when every muscle in my body was shaking uncontrollably.

I ran a high fever until Sunday night. Finally giving voice to the old bet and how much it hurt me, saying everything out loud, should've been liberating, but it wasn't. I hate that I succumbed to fever—proof of the extreme stress I've been suffering for so long. Delirium set in. My body felt like a conflagration. Maybe it wanted to burn away all my embarrassment and humiliation over the fact that something so inconsequential that Grant doesn't even remember has the power to hurt me still.

But by dawn on Monday, my fever breaks.

I shower, then run a bright red lipstick over my mouth to cover how pale I look. Nothing can hide the dark circles under my eyes or the ghostly pallor of my mildly hollowed cheeks, so I figure to hell with it. I haven't eaten anything since lunch on Saturday, but I'm not particularly hungry.

I go to GrantEm early, since I'm done getting ready and don't want to stay in my depressingly dingy apartment with its smell of sweat and illness. Morning traffic is light, which is nice, but I'm dreading the coming day. As much as I wish I could quit, I can't. I need the money and the eldercare benefit.

Act calm. Act cool. You've handled Grant all this time. Nothing's changed. He's still the same dickhead.

If he brings up forgiving me again, I'll just shrug. If he expects gratitude... Well, he'll just be disappointed.

After work, I'll drop by the bar and tell Jenna I'm quitting, if she hasn't fired me already. I don't want Zack to have to give up a job because of my conflict with Grant. I can find another part-time bartending position. Grant can't buy up every bar in the city, and I don't want another job where he's my boss.

I grab a fresh mug of coffee from the breakroom and head to my desk. The floor's empty on Grant's side, which is weird. A lot of people should be here by now...

Oh, wait. Since he's been working everyone hard for weeks, Grant made show-up time at ten today. The associates looked at him like he was the second coming of Christ.

His request slipped my mind, but even if I remembered, it wouldn't have made much of a difference. Unlike his MBA people, I get paid hourly. I can't afford to work fewer than forty hours, especially when I've lost the bartending income from the weekend.

As I get closer to my desk, I can hear a conversation coming from Grant's office through the open door. Guess he ignored his own edict as well.

"It's about our bet," Grant says.

"Our bet?" It's Emmett voice.

"The one about Aspen."

I stop and hold my breath, even as tremors start again. But I'm not feverish like before. I'm not cold, either. My head is oddly clear as I accept the possibility that Grant might've at some point bragged about being my first to his brothers, too.

"I lost," Grant says.

What?

"I must be a lot more tired than I thought, because I swear you just admitted defeat. Don't we still have time until the three-month mark?"

"We do, and I did."

"Weird. You hate losing more than anything."

No kidding. He spent tens of thousands of dollars to be my first and win the bet in college.

"So you aren't going to get her to quit?" Emmett asks.

Out of reflex—maybe because I don't want to hear the rest of a debasing conversation about me—I take a few steps back. My entire body feels achy, but my throat hurts the most, like it's covered in frost.

So. When I joined GrantEm, Grant made a bet with his brother —this time to force me to quit. That explains so much about his unreasonable requests, and how furious he was when he realized I was getting paid overtime. He thought I'd quit out of exhaustion and being overworked.

Maybe his offer to "forgive me" was a last-ditch effort to get me to quit. And then he banged on my door on Saturday and Sunday. What would he have said if I'd opened the door?

I've simply been a source of amusement for him. My struggle, my dreams, my aspirations are just a big, fat joke. Otherwise, he wouldn't have started another bet with his brother.

Is he going to streak around the office? I wonder cynically, then decide I don't care. I walk back to the breakroom, dump the coffee and leave the mug in the sink. Bracing my hands against the edge of the counter, I stare at the brown puddle on the otherwise pristine stainless steel. Maybe I'm like coffee to him. Nice when it's fresh enough, but as time passes, it becomes gross.

I almost laugh at the ridiculous analogy. I must be tired. Or something. My vision blurs. I blink and feel tears fall. I swipe my fingers across my cheeks to dry them. My head now feels like it's full of soggy noodles, but I have only moments to gather myself before I have to act like I'm not hurt. That nothing Grant does can ever affect me.

Thank God nobody from his team is in early. Otherwise, so many people would've heard. Or maybe they already know. After all, I was the only one who didn't know back at school, and Grant has even more power here. GrantEm is his kingdom.

I rub my hand over my heart, where a dull ache is starting. *It's just the stress,* I tell myself. It has to be. Otherwise, it's too unfair.

My phone pings in my purse. I pull it out and glance at the screen, wondering if it's Grant texting for the ten thousandth time. But it's the Orange Care Center.

–Orange Care Center: We think you should come in. Kenny's deteriorating rapidly, and he's asking for you.

I sway. Ice seems to run through my veins. Grandpa looked fine on Saturday. He mistook me for Grandma, but he always does that. He even tangoed with me, humming and laughing.

How can he be deteriorating?

I can't lose him. Ugly, monstrous panic and terror pulse inside me, and everything burns painfully, like I'm inhaling a cloud of acid. Shaking, I grab my purse and dash toward the elevator, while calling the center.

They're probably overreacting. *I'm* probably overreacting. It's just some kind of legal thing they have to do, just in case, to prevent a possible lawsuit.

I hit the button for the elevator repeatedly, willing it to come faster. The phone continues to ring. Come on, come on!

"This is Gi-Hoon at the Orange Care Center. How can I help you?"

Finally! "It's Aspen," I say hurriedly. "I just got your text." *Tell me you screwed up!*

"Oh." The single, sympathetic syllable dashes all my hopes. "I'm so sorry, Aspen."

"What? What are you sorry about?" *Tell me you're sorry you made a mistake!*

"I really think you should come if you can. The doctor's here, but Kenny's been asking for you."

My knees shake. I brace myself against the wall next to the elevator to stay upright. "Since when?"

"He was okay until last night, but this morning..."

"Was there an accident? Did he fall or something?"

"No. He complained about being lethargic, then..." Gi-Hoon sighs heavily. "I'm so sorry."

The elevator finally dings and opens. I stumble into its maw, hit L and squeeze my eyes shut. Something sour and bitter pushes up from my belly to my throat, and I swallow, covering my mouth. I can't believe this is happening. This just *can't be happening to me.*

As I fight the rush-hour traffic to reach the center, I curse at life. At the cars. At the fact that today's Monday. And the fact that the universe is so *fucking* unfair.

All I have is Grandpa. Why can't I keep him? Why must it take him away from me, too?

"Fuck you!" I rage in the car at some force in the universe out to torment me. "Fuck you and your fucking injustice! Fuck you!"

Then abrupt fear slashes at me. What if the unseeable force is about to take pity on me, but hears me bitching?

"I'm sorry," I say like a lunatic. "I didn't mean it. Please."

Don't take him away, I pray fervently. *I'll do anything!*

When I reach the center, I park my car and run to the lobby. Gi-Hoon stands when he sees me running in, grabs a fistful of Kleenex and gives them to me. Only then do I realize I'm crying.

"Thank you," I say between panting breaths. I dab at my face. I don't want to show up with teary eyes, looking like a mess. It'll worry Grandpa. Stress isn't good for him.

I check my reflection in the small mirrored wall in the lobby. My eyes are red, and my face is blotchy. I blow my nose and put on some powder, hoping it helps cover up the panic and pain.

Then I go to Grandpa's room on the third floor, desperately praying for a miracle. Dr. Benton's saying something soothing to my grandfather, but he keeps saying, "Where's my baby? Where's Kat?"

I step forward, forcing a smile. My chin trembles, and I tighten my jaw. "Hi."

Grandpa's eyes swing to me. "Kat!"

My eyes burn with tears, but I hold them back. He looks unbelievably frail. It's like he's lost half his weight, and his soul is ready to take leave of his body. "Hi," I croak.

"What's wrong with your voice?"

"I was singing late last night, and I strained my voice a little."

"Want some hot lemon tea?" He swallows with some effort. "With honey?"

"Yes. I'd love that."

He starts to push feebly at the sheets.

I put a hand over his. His skin's so cold, like he's already half-dead. *Please...* I hold his hand in mine, trying to warm it, as though that will keep him here longer. "Later."

"You sure?"

I nod because I can't bring myself to speak.

He blinks, then nods. "Okay." Then he's quiet for a moment.

I use the silence to compose myself, breathing over his hands, hoping I can warm him. A person who's warm can't be dying, right? But even as I want to deny it, I know I have to say goodbye. Except I don't know how.

He's been my guardian. My rock—my everything. Can a dolphin say goodbye to the ocean? Can a morning glory say goodbye to the sun?

"I love you so much," he says quietly. "You shouldn't be sad, Aspen."

He recognizes me, and my face crumples.

"Old people die," he whispers. "That's the way of the world. Your boyfriend..."

Boyfriend? It can't be Zack, because he would've said the name. I wonder how far Grandpa's gone back in time.

He continues, "He likes you. He'll be there for you. He's a good, solid boy. I feel like…" He swallows again. "I can count on him. Count on him to take care of you. He promised he would."

Nobody made that promise, Grandpa. You're the only one I have left. If you leave me, I'll be alone.

But he looks so light and free that I just nod with a smile. "Yeah. He's a good guy," I say, even as my heart is breaking into pieces. I know I need to do this for him. "I'll be fine."

"Good." He smiles. "Think I'll…rest a little." He closes his eyes, his lashes fluttering. After a few moments, his hand goes limp in mine.

Hot tears burn my cheeks. I bury my face in the crook of his neck.

I'm truly alone.

55

GRANT

When Aspen doesn't show up at the regular time, I tap my desk, wondering what's going on. Then I remember: everyone's coming in at ten today.

She must be taking advantage of that. She's been avoiding me, and she isn't going to come in a second sooner than she has to. That's fine. It gives me more time to compose myself and what I need to say.

My anxiety ratchets up, though. I feel like words won't be enough, but I don't know if buying her something expensive is going to convince her I'm serious. Flowers, maybe? Then it hits me—the reason Aspen and I visited her grandparents' home in the first place!

I contact the concierge service and ask them to get me as many jars of organic strawberry jam from Sun Valley Farms as possible. My gut tells me that little but thoughtful things like this are what's going to convince her I'm not screwing around. She loved the jam fourteen years ago, and I hope she still loves it.

But she doesn't come in by ten. I check half an hour later—still nothing.

I pull out my phone to text her, then notice an unread message on my messenger. It's Leah from HR.

–Leah: FYI, Aspen called in sick.

That's a lie... Isn't it? She's been avoiding me, and she's doing it again. But I can't tell Leah that.

—Me: Did you get to talk to her on the phone? How did she sound?

—Leah: Terrible. If she's half as bad as she sounded, you would've had to send her home.

Okay, so maybe Aspen really is sick. Or maybe she sounds like crap from screaming expletives at me. But I put more credence in her being sick. She wouldn't want to give up pay after not working at the bar over the weekend.

—Me: Does she have any sick days she can use?

—Leah: She has one day accumulated.

My first instinct is to offer money to Aspen to make up for it, but she'll just refuse, regardless of whether she's decided to forgive me or not. I should give her some overtime hours.

Or actually...I should use the charitable foundation Sebastian's family funds.

—Me: Seb, didn't you say your family has a foundation that helps pay for eldercare for the needy?

—Sebastian: Yeah. Why? Wanna donate? Grandmother's always looking for new donors.

—Me: Yes. But I want some of my money to go toward a very particular recipient.

—Sebastian: Who?

—Me: Aspen.

A small pause.

—Sebastian: Isn't that the assistant you're trying to get rid of?

Of course he'd remember that.

—Me: Yes, but things are different now. She worked out.

—Sebastian: I can see what I can do, if you can get Jeremiah to take a case for me.

—Me: Why don't you ask her directly?

—Sebastian: I did, and she said no.

Whoa. Jeremiah wouldn't turn one of us down. Not because she's fond of us, but because she knows we can afford her rate. On top of that, we aren't idiots who bring her migraine-inducing cases.

—Me: Did she say why?

–Sebastian: I already know why. But I want you to convince her.

–Me: That's an unfair trade. You know she never changes her mind.

–Sebastian: I can't get married! I refuse!

I stare at the screen, at a loss for words. Finally, I type:

–Me: I'm at a loss for words.

–Sebastian: It's complicated, but I need Jeremiah and her minions to undo a stupid contract my grandparents signed! They did it without consulting me! It's gotta be illegal.

Poor Seb. At least none of the Grants signed me away in a contract.

–Me: I'll lobby via Hux. He might get a better result.

–Sebastian: Tried that. She told him to mind his own business or join the firm if he wants to help out.

Hux will never join Huxley & Webber, not even for Sebastian. He fought so hard for the freedom he has, away from the family law firm.

–Me: Okay, I'll TRY. I'll ask Jeremiah, but no guarantees.

–Sebastian: Thanks. It means a lot. She won't even answer my calls. I think she's blocked my number.

Ouch.

–Sebastian: I'll talk to the foundation people. Just send me the details.

–Me: Okay. I'll send everything over before lunch.

I pull up Aspen's HR files and grab the info she filled out to get the eldercare benefits. I forward that to Seb, along with instructions to my accountant to distribute some money to the foundation. This should lift the financial burden on Aspen. And I'm donating enough to pay for ten other needy families, so it's a good outcome. On top of that, Aspen's situation qualifies for the foundation's criteria for helping out, so it isn't like she's getting assistance she doesn't deserve. She just didn't know about the program. I make a mental note to see if Huxley's agency will take on the foundation's PR to promote what they do.

After work, I drive over to Aspen's place. I don't bring anything, since I don't know what she needs. But I want to check and make sure she's okay.

But the lights are out in her apartment. Maybe she's resting...?

I watch her apartment windows for some time until the units next to her start to turn off their lights. I check the time. It's already eleven.

I send her a quick text.

—Me: I heard you're sick. If you need anything, let me know.

She doesn't read it or respond. I sigh.

Probably still mad. But maybe enough time has passed that she's calmed down a little. Mom usually cools off once she's thought things through. I hope Aspen's like that, too, so when I tell her the full truth about the bet, she'll be able to listen without jumping to the absolute worst conclusion.

But she doesn't show up on Tuesday...or Wednesday. Leah doesn't update me. When I contact her, she says Aspen hasn't called in sick, but maybe she's too sick to even do that.

—Leah: Sometimes it happens. She lives alone. But I'll call and see what's up.

Since Aspen won't even read my texts, it's probably the best plan. Unease settles in my gut, though. This situation is an eerie mirror of what happened after Heath and Will streaked, except the circumstances couldn't be more different. What happened on Saturday wasn't bad enough to warrant her abandoning Kenny. Hell, she should be here in the office, kicking my ass.

Even as I try to reassure myself, what Kenny said about her being a marshmallow instead of a prickly pear comes back. She's soft and sweet if she decides you're worthy of being in her inner circle. I'm not there now, so she won't let herself be vulnerable to me. She'll show up at work, pretend nothing's wrong and do her job, while driving me crazy with her you-don't-matter-to-me act.

My messenger pings.

—Leah: She's still sick. She sounds bad. Not as bad as Monday, but still bad.

Okay... So she's just still sick...and she doesn't want to deal with me because she isn't reading my texts. Fine. I'm not going to hound a sick woman like some asshole.

By Thursday, I receive a case of the jam I asked for. I take a jar—since the security at her apartment is crap, and I don't want to risk having the entire case stolen—and leave it outside her door with a note on the lid.

[I'm sorry about everything. Can we please talk?

–G]

She ignores me—or maybe she didn't see the jam and note. Neither possibility is good. She doesn't come in on Friday, either. Now I'm outright alarmed. I contact Leah again.

–Me: What's up with Aspen?

–Leah: Still down. She said she has some stomach bug, which can get nasty.

But *five days?*

It pisses me off that Leah's so blasé about Aspen's situation. She lives alone. She could need somebody.

I attend all the morning and lunch meetings, but my mind's only half there. I can't quit worrying about Aspen, but can't figure out how to reach out to her, either. She won't respond to calls or texts, and she doesn't answer the door when I go by. Her lights are always off—I literally don't even know if she's home.

By six, another possibility strikes me. Something could've happened to Kenny. Aspen is intensely private about her life and Kenny, and she might've lied about being sick while taking care of her grandfather because she knows HR will convey whatever she tells them to me.

I immediately get to my feet and start to head out.

Larry jumps from his desk. "I need just a couple of minutes to wrap up the due diligence!"

Due diligence on what? I don't remember, and I don't care. "Email me," I say as I trot to the elevator.

I can feel everyone's eyes. They've never seen me run in the office. I've never had to.

I call the Orange Care Center as I reach the lobby.

"Hello, this is Gi-Hoon at the Orange Care Center. How can I help you?" a pleasant male voice says.

I try to speak, but my throat's too dry. I swallow. "This is Grant Lasker. I'm calling regarding Kenny Hughes. I'm a family friend, and I swung by a couple of times." *Please tell me he's fine.* I don't know what Aspen will do if anything's happened to him.

"Oh." That one syllable rings with sympathy.

Fuck. Don't show me sympathy. Don't—

"I'm so sorry. I guess you haven't heard...?"

"Heard what?" Dread pounds in my chest.

"He passed away Monday morning." His voice is gentle.

"What? But he was fine on Sunday. I saw him."

"His heart gave out. It was rather sudden, but peaceful. Thankfully, he had a chance to say goodbye to his granddaughter."

I run a hand down my face. Kenny died. Aspen should've said something... We have a separate leave policy for people who lose family members—

To her, you aren't the kind of person she can talk to in a situation like this.

To her, I'm just an asshole who took her virginity to win a bet and then tormented her endlessly the next time our paths crossed. She must've thought I was the scum of the universe when I offered to forgive her so we could "start fresh."

So much regret wells up that it turns into anguish. My chest hurts, like my ribcage is being pushed open from the pressure. I put the heel of my hand against my breastbone, trying to contain the pain, but it cuts until I feel shredded.

While Aspen has been dealing with Kenny's death, I've been patting myself on the back for taking care of her bills at the center. What an idiot I've been. Why is it that I'm always a step behind?

"Did she have anybody with her?" I ask, praying Aspen wasn't alone when Kenny passed.

"No. It was just her."

56

GRANT

It's started to rain by the time I come out of the GrantEm building. My whole body feels numb. Did Kenny know he was dying? Is that why he asked me to be with Aspen? To make sure she wouldn't be alone?

His death feels so sudden. The shock and grief Aspen must be feeling... I don't know how she managed to remember to let the firm know she couldn't come in.

The drive to her place is slow and painful, with SoCal drivers crawling on the rain-slickened roads. Two pileups on the way create even more congestion. Frustration mounts with the need to reach her, but there's nothing I can do to make these desert dwellers go any faster.

My eyes involuntarily go to the dashboard when the sound system starts playing "Only Love Can Hurt Like This." Aspen hated it, which is precisely why I put it on an infinite loop when I drove her to Lola's, just to be a dick. As Paloma Faith's words flow out, my heart aches. I know now why Aspen hated to listen to it, especially with me around. The song is a reminder of how she's misjudged me. How toxic I've been for her. And it doesn't matter that I didn't mean to be, because the result is the same. Conscious volition or no, when you step on a baby bird, it dies. I was a capital-A asshole. A complete and utter bastard. If I could, I'd kick my own ass.

When I finally reach Aspen's place, it's after ten. I park my car and get out. The rain seeps into my clothes, chilling my skin.

I scan the building, looking for lights in her apartment. It's dark. Is she with a friend? As much as I want to speak to her, I also hope she's with somebody who can soothe her pain.

Something moves on the metal balustrade on her balcony. Son of a *bitch. Is somebody trying to break into her place?*

I start forward, ready to defend her against the intruder, then stop. It's *Aspen*, straddling the balustrade, one leg on each side. Her hand is wrapped around an urn that's propped on the railing between her thighs, and she's holding a bottle. The chill from the rain suddenly fades into the background as an icy dread spreads through me.

I open my mouth to tell her to go back inside, then stop. She lifts the bottle and takes a swig, her torso swaying. Cold sweat covers my spine. She's probably drunk. If I call out, she might turn or lean toward me to see what's going on, then lose her balance on the wet balustrade and fall. Even though her apartment is only on the second floor, she could be seriously injured.

My heart racing with panic, I run into her building and up to the second floor. Hopefully if I knock, she'll answer. And she'll be out of danger...

I lift my fist, then pause. *Her door is ajar.* What the fuck? Fury overwhelms the panic. She's a woman living alone! Doesn't she know how dangerous it is to leave her door open?

I want to shake her and yell at her to be more careful, but now isn't the time. I slip inside, making sure to close the door and lock it firmly. Since it's so dark, I turn on the light.

"Aspen?" I call out so she knows it's me and not some criminal.

She doesn't seem to hear me, even though the sliding door to the balcony is wide open. She merely lifts the bottle to her mouth again. Rain glistens on her skin; her white T-shirt and jeans are wet and plastered to her body. Her lips have no color, and her eyes are slightly unfocused, like she's gazing at something far away in the night sky.

I walk toward her, keeping my steps measured, hiding my churning emotions. Taking care of her is the priority.

"Aspen," I say again, my voice gentler. I stop at the sliding door, afraid she might do something rash if she thinks I'm too close. She ran on Saturday and refused to see me. I don't know how drunk she is right now, and she might just tilt backward off the balustrade.

"Grant?" She turns her head in my direction, and her body sways again. My heart leaps to my throat.

"Come this way, please." I slowly extend a hand.

She raises her bottle like a shield. "Why should I?" Her words are slightly slurred.

"We're two stories up. It's dangerous."

"So? Why do you care? You aren't my boss anymore." The smile she gives me spikes my anxiety. It's the hopeless smile of someone who has nothing left to lose.

"Yes, I am. Look, I'll pay you overtime if you'll just come this way," I say, hating that money is all I can use to lure her off the balcony. If I hadn't been such a moron, I could tell her I care about her...that I love her. But she wouldn't believe me now.

"Nope. You can't. I emailed my resignation this afternoon. Didn't you see it?" She frowns. "Maybe I sent it to HR." She brightens. "But hey, congrats! Now you can get an assistant you really want."

Of course she did. She doesn't need the job anymore. Despair descends on me over the realization that not even my money is of use to her. Still, I keep my voice mild and shake my head. My priority is ensuring her safety. "You're the one I want."

"No, no. I'm the one who cost you. But don't worry. I'll ship you back your dresses and shoes. Aw, shit." The rain on her face makes it hard to tell, but her expression crumbles, and I swear tears are falling from her eyes. She puts her forearm over her face, pulling the urn closer with her other hand until it's cradled against her lower belly. "Fuck. I'm not... This isn't how my life was supposed to go."

"I know. You've had a really rough time. So come on over here. We'll figure out how to put your life back on the right track, okay?" I need to penetrate her drunken grief, but—

"What's the point? I have nothing. I'm really alone. And it's all your fault." She points at me with the bottle and shifts a little bit more toward the wrong side of the balcony.

My gut feels like it's been chopped into little pieces. "I know. It absolutely is. But please. Come inside and blame me."

"If I hadn't met you... Or at least hadn't *slept* with you..." She shakes her head. "You're *such* a dick. And you haven't changed."

She isn't saying anything I don't know already. But it cuts deep anyway. "So come here and kick my ass. I promise I'll let you kick it as much as you want. Just come in from the rain."

"No. I'm not going anywhere near you. You're bad news, Grant. Every time you're around, bad things happen."

"I'm sorry about the bet in college," I say hurriedly, praying she'll accept my apology and come inside. "I was roped into it by circumstance, and I didn't even remember it until I ran into Will at the airport and he brought it up. I thought I could hide it from you."

"How could you hide something like that? They were naked! And running!" She waves the bottle around.

Every muscle in my legs quivers with the need to lunge and grab her. The problem is that I might not make it in time, and she might just fall over. "I asked them not to do it. I didn't care about the bet. You were what was important to me. You still are." I run a hand over my mouth. "I should've come clean before anything happened. I was scared that telling you might make you hate me or think the worst of me. I was so afraid of destroying your trust. But I swear to you, I never spread the story about the bet or told anybody about our time in Malibu. It was too special for that." I tilt my head, pointing at my cheek. "Please, come here. Slap the shit out of me. Fourteen years is a long time to hold something inside. I wish you'd done it back then."

"I couldn't." Her voice is awful. "Grandma died."

I squeeze my eyes shut at the pain cracking through her words. I failed as a boyfriend in so many ways back then. I should've been there for her. I should've done everything in my power to reach her, talk to her, figure out why she left the way she did, instead of jumping to conclusions.

Her gaze drops to the urn in front of her. "She didn't make it. So confronting you wasn't a priority." Her fingers slowly stroke the urn.

"You want to know what I did with the money I got from selling the things you gave me? I used it to pay off the hospital bills and her funeral expenses. My grandparents didn't have health insurance, so...once I did that, there wasn't much left. But at least she got the best casket money could buy."

I'm an idiot. A dumbass. I wish I could go back in time—when I made comments about her being materialistic and what she must've done with the two hundred thousand—and strangle myself.

"I'm glad," I say.

My throat feels like it's full of sand. Now I finally understand why she didn't add up. I was trying to fit her into the wrong mold. I treated her like she was one of the numerous women who used me for my money, my body or my connection to Ted Lasker or Athena Grant.

Aspen tilts the bottle into her mouth again. "Grandpa's not going to get one. I had to cremate him. They were pretty quick about it. I think they felt sorry for me." She takes another swig.

"We'll do whatever's right for your grandfather." I wish I could take away some of her pain. She already cremated Kenny, but we might be able to do something—a burial or wake or whatever she needs for closure.

"I also know about your bet with Emmett," she says flatly, her eyes still on the urn.

Jesus. That too? Dread slices down my spine. "How?"

"I heard you and Emmett talking in the office. Can you imagine? If my grandfather had died even a day earlier, you could've won."

"No," I say, hating that I put that kind of pain into her. "I would've still lost. The bet was for three months, and I still had time. I forfeited."

She blinks, finally tearing her gaze from the urn and turning her head toward me. "Why?"

"Because I didn't want to win. It didn't matter anymore." I exhale heavily, but the weight on my chest doesn't ease. "I thought you had used me for money back in college. But even then I couldn't stay away from you. I wanted you. I..."

My heart is pounding against my ribs so hard, they feel like they're about to snap. I like to be strategic. I like to win. But what I want to tell her... I'm afraid it'll only come across as a pathetic, blatant attempt at manipulation. She already thinks I'm the kind of asshole who'd pick winning a bet over her grandfather living longer.

But she deserves to hear this because it's true. And if she uses it against me, so be it.

"I didn't want to admit it, and I fought so hard against it, but I love you. When I asked to start fresh, it was more for me—because I can't fight what I'm feeling for you anymore."

She blinks at me, but I don't think anything I said is penetrating. She frowns, confusion fleeting through her sad moss-green eyes.

Finally, she says, "You don't have to say that because you feel bad for me, Grant. It's okay. I knew I was going to be alone when he...was gone. Your pity won't change the fact that I have no one left."

Her rejection is like a hard kick in the balls, but I bear the pain. It's the least I deserve. And whatever I'm feeling is nothing compared to what she's suffering. I'd give up everything to relieve her agony.

"I saw Kenny on Sunday before he passed away."

"What?" Her eyes flash. "I told you to stay away from him!"

"I had to. I thought you might be with him, and...we needed to talk."

She stares at me for several long moments, then finally her shoulders sag. "Well, it doesn't matter now."

"He was worried about you. He didn't want you to feel alone. I promised him I'd be there for you."

"I don't believe you."

"And I don't blame you. But I did." I keep my eyes locked to hers, willing her to believe me on this one point, if nothing else. "I love you, Aspen."

"What if I hate you?" she demands.

"It doesn't matter. I still love you. I'll never, ever leave you to be alone."

She takes another swallow, her eyes still on me. I wish I could read her better, but she's so volatile. And I don't know how to make her believe me.

Then I see the jam I brought her on the counter. The sticky note is still on the lid.

I turn my focus back to her. "I know you don't believe me, but I want you to know you're my everything. I remember every second of our time together. I was riding Starfire when you chased me on the polo field. We danced to 'La cumparsita' for the first time, and again when we were in Malibu on that rainy night."

Her expression is unreadable. But she's listening.

"Our first real date was at an Italian restaurant named Benedicto's. You were in a white Aquinas College T-shirt and denim skirt. Your hair was down, and you looked absolutely beautiful. We sat at the table by a window that overlooked a garden full of flowering rosemary. You had clam pasta, and I splurged and had the chicken parm, then we split a tiramisu for desert because you said it was the best in the state. And you were right." I smile a little at the memory. I'd give everything I have to be able to go back in time, erase all her hurt. "Your favorite fairytale princess is Belle from *Beauty and the Beast*. And I was the Beast, according to you. All roaring gruffness. And just like him, I didn't make the best first impression."

Her mouth forms a small O.

"Your favorite jam is an organic strawberry jam from Sun Valley Farms. Your grandmother told me you also like their blueberry jam."

Her gaze lands on the jam on the counter briefly, before lifting back to me. Pain and confusion fleet through her eyes.

I continue, "I asked because I wanted to get some for you, since you said it was hard to come by. During our visit, your grandparents danced to 'Por una Cabeza,' and you and Kenny tangoed to 'Danzarin.' All of you looked so happy together, and I longed to belong with you."

Aspen abruptly lowers the bottle and lurches. My heart drops, and I swear I can feel my hair graying.

She drops the bottle, which lands with a thunk, and extends her free hand. "Can you help me? My legs are asleep."

"Yes."

Thank you, thank you, thank you. I give a silent offering of gratitude to whoever or whatever is up there watching over us.

I want her to let me have the urn, but she's holding it tightly, her fingers white. I wrap my arms around her and gently lift her off the balustrade. She's so cold. Uncontrollable shivers rack her body.

I carry her into the living room. Under the better light, I can see her lips are blue. They're quivering, and her teeth start to chatter.

"You're freezing," I say.

"So...are you," she manages.

"Why don't we get you warm?"

She nods jerkily, still holding on to the urn.

"Is it okay if I put the urn on the table?" I ask.

"Yeah."

I take it from her and place it in the center of the table. It must be horrifically painful to realize that a man of such vitality could be reduced to this.

"We need to get you out of those wet clothes," I say.

"Okay."

"Let me run the shower." I go look for the bathroom in the tiny apartment so she can strip out of her T-shirt and jeans. The bathroom's in the back with a shower stall so tiny, it could fit into a commercial airplane's lavatory. I twist the faucet and give it a few moments, but the showerhead continues to spew icy water.

I go to Aspen. To my concern and annoyance, she's still in the wet clothes, shivering.

"How long does it take for the water to heat up?" I ask.

"Not that long."

"It's still cold."

"Oh yeah..." She blinks slowly. "The heater broke a couple of days ago."

"The landlord hasn't fixed it?" That's gotta be illegal. I'm going to sue the bastard.

"I never had a chance to tell them." She gives me a small shrug. "It didn't seem that important. Cold showers aren't that bad."

"Well, you aren't taking another one." It's incredibly sad that she was too lost in her grandfather's death to even take care of herself. And I'm even more exasperated with myself for not having been here for her sooner. "Come on. Let's go."

57

ASPEN

Grant opens my closet, then pulls up short at the first thing he sees. It's the green dress I wore *that* day. He flinches, probably because he remembers what happened that morning in the office, and tries to move past it, but I extend a hand.

"That one's fine. I'm not picky." Certainly not about an outfit—well, about anything, really.

"Let's find you something else," he says, rummaging through my things and fishing out a gray sweatshirt and green yoga pants. *Why are they in the closet?* I've been meaning to wash them. "These'll be warmer."

"Okay." I'm too cold and exhausted to care that they aren't that clean. My skull's numb from the frigid rain. Who would've thought L.A. could get so chilly? "You mind?" I say when he stays rooted to the spot, looking at me like I might do something to hurt myself.

"Sorry," he says, then turns around and moves toward the kitchen, making sure to face the fridge.

I look at the tiny bed with its old, faded sheets and the nicked and wobbly dresser from my high school years. The only nice thing I can say about the space is that it's tidy.

My fingers are stiff, and my head feels like it's full of seaweed.

The cheap tequila probably wasn't a great idea, but I couldn't resist when it called to me in the store.

After a lot of fumbling, I manage to shed the wet clothes, including my underwear, and put on the sweatshirt and pants. As I turn around to grab my phone, I catch my reflection in the mirror. I look like a drowned rat. A *pallid* drowned rat.

I shove my feet into the first pair of shoes in the closet—neon-orange flip-flops. They don't match the outfit. But I can't think of a single reason I should care.

"I'm ready," I say.

Grant turns around. If the mismatch of my outfit and shoes shocks him, he doesn't show it.

He puts his hands on my shoulders. "You good?"

"Yeah." I take the urn again, hugging it close.

He puts his hand at my back, like he used to when we were younger. He escorts me out the apartment and makes sure I lock it properly, and then we get in his car and drive off.

He fiddles with the controls, and my seat grows warm. The vents exhale hot air over me. The speakers in his car are quiet, and it's just the sound of our breathing and the car engine. The streets are pretty empty, although they're slick with the rain that keeps on falling.

"You're going too fast," I say listlessly.

"I'm not. Unlike the people in this town, I know how to drive in the rain." He starts to lift a hand and move it toward me as though he wants to stroke my arm, but catches himself. "Trust me."

I look at his hand resting between us. He doesn't seem to know what to do with me, except get me warm and take me to his place. I don't know what he thinks we should do about Grandpa. Did I tell Grant I couldn't even get the plot next to Grandma's grave because the price was so outrageous? I don't know if holding on to the ashes is a good idea, but I don't want to scatter them. Grandpa wouldn't want to be anywhere except by Grandma's side.

Grant pulls into the garage at his mansion. The rain makes the place look like a safe haven, where you can relax and catch your breath before you take your next step. I wish I knew what *my* next step was going to be. I wish I didn't feel so strangely detached about everything.

Grant opens the door for me, and I step out of his car.

"This way," he says, escorting me.

I look at him. His hair's mussed and his clothes are damp from the rain. He was wet even before he came into my apartment. Is he cold too? His palms feel much warmer than mine, but that doesn't mean he isn't chilled.

The garage is connected to a foyer. He leads me past a vast kitchen and living room. I stop. "Where should I leave this?" I ask him, lifting the urn in my hands. I don't know if he wants the ashes too far into his home. He might get weirded out about it.

"Anywhere you want," he says.

There's a coffee table in the living room that overlooks the lit garden. Grandpa would like the view. "How about on the table over there?"

"Of course."

I trudge over and place the urn on the table, then stroke the top as if it were Grandpa's hand. The garden has a lot of pretty flowers, so... Yeah, it's a good spot to leave him for the moment.

Grant leads me up a winding staircase. Unlike the Malibu place, the staircases here are sturdy, with wooden railings and steps.

"Which one's your room?" I ask, looking at multiple doors in the hall.

"There at the end." He gestures. "I also have four guest bedrooms."

Does he want me to be in one of the spare bedrooms tonight? That feels logical. He said he loves me, but he doesn't know the real me. He only knows me from college and work. And I'm a complete mess right now.

But I really don't want to be by myself, especially in a strange place, not when the rain's dripping down the windows and my heart's too heavy to dance. "Is it okay if I stay with you?"

His hand twitches against my back.

"I'm not talking about sex. I just... I don't want to be alone."

"You can have whatever you want," he says, his voice a little hoarse.

His bedroom is spacious, with a huge bed and nightstands on each side. On the wall are a few artistic photographs—maybe his mother's—and a vase of white lilies sits in the corner.

"Flowers?" They don't fit my image of how his bedroom would look.

"The housekeeper picks them out. If you don't like them, I can toss them."

"No, no. They're pretty." I reach over and pluck a blossom. The divine scent soothes the jagged edges in my chest.

"You can use the shower first." He takes me inside a gigantic en suite bathroom, complete with a Jacuzzi tub and a separate stall. Everything's shiny and spotless. Top of the line.

"The towels are fresh. Housekeeping swaps them out every day. Here are the spare dental kits, including a toothbrush. If you need anything, just holler."

"Okay."

Once he's sure I'll be all right, he leaves. I brush my teeth first, trying to get the taste of cheap tequila out of my mouth.

Here, the hot water comes out instantly. I slip out of my flip-flops, strip off the sweatshirt and pants, then stand under the scalding water. My fingertips and toes prickle as they warm up. It feels *amazingly* good. Reminds me that I'm alive, and life has to go on.

My eyes burn, and I let the tears fall again. It feels liberating to cry. And to feel kindness from somebody who knows me and my grandparents.

Since Monday, so many people tried to show me sympathy, but I could sense their unease, something people often feel when a person they don't know has died and they aren't sure of the appropriate level of sadness to display to avoid looking fake.

All Grant has shown is true grief, like he's sharing the pain I'm feeling. And the burden and grief I've been carrying since Monday seem a little less crushing now.

I use the body wash and shampoo in the stall. They smell like fresh pine forest—like him. When I'm done, I notice thick, fresh towels hanging on what looks like a short ladder attached to the wall outside the shower stall. I take a towel, and it's *warm*. It feels positively toasty on my bare skin, and I sigh how the little luxury makes me feel more human.

I dry myself and slip into a bathrobe. I'm pretty sure it's Grant's, but I don't have anything clean to wear.

I step out of the bathroom, my hair a little damp. I still feel raw, but at least I'm warm. Seeing Grant makes me feel... I don't know what I'm supposed to feel. But knowing that there's somebody with me is mildly comforting.

"It's all yours," I say.

He points to a hair dryer on the bed. "You can use that. I'll be right back."

He hurries into the bathroom, and the spray starts.

I dry my hair, then perch on the edge of the mattress and stare out the window at the dark sky. Raindrops continue to streak the glass. It's quiet and peaceful in here.

How many women have been in this room? Yvette, most definitely. Even though she was worth only two hearts, she was his girlfriend. I suspect there were more, but I didn't check for other names with hearts next to them.

"What are you thinking about?" comes Grant's voice from behind me.

I gaze at his reflection. He's only in a towel, since I took his robe. I consider not saying anything, but why hide it? "I was just thinking about all the women who were here before me."

He sits next to me. He smells amazing, clean and woodsy. "I've never brought a woman into this bedroom. Actually, nobody's really been allowed in my home except the staff, my brothers...and my mom that one time."

I raise my eyebrows. "Not even your father?"

"*Definitely* not him."

He shifts, and I notice tattooed lines on his shoulder. They weren't there before.

"What are these?" I ask, tracing the first few with my index finger.

He tenses for a second, then lets out a small laugh. "They're to mark each year I was away from you. There are fourteen total."

I lift my head, stare into his self-deprecating gaze, then count the lines on his shoulder. Sure enough, there are exactly fourteen.

He continues, "I told myself I did it to celebrate that I was impervious to you, but in retrospect, what I was really doing was marking time. Like a prisoner stuck in a dungeon without windows, wondering when he'd be let out."

I run a fingertip down the lines. My heart flutters, more than when he told me he loved me, more than when he recited all the little details from our past. A small, cynical and cautious part of me clung to the thought he was just saying that to get me to come down off the balcony rail—that he couldn't really mean it. But this... It's obviously been done over a long period of time, and the first one on the top is slightly lighter than the one on the bottom, which must've been done more recently.

I kiss the faintest line inked to his warm skin fourteen years ago. Maybe Grandpa knew how Grant felt about me, whether he said the words or not. My grandfather was always wise about matters of the heart, which is why he asked Grant to take care of me. He needed to make sure his baby girl was going to be okay, and he'd never entrust me to the hands of somebody he deemed unworthy. And he did his best to reassure me as he was passing away that I wouldn't be left on my own.

I touch my lips to the rest of the lines that represent all the years we've lost. All the years we hurt. Grant wasn't the only one stuck in the past. I was too. I couldn't believe I could love, make myself vulnerable again.

Grant's muscles flex and move under my mouth. I place my forehead on his shoulder with a sigh. What little tension remains inside me eases completely. Though I'm scared to trust him again. To start fresh, like he said on Saturday. On the other hand, I don't want to be the only one stuck in the past, unable to move on to a future that could be brilliant and beautiful, if I'd just be brave.

He strokes my hair, the touch gentle, like he can sense my hesitation and doubts. "I'm never going to leave your side," he whispers somberly. "I'm always going to be there for you. I'm going to prove myself to you even if I have to walk across broken glass to do it."

I let his words sink into my mind. *Just take the next step.*

My blood pumps with fear and embarrassment. I thought I had nothing to lose after Monday, but I'm realizing that I still have something—my heart. It broke all those years ago. I thought I'd buried all the pieces with Grandma, but I've been kidding myself. All those pieces are still with me, just not very well mended. Now my heart is jagged and scarred. I'm too ashamed to show it to anyone, especially Grant. How will he react when he learns how damaged it is, how fearful I am? He's always been so bold that I don't know if he's going to understand.

I lift my forehead from his shoulder. "Is there something for me to wear?"

He looks at me like he's already missing the sensation of my leaning into him. "Um, yeah. I have some shirts."

He stands up, and I follow him to the closet. He opens the door, and I blink at the sight of my old things—the stuff Suyen auctioned off for me. The dresses are hanging from the hangers, and the bag and shoes lie underneath. Not a speck of dust sits on any of them.

It's like the world suddenly turned upside down. "How...? Why are they here?"

"I bought them when Marketta told me about the auction listing. I was going to ignore what you were doing, but I couldn't. And when I saw a bunch of assholes bidding on your stuff, I couldn't let it go."

"I'm pretty sure it was women bidding."

"I don't care," he says stubbornly. "I couldn't imagine somebody else wearing them. They were for you, and you only. Jesus, we danced in one of them. I peeled you out of it when we had sex for the first time."

I stroke his arm, surprised at how sentimental he is. "I didn't know."

He shrugs. "I didn't want you to."

"Why didn't you throw them away?"

"I don't know. I just...couldn't. It's like my subconscious was trying to hang on to the most beautiful memory of my life, even if, at that time, I thought it was fake."

I look up at him. How can a guy make a girl's knees weak without using the L-word? Grant's the first. And only.

"I wish…I wish I'd sent you a hate text after Grandma's funeral. That way…we could've had this conversation fourteen years ago."

He turns and cradles my face in his hands. "No, Aspen. Never, ever blame yourself for what happened. That's all on me." When I stare back mutely, he says, "Say you agree with me."

"But I don't."

His face twists like he wants to cry, but he laughs instead. "You're always so goddamn stubborn."

"It's the basis for my charm."

Still laughing softly, he pulls out a cotton T-shirt for me. It probably fits him, but on me, it's going to be enormous, reaching a couple of inches above my knees. "Here. This should do it."

"Thanks."

I go to the bathroom to put on the shirt and hang the robe where I found it. When I come out, he's in a white T-shirt and loose black shorts, and the curtains are drawn.

"You want to eat something?" he asks.

"No, thank you. I'm not hungry." I slip under the covers, more exhausted than anything. I haven't had much sleep since Monday, and sleep seems more urgent.

He turns off the light and joins me in bed, and we lie there without touching. It isn't that difficult, given the size of the mattress. And I know he'll give me whatever space I need, for as long as it's necessary.

I stare into the darkness, feeling the air move in and out of my lungs, and hear the quiet sound of Grant breathing. I think about all that's happened since he walked into my apartment just hours ago. What I've discovered—his holding on to our memories, the tattoos and the things from college. How much he blames himself. How his very presence soothes me, so the pain is no longer overwhelming. Even the acidic ache in my heart that's been present for the past fourteen years is gone. It's like I'm starting to heal.

"Can you hold me?" I ask quietly, turning so I'm lying with my back to him.

Wordlessly, he spoons me, his face buried in my hair. He cradles me protectively, like he'll always keep me safe from the world. His body heat seeps into me, and I sigh, slowly relaxing.

Since Grandpa's death, I've felt like a balloon that's been cut from its string, just floating away into the sky—up, up, up, until I'm so far from everyone and everything that I can never be okay again. But now, I'm feeling anchored. Safe.

And I realize this is where I've always wanted to be—within his arms.

I lay my hand over his and link our fingers. Then I notice something else... His erection pressing against my ass.

"Um..."

He groans. "Sorry—biology. I know you've had a tough time of it the past few days. But I'd have to be a zombie to not get interested when I'm holding the only woman I've ever loved."

The "I love you" from earlier didn't have the full impact—I was a tad too cynical. But right now, this declaration of love knocks on the door of my heart, and I feel the wounded little organ opening up a little, ready to give us another chance.

I shift and turn until I'm facing him. I can't see much in the dark, but I can definitely feel how hot he is. How much he wants me, and how much he's controlling himself because he doesn't think I want it.

I cradle his face in my hands, and the heat sears my palms. I kiss him tenderly. He responds, using only his lips, as though silently asking, *Are you okay? Are you sure?*

I kiss him a bit more deeply. *I'm okay with you. I'm sure with you.*

His mouth fuses with mine, and his tongue glides in. I meet it, and realize how much I've missed the tenderness of his kiss.

His warm hands cup my face like I'm the most precious treasure in his life. Hot shivers run through me, pushing out the cold loneliness I've been feeling since Monday. When he's holding me like this, kissing me like this, I feel like I'm never going to be alone.

I slide and roll up on top of him. He weaves his fingers into my hair, then glides one hand down, stroking my neck and back in a smooth, surprisingly soothing, movement. I wriggle against him until his cock's pulsing against my lower belly.

He groans again, the sound muffled against my mouth. Sweet

longing pierces me, and I deepen the kiss as heat rises between our eager bodies.

He slips his hand under the shirt I'm wearing. My nipples ache with anticipation. He cups my breast, and the calluses on his palm graze the tip. I moan deep in my chest, feeling the liquid heat gathering between my legs.

He touches me tenderly, taking his time, as though he's relearning my body, its shape and weight and feel. He holds my nipple between his index and middle fingers, applying a subtle pressure. I rock against him, seeking the pleasure only he can give.

He pushes the shirt out of the way, and I pull it up and off and throw it somewhere, then tug at his. He uses his neck like a wrestler to lift us both off the mattress as he rips it over his head, then lifts his face, taking my breast into his mouth, sucking hard. My back arches at the shocking heat, and my toes curl against the sheet. His hands move over my body constantly, letting me know how much he adores me, how much he wants me.

I'm going out of my mind. The air in my lungs grows thicker, and my heart races with joyful bliss. Blood roars through my veins. My God. I feel so alive.

He makes me feel alive.

I cradle him between my legs and rock against him through the thin fabric of his shorts. His shaft is unbearably large, and it pulses with want.

I slide downward, tug his shorts off and dispose of them. I can only make out the faint outline of his cock in the darkness, but I can feel so much heat radiating from it. It smells like him and desire, and I take the tip into my mouth, wanting to taste him, feel his lust for me in my mouth.

There is a sharp intake of breath from above. I love what I'm doing to him, the rapid throbbing of his shaft. Slickness coats my tongue. He tastes of hot, salty, needy male.

I pull him deeper, stroking his thickly muscled thighs, then gently hold his balls in my hands. His belly jumps and his legs twitch as he fists the sheets. He braces his feet flat on the mattress and shallowly thrusts into my mouth. I use my lips and tongue, giving him the pressure he wants. Feeling his bare desire heats me up, and I'm soaked between my legs.

Suddenly, he grips my shoulders and pulls me up for a hot kiss. He plunders my mouth, like he can't get enough—he'll never get enough.

He lowers a hand, slipping a finger between my legs and finding me wet and slippery.

"Sucking your dick did that." I feel wickedly confident. I know I can say anything honestly, and he'll accept it.

He lets out a rough breath. "If you keep talking like that, I'm going to embarrass myself."

"How?"

"I think I'm going to come before you do. And we can't have that." He reaches into the bottom drawer of his nightstand. I can hear things rattle, like he's looking for something in a box. Finally, he pulls out a strip of something. "Condoms," he explains, before ripping one open and sheathing himself.

I watch him, appreciating he's thought of protecting us. Then I put a hand over his chest when he tries to roll us over. "Uh-uh."

I position myself over him, lining us up. I sink onto him inch by delicious inch, biting my lip at the unbelievable pleasure starting between my legs. But what's most amazing is the aching tenderness swelling in my chest.

I reach down and thread my fingers through his, holding him tight. "You're mine," I say as I start to move up and down.

"I will always be yours." His eyes glitter in the dark as he responds. His vow promises more in the silence of the night. *I'll never leave you. You'll always have me. You'll always be mine, too. Mine to love, mine to protect, mine to cherish.*

I don't know how I can know all that, but I do. It's as though somehow our hearts are linked, and each of us understands exactly how the other is feeling.

The pleasure mounts, and I grind my hips against him as I move up and down. He thrusts with controlled power, deepening our connection. I arch my back as I climax, all my senses spiraling out into space as I shudder over him and around him.

He joins me at the peak, his pelvis pushed upward, driving into me until he can't come any deeper. My name tears from his lips, like the lost piece of his soul he's finally reclaimed.

I collapse on his chest, wrapping my arms around him. He holds me, stroking me tenderly, then swipes his thumb across the skin underneath my eyes.

"What's wrong?" he whispers. "Are you...okay with what we just did?" The question's tentative, but he's hiding his uncertainty and sadness well.

I nod. "I don't regret anything. I didn't even know I was crying." I sniffle. "I don't know why, but really. I'm fine." I tighten my hold around him, and he pulls me even closer. "All I know is I just feel lighter. Like everything's going to be okay. I don't know how to explain it."

He presses a gentle kiss on my forehead. "I'm glad." But underneath those two simple words, I sense determination—that he *will* make sure everything's going to be okay.

58

ASPEN

When I open my eyes, I'm alone in bed. I try to sit up and find that Grant tucked me in tight before he left. It's an effort to rise against the sheets.

I don't know how long I slept, but I feel well rested. My eyes don't feel awful, and my head doesn't ache much. I smile a little. That's one way I took after Grandpa—no hangovers. And weirdly enough, thinking of him doesn't make my heart feel like it's about to rip into pieces. I look up at the ceiling, blinking slowly.

I think I'm going to be okay.

My stomach growls like an annoyed and unfed kitty. I struggle and finally get one edge of the sheets to come free from under the mattress. The T-shirt Grant gave me last night is on the pillow next to me, neatly folded. I put it on, letting it hang like a loose dress.

I brush my teeth, splash some cold water on my face, then pad out of the room. My bare feet are silent, and nothing creaks in this home. With the brilliant SoCal sun pouring inside, the hallway looks bright and inviting. As a matter of fact, the whole place looks lovely. But then, Grant has excellent taste.

As I go down the stairs, I hear him on the phone. I can't make out what he's saying, but he sounds exacting and commanding. I smile a little. He sounds *hot*. And supremely confident, as though he's convinced that he'll always get what he wants.

I find him in the living room, casually standing by the window and looking at the garden as he speaks on the phone. He's in a V-neck shirt as blue as the Pacific and worn jeans. His feet are bare, like mine. A layer of stubble covers his chin, and I like how relaxed and at home he looks. It reminds me of how he was all those years ago.

He wraps up the call as soon as he realizes I'm downstairs. His eyes collide with mine, then he takes me in. He goes still for a moment and expels a breath. "I don't think I'll ever get used to the sight."

"What?" I look down. "What sight?"

"You in nothing but my shirt, in my home." It isn't just desire that glitters in his gorgeous eyes, but satisfaction—that everything's right with the world. I know I'm the reason he feels that way, and pleasure warms my heart.

"Maybe after a couple of days...?" I suggest with a wink.

He shakes his head. "Maybe after a century or two."

"I don't know. I'm going to get old. You may not be so awestruck then."

"Aspen, your hair can go gray and you can be covered in wrinkles, and I'll still think you're the most beautiful woman in the world. And I'm going to think what a lucky bastard I am to have you in my life."

He wraps his arms around me, and I melt into his embrace.

"How's your head?" he asks.

"Great. I don't get hangovers."

"That's useful. So, are you hungry? It's late." He glances at the wall behind me.

I look back and see a clock. It's almost eleven. "Wow. I can't believe I slept for so long."

"You probably needed it. I have some bagels, cream cheese and lox. If you want something fancier, we'll have to hit a brunch place." He straightens a little. "Actually, Nieve has a great champagne brunch—"

"I'm fine with a bagel and cream cheese, as long as the bagel can be toasted first, and I get some strong coffee with it."

"No problem. Lox?"

I wrinkle my nose. "Is that the salmon thing?"

"Yeah."

"No, thanks. I don't know about having fish first thing in the morning."

He laughs and takes me to the counter in the kitchen. It's huge, with copper pots and pans hanging from above. The stove has six burners, a huge griddle and an indoor grill. I count two ovens and two microwaves, but there might be more. Everything in the kitchen, including the double fridges, is spotless and shiny. Like it's never been used before.

"Do you cook?" I ask.

He starts the coffee. The machine begins to fill the area with the bittersweet aroma. "No. I have a chef who comes over and cooks when I know my schedule's going to be easy, but that's not very often," he says, pulling out a tub of cream cheese from the fridge and throwing two pre-cut bagels into a toaster.

"So why do you have a kitchen this fancy?"

"My interior designer. He thought I should have everything I could possibly want, just in case." He glances at the copper above him. "And, you know. It looks nice." He shrugs.

I look up at the pots and pans. They not only look nice, but expensive. I wouldn't dare touch them, lest I scratch them. The interior designer probably went crazy.

Grant serves two mugs of coffee, giving me one. When the toaster spits out the bagels, he puts them on two porcelain plates and hands me a bread knife. "By the way, do you want some jam?" Moving with elaborate casualness, he pulls out a jar of Sun Valley Farms' organic strawberry.

"Yes. Thank you," I say with a smile. I haven't had it in *so* long. It wasn't something I could afford once Grandpa had to move into the assisted living center.

We sit in a comfortable silence. I take the jam, feeling like I'm back in time when everything was okay. It continues to surprise me that the smallest luxury can have the power to make me feel better.

But it's not just the luxury aspect—it's the thoughtfulness behind it, the kindness.

After I finish more than half my breakfast and most of my coffee, Grant says, "There's something I want to talk to you about."

"Yeah?" I take a sip of the coffee, looking at him over the rim. His expression's too serious, and that's making me nervous.

"I was looking into the situation with your grandmother's grave. There's a plot next to hers, and my people are already on it to get it for Kenny if you still want it."

I stare at him, stunned. "It's only been a day. Not even. And it's Saturday."

"Things can happen fast if you're willing to throw some money around." He gives me another mug of coffee.

My first knee-jerk reaction is to decline. I don't want to give Grant any reason to think I could be here with him for his money.

"I want to do it for you." It's like he read my mind. "And for Kenny and Kat. They were in love, and I admire them for always being there for you. It's the least I can do."

"But...it's too much."

"No." He reaches over and holds my hand in his, tracing the diagonal line on my palm with his thumb. "It's actually very little. Besides, if the situation were reversed, you'd do the same for me, right?"

"Well... Yeah, but—"

"So don't reject me."

He knows exactly how to convince me. I sigh. "Okay. Thank you."

A smile breaks out over his face. It's as bright and mesmerizing as the sun emerging from the clouds after a long storm. And I know I've made the right decision.

———

When Grant said things could happen fast, I knew he could move the process along faster than I'd been able to when Grandma passed away. But the speed at which his people take care of it is stunning.

By Monday, everything's arranged and we're ready to place

Grandpa next to Grandma. The headstone, unfortunately, is going to take longer because an appropriate slab of marble has to be picked out—to match Grandma's—and the text needs to be etched onto it. But I'm so grateful to have my grandparents together that it doesn't really register as an issue, although Grant looks mildly annoyed with the delay.

A crew he hired has already dug a hole deep enough for the urn. I place it into the grave with care, and it takes no time before fresh dirt covers the glazed jar. It feels bittersweet and final, but part of me is glad he's going to be with Grandma, like he'd want. He was without her for so long.

Unlike Grandma's funeral, this time it's just me and Grant. As I gaze at my grandparents' graves, I try to smile. Grief is still in my heart. Regret, too, that we couldn't have more time together. But I'm grateful to both of them. And I wish I could hug Grandpa for worrying about me until his last moment.

I reach over. My fingertips brush Grant's, and I link my fingers through his.

"Thank you," I say. "For this, and for making that promise to my grandfather. I'm sure it alleviated his worries."

Grant squeezes my hand. "You're welcome. But I would've done it even if Kenny hadn't asked me to."

I look up at him. My vision blurs, and he holds me. He softly hums "Por una Cabeza" in my ear, and my lungs seem to shudder as my heart swells with love and sorrow.

He doesn't ask me to stop crying. All he does is hold me and let me hear the music from that moment—when all four of us were together and happy.

As Grant continues to hum the soulful strain, I look up at the cloudless sky. My tears continue to fall, taking the raw grief with them. I just know my grandparents are dancing in heaven, gazing at each other with love.

59

ASPEN

"Do I look okay?" I ask for the hundredth time since four.

"You look perfect." He pulls me close, running his hand from my shoulder down along my spine. It rests on my butt, and he squeezes. "Hot enough to make me want to rip that dress right off you."

"No!" I pull away instantly, crossing my arms over my torso. He's not going to rip this chartreuse Fendi dress! Josephine and I spent over two hours going over my options, and I'm not going to show up for dinner with his brothers and their wives in something less impressive. The Fendi is classy and elegant, with a fitted bodice and slightly loose asymmetric skirt. Josephine assured me it's the one to wear to make a good impression.

And I desperately want to make a good impression on his brothers and two sisters-in-law.

"Hey, okay. I'm not going to do anything." He raises both hands.

"You better not," I say sternly, but continue to maintain my distance. I don't trust his hands-raised gesture. He's quicker than lightning when he wants to be, and he's fooled me twice since I sort of moved in with him two Fridays ago.

Although we never talked about it in detail, he refused to let me return to my old apartment. I suspect he's still a little traumatized

440

about seeing me straddling the balcony railing. I'm not sure why, since it isn't like my apartment is on the tenth floor. The worst injury I would've sustained might have been a broken ankle.

However, he still acts like I was playing hopscotch on a rickety bridge over molten lava. Probably a psychological thing. And when it comes to me, Grant seems to be more psycho than logical. He sent a crew to grab all my stuff from my apartment, leaving the furniture behind. I'm sure he's going to have his lawyer deal with the property management. He's already annoyed that there was no hot water and the carpet is so thin it might as well have not been there.

"Why don't you check on the caterers?" I ask, inspecting my makeup again. Emmett and Amy know me already, but the others don't. I was a little uncomfortable about seeing Emmett, especially knowing about the bet. But Grant's explanation about what Emmett did when he forfeited the bet eased my nerves. Emmett wouldn't have done that if he didn't wish us the best.

Now I just have to convince the rest of his brothers and their wives that I'm cool. Just hearing about them from Grant in the last few days made my head spin at their impressive lives.

I'm really not that...grand. A college dropout, and not even working at the moment, to boot. Grant told me to take time off, take care of myself and think of what to do next.

"And you're going to put up with Marjorie?" It was kind of a joke and kind of not. I know how much he dislikes her.

"Making sure you're okay is more important."

To be honest, taking a break is exactly what I need, because after that conversation, I realized I haven't had any time off in...years. I was too busy running from one job to another, trying to make enough to pay the bills. Just having the time to get enough sleep and think things through without worrying about the next bill helps me clear my head.

"The caterers are fine," Grant says. "I already checked."

I turn to him. "I'm so nervous." I wipe my clammy hands on a small towel. "What if your brothers don't like me?"

"They'll adore you," he says.

"You're biased."

"I'm objective. If they don't like you, I'll tell them to go fuck off—"

"No!"

"—because they aren't the brothers I thought they are. I don't hang out with idiots with bad taste." Grant tilts his head. "You need a bracelet." He reaches into the huge island in the closet and pulls out a gorgeous string of rubies. "Here." He loops it around my wrist. The platinum hook has my name engraved, along with an infinity symbol next to a heart, to indicate I'm worth infinite hearts. "The cherry on top, even though it's kind of in the middle."

I laugh and give him a hug. The intercom announces the first arrival.

Grant checks the security app. "It's Noah. Let's go say hi."

———

Noah isn't the only one there by the time we make it to the first floor.

"Noah. Huxley. Nicholas. Say hello to Aspen." Grant puts a protective arm around my shoulders.

Noah beams, then hugs me. He looks vaguely familiar. "We saw each other at the steakhouse."

"That's it!" I smile.

Huxley and Nicholas hug me, too, although I get the feeling Huxley isn't really a hugger. His embrace is both stiffer and briefer than his brothers'.

More people show up quickly. Emmett and Amy. Sebastian. Griffin and Sierra. I'm fascinated that Sierra is the CEO of an adult toy company. I looked it up, and it's super popular. Not only that, it's considered one of the best family-owned businesses to work for in California.

We sit at the table. Emmett smiles. "Welcome to the family."

I look around, a little confused. Grant and I are just living together at the moment.

"Totally," Huxley says.

"But..." I pause.

"Grant used to say love didn't exist," Griffin puts in.

442

"Hey, that was before," Grant says. "And due to a *very* large misunderstanding—"

"He never had us meet a girlfriend until now," Emmett adds with a warm smile. "Or let anyone live with him."

"So you might as well be part of the family," Nicholas says.

I smile, relaxing at their ready welcome and explanation. Grant squeezes my hand.

"She'll be like the sister you never had," Grant announces.

"Why sister?" Noah says.

"That way you don't feel anything inappropriate about her," Grant says, with a dangerously possessive glint in his eye. "I'd hate to have to kill you."

His brothers groan, and we end up laughing. Although Grant said he and his brothers all have different mothers, there are remarkable similarities. It's the hair color and the square jaws. And the air of wealth and power—like they know they can get whatever they want.

Except Noah. He's a bit distracted the entire time. In addition, he seems to blurt out whatever comes to mind.

Like...

"Don't tell me you cooked," he says to Grant, looking at the massive spread.

"Of course not." Grant passes me the mashed potatoes I've been eyeing.

"And you didn't make your girlfriend do it," Noah says.

"I would never. She's my girlfriend, not my chef."

"I wouldn't be comfortable cooking for this many, although if you really want to have a holiday meal, I suppose I could try something for Thanksgiving?" I say. I used to help Grandma with hams and pies.

The table goes quiet. Somebody's phone pings, but is ignored. Sierra and Amy look at me like an angel, while the brothers appear stunned.

"You do Thanksgiving?" Noah asks.

"Well...yeah. Of course. Don't you?" I say.

"It's just that...we eat out," Nicholas says.

"Not me." Sebastian's tone says he wishes he could eat out.

There's another ping.

"I'll join you for holiday meals," Noah says eagerly. "I never say no to free food."

I laugh. All of the brothers are apparently extremely well off. It's amusing that Noah's acting like a poor college kid.

"Ignore him," Huxley says to me. "He's always on social media, which, unfortunately, has rotted his brain."

"Stop bad-mouthing Noah," Sierra says. "He's great."

"Thank you," Noah says.

"Facts aren't slander," Huxley says.

"Listen to my wife," Griffin says.

Another ping.

"Do you ever *not* say 'listen to my wife'?" Nicholas asks.

"I might, if she were ever wrong," Griffin says.

That's sweet. It's something Grandpa would say. And surprisingly enough, thinking about Grandpa doesn't hurt as badly anymore. It's like...I'm okay, even though earlier today, I thought about visiting him because it's Saturday. It's been such a longtime habit, it took me a second before I remembered he wasn't around anymore. So Grant and I held each other and watched a movie in bed instead.

Huxley makes a whip-cracking noise.

"You want to step outside and do that?" Griffin says with a thin smile.

"Nope. I only do it in civilized settings. Like at a dinner table with ladies."

Grant leans over. "Griffin does kickboxing. You don't want to mess with him."

"Does he ever kick your butt? Or your brothers'?" I whisper back, surprised that Griffin's that...scary. He looks like a proper professor. Slightly disapproving but otherwise intellectual.

"No. He just acts like he will." There's warm affection in Grant's voice.

"Thug," Noah says. But he's looking at his phone.

"He's a respectable professor," Sierra says.

I don't think Noah hears her. Were all the pings for him?

"What's so fascinating?" Sebastian says.

"It's a sale at Bobbi's Sweet Things," Noah says. "The cupcakes in the picture look so good." A phone pings again, and he doesn't tear his gaze from the screen or move his fingers.

"She's amazing, isn't she?" I say.

His head comes up. "You know Bobbi?"

"Sure. Her bakery is where my grandparents' dance studio used to be. I first met her when she came by to talk to Grandpa."

"So you guys are friendly?"

"Yeah, of course."

"Then can you please buy me one of her croissants?"

What an odd request. "Why can't you do that yourself?"

"She hates me. And every time I try to send somebody else, she just seems to know."

"What did you do?" Nicholas asks.

"Nothing!" Noah protests. "You know me."

"Probably posted a shot of her ass on social media," Huxley says.

"Unlike you, I don't let my phone get hacked," Noah says.

"What do you mean, 'unlike me'? My phone's never been hacked."

A phone pings again.

"Whose phone is that?" I say. "It could be important."

"It's mine," Sebastian says. "And don't worry, it's nothing. Actually, let me just put it on mute."

"How can it be nothing when it's probably your fiancée texting you?" Noah says without looking up from his phone.

"What? Since when?" Emmett's eyes are wide as he stares at Sebastian.

"It's BS," Sebastian grouses.

"Lucienne Peery isn't BS," Noah says, finally placing his phone on the table.

Lucienne Peery... The name sounds vaguely familiar, but I can't place it.

"She's crazy," Huxley says. "Why the heck would you marry her?"

Then I remember: the jewelry heiress. Totally wild and out of control, too. And Sebastian is engaged to her? Wow...

He groans into his hands. "It's complicated. I'm trying to get

Jeremiah to fix it, but she refuses. Andreas won't return my calls, either."

"Well, yeah. Peery Diamonds is an important client," Huxley says, not wholly unsympathetic. "And if you don't know, the company's new to the firm. So Mom doesn't want to do anything to upset them."

Sebastian straightens. "I don't care what the deal is, but Lucienne's going to call it off, and we're going to go our separate ways."

"Why don't *you* call it off?" I ask tentatively.

"It's complicated," he grumbles.

"Guess this means you won't be introducing us to her?" Griffin says.

"I'd rather choke on cat vomit."

Wow. I feel sorry for the woman, to be rejected by her fiancé and his entire family. None of the brothers look like they want to be on her side. If she were on fire, they'd just watch. Noah might pull out some marshmallows.

On the other hand, I feel sorry for Sebastian, too, for having to marry Lucienne Peery. There's no scandal she isn't attached to somehow. And apparently she goes through men like tampons.

The brothers start tossing out suggestions to get her to break off the engagement. Amy reaches over and squeezes my hand. "Don't worry. Whenever these guys get together, they get a bit over-dramatic."

I glance at the lively discussion among the men on how to "protect" Sebastian. I'm not sure if it's overdramatic. More like overprotective. Sebastian seems like a capable guy, even if his fiancée is as awful as Huxley claims. But seeing how much they care about each other is sweet. It makes me adore Grant more, if that's even possible.

"All of them take everything that happens to any one of them personally," Amy adds. "And they do the same with what happens to their women, too."

Sierra smiles. "I love it. They didn't come from the most normal family, but they're *family* in the truest sense of the word. They have your back. Always."

I smile. "Good to know."

"So, when's the wedding?" Amy asks.

"I'm not sure. We aren't even engaged yet," I say with a smile. Grant's taking his time. I think he's ready to ask, because he looks at me like he's dying to say something before catching himself. Maybe he wants to make sure I'm emotionally ready. He knows losing Grandpa messed me up. But he doesn't seem to realize that having his unconditional love has helped me heal faster. Every day, I feel a little bit more surefooted. A little happier and more optimistic.

"Knowing Grant, he'll propose soon," Amy says before taking a bite of roast beef. "When he wants something, he goes for it. If anything's in the way, he steamrolls it."

"You may be right," I say. "He's agreed to have me meet his father tomorrow."

"*You're going to meet Ted Lasker?*" Amy nearly shrieks.

An abrupt silence falls on the table. All six brothers swivel their heads at Grant, then at me, then back at Grant.

Noah looks stricken. "I thought you said you loved her."

Emmett shakes his head. "You're either really brave or really stupid."

Sebastian gives Grant an expression full of mourning. "I hope her love can overcome what you're about to do to her."

"What?" I say. "I told him I'd love to meet his dad, and he said okay. Why should he hide me from his father?"

"Oh, it isn't that he's hiding you from Dad," Nicholas says. "More along the lines of hiding Dad from you."

I frown. *That's an odd way to put it.* Grant did seem a little nervous when he agreed to introduce me to his father, but his brothers are acting like Ted Lasker carries both Ebola *and* the Black Plague.

"It's okay," Huxley says to me. His tone is extra grave. "No matter what happens, we've got you. You're one of us now."

60

GRANT

If I had it my way, Aspen and I would be doing anything other than meeting my dad. And if we had to suffer the ordeal, we'd do it in a cabin on top of a mountain so remote you couldn't get cell reception.

But no. He insisted on having a Sunday brunch at Jean-Georges. So everyone's going to see us. Maybe even take photos.

After all, that's where you go to be seen. And to be honest, I prefer not to go there, because it reminds me of how colossally I screwed up fourteen years ago. But she said yes to everything Dad asked for.

Ugh. Just *ugh*.

My phone pings—again. My brothers sent dozens of texts last night after leaving my place.

–Griffin: You really sure about this?

–Noah: I have a way to slip an elephant laxative into his coffee before he leaves home. Just say the word.

–Huxley: That's disgusting.

–Noah: But effective. He won't be going anywhere.

–Sebastian: Hire somebody to sabotage his cars so they don't start in the morning.

–Emmett: All of them? Too iffy.

–Nicholas: What if something happens to Joey? Dad can't tie

his own shoes without that weasel. I suggest getting a hooker to distract him.

–Griffin: Do it! Hell, I'm gonna get a hooker just to screw him.

–Emmett: Don't have her screw him. The woman will deserve better. Have her stab him with a tranq dart.

–Me: Thanks, guys, but stand down. I need to do this. It's important to Aspen.

She didn't grow up like us. She was raised by good people. To her, meeting the parents is a natural progression in a relationship. She wouldn't understand if I refused to have her meet Dad, and I don't want her to feel inferior or somehow "less" because of my father issues.

Mom's in Greece right now—and thank God, because she doesn't get along with Dad or Joey. I'd hate to ask the waitstaff to clean blood up off the floor.

Aspen and I dress with care. She wants to make a good impression. I just want to look great so she doesn't dump me on the spot after having to endure Dad for an entire meal.

She's in a deep emerald top and skirt, which look amazing on her. Her outfit is pretty conservative, and that's on purpose—I don't want to give Dad any weird ideas about her wanting to break into Hollywood. He thinks every woman wants to be in movies.

Dad and Joey walk in together. Joey takes a left turn and takes a table a few yards away, like a dog that isn't allowed to sit with its owner. Dread has been coiling in my gut, but at least Dad's dressed like a respectable human being in a white dress shirt, charcoal slacks and sports jacket. He's clean-shaven, so that's good. He could lose the smarmy smile, but at least he doesn't look high or hungover.

"You must be Aspen," he says, reaching over and taking her hand in both of his. Then he pulls her up and hugs her.

On the second heartbeat, I swat his hands on her back. "That's long enough, Dad."

He reluctantly lets go. "I'm just overcome. Finally getting to meet the girl who brought you to your knees."

"It wasn't quite like that," she says with a smile.

"I'm Ted. So happy to meet you." He sits down. "You can't

imagine how happy I am. I was never introduced to Jenny and Sarah properly."

Oh for God's sake. "Amy and Sierra." He can never remember their names.

Concern clouds Aspen's face. "Does he have the same problem my grandpa had?" she asks, *sotto voce.* She shoots a look of under-served sympathy in Dad's direction.

"No. He's"—*too lazy and self-centered*—"just terrible with names."

"I think she likes me," Dad announces. He takes her in with his eyes.

Our server comes over with a pot of fresh coffee. I order pancakes and bacon, and she asks for French toast. I push cream and sugar in her direction. Dad gets the eggs benedict with organic berries.

"Get her the berries too. Women always love berries," he says, deciding for her because that's what he does for everyone.

When our server leaves, his smile grows wider, his eyes twinklier.

I don't like that. Not even a little. I brace myself for a tsunami of embarrassment.

"So. Where's my invitation?" he asks.

Aspen seems momentarily nonplussed. "Invitation?"

"There is no invitation." I'd rather perform a naked pole dance in the middle of the office.

"Nonsense! Every wedding has invitations." He's as outraged as if I'd said some other producer bangs more chicks.

"I'm not sure we're quite that far along yet," Aspen says.

Dad narrows his eyes. "Is that how you want to play it?" He waves a hand. "Fine, I'll cast you in my next movie. A leading role! You can also select whoever you want for your love interest. If you can't decide, I can cast somebody. Maybe two somebodies. And I'll let you have sex with both of them."

Aspen chokes. I grip the knife. Is Huxley & Webber good enough to get me off if I stab my dad right now?

"I'm not going to cheat on Grant!" she says.

"It's not cheating if you do it on a set," Dad says. "It's art! With a director, lights, sound—"

"You want me to cheat on Grant—"

"Nah. Just film a sex scene or two."

"—in front of everyone?"

"No, no, no. Just the crew. Grant can watch the scene, too. He'll appreciate it because he knows I don't make porn. Tell her, Grant."

Aspen's jaw slackens.

Before I can make a cutting remark, Aspen says, "I can't invite you because we aren't even engaged."

"What?" Dad stares at her, then at me. "What the hell is wrong with you?"

"*Me?*" He tells her he wants her to make soft porn and then wants to know what's wrong with *me?*

I haven't had the courage to ask because she hasn't told me she loved me yet. The ring I've been carrying in my pocket is calling me a pussy, but I don't care. I'm not botching this move. It's too important.

"Why don't you have a wedding date yet? Are you too stupid to ask, 'Will you marry me?' I thought I raised you better!"

I'm going to kill him.

Aspen places a hand on my forearm, which is so tense it's quivering. "Actually, Grant is maybe the smartest man I've ever met. And I hate to say this, but I think I have a stomachache."

"What?" Dad shouts at the same time I say, "Are you okay? Why didn't you say something?"

"It seemed like meeting your dad was more important. But we've done that now." She turns to Dad. "I'm sorry. I think I have to go." She stands. "Can we go together, Grant?"

Hallelujah! I jump to my feet. "Of course. Let me see if I can get someone to make a house call."

We take our leave and don't speak until we're safely inside the car.

I reach over and hold her hand. "You aren't really sick, right?"

"Nah." She turns to me with a small smile. "I don't look sick, right? I could never pull it off. My grandparents always knew when I tried that as a kid."

"I had to be sure." I kiss her hand.

"Let's go home."

Home. I love it that she considers the mansion her home. I maneuver the Maybach through the traffic. "Are you okay with the way the visit ended?"

"Yup. I got to meet him, so it's all good." She sighs. "I didn't realize how badly it would go. I thought Amy and Sierra were exaggerating."

"Not at all. And that's him on his *best behavior.*"

She chokes a little. "Oh my God. I don't... I can't... Really?"

"Believe me, we got off easy."

"Wow." She lets out a long breath. "Wow."

"You aren't really disappointed, are you?" I ask.

"No. I'm just... I thought you had a charmed life with a famous and powerful dad and all that. And now I see maybe I misjudged you."

"I can't complain about my life. For one thing, it's led me to you."

She tightens her hand around me. "I know *exactly* what you mean."

When we're home, she takes me to the living room.

"Aren't you hungry?" We didn't get to eat anything except a couple of pieces of toast early in the morning.

"Yes, but I want to dance first." She fiddles with her phone. "Put some order into this chaos."

I indulge her. I want her to feel free to do anything she wants. "La cumparsita" starts playing from her phone. She approaches me, her steps sexy with her hips loose, her eyes on mine the entire time. I turn with her, extending my hand, palm up. She places hers on it. I feel the corner of my mouth quirking up, and I pull her into my arms, spinning her like a dandelion puff in the air.

A lovely flush colors her cheeks, and we dance to the music. We haven't tangoed in fourteen years, but we move like our dance in Malibu was only yesterday. Her legs brush against mine, and her feet trace the curve of my calves. Then she's pressed so close against me that I can feel our hearts beating in complete unison, as though they truly are one.

And as happiness fleets over her, I feel calmer too, the awkward time with my dad fading away.

She turns, and when she stops, I dip her to the final note. She laughs.

I straighten us up. She wraps her arms around my neck. I love intimate moments like this. We don't have to have sex or talk about life to feel like I'm one with her.

"Grant," she murmurs into my ear.

"Mmm?" I speak just as softly, luxuriating in the feel of her in my arms. I could stay like this forever and die a happy man.

"I love you."

Her declaration lances me like an arrow, sweet and irrevocable. A thick lump forms in my throat. No matter how many times I told her "I love you" since that Friday, she never said the words back. I thought it was because she wasn't sure yet—after all, I have a lot to make up for.

"Marry me," she says.

I stare, not comprehending. The ring in my pocket pricks my thigh.

Her smile grows broader. "I figured I should propose, since you told me you loved me first."

My inside swells until it's so full of love it's about to burst. I run a hand over my mouth, then over my racing heart, so it stays put in my chest. Pulling the ring out of my pocket, I drop to a knee. "Yes." I put the ring on her finger. I kiss her hand, then rise to my feet. I cradle her face and kiss her, then hold her hand, then kiss her again, as she laughs like the happiest woman in the world.

The ten-carat diamond on her finger glitters as brightly as our beautiful future.

61

GRANT

Aspen and I decide to have our ceremony on a yacht, cruising along the Pacific coast. She said she'd love to do that again, and I thought it'd be perfect. A ship is highly defensible against uninvited guests.

The entire vessel is decked out in ivory silk and lace. Thousands of pink roses cover every surface, their heady scent mingling with the brine of the ocean. We opted for an evening cruise, and the sun is blood orange as it touches the far edge of the sea.

We kept the ceremony small. Aspen invited her nosy Asian neighbor lady from her old apartment, Suyen and her family. I invited my brothers and their wives and a few friends. Mom shows up with a camera, as usual. She said she was going to take some photographs to celebrate our wedding and give them to us to keep. Aspen almost fainted with excitement.

Aspen is absolutely gorgeous in a white Queen Anne dress. The skirt is layered with chiffon. Although it looks simple without a huge train, it's covered with tiny pearls and diamantes, and they shine and glitter with every step she takes.

When we exchange vows, I get a little choked up. My idiot mistake cost us fourteen years, but here we are. She smiles, then kisses me. "Love you."

"Love you more. I'm the luckiest guy alive to be with you right now," I say as the quartet plays Mendelssohn's wedding march for our first walk together as a married couple.

Suddenly the sound of tense strings overlays the music. Then the brass blasts the all-too-famous tune of Wagner's "Ride of the Valkyries." And the sound is coming from...the sky?

Aspen puts a hand over her eyebrows and looks up.

Under the music, the thrum of a helicopter cuts through the air. "What the hell...?"

Emmett runs over, holding my phone. "Here."

I look at the screen.

–Dad: I told you I'd come!

–Dad: And I arrive in style!

–Dad: You'll never forget this entrance.

–Dad: Or the wedding.

–Dad: I know dramatic.

–Dad: Majestic, too.

Oh, you bastard. What the hell does he think he's doing? It looks like a re-enactment of *Apocalypse Now.*

I should've known he was going to pull something like this. I tried to keep the details of our ceremony quiet, but it's nearly impossible to hide charting an entire yacht for three days.

"Tell them to start the festivities early," I shout to Emmett, so he can hear me over the chopper and the Wagner roaring over us as Dad buzzes around the yacht.

"Got it!" He grins and runs off.

"Wow. I guess your dad really wanted to come," Aspen says, squinting at the helicopter in the dusky air.

"Yes, but he's not going to be able to join us."

The chopper circles and starts to return. *Oh no, you don't.* I look in the direction Emmett ran off to. *Come on.*

Suddenly there's a huge *boom!* and the sky lights up.

Yes!

The chopper swerves. Out of a thousand flowers of light, a huge heart appears in the sky. The crew continues the fireworks.

"Isn't that dangerous?" Aspen asks, her eyes wide.

"They aren't going to hit the helicopter. Just scare him a little."

And sure enough, Dad's pilot is smart enough to know what's good for him. The chopper turns and starts to fly away.

"Wow. That was...something."

"Sorry about that." But I'm not. I'm proud I managed to scare Dad away, so now we can wrap up our ceremony and have a good time with our family and friends.

She laughs. "It's something we can tell our grandkids."

"You're the best."

"And the luckiest. And the happiest." She puts her hands over my cheeks. "Because I have you."

62

–Heath: Is it true you blocked all my funding options?
–Heath: Don't deny it! I heard from a reliable source.
–Heath: George told me.
–Heath: Come on, man! I didn't sue you for breaking my nose!
–Heath: Without the additional funding, I'm gonna be ruined!
–Heath: Hey asshole! Answer me!
–Heath: Is this about the bet? It was 14 years ago, man!
–Heath: Is that why you cut off funding for Sadie's company too after giving her money to expand her business?
–Heath: I saw you married Aspen! So what's the big fucking deal?
–Me: 14 years. That's the big fucking deal. If you need to reach me, do it through my attorney's office. You're blocked.

63

ASPEN

Grant doesn't often have time for polo matches, but he rides when he can. And today happens to be one of those days.

I should wait for him to come home, but I just can't. I feel like I'm going to burst if I don't talk to somebody.

I check the time. He's going to be at the club for at least a couple more hours. My mind made up, I get in the creamy Rolls-Royce he gave me last Christmas and drive. I start to speed, then remember that I can't be reckless with my safety and slow back down to the speed limit.

The drive reminds me of the first time we met—when I chased him down at the polo club to force him to do a project with me. Of course, I don't have to chase him down for anything now. We've been married for three years, and he's always there for me.

I look at the gorgeous sky while stopped at a light. Two birds fly together, swooping up and down, like they're playing. Or wooing one another.

I'm so happy, Grandpa, Grandma. I love you so much.

Although they aren't with me in person, I know they're watching over me. There's no other way to explain all the amazing things that have happened.

I park my car in the huge lot and head inside. A sharply dressed receptionist smiles. "Good morning, Aspen."

"Hi." I smile. "Is Grant still riding?"

"I think so."

"Thanks." I head to the track. The air here feels different from the city. So much nature—trees, soil and cut grass.

Grant is on his horse, galloping. He's still an amazing rider. Actually, he does everything so well, it's hot to watch him. I didn't know that simple physical competence could be sexy until I got to live with him.

I wave with a smile.

He slows down, then dismounts. "What are you doing here? Is everything okay?"

"Yeah. I just couldn't wait," I say, trying not to smile too much and give myself away.

"What is it?"

I grin. "You remember how we were going to tell our grandkids about what your dad did at our wedding?"

"Yeah..." His eyes widen. "Holy *shit*."

"Yup." I grin. "Just found out."

He looks at my belly, then at my face. "Is it a girl or a boy? How far along?"

I shrug with a smile. His reaction is priceless. "I don't know. Over-the-counter pregnancy tests don't tell you that kind of detail."

He hugs me, then drops to his knees, pressing his face against my stomach. "Every time I think I can't get any happier, you prove me wrong. I love you so much."

I place my hand tenderly on his head. "I love you too."

TITLES BY NADIA LEE

Standalone Titles

The Ex I'd Love to Hate

My Grumpy Billionaire

Baby for the Bosshole

Beauty and the Assassin

Oops, I Married a Rock Star

The Billionaire and the Runaway Bride

Flirting with the Rock Star Next Door

Mister Fake Fiancé

Marrying My Billionaire Hookup

Faking It with the Frenemy

Marrying My Billionaire Boss

Stealing the Bride

———

The Sins Trilogy

Sins

Secrets

Mercy

———

The Billionaire's Claim Duet

Obsession

Redemption

Taken by Her Unforgiving Billionaire Boss
Pursued by Her Billionaire Hook-Up
Pregnant with Her Billionaire Ex's Baby
Romanced by Her Illicit Millionaire Crush
Wanted by Her Scandalous Billionaire
Loving Her Best Friend's Billionaire Brother

ABOUT NADIA LEE

New York Times and *USA Today* bestselling author Nadia Lee writes sexy contemporary romance. Born with a love for excellent food, travel and adventure, she has lived in four different countries, kissed stingrays, been bitten by a shark, fed an elephant and petted tigers.

Currently, she shares a condo overlooking a small river and sakura trees in Japan with her husband and son. When she's not writing, she can be found reading books by her favorite authors or planning another trip.

To learn more about Nadia and her projects, please visit http://www.nadialee.net. To receive updates about upcoming works, sneak peeks and bonus epilogues featuring some of your favorite couples from Nadia, please visit http://www.nadialee.net/vip to join her VIP List.

Printed in Great Britain
by Amazon

18218750R00274